Tira's Education
Twelve Dancing Princesses Book Eleven

Christine Young

ISBN: 978-1-62420-469-2

Credits
Cover Artist: Designs by Ms G
Editor: Christie L. Kraemer

Chapter One

Baltimore 1821

On board the ship taking her to Baltimore, Tira Hepburn watched the land grow closer until the boat finally docked. Her trunk was unloaded and she walked down the gangplank with a small valise in hand, her heart in her throat. This was her new life, and it was the first time her twin Tavia was not by her side. She inhaled a long deep breath, breathing in the fresh clean air so unlike that of London and listening to the sea gulls as they flew overhead.

"Tira, over here. Tira."

She smiled seeing her cousin jumping up and down, waiving her hands in the air. Aidan McLellan, strands of wild red hair flying in the breeze off the ocean waited by a wagon, ready to take her to the home their families owned in the city. When Aidan finally finished jumping, she ran to her, arms outstretched.

With hugs, "You're here. You finally made it. Auntie wrote to me when you would come. Mr. Lundin sent word this morning that several fishing boats had sighted the ship and relayed messages. I've been waiting impatiently for an hour at least."

"Have you heard from Blade?" Arm and arm, Tira and Aidan walked to the wagon. A dockworker helped put the trunk on the cart. "He left London almost to the same day that you did."

"No, thank goodness. If I never see that man again, I'll be happy." Aidan looked behind her as if the man she spoke of would turn up. "But I'm truly afraid it's just a matter of time before he finds a way to humiliate me again. If he arrives in Baltimore and does that..." She let the sentence hang and Tira put her own meaning to the words.

Tira was pretty sure Aidan wanted to see Blade at least one more time. She loved him but she probably wanted it on her terms and where Blade was concerned, that wasn't going to happen. For years their relationship had revolved around Blade's ideas and what he wanted or thought was best for Aidan.

"You must live each day wondering if he'll come after you. I know I would find you if I were him. He's always tried to protect you. You have to figure out how you're going to deal with his antics when he does show up." Tira hated the thought, yet she knew Aidan loved the man. When the two of them got together for good or bad, their relationship would most likely be defined as a match made in hell.

"He won't. If he hasn't come yet, I doubt if he will. That last incident drove the point home for both of us that we're not suited to each other and never will be. At least what happened before Ella's wedding made it perfectly clear to me. He's never going to see me as a woman, always as a little girl."

"Lundin Ships," Tira read as they stepped passed the building. "Experienced ship builder needed." She turned to Aidan, "I'm going to apply first thing in the morning. This is heaven sent for me." She clapped her hands together excited by the prospect. Her dreams were about to come to fruition. She so wanted to learn how to design and build ships, and Jamie Lundin was just the man to teach her.

"You don't really believe Jamie Lundin will give you a job, do you?" Aidan stared at her, a skeptical expression of her face. "No one hires women for ship building jobs."

"I can only hope. I'm going to go dressed as a man. Tavia and I bought pants and men's shirts in London. Tavia sailed on a ship as a cabin boy. She even cut her hair short. Haven't heard from her though I've been thinking about her constantly."

"Tavia Hepburn, your twin, she did what?" Aidan asked, seeming shocked at what Tira said. "She's more impulsive than me and you also. Look at you, trying to be like a man. I've been trying for years to convince Blade I'm a woman grown and less than a year ago he still thought I was a little girl. I would never masquerade as a man."

"Perhaps you should have tried wearing pants. I heard the ploy worked well for Ella. Remember how Drake had her wear britches when he was trying to figure out if he wanted to marry her." They were alone, of course, at Drake's hunting lodge and no one else saw her.

"Ella Hepburn, now Montgomerie, she's a duchess. Are they doing well, she and Drake?"

"They were when I left. You know, Blade searched London for you. No one would tell him where you disappeared. We all kept our promise to you even though it was hard," Tira said. "Then he vanished without a trace."

"That's a relief, I'm glad everyone kept silent. I need time to figure things out, and the last person I want showing up on my front door is Blade McPherson. I've had a few outings with some men I've met, but none of them make my heart rush with desire or even beat a tiny bit harder. I don't know how long it will take me to get over him. If I ever do."

"Before I left, I heard Blade was called home. His father was ailing. So, you may have a longer reprieve than expected." Tira watched Aidan for a reaction. All who had known these two over the years hoped someday they would find a way to get over their differences. Aidan had been in love with Blade since she was thirteen.

Aidan pulled in front of the house, stopping the wagon with a huge sigh. "Did you realize it's been over six years since I first met him. I wish he never showed up at the castle that day with his friend, Hunter. If I never met him, I might be happily in love now and not pinning away for someone I can't have."

"You've been in love with that man for so long. Have you even been kissed by another man?" Tira was sorry she asked that question. After all, she'd never been kissed.

"Have you?" Placing one finger on her lips as if she remembered how Blade kissed her that first time in the gazebo at the Montgomery estate, Aidan turned the question back on her cousin.

"No." Tira didn't want to talk about it. Since Ella and Drake's wedding, Jamie Lundin had caught her eye when he escorted Tavia, her twin. She had dreamt of his kisses. Now she meant to parade herself in front of him in men's clothing. He'd never treat her as a woman if she did that.

Aidan laughed softly. "Here we are virgins who've never been kissed." She choked back her thoughts. "Well, I've been kissed that one time when Blade managed to humiliate me in front of all my family. I liked it when I thought he was sincere."

"Maybe that's why we fled London. There are no opportunities left for us in England," Tira said, looking over her shoulder and trying to see Jamie's building while wondering what would happen tomorrow.

"Hello, welcome. I hope you feel at home here." Lilly, the black woman Amorica rescued from slavery stepped from the door. "Do you need help? I can call Joshua. He can get your trunk."

"Yes, please," Aidan said, smiling. "It's the only way we'll get that trunk up the stairs. If not, we'll have to take each piece of clothing a couple at a time."

Tira followed Aidan into the home and up the steps. "So, this is the house." She inhaled a long deep breath, closing her eyes for a moment. Here, she was truly independent. She didn't have to answer to anyone except herself and her conscious. She could come and go as she pleased.

"I'll show you to your room and you can freshen up before dinner." Aidan looked over her shoulder at Tira as she followed behind.

Inside her new bedroom, Tira held her breath, looking over the place where she was going to stay indefinitely. Second thoughts about what she was about to do assailed her. She wanted Jamie to court her properly, but she had serious misdoubts about that ever happening.

She plopped down on the bed, staring at the ceiling and thinking about Tavia. Where in the world was she? They'd never been separated before, and now she hadn't seen her twin for closing on seven months. Was she still alive? Tira was pretty sure if something happened to her, she'd know. They always had a way of communicating without speaking. They shared an unbreakable bond no one else understood.

A knock on the door brought her from her introspective thoughts to the present. The door creaked open and Lilly peeked inside. "I've hot water. Would you like a bath?"

"Oh, yes. Yes, yes, yes, that would be heaven." Tira sat up smiling, her hands clasped under chin. The trunk was brought in behind the hot water as her bath was filled.

Once the door closed and she was alone again, she slipped out of her clothes and into the bath. Famished, she washed quickly then dressed in clean clothes before skipping down the steps.

"Hello..." She peeked into the parlor.

Aidan met her with a glass of wine. "Come, dinner won't be ready for another hour. Let's go into the parlor and have a few dainty dishes before the meal. Lilly loves to put tiny bits of meat in pastry shells with a cream sauce. They are really very good. I have to be careful not to fill up on them before dinner though."

Tira sat back, her eyes closed, wondering what the morning would bring and if Jamie Lundin would hire her and if she could pull off her disguise. "You know, I'm...I guess I'm a bit afraid for tomorrow. What if he recognizes me? What if he doesn't think I'm a man?"

"Honestly, I don't see how you can change yourself enough so that anyone who has met you would not recognize you," Aidan said, blunt as usual. "And if Tavia tried to pass herself off as a boy, I'm sure her true identity will be or already has been discovered. This is all foolishness, but time will tell. If he doesn't recognize or know that you're a woman at first site, I have serious doubts about his character."

"That's what I'm afraid of too. Tavia cut all her hair off. Do you think I should do that?" Tira didn't want to go to that extreme even when she knew it would grow back.

Aidan choked on her sip of wine, spewing liquid everywhere. "Absolutely not. Don't you dare. Put lots of pins in your hair to keep it in place and wear a beanie of some sort. Do you have one?"

Tira pursed her lips, staring at Aidan and her look of concern. She had more than second even third thoughts about this crazy endeavor, wanting Jamie to see her as a woman not a man. "I do. I have material to wrap my breasts too. Tavia and I practiced winding the fabric around our torsos, but it hurts. I'm not sure how long I can put up with the bindings."

Again, Tira's thoughts turned to her sister who could have had the same problem. At least she had a home, a place where she could go and unwrap the fabric confining her, but on board a ship Tavia would have none of that, no privacy what so ever.

"This is all foolhardiness. Never, never lie, you know that. Go to him just the way you are and maybe he will see that you're sincere. Men don't like to be deceived, and they can hold it against you forever," Aidan voiced her opinion. "I should know better than anyone."

"You speak from experience?" Tira questioned, wondering what Aidan lied about with Blade. It certainly wasn't her age.

"Not personally but I've watched my sisters and my cousins. Lies tore them apart from the men they loved. In the end they found their way back to each other, but the truth would have served each of them better. I am never going to tell a lie to the man I love."

"Not always real lies but misunderstandings and lies of omission," Tira corrected, knowing as soon as she showed up at the Lundin ship building company requesting a job, she would be in the middle of a lie of omission. "And I can't risk going to him as a woman and asking for a job. He would never hire me if he knew I was female."

"A man's job."

"A man's job," Tira agreed with a huge sigh. "I don't know what to do. I spent the long voyage here believing I would learn how to design and build ships. This is the only way and I'm determined to make it work. He has to believe I'm a young man and give me a chance." Tira picked at the little pastry in front of her, the huge appetite from minutes ago vanishing with her outstanding worries. She sipped her wine, staring over the rim and out the window toward the building, Jamie's building.

"Alright then, you think he'll believe you're a man. What will you do when he sees through your disguise and he will?" Aidan posed the question.

"If."

"If he doesn't know who you are the minute you stand in front of him, I'd be shocked. You have delicate feminine features that no man would have. Of course you could say you were fourteen, but he wouldn't hire you then either," Aidan pointed out.

"I really don't want to think about it right now. Thinking about tomorrow makes my stomach churn and tie in knots. Have you figured out what you will do when Blade turns up here to protect you from yourself just as he always does?" Tira challenged Aidan, determined to change the subject from her and the very real probability Jamie would recognize her.

"Good ploy, change the topic." Aidan laughed, finishing off her wine and pouring them both another drink. "If he turns up, I will dissuade him in the best way I know how."

It was Tira's turn to chuckle. "Have you ever dissuaded him?"

"No. I chased him until he mortified me. If I ever see him again, I will play hard to get. Not sure if I can do that, but I'm certainly going to try. Actually, after what he said to me, I'm not going to forgive him easily. Besides, I've a few suitors here in Baltimore."

"Any you can be serious about?" Tira asked, pretty sure she knew the answer to her question.

"No, but they escort me places and keep me from getting too bored. Lilly has all the chores done by the time I think about them. I go for long walks by the small lake down the hill. Other than that..." She shrugged. "I miss everyone so much and would almost welcome Blade just so we can have a big fight. He challenges me and keeps everything exciting. I really don't want to say this but I miss him more than I care to admit."

"Don't you wish life was easier?" Tira asked thoughtfully, knowing anything worth having was worth working for. "I certainly do. All I want is to learn how to build ships. I don't care about anything else." But she did, she needed a family and love.

"You will when you find someone to love. Do you care about Jamie at all?"

"Right now, yes. Jamie did touch my heart a tiny bit when I met him at Ella's wedding, but he held himself aloof. He's not approachable. I doubt if he's looking for a permanent relationship or a relationship of any kind for that matter. I had the distinct feeling he was hiding something. Do you know if Drake knew what it was?"

"He was merely an acquaintance Drake knew from his ships and business. He asked him to be part of the wedding party so he could tell his brother he didn't need anyone."

"Are you in love even a little bit?" Aidan asked. It seemed her curiosity had risen several notches.

"Not right now and certainly not with Jamie Lundin. I barely know him. How did this conversation change from asking for a man's job to a possible husband? Have you heard from Amorica recently?" Tira changed the subject to her oldest sister.

"She and Damian were here a couple of months ago. Their children are growing like weeds and the two of them are still so much in love..." Aidan let that thought hang in the air. "I so wish I could have what they have." She paused, thinking, "with Blade when I finally forgive him."

"I need to fall in love first," Tira said pensively, wondering what it would take to catch Jamie's attention. Could she work as a man on his ships during the day and meet him at night as a woman?

"I've been in love for over six years, and he's thought of me as a little girl for that long. What can I ever do to change his mind?" Aidan let a heavy sigh emanate from her.

"Blade doesn't deserve you."

"Tell him that."

"Dinner is ready, any one hungry?" Lilly stood in the doorway, hands clasped in front of her, a smile on her face.

"Famished, even though the pastries were wonderful." Tira strode to the dining room relieved to put the conversation behind her and eager for tomorrow morning so she would know her fate.

"Lilly, will you and Joshua join us for dinner? I understand you don't feel comfortable eating in this house, but you and your fiancé are so welcome." Aidan took Lilly's hands in hers obviously hoping she would finally get over the slave versus free person status.

"I will ask him, but he is newly emancipated and I know exactly how it feels to have to bow down to a white master." Lilly spun, "I'll be right back."

Aidan turned to Tira to clarify, "When Damian first came here, he bought Lilly and emancipated her. Now he has done the same for Joshua. Because of intense prejudices, they must be very cautious and don't dare go very far from this property. The townspeople understand they are free, but the farmers and plantation owners in the surrounding lands will not accept it unless they see proof. If they go anywhere, they have to carry their papers and in doing so they risk losing them or having them stolen."

"There is risk in everything they do." Tira was appalled at the revelations.

"Many will strive to keep these two apart and put them in chains again. There are several copies of their papers just in case. Amorica also has duplicates in her home. There is a reproduction in the safe here and they both have copies of their own."

"My goodness..." Tira was shocked by Aidan's words. "I would have never believed one would have to go to such lengths to prove they are free. Everyone should be free. This is the eighteen hundreds after all."

"The people here use the slaves to plant and harvest their crops. They are not free and it seems never will be unless some wealthy person buys them and gives them their freedom."

"That's awful."

"No, it's inhumane."

Lilly returned. "I'm sorry. He wants to give his apologies, but he doesn't want to intrude on your privacy. So he declines. I will eat with him and I will see both of you tomorrow morning."

"I understand. Amorica told me it took years for you to feel this comfortable even to consider eating with us, but I want you to know that we are not above you in any way. We are all the same, equal in every way. What happened to you and Joshua is a travesty that in a better world would be stopped immediately." A tear slipped down Tira's cheeks, wearing her feelings for everyone to see.

"It won't though," Aidan said thoughtfully, placing a hand on Tira's. "Having been in this part of the world for only a short time I understand what drives the men who keep slaves. They are all greedy men who want free labor. Most believe they couldn't afford to farm their huge crops without the slaves who work for them. They think they would go out of business if they paid anyone to work their land. Your Jamie Lundin is not one of them. His farm is slave free."

"I must go. Joshua is very apprehensive. He has a hard time believing Tira came from across the ocean and she is not his enemy. He is constantly looking over his shoulder, believing his master is hunting for him," Lilly said, also looking over her shoulder at the back door.

"Take enough food for both of you then and enjoy," Aidan said, having assumed the role of the lady of the house. "He had the same reaction to me the first time we met." She turned to Tira.

"Thank you." Lilly curtsied then packed a basket of food before leaving for the kitchen then their little cottage beside the big house.

"So, let's talk about tomorrow." Aidan leaned forward, elbows on the table, her chin resting on her hands.

"Tomorrow?" Tira feigned innocence, anticipating and excited but dreading the moment too.

"Yes, you've got this notion you can wrap yourself up all by yourself. If you're going to wake me up at the crack of dawn, I'm going to be very unhappy with you, Tira Hepburn."

"I promise you I can do it." Tira smiled before taking a bite of food. "But perhaps I should practice. If I can't do it by myself tonight, I'm going to want you to help me. I'll just sleep in them."

"You mean lie awake staring at the ceiling all night long, but yes, I'll help you because I don't want you waking me up before the sunrises."

"I promise I won't wake you up."

Finishing dinner and clearing the dishes the cousins strode upstairs. "Lilly will clean this up in the morning or later tonight. She berates me if I try to take over any of the chores she considers her duty."

In Tira's bedroom, "Here are the bindings." Tira pulled out a long length of fabric cut about five inches wide. "And here are the shirt and pants I plan on wearing." She held them up, grinning.

"Oh bloody eyes, this is scandalous. Jamie Lundin is going to be shocked at your brazenness. There is absolutely no way you can hide your curves in those garments."

"He won't know I'm female. Tavia and I planned everything." Tira was determined to make this work, and if she had to tell herself the same thing over and over, she would. Aidan shook her confidence and she wasn't at all sure anymore if he would believe she was a man.

"Keep saying that and maybe you'll convince him."

Aidan plopped down on the bed to watch Tira try to wrap herself in the fabric and fasten the bindings. Twenty minutes later, Tira frowned at her and lay down on the bed. "This isn't as easy as I thought it would be."

"Thought you said you practiced."

"We did but we weren't able to do any better than this. I kept going over the process in my head, and I thought I had it figured out, but my hands and my fingers just don't work the way I think they should." Tira felt the weight of her plans begin to implode on her.

"Obviously you don't. What now?"

"You wrap me up now so you won't have to get up in the morning." Tira smiled, one eyebrow lifting in silent speculation.

"I want to see you completely dressed." Aidan stood back to look Tira over when she was done with the bindings.

Tira pulled the britches and shirt from the trunk and after putting them on, "How do I look?"

"Like a woman. Your hips are too wide, Tira, and even with your hair pulled up and tucked under the cap, your features are all female. There is no way Mr. Lundin will believe this ruse. You wouldn't even believe you were a boy. I'm sure Tavia had the same problem."

"Well, I have to try. You knew who I was, so this test wasn't fair in the least." Tira protested, her hands on her hips. "I've got to keep believing he won't see me as a woman."

"Don't do that if you want to ape a man. The way you're standing makes your hips stand out even more and I have a feeling you better not bend over either. Try to pose like a man would."

"And how is that?" Tira asked thoroughly out of her element.

"How would I know?"

"Well, you brought it up. How does Blade stand when he's acting all male?"

"Chest puffed up and feet braced apart. He usually has his hands on his narrow hips. Don't think you should puff up your chest or bring his eyes to your wide hips."

~ * ~

"What the devil," Jamie mumbled after the incessant knocking woke him up from a deep sleep. "The town must be on fire...the docks, the ships." His heart racing, he slipped on his buckskins and running his hands through his hair then racing down the stairs, opened the front door.

Tira Hepburn, what the bloody eyes was she doing at his front door at five in the morning and what was she doing aping a man? For that matter, what was she doing in Baltimore? Tira must have been the reason her cousin Aidan was inquiring about the ships coming in from London. "Can I help you?" he asked out of politeness but wishing he still lay in bed sleeping.

"I'm here to apply for the job."

"What job?" Sleepily, he ran his hands through his hair, unable to take his gaze off the woman on his front porch wearing men's clothing. Even dressed in that ridiculous outfit she mesmerized him. The only job he knew of was the one for an experienced ship builder.

"The one building ships." She smiled, puffing up her chest and settling her hands seductively on her hips.

Obviously, she had no idea how the simple gestures emphasized her femininity.

If he didn't miss his guess, she sounded indignant, but for some reason he couldn't fathom, he didn't want to end the conversation this instant. He had no choice though. His six-year-old daughter was asleep upstairs and needed breakfast before he could continue with this strange encounter. "Come back at eight o'clock. Not here but at the shipyard. I'll speak with you then and not a moment before."

"I went there to begin with but when no one answered my knock, I came to your house. I need this job." Her voice filled with indignation.

You need this job my ass. "Come back at eight and we can discuss this civilly." He started to close the door.

"Promise me you won't give the job to someone else before the interview." She smiled at him.

"Doubt if anyone in town besides you wants the job. The sign has been up for over a month. Besides, there aren't very many skilled ship builders in town. Are you skilled?" He challenged, hoping she would back down and he wouldn't have to be at the office at eight.

"Papa, who is it?"

"Go back to bed, honey. It's no one you need to concern yourself with." Yet he suddenly knew what he wanted Tira Hepburn for. She could be Annie's nanny. He reminded himself none of the Hepburns could possibly need a job. He was eager to find out more, and the upcoming interview with Miss Tira could be enlightening. Getting to the bottom of this made the day a bit more interesting than he thought it would be. Suddenly, he was eager to start the day and discover what would come of this chance encounter.

"Papa." Annie stood beside him, tilting her head slightly and pursing her lips.

"Who is it?" Tira shifted her position as if she was trying to see beyond his shoulders.

"She's no concern of yours," he told Tira a bit too harshly, his protective nature kicking in. Where Annie was concerned, he would guard her with his life and make sure nothing bad happened to her, ever.

"I'm sorry," Tira said weakly. "I didn't mean..."

"Of course you didn't. Come back at eight. I'll meet you then." He was surprised at her smile and how that simple gesture affected him, touched his heart in a way he didn't understand. What on earth was she doing to him?

Awkwardly, she backed away and nearly fell off the porch before she turned and headed away from the shipyard, her hips swaying provocatively as she walked. He felt a crazy urge to run after her and then what? Drag her into his arms and kiss her?

He remembered her from Drake and Ella's wedding months ago. She'd been the first woman who found a way beneath his hardened heart since his mistress died in childbirth and left him to raise Annie on his own. Tira Hepburn was not a candidate for his mistress, a wife maybe...

Lizzy, his mistress, had never wanted to become his wife and after his first marriage, he sure as hell never wanted to be wed again, but he cared for Lizzie and mourned her loss. Before she died, he promised her he would take care of Annie and make sure she would never have to sell her body to make a living.

He was too awake now to go back to bed, so he walked Annie to her bedroom. It seemed she was awake now too.

"Would you like a big breakfast this morning?" He ruffled his daughter's hair and delighted in her smile and laughter.

"Pancakes," she asked, "and bacon too? Anything but oatmeal."

"What ever you want today but don't get used to this royal treatment. Get dressed and by the time you get down for breakfast, I should have most of it cooked. We can talk then about the rest of the day." He loved her more than life itself.

"Who was the lady?" Annie asked.

He chuckled softly. Even his five-year-old daughter knew the person at his door was a woman, not a man. For a quick second the thought of going along with her ruse crossed his mind, but he shrugged it off. Truth was always better than lies, and if he let her work for him, he could risk her life. He wasn't about to do that. Damian Andrews, her brother-in-law, would have his hide if he hired her. Truth be told, he was more afraid of her sister Amorica.

Annie stopped at the top of the stairs. "Are you going to get dressed before breakfast? Did you know she was staring at your chest, Papa? Why was she doing that?"

For a moment he choked back an answer. He'd been staring at her chest or lack of breasts too. That wasn't the way he remembered Tira. "After breakfast, maybe we can talk about where she was looking." Given time his Annie might forget her question. He certainly didn't want to answer it.

He remembered Tira's form from that one time he saw her in London, and she was not flat chested. She must be horribly uncomfortable. It was another reason to let her know she couldn't fool him.

"That's not an answer," Annie said, standing at the bottom of the steps. "Don't forget I want to know why."

Laughter threatened to bubble up from his gut, "Guess I don't know. Now run along and dress." Jamie couldn't help but chuckle at his daughter. He felt a strange sense of elation that Tira liked his body.

With the bacon cooking on the stove, he mixed the pancake batter. He thought about eggs and potatoes but decided with just the two of them that was too much food. For a moment he thought about inviting Tira but shrugged off the thought. Asking her to breakfast was too much too soon.

"You're not done." Annie raced into the room laughing. "I knew I could beat you." She ran to him and hugged his legs. "I brought you a shirt." She folded it across the top of a chair.

He bent over, lifting her into the air for a quick toss then a kiss before setting her on a chair. "Be patient, little one, and thank you for your thoughtfulness. This shirt is exactly the one I would have picked."

"Do you think the lady is hungry?" Annie asked.

His heart stopped for a moment. "Why do you ask?"

"She's sitting on the stoop at the shipyard office. Every once in a while, she stands and stretches then sits down again. I feel sorry for her. We could invite her to breakfast. If you have your shirt on, she might not stare at your chest."

"Probably not a good idea. She's looking for a job. We don't mix business with pleasure." Tira Hepburn was clearly muddled if she thought he would hire a woman.

"What kind of job?"

"She wants to build ships."

"That's man's work," Annie said, a serious tone edging her voice. "She can't do that."

Those three words shook him to the core. While he didn't want Tira Hepburn in his shipyard distracting his men, he wanted Annie to be able to pursue any dream she had.

"Annie, I want you to think beyond what men and women should do for work or with their lives. Your mother wanted you to pursue whatever dreams you had." Actually, her mother wanted her to find a man to marry and support her, but Jamie found he wanted more for his little girl. He wanted her to have a voice in her life.

"Why would you want that? I want to be a wife and a mother, well, that's what all my friends say they want. Do you want to know what I really want to be?" she asked, eagerly watching him it seemed for a reaction.

"Tell me." Jamie flipped a pancake on to her plate and pushed the syrup and butter toward her. He gave her a piece of bacon then heaped his plate with food.

For a couple of seconds, she pushed her food around on her plate before she looked up. "I'd like to be a doctor."

"Really. That's incredibly special. Why?" He didn't want that for her. Hypocrite.

"Because they help people when they are sick," she told him in such a matter of fact manner. "I want to know how to do that."

He was suddenly frightened her dream would come true. Doctors took risks with their lives to help people. "That's noble of you." He meant to encourage her even though he wanted anything else for her. He knew through the course of a person's life, they changed their dreams. When he was a boy, he wanted to be a lawyer.

"If she can't work in the shipyard, could she be my nanny. I like her. Well, I think I'll like her. You told me you were going to hire someone, but that was months ago."

"You don't even know her, but I met her when I was in England and I liked her too. I'll ask her if she'd like that job."

"When you fire her from man's work."

"Yes, poppet when I refuse to hire her because she's not strong enough to work in the shipyard. I'll ask her if she wants to be your nanny."

"Thank you."

"Eat up. I've got to go to work and you will need to go with me." Except when Mooney's wife wanted to watch his little girl or school was in session, Annie went to the shipyard with him. Today would be no different.

He cleared the dishes, leaving them in the scullery for his housekeeper. "Are you ready?" Jamie held out his hand and Annie let him take her hand in his. She was so precious, the best thing that ever happened to him. "Would you like to go swimming after work today?"

"Yes, the little swimming hole behind the Andrews house? I love it there. You can help me learn to float on my back."

"The very one." He stopped in front of Tira who stood when they approached. "I see you waited here. Nothing better to do?"

"I did." She nervously wiped her hands on her pants. "Stay."

Inwardly he groaned, noticing the beautiful curve of her hips and imagining the sway of her breasts if she hadn't bound them, and he sure as hell hoped she didn't cut off her hair. He opened the door and waited for Annie and Tira to walk through the door. "Go up on deck. Your things are still there. Practice tying the knots I showed you last week. Now behave yourself until I'm through with this interview. Call me if you need anything."

Jamie walked into his office, Tira following him. He sauntered around his desk and sat then motioned for her to take a seat. For some reason she fascinated him. "What can I do for you?" The only real question was how long he was going to let her think she was fooling him.

"I'm looking for a job." One more time, she ran her hands along her thighs then back. "I want to design and build ships. Wanted to learn how to do that for as long as I can remember."

He couldn't help himself, that small gesture made him think about doing just that to her. He cleared his throat, pushing those thoughts to the back of his mind, trying to focus on her eyes instead of her lips. "So, you're an expert ship builder. Any credentials?"

"No, but..."

"But?"

"I want to learn. It's all I've ever wanted to do and I'll work hard," she repeated. Her voice grew soft, almost wistful.

"The job description calls for an expert. I don't have time to teach someone." He watched her expression change from hopeful to full disappointment. "I need this person who I hire for the job to be there for me, so I can spend more time with my daughter."

He watched her squirm in her chair, her lips tilting downward. "I see. So there's no chance you will give me the job."

He leaned forward, hands clasped, "However." He peered heavenward searching for divine strength, "Lady Tira Hepburn..." he paused, seeing her sit up straight, her demeanor changing to obvious anger and her lips pursing. Red colored her cheeks. "Yes, I know who you are. I don't know why you want to ape a man or why you need to work, but I could hire you as a nanny."

"Please." Annie stood at the door, jumping up and down, clearly excited about the prospect. "She's pretty and I want her for a nanny. I bet she'll be more fun than my last one. I don't even care if she stares at your chest."

"Stare at your chest? I didn't." She turned even redder, if that were possible.

"Yes, you did, but it doesn't matter."

"I didn't know you had a little girl." Tira looked from one to the other. "She has your eyes."

"I don't keep Annie a secret nor do I advertise the fact at a wedding in London," he said, his voice curt, his brows drawing together defensively.

"I'm sorry. I didn't mean to imply...well, I suppose I should go." She rose, hesitating a moment to address Jamie. "What gave me away?

How did you know I was Tira and not my twin?"

He sat back, relaxing in his chair, looking her up then down, understanding the advantage was his. "Anyone who looks at you would know you were aping a man. Even Annie knew you were a woman. As to how I know which twin you are, you have one tiny dimple on your cheek next to the corner of your lips. Tavia has none."

"Oh." She backed toward the door, clearly distraught, moisture forming in her eyes. She turned and in her haste, ran into the wall.

Before she could leave, "You didn't answer my question. Would you like to be Annie's nanny?" That would mean he would spend more time with Tira. He wasn't adverse to that notion. She had intrigued him the first time he saw her and now dressed in men's clothing, she captivated him even more.

"You're right. I don't need to work. I've always wanted to learn how to build ships. I did build a small sailboat about six years ago. The vessel didn't sink." Tira turned to glance at his little girl. "I could be her nanny for a little while. I don't want to go back to London right away, and I will need something to do with my time. Why not?"

"Good, then you can start today. She was supposed to be playing in the captain's cabin aboard the ship. Instead she chose to eavesdrop on our conversation. The vessel is nearly finished." He slanted Annie a stern look.

"I couldn't wait to find out what she'd say. I promise I won't do it again," Annie said, in her defense.

He led the way to the gangplank, which stopped at the ship's deck. Once on board, he showed her the cabin. "Annie has a few toys she likes to play with inside. When she's hungry, you can take her home and fix her whatever she wants or whatever is in the pantry."

"Anything else?" she tilted her head prettily to one side. "Will you be there for lunch too?"

He vowed he'd never get involved with a woman other than a willing widow or someone who would be a mistress. Tira Hepburn was not that woman. So why was he letting her move him in ways he was hard pressed to resist? "If I can spare the time.

"I think Annie can fill you in if you have questions, and I'll be in my office finishing some paperwork if either of you need me." He turned and left, shaking his head and thinking about his life in a completely different way than he'd seen it when the pounding on his door woke him up this morning.

In his office he poured himself a cup of coffee, realizing Mooney, his assistant, had come to work early this morning. The man must have seen and heard most of the conversation between Tira and himself. Jamie groaned, unready to answer questions and knowing the man would be relentless when he wanted to know something.

"Who's the little gal and why's she dressed like that?" Mooney stepped through the door, rubbing his bearded chin and holding a cup. "I see she caught your eye. 'Bout time you found someone."

"Lady Tira Hepburn." Jamie turned slowly, unable to stop smiling. "She thought...she wanted a job building ships so she thought she could fool me with that get up. I met her on my last trip to London."

Mooney's jaw dropped. "You'd have to be blind as a bat for that to happen. Don't see a lady in britches too often but..." It seemed he couldn't say anything more. He poured coffee into his cup.

"She's going to be my...Annie's nanny," Jamie put in, thinking how ridiculous that sounded.

"You're going to employ a real lady, a member of the British aristocracy, to be your nanny. She on hard times or something?" Mooney gazed out the door as if he wanted to get another look at a real lady.

"Looks like it. Annie likes her. No hard times as far as I know." Jamie didn't want to explain himself. He sensed a note of disapproval in Mooney's voice. He couldn't help but wonder at his motives, and if that was what Mooney was thinking too. He and his daughter were going swimming after work, and he wondered how he could convince Tira to come with them. Those thoughts went directly to motive.

"Well, it appears to me, you're lookin' at a lot of trouble. Thought you told me once you're not the marryin' kind. You keep lookin' at her the way you were just doin, well..."

"I did say I don't intend to embrace that popular institution. You don't have to remind me. Annie likes her and she usually gets whatever she wants," he said again trying to convince himself he didn't have ulterior motives where Tira was concerned.

After his first marriage and the way it ended, he knew he would never give that institution another chance. Three months after they tied the knot, his wife ran off with another man.

Mooney's roar of laughter echoed in his ears, "Bet you're wed before the end of the year. She's not Lizzy and she's certainly not like your first wife. She's not going to sleep with you and have your child without a ring on her finger."

Jamie stiffened. Mooney's words hit too close to his thoughts, and he couldn't figure out why he was regarding Tira in that same light. Two chance meetings and Mooney had him married. "You know I don't gamble."

"She's a pretty little thing, even in those clothes. Wonder what she'd look like dressed in proper female clothing?" It seemed Mooney tried to goad him.

He was about to say something back when Annie's scream caught him by surprise. He dropped his coffee cup and ran.

~ * ~

Mathew Dutton surveyed the inside of the house. It was opulent, designed in golds and reds, a mirror on every wall. The women of the house were all beautiful and scantily clad, yet in ways more discreet than in most brothels. They showed their curves but not their bodies. A man had to pay handsomely to play with one of his girls. His was what he called a high-class operation.

Beside him the madam of the house sipped a fine brandy he'd imported from Scotland. Kendall was his first. No one else touched her unless they paid more than handsomely. She'd given herself to him years ago, claiming she never wanted conventional things for herself, not marriage and certainly not a family.

"Kendall, I've a new girl in mind, but I don't think she'll come along as easily as most. I'm not sure. I'll have to look into her situation more extensively. At first look she appears to be British aristocracy."

"Who is it? Do I know her?" Kendall Mackenzie asked.

"No, she's new in town. Just arrived yesterday. Heard she asked for work at Lundin's shipyard."

"What's the problem? If she looked for work there, she must be down on her luck." Kendall sipped the brandy, sliding her hand along Mathew's leg, her meaning clear.

"We could take this upstairs?" Mathew said, catching her exploring hand and kissing the back before she could reach her destination.

She moistened her lips. "Not until I know who you're talking about and why there might be a problem. You've always had a way to convince the ladies. Besides this job at the shipyard had to be gossip. No member of the British aristocracy would stoop so low." Kendall sat back, pouting provocatively and letting him take full advantage of the view of her cleavage.

"Don't know her name, working on that little piece of information, but Aidan McLellan picked her up at the docks and took her to the Andrews home. Could be she's connected to that clan in some way."

"You think she's kin. We don't want to mess with any of them. They've got too much influence here and in England. Andrews and Lakeland could have me run out of town if we provoked them. I like it here and I don't want to move."

He trailed a finger along her bodice. "I don't want that either. I'll make sure I understand who it is before I take action. She'd make a beautiful addition to the stable of girls we have here. She's looks aristocratic, long black hair and enticing curves. I couldn't get close enough to see her eyes, but I will."

Kendall swatted his hand away. "We can take this upstairs later. Need I remind you, I've a business to run?"

She rose and flounced away, greeting a customer before calling for one of her girls. The man and the lady disappeared upstairs. Mathew's gut tightened. He downed his brandy, standing. On the front porch he leaned on the railing, looking over the town.

Meeting Kendall had been a godsend. Together they built this brothel as well as two others in neighboring communities in addition he just purchased one in London. When he met her, they were both dirt poor. Now he could buy anything he wanted, and he wanted the girl he saw yesterday.

Kendall wasn't like most women. She had a fire inside that couldn't be tamed. At first, she had been the main attraction, now she only serviced him, unless someone came to the home she was attracted to. He knew she had been intimate with more than just him. Of course he saw other women too. He looked forward to making love to the new girl in town. Mentally, he undressed her, his breath quickening in anticipation.

The evening was clear, barely a cloud could be seen. A few stars shone in the darkening sky. A crescent moon rested on the horizon and a cool breeze blew off the ocean.

Kendall appeared at his side, two glasses of brandy in her hands. She handed him one. "You really smitten?"

"I don't know what it is. I thought I was too old and too experienced to feel this way. She's just another woman."

"You're going to have to find a way to convince her this is the life she's been craving."

"It would help if I understood why you chose me and all this." He gestured with his hands.

She paused, seeming to think. "I've never told you this, but my mother was never happy. She married a bastard and had his children, one after another until he left her. I didn't want a bastard dictating my life. When I met you, I'd slept with several men and I liked it. The thought of having to make love to just one man my entire life wasn't appealing."

"Variety is nice." His hand rested at the small of her back. "No regrets?"

She gasped when his hand slipped beneath her skirt. "None." She turned in his arms.

His lips molded against hers as her tongue swept the inside of his. He groaned low in his belly, letting his other hand find her breast, teasing a nipple. "Can we take this upstairs yet?" He touched the length of her neck with lips and tongue.

"Another hour perhaps. I'll leave Jessica in charge if we get any new customers."

"Go on then." He stood back, watching her leave and anticipating the night with her in his arms.

Chapter Two

Perched at the top of one of the main masts, Tira could see most of Baltimore and far out to the ocean as well. During the trip from London, she'd wanted to scale the masts and she was sure her twin, as a cabin boy, had done just that, the thought making her jealous. Now she sat in the crow's nest, content to breathe the fresh air and watch the waves lap at the beach while seagulls flew in the brilliant blue sky.

"Papa, Papa, look at what Tira can do. I want to try," Annie cried out, pointing skyward.

Tira looked down waving and wondering what the confusion was. When Jamie arrived on deck, a large burly man behind him, Annie was dancing up and down on one foot then the other pointing to the sky.

She waved at Jamie, grinning shamelessly. "Hello down there. You didn't have to come. I've everything under control. I know Annie screamed, but she was so excited she couldn't help herself."

"Come down this instant before you fall and kill yourself." Jamie's voice thundered upward.

"Why?" She bristled at the unfeeling command. Authority from another person had never been a part of her life. "I don't want to and I'm not going to fall. I never fall. You have no reason to command me and expect me to obey your order."

"Never say never. You can't take care of Annie if you're putting dangerous thoughts in her head or if you have broken body parts," Jamie yelled. "And as long as I'm your employer, I can command and expect obedience."

"This isn't dangerous," she called down, bristling at his tone as well as his words. "I've been climbing things all my life. This was easier than most trees and easier on the hands." Feeling as if she was making a bad impression, she swung her legs around and nimbly climbed down, landing on her bare feet in front of Jamie, dusting her hands off and smiling inwardly.

Stepping forward, he tripped over one of her shoes. "Good god, woman! Put these back on." He held them up to her. "You frightened everyone. What did you think you were doing?" He ran hands through his black hair, pacing the deck. "You're not to do this ever again. I won't have it and I don't want to find you lying on the deck unable to move."

"Tira didn't scare me. I would've gone up too but she told me no." Annie sounded indignant. "You said I should follow my dreams. If I were a boy, you wouldn't have reacted like that."

Jamie, looking at Tira, quickly took his jacket off. "Put this on," he growled and turning to Mooney, "Best you go back to the office."

Mooney nodded then left, a huge grin on his bearded face. "One year, mark my words," he called out.

"Whatever for?" Tira held the jacket in front of her staring at it as if it were vermin.

"Just put the damn thing on. Do you always question everything?" he asked clearly furious.

Frowning she slipped the jacket over her arms. "I would still like to know why?" She glanced Annie's way in hopes the little girl could shed some light on her father's strange behavior.

Annie shrugged her tiny shoulders. "Papa is kind of funny about some things. He didn't seem to care earlier, before we unwrapped you."

She felt the heat to the tips of her toes, needing to defend herself and realizing she should have paid more attention to the state of her undress. Her heart thundered in her ears, blood pumping to her face, "I was uncomfortable and since there was no longer a need to conceal my breasts..."

"You thought you should show them to the world instead." His smile seemed smug as he gazed at her. "You can show them to me anytime."

She bristled at his words, not liking his expression or the meaning of his not very subtle innuendo. "You are not the world and I'm sure they are not the first ones you've seen." Trying to get an advantage without disagreeing with him, she smiled when she saw him blush.

"Are you always this incorrigible? I'm not sure you're suitable for a nanny. But you might be suitable as a mistress if you have the skills," he taunted her and it seemed to provoke.

"Papa." Little Annie had her hands on her hips, staring furiously at Jamie. "I'm not real sure but I think your words hurt my new nanny. She turned pale as a ghost. You need to apologize."

"Go to the cabin." His vice so stern it surprised Tira.

Annie's head fell and dragging her feet, she started to obey. Jamie was in front of her before she reached the room. "I'm sorry, little one. I didn't mean to hurt your feelings but this is adult stuff, and I don't want you to hear me get angry and I'm afraid I'm terribly close to losing my patience right now as well as my temper. But not with you, sweetheart, never with you."

"Don't you be mean to Tira. I'll never forgive you if you make her cry. She likes to play with me." Annie straightened her back, stepping more quickly to the cabin then closing the door behind her.

Tira would have smiled if she dared, but Jamie was very angry. She just wasn't used to a man caring what she did or didn't do. For her, this scenario had never happened before.

"I'm not incorrigible as you said. Ever since I can remember no one has told me...well, no one has cared what I do. I don't know how to react, but it seems to me this is not your business."

"When you're with my daughter, I care and even when you are not. Rumors spread easily and your reputation can be damaged by the smallest mistake. You're lucky that Mooney won't say anything."

"I would never believe climbing something would cause people to talk. I didn't know you were such a prude." She shot back, not caring how he would accept her criticism.

"This has nothing to do with climbing the mast. Good god, woman, I could see your breasts, your nipples. Is that how you're accustomed to displaying yourself?" He turned striding to the railing and looking toward the ocean, his back stiff and his shoulders tense. "And so could Mooney."

"You don't have to be so rude." She stood beside him, her legs shaking. "I don't mean to be flippant but I fight back when I'm attacked. It's a natural instinct. When you grow up in a family of all girls and with a father who is so deep in mourning he doesn't care what happens to you, men don't tell you what to do. I apologize for embarrassing you. I'll try not to let it happen again."

"There was no embarrassment on my part. When I saw you... I probably shouldn't divulge what I was thinking. I am a gentleman."

"Are you?" she queried, thoughtfully turning to regard him more closely. "What makes a man a gentleman?"

"I don't know. I like to believe I'm a nice person."

"Oh, then you are a nice person and does that imply you're a gentleman too? I think Drake Montgomerie is a nice person, but where Ella, my sister, was concerned he was no gentleman."

"Montgomerie had his reasons."

"Every man thinks he has his reasons and that no one should dispute them. His word is law. Would you do the same to me?" she challenged, expecting an answer but unsure what it would be.

"If you were amenable, I suppose I would. What did he do?" he asked, a puzzled expression on his face.

Tira laughed, enjoying this moment. Evidently, he wasn't in London long enough to hear the gossip surrounding Ella and Drake. "I am amenable. Before they were married, he took her to his cabin in Scotland to see if she was passionate. He had his reasons but was unwilling to share them with my sister."

She thought the gesture telling when Jamie rubbed the back of his neck, his brows furrowing. "That was not well done of him." It seemed he ignored the fact she told him she was open to his advances.

He surprised her when he ran a calloused fingertip along her jaw. "This boat will launch in two days. Perhaps we should take a week to find out if you are passionate, Tira Hepburn. Although personally, I'd rather know if you could spend a week with me without an argument."

She felt the impact of his words to the tips of her toes and stepped backwards without looking. Tripping over something, she landed on her derrière, the jacket falling off her shoulders. He stood over her, a hand extended, a manly grin on his handsome face. It seemed he won that round.

"You don't mean that." She accepted his help before realizing she lost her covering.

"I do. You have fascinated me since the first time I saw you. But if you sail with me, know I won't wed you, passionate or not. I vowed a long time ago to never take a wife. You could, however, become my mistress."

She inhaled a shocked breath of air. "You don't mean that. What about Annie's mother? You wed her."

"No. I did not."

"I don't understand."

"Lizzy was my mistress and she was perfectly fine with that status. She didn't want to marry either."

"Well, neither do I. Marry that is. I just want to build a ship." She lied though and didn't like the feeling. Marriage had always been something she wanted, but for some reason she didn't want to admit the fact to Jamie, particularly after this disclosure.

"Then you'd become my mistress if I teach you how to build a ship?" he asked, easily smoothing a lock of hair behind her ear, letting his hand linger a bit too long on her shoulder.

She straightened her shoulders, realizing her breasts were there for him to stare at. She tried to ignore the fact. "I might if the terms were agreeable." She turned around and picking up the jacket he loaned her, slung it over her shoulder and walked toward the cabin.

"Then payment begins right now and we'll talk terms later." His hand on her shoulder he turned her.

Surprised, she gave a tiny cry at his actions as he pulled her to him, his hand on her waist. Her breast brushed his chest and his mouth settled on hers. His lips soft and wet molded sweetly to hers.

Bloody hell, what had she gotten herself into? The heat of his hands running up her back then down sent a shiver of warmth sliding through her. Before she realized his intentions, his hands settled on the flesh of her back and when she gasped at the startling sensations, his tongue swept inside her mouth exploring her; delving, stroking urging a response.

In the back of her throat, she made a tiny sound and wondered if it was her or someone else making the noise. She closed her eyes, succumbing to the passion he ignited so easily within her. If Drake did these things to Ella, no wonder she gave in to the passion.

He stopped suddenly, withdrawing less than an inch from her face.

His words whispered heatedly against her. "First installment. I intend to collect at my whim. For now though, I've business to take care of."

Shocked by his arrogance, she stepped away from him, swinging her hand at his face with as much force as she could muster. He easily caught her wrist. They stared at each other for what seemed like hours. "I didn't agree to insults. And I won't be at anyone's whim. And Jamie, if we do this, I will have a say in what those terms are."

"But seduction is fine?" An eyebrow rose in speculation.

"If this is going to be a partnership, I will have a say as to when and where." She didn't understand what drove her words. She wasn't going to be his mistress now or ever. Figuring a way to get what she wanted without becoming his whore was at the forefront of her thoughts.

"I never said anything about a partnership. By the way, if you wish to wear these clothes while you're working here, I've no objections as long as no one else sees you."

Truth be told his kiss left her spineless and yearning for something more and while she shouldn't, she liked the idea of the pants and shirt when he was the only one around. The risk was too great though. Anyone and at any time could come to speak with him and see her.

Suddenly reluctant to allow him the view he seemed to covet, she crossed her arms in front of her.

"I wonder," he paused, taking her wrists and putting them by her sides. "How much you are willing to give up in order to receive the prize you crave. Is it worth your reputation and all you hold dear?"

"A reputation is nothing. It's what is in your heart that counts. To answer your question, I would give up just about anything for my dream. My sister, Ella, gave up everything for her dream and in the end, she found everything she ever wanted."

"Papa, can Tira come play with me now. I'm tired of practicing knots. I want to have something to tie up. She likes to play dolls with me, and I found my favorite one upstairs under my bed. You know the one I lost last week." Annie tugged on Jamie's pants. "Please."

"I suppose so. Perhaps you should go home and change your clothes. Annie can go with you." He turned to his daughter. "Would you like that, Annie? You can see where Tira lives and meet her cous in Aidan."

"We can have a tea party!" Annie jumped up and down, excitedly clapping her hands.

"Yes dear, Aidan would love to have a tea party and maybe Lilly will join us." With fondness, Tira remembered those days when the three of them would have tea parties. Amorica rarely joined them though. She smiled, knowing what Amorica would think about Jamie's outrageous proposition and what Damian would do if she followed through with his suggestion and joined him on board this ship for a week. Damian had a huge protective nature.

Jamie swept Annie into his arms with a gigantic hug and kiss on her cheek. "You be good and make sure you mind Tira." He slanted her what she thought was a wicked smile.

"Come along, Annie. Let's leave your father to his work while we play." She tilted her head flirtatiously and winked at him. Her actions were outrageous and she realized he wouldn't let her win this game, but she meant to challenge him at every turn.

Tira held out her hand to Annie who eagerly accepted it. With his coat thoroughly covering her, they left the shipyard and within ten minutes they walked into the Andrews home.

"There you are," Aidan greeted them, "And this must be Annie. I've seen you in town with your father." Aidan knelt to welcome her. "To what do I owe this pleasure?"

"Tira has to change her clothes because I unwrapped her, and Papa didn't like what he saw. She said we can have a tea party," Annie finished, sitting down on a chair, hands folded in her lap.

"Oh, my," Aidan said, staring at her cousin. "He saw you, your..."

"He knew who I was before I even got to the interview. This little one knew I was a lady the first time she saw me. Do you think Tavia was found out in this way?" Tira was suddenly frightened for her sister and what might be happening to her. She had no safe haven to run to if she found herself in trouble. She'd be on board the ship with nowhere to go.

"What about the unwrapping? He didn't like what he saw?" Aidan urged, looking as if she was sick.

Tira looked at her feet then Annie, "He obviously wasn't going to hire a woman for man's work, so he hired me..."

"As my nanny," Annie chimed in, grinning.

"When I went with Annie to play, I was uncomfortable so Annie helped me get rid of the bindings. I made the mistake of showing off for Annie."

"What did you do?"

"I climbed—"

"The mast," Aidan finished for her, her eyes wide. "Was it fun? I would have wanted so much to be up there with you. It's like being on the top of the world, I'm sure."

"Amazing. I could see so far. But Annie screamed because she was so excited and Jamie came running to see if his daughter had died," Tira finished on a somber note.

"And..."

"Well, I didn't realize the shirt didn't conceal anything. He was furious about both; the climbing and the sight of my breasts. He's allowing me to be Annie's nanny as long as I don't do anything else outrageous." She wasn't about to tell Aidan about the proposition and what she'd agreed to. That agreement was the most shocking thing she'd ever done. If she did, Aidan would send a message to Amorica and all her dreams of learning how to build a ship would end. Jamie was her last hope. She would figure out a way to keep from becoming his mistress or succumbing to his kisses. Giving in to his seductive passes was not part of her agenda.

"We'll have our tea party with lunch. Tira can join us after she changes her clothes." Aidan led Annie into the kitchen where Lilly was humming and fixing sandwiches.

Annie sat down at the table. "Will you fix some tea too? We're going to have a tea party with little sandwiches and cookies. Do you have cookies? Will you join us? Tira is changing her clothes."

"Of course I'll join you," Lilly said while she set the table then found a teapot and cups. "We have shortbread cookies, but you have to eat your lunch first. You know, I've never been to a tea party."

"Can I just have a cheese sandwich? I don't like ham." She sat down, making herself at home.

"Of course you can."

Tira swept into the room dressed casually. She found a dress that didn't require a corset and was eager to enjoy the fashion that was not dictated by English aristocracy.

"Really, Aidan, I could come to enjoy the freedom of no corset. I'd like to find a shirt that isn't so see through though."

"There's something you haven't told me. Maybe tonight you can say what's really on your mind." Aidan sipped her tea.

"We're going swimming after Papa's finished with work," Annie blurted. "Tira's coming too."

"I'm not, Annie. I don't have anything to wear. Never thought to pack a bathing suit."

"I have one. It might fit you if you really want to join them." Aidan raced up the stairs and appeared a minute later with a garment in hand.

Tira looked at it with a bit of disdain. "I don't know. I've never swum in anything before, and I'm not sure I want to spend time with Jamie tonight even if Annie is there."

"Well, we don't have the privacy of our lake near our home and we do have to adhere to the dictates of society. I don't think Jamie would appreciate you swimming in nothing."

Too bad Aidan didn't have the ability to see into the past. Tira was sure Jamie would love it if she swam naked but not in front of her daughter. "I'll take it but I'm thinking I'd be better off if I just put my feet in the water."

"Probably so," Aidan agreed reluctantly, eyeing her critically.

Tira was sure Aidan was seeing things she wasn't saying.

~ * ~

Jamie sat at his desk, his head in his hands. He acted horribly, baiting Tira, and he didn't understand what drove him. This was not who he was. And what was it about the young lady that put him on edge and tempted him in ways he never before experienced. Even Lizzy had not tempted him to put aside all his values, and he'd thought himself half in love with her.

He had been looking forward to swimming with Annie but now Tira would be there and he didn't know what outlandish thing she would say or do. For that matter he didn't know how he would react. She pushed, challenging him in ways he didn't understand.

Tossing his pen on his desk, he rose, pacing the room, unable to concentrate on anything but the site of Tira when she landed on the deck so effortlessly after climbing to the top the mast. She was an enigma he couldn't unravel, but did he want to?

Then there was the kiss and the outlandish proposition. Tira Hepburn was no man's mistress. He knew that. So why did he hope? What was it exactly that he wished for?

"Boss?"

His foreman, Clay stood in front of him. Clay never came to town unless something went wrong on the farm. Jamie had a small plantation outside town. He inherited it from his parents but he didn't like working the land. The sea was in his blood. So he let Clay handle the day-to-day issues.

"What is it?" Jamie felt the darkness from his man, understood there was a problem even before Clay spoke.

"There was a small fire at the worker's quarters. We think it was arson but can't prove it. We'll need to rebuild so I thought you should come take a look and give suggestions."

"Mooney!"

"What is it?" Mooney had this way of showing up in the split second he yelled his name. "You called?"

"I have to go out to the farm. Will you go to the Andrew's house and explain to Annie that we're not swimming this afternoon? I will make it up to her. Tell Tira that she needs to bring Annie home and stay there with her tonight." He liked the idea of Tira spending the night in his home. If he were honest with himself, he'd spent time trying to figure out how he could do that very thing without causing gossip.

"You think she's going to agree to that?" Mooney asked with a note of skepticism in his voice. "Maybe Annie should stay in the Andrew's house with the two ladies."

"No. I want Annie at home and in her bed." *And for some reason I want Tira there also.* "Tira can pick one of the extra bedrooms. There are at least four to choose from. On second thought tell her to take the room next to Annie's. I want her close to my daughter."

Jamie welcomed the chance to get out from behind his desk and do something physical. He pushed his horse, enjoying the freedom of riding outside the city and wondered if Tira liked to ride.

When he rode down the lane toward his farm, he saw smoke billowing from one of the outbuildings. Clay had ridden ahead of him and now he greeted him in front of the smoldering worker's quarters.

Jamie dismounted and for a few moments he surveyed the area. "Do you have any idea who set the fire?"

"No," Clay was shaking his head. "Just a dark shadow early this morning. We've had issues with the farm next door, but there's no proof anyone from that plantation set the fire."

"What are the issues?" Jamie was pretty sure he knew the answer, but he didn't want to put ideas into Clay's head.

"Don't like the fact that the blacks working for you get wages. Think you're setting a bad example for the rest of the folks in this region."

"I won't have slave labor."

"Probably why you're not making the money other farms are but it's your place. I'm not exactly keen on slaves either. Something about it is just not right in so many ways."

"That it is. When you're not paying people to work the land, you make more money. I'm not running this farm to get rich. We've got to rebuild. You can make a list of everything we need and run it by my office tomorrow and we'll buy what you request."

"Everything?"

"That's what I said and set up guards around the main house and the other out buildings. I'm going to pay the Wilson's a visit then I'm heading home." Jamie mounted, determined to get to the bottom of this.

His visit with Mr. Wilson didn't shed any light on the fire, but he understood the animosity the man and his family felt towards him. The Lundin farm employed anyone who wanted to work and paid them equal wages. Mr. Wilson clearly disliked him, but he wasn't willing to admit any part in the fire.

It was late when Jamie rode into town. Dark clouds were building in the south and a strong breeze whistled around him. He knew Tira and

Annie would be asleep in his house and that gave him a good feeling. He marveled that he took comfort in knowing Tira slept beneath his roof. Strangely he never wanted Lizzy to sleep in his house. He still owned her house and had thought to give it to a new mistress but that was six years ago.

"Tira?" he whispered into the darkness of the night. This ploy could go too far. Tira would never be his paramour and he understood that fact, yet he couldn't help himself from wishing. For now he would enjoy her charms from a distance, if that were possible.

Inside the barn, he brushed down his horse, watered and fed him then set his footsteps to his house eager to see his daughter and Tira. They would be asleep, but he meant to look in on his daughter and brush a kiss on her forehead. He would check in on Tira too and perhaps kiss her also.

Stepping inside his home he felt a moment of contentment. His two girls were asleep upstairs. Well, that was a bit early to make a pronouncement or an assumption. He had a lot of convincing to make Tira his girl. If she didn't like Lizzy's house, he'd build her a new one and rent out the first.

In the bathing room upstairs, he splashed water on his face and hair then towel dried it. Stepping into Annie's room, he froze. On the tiny bed, both Tira and Annie were curled up together. Annie was sound asleep, but when he stepped inside, Tira sat up, pushing raven black hair from her face. She wore one of his nightshirts. He sucked in air when it slipped off one shoulder revealing creamy white skin. Sleepy eyed and beautiful he was hard pressed not to pull her into his arms and carry her to his bedroom.

"Hush," Tira said as she slowly sat up, trying to scoot from the bed without disturbing Annie. "It took her forever to fall asleep. She missed your goodnight kiss, and I had to promise to stay in bed with her until you got home. I'll go now," she said in a whisper.

"Thank you," he told her knowing he'd done well when he hired her as a nanny. "I need to talk to you first." Where had that statement come from? What he wanted was Tira in his arms as well as his bed.

"I'll wait in the parlor downstairs. I hope you don't mind. I borrowed a few things." She grabbed a robe, his robe, before she left the room, shutting the door softly behind her.

He smiled, closing his eyes as if the image of her in his nightshirt was emblazoned in his head. Swiftly, he walked the short distance to Annie's bed. Kneeling beside her, he kissed her on the cheek. "Goodnight, little one. I love you. Sleep tight."

Annie opened her eyes then smiled before closing them again. Seeming content, she turned over and Jamie pulled the covers to her chin. Lingering, he watched her, mesmerized by the miracle he helped create. Then his mind focused on the beautiful woman waiting for him downstairs.

When he strode into the parlor, Tira was curled up on the sofa, a glass of brandy in her hand. She appeared sleepy and definitely tempting. He couldn't picture her in the house he kept for Lizzy or in another home. He could only see her in this house with him and Annie.

"I'll get dressed. I should go home now," Tira said but she didn't rise from the sofa. She watched him over the rim of her glass.

"No." At the sideboard he poured a glass for himself before settling next to Tira. "No, you can't walk home in the middle of the night by yourself. I can't leave Annie alone. You understand."

'Why do you have to go with me? I'm a big girl." She set her drink on a side table. "Really, I should leave before people know I spent the night in your home when you were here."

"If you're going to be my mistress, what does it matter?" He didn't like himself very well at the moment. This woman deserved better than what he could offer. She deserved a husband and children, if that's what she wanted. He should leave her alone and purge the unchaste thoughts he had for her from his head.

"I'm not going to be your mistress." She smiled at him, seeming to wait for his reply.

A surge of anger swept through him but he tamped it down. "I thought we had a bargain. You don't mean to renege on it now do you?"

"I suppose I do." She looked away, staring into the darkness outside. She rose then and walked outside. Sitting on the porch swing she pushed it gently. "I couldn't live with myself if I sold my body to someone I barely know." She shrugged her tiny shoulders, staring into the night.

"Why? You want to learn ship building. It was our bargain, remember?" He grabbed a quilt and wrapped it around her shoulders, sitting down beside her while he waited for an answer. "You don't want to take a chill."

Tira turned to him, touched a slender finger to his chin. He caught it, holding her small hand within his. What he wanted was to taste the tip, suck it deep into his mouth.

"Jamie, I won't be your mistress, but I will sail with you when you take your ship's maiden voyage. As with Ella, one week should be enough."

"Enough for what?" At least he would get part of the bargain, but he didn't believe one week with Tira would ever be enough, at least not for him. He wanted a lifetime with her.

"Enough payment, my reputation for my dream." Her voice dropped and he needed to move closer to hear her.

She sounded sad to him. "I don't need or want payment. Come with me on the trip if you want and whether you give yourself to me or not, I will put you to work when our next ship is commissioned. This agreement was never meant to hurt or intimidate you."

"I'm sorry. It's just that..." She swallowed, her lashes lowering, fanning across her cheeks.

If she would take comfort from him, he would pull her into his arms and hold her. As if understanding and accepting his thoughts, Tira leaned into his body. He held her close, the swing gently moving in a soothing rhythm. Time seemed to standstill as rain began to fall. The southern breeze changed and blew harder yet they remained on the swing.

"It's just what?"

"I was being flippant when I agreed to the terms you asked. I wanted to challenge and win. But the sacrifice is too great. Where you're concerned, I don't know what I want. You've changed me in ways I don't understand and I've hardly known you more than a day. I'd probably go to hell and back with you if you asked."

Touched, he stroked her back, vowing to do right by her. Thoughts of seduction evaporating, "We should go inside where it's warmer. We're in for a big storm tonight." He kissed her forehead and helped her stand. His arm around her they walked inside.

"Do you need help with the shutters? I've heard Amorica talking about the hurricanes that can sweep through here this time of the year. We need to close them before the winds get too strong."

"You think this is a hurricane?"

She shrugged her slender shoulders again, the cover slipping. "I don't know. I've never been in one. Could be, I suppose."

"Yes, to the shutters. It will go much faster. If you take care of the upstairs, they're on the inside, I'll go outside and close the downstairs shutters."

The wind had picked up and Jamie struggled with the last few before he finally finished. Inside the parlor, Tira was laying on the sofa a blanket over her seemingly ready for bed.

"There are plenty of bedrooms." He sat down beside her. "Don't feel compromised if you take one of the guest rooms."

"Have you seen them lately? The rooms?"

The expression on his face changed to remembrance. "They're filled with the things from Lizzy's home. I haven't had the chance to sell anything. For a while I thought about putting the house up for sale which is why I brought everything here."

"You've had no need to do anything with them. I'm sure it must be hard to get rid of things that were hers."

He realized it wasn't hard because while he enjoyed Lizzy's company, he never loved her. He just didn't bother. "You can take my bed."

"No, you must need your sleep. You've been up most the night." She looked at the grandfather clock. "It's after four am."

"We can share my bed. It's big." He waggled his eyebrows at her. A man could always hope.

"No," she whispered softly. "That will just not do."

"It's time to be practical. I'll put a row of pillows down the middle and I promise not to touch you."

"I don't know if I can promise not to touch you." She regarded him, her wide green eyes sparkling with fire. "And I'm not sure if I was lying in bed next to you, I'd be able to sleep."

"Why not?" He needed to hear her say the words. He sat beside her and pulling her into his arms, his mouth found hers. Her lips were soft and moist beneath his and the whisper of her warm breath sent his heart racing.

He felt her fingers wind into his hair, exploring then resting on the back of his neck, tiny nails moving with exquisite precision.

He pulled away, his hands still resting on her narrow waist.

"Because." She moistened her lips and he needed to taste her sweetness once more.

"Because why?"

She closed her eyes. "You make me feel as if I'm melting, and I want you to hold me and never let me go. Your kisses heat my body from the inside out and I know if I tried to sleep, I wouldn't be able to think about what comes after the kisses. Until you, I've never been kissed or touched in that way."

"Did you know I feel the same? Right now, this instant I need you in the most elemental way. If I told you what I wanted to do with your body, I'd shock you to your core."

"You've shocked me before."

"Are you encouraging me?" He ran his hands up her ribcage to just below her breasts, enjoying the rapid beating of her heart and the shallow quick breaths.

"I can't encourage you even though I'd like to."

"I'm beginning to feel as if I want to know more about you. Why can't you encourage me?"

"The Duchess," Tira said.

"The Duchess, she's across the ocean. I don't see her in this room. I hear she wields a strong cane."

"She does, but even though The Duchess isn't in the room, she's very much inside my head telling me that a kiss is fine but nothing else. Don't let a man touch you anywhere but on the lips."

He chuckled thinking about Tira's confession. "So, The Duchess had sex talks with you since your mother could not. She has a powerful hold on you then. I know your sisters did not adhere to her rule so why you?"

"Amorica wasn't with The Duchess long enough to find herself under The Duchess's thumb, and I don't think Auntie Charlotte thought she needed to do that—give sex talks. But she didn't get the desired results with the first three who came to live with her so she changed tactics and Ella was given a choice by Drake; go with him or never see him again."

"Your cousins?"

"Pretty much the same thing. Ravyn and Christel didn't get the talk. Storm was too far away and fell in love without coming to London. As for Fayth, she wanted to be ruined. She sailed away with Jarret so she wouldn't have to be a debutant in London."

"What about you?"

"I don't want to be ruined, but if I find the right man, someone I could fall in love with, I don't care if I am. However, I'm not in a hurry."

Strangely where Tira was concerned his thought process had changed and he wondered things he'd never thought possible. "You do know if you sail with me, you'll be ruined whether or not I take your virginity."

It seemed her eyes crossed. "You would do that?"

"What?" She had a way of changing the subject and confusing him.

"Take my virginity. The Duchess didn't talk about what that entailed. I'm not sure if it's something she would like."

He choked back a laugh. Her sex talk had not been very thorough. "She told you nothing about what happens between a man and a woman. Her only advice was to tell a man no if he did anything but kiss."

Tira was nodding her head with her bottom lip caught beneath her upper teeth. "She did tell us she didn't obey her rule when it came to the Duke, but she was lucky because he fell in love with her and married her. She said not all men would do that."

"She did?" Now he couldn't help the laughter. "I would love to hear some of her other stories."

"She has a lot of them, but I think Ella and Eveleen heard the most. Like Amorica I didn't stay in London long enough to thoroughly enjoy the time with her."

He had to find out what she would do if he touched her more intimately. His hand rose to cover her breast. While he watched, her eyes widened then his mouth closed over hers, sweeping his tongue inside. His body hardened with the feel of her nipple tightening beneath his touch. He paused a moment, waiting for her response. He rolled the tiny bud between his fingers. And the small sound coming from deep in her throat delighted him.

"The Duchess says no."

"What do you say, Tira? Do you have a mind of your own?"

"No, no mind at all right now."

Tonight, he knew he could seduce Tira, take her and she would give all that she knew how to give. Tonight, he could make her his, but he wanted their lovemaking to come from her heart. This evening however, he could teach her one more thing.

Slipping the robe from her shoulders, he quickly unfastened the shirt she wore. It fell open, the rounded globes of her breasts just visible in the opening. Kissing her again, his hand settled on her breast, touching the nipple lightly, teasing it until she moved against him, her hips arching, searching for something. He could almost hear her asking for more.

He drew apart from her then slowly and watching her eyes for as long as he could, he lowered his head and sucked her nipple into his mouth biting gently, the texture so exquisite. Her nails dug into his neck while her hips rose again.

He looked at her then, "What does Tira say?"

"That I don't think I can walk. That...I don't know." Her voice was a thin wail. "I don't want to say no."

At last The Duchess had vacated the room. "Time for you to go to bed. I'll carry you since you can't walk."

With nothing more said, he swept her into his arms and up the stairs. He set her on his bed then kissed her forehead just as he had his daughter. "Sleep well tonight, my sweet temptress."

She reached for him, but he backed from the room, "I'm sleeping downstairs on the sofa. No arguments. Tonight, I'm saying no. Hardest damn thing I've ever done though."

While he should be exhausted, he wasn't. Opening the outside door, he walked to the swing and sat down while the wind howled around him. The first half of the storm should sweep through by sometime tomorrow morning or early afternoon. Then the sun would shine before the second half hit land.

A different type of hurricane by the name of Tira Hepburn swept into his life. He truly didn't know how he was going to keep his eager hands to himself or his intentions noble. To do that he would have to have the help of The Duchess because Tira could not tell him to stop any more than he could say those words to himself. Good god, what had happened to his life in one short day? The cold wind and rain were what he needed. He'd go for a ride but..."

He sat on the swing until the day lightened enough for him to know it was morning. With a groan as he stood from aching muscles, he stretched then headed for the kitchen. Time to make breakfast. Annie will be downstairs and hungry before he could blink. He wondered how long Tira would stay in bed. Was she an early riser or did she sleep in? Unable to stop himself, he whistled, feeling truly happy for the first time in years.

He put wood in the kitchen stove and lit it then found the frying pan.

"Papa, you're back. I thought I saw you in the middle of the night but Tira's in your bed. Why?"

"Tira didn't have a bed to sleep in last night so your father gallantly gave her his." Tira strode into the room wearing the same dress as she had the day before. "I see it's still raining."

"And the wind is blowing," Annie finished excitedly. "We can't do anything but stay in the house until the storm blows over."

~ * ~

"Did you see that? Wanton hussy. While I understand Mr. Lundin is lonely, she has no business enticing him in britches." Louise Miller asked earlier, the afternoon Tira applied for a job. She was sweeping the walkway in front of her house and visiting with her friend.

"See what?" her friend Edna asked.

"That new girl to town, the one who moved in with Aidan McLellan in the Andrews house. She was dressed as a man early this morning. And she's still in that house. It's after suppertime. Someone should look after Annie a bit more or bet you Annie will be a whore just like her mother. I won't let my Sara play with her and neither will anyone else who knows her story," Louise said indignantly.

Edna shrugged, looking at the Lundin home. "Doesn't make much difference to me what he does. Must be his new mistress. He's been without one for nearly six years now. Everyone thought he'd move someone into Lizzy's home within a year after she died."

"But he didn't, did he?" Louise asked. "That girl needs a good and decent role model like my daughter."

"Do you really think you should judge the little girl by her mother's actions? You know, Louise, he's never looked a second time at your daughter. If he'd been interested in her, he wouldn't have waited six years to do anything about it."

"It's scandalous if you ask me. When you have a father who keeps mistresses, what do you think will happen to his daughter? Damian Andrews needs to know what's going on right under his nose and put a stop to it." Louise put her hand above her eyes to shield them from the dimming sun while she stared at the Lundin home.

"Well, who do you think is going to ride way out there to tell him? No one we know. Besides, Jamie Lundin does what he wants when he wants. Doubt if Andrews can stop him."

"He's going to have to wait to find out what's going on in his house until he makes one of his few trips into town. I'm sure Amorica would have something to say. I heard the woman is her sister. Do you think that's true? Amorica wouldn't want all this gossip."

"I believe it's up to us to let him know. I'm going to find someone who feels as outraged as I do," Louise said. "Then I'm going to send a message to Amorica and Damian. Tell them exactly what's going on over there."

The wind whipped up a small funnel of dirt and debris. "You're going to have to put all your outrage on hold for a while. Looks like a storm is brewin'. Probably time to close the shutters before it gets worse."

Louise held her hand to her eyebrows, staring at the darkening horizon. "I'm not going to forget this. As soon as this storm blows itself out, I'm going to get a message to her sister."

Chapter Three

"Alright then, what will we do?" Tira asked as she watched Jamie cut potatoes into little squares, her mouth watering. "Can I help?"

"Don't have any idea," Jamie said while he put bacon in the pan. "Can you cook?"

"Do you like to play cards?" Tira asked, eyeing him critically and shrugging.

"Not very well."

"Don't know how to play cards. We can play with my dolls. Papa likes to do that. Don't you, Papa?"

Tira slanted Jamie a glance then laughed when he shrugged his broad shoulders. "I'm sure he loves playing dolls, dressing them, feeding them, putting them to bed."

"You could practice tying your knots," Jamie volunteered from his place in front of the stove.

"I don't like to tie knots," Annie said crossing her arms in front of her, head down and a tiny pout to her lips. "Knots are supposed to tie things up, not just sit there ready for your inspection."

Jamie laughed before changing the subject and the focus of this conversation. "When the storm lets up, I'm going to take a walk around town, survey the damage. The second half of the hurricane will run roughshod over anyone who's already in trouble. If the shipyard has fared well, anyone needing shelter can take cover there."

"Do you want company?" Tira felt the confinement to the tips of her toes. With the windows shuttered one had to poke their head out the door to see anything but the walls. Walls, which seemed to close in on her.

"Can't leave Annie alone and she can't come with us if that's what you were about to ask." He slipped the potatoes into the frying pan.

"Maybe I can work with her on her knots." Tira regarded the little girl with new motivation. Jamie didn't believe women could do a man's job, but he thought his daughter should learn something only men learned. Where would she ever use that knowledge in Jamie's world?

"That would be nice. Do you know how to tie any?" His voice held a tinge of cynicism but he grinned anyway.

"No." She paused in thought, searching for a way to combat his sarcasm, "but I can watch her. She's such a sweet little girl and I enjoy spending time with her and I do enjoy playing dolls with her. If you're out, could you stop by and see how Aidan and Lilly fared during the storm? Maybe get me a change of clothing also."

He nodded while he scooped the potatoes from the pan. The sausage was done too.

He must have bought a loaf of bread the other day because a fresh loaf was cut and sitting on the table.

"Martha, the lady who runs the boarding house and little café near the docks brings me fresh bread every day. This was yesterday's." It seemed Jamie read her thoughts.

"What do you say we have another tea party with our breakfast? Run upstairs and bring down a couple of your dolls, your favorite ones of course. I'm sure they'd love to be a part of this early morning feast," Tira said hoping to put a smile back on Annie's little face.

Annie jumped from her chair and raced up the stairs.

"You have a way with her."

"Your daughter is a sweet child. I enjoy spending time with her. Aren't there other children her age she can play with?" In so many ways playing with Annie reminded her of her childhood, but the little girl needed someone other than adults to form bonds with.

"How did you sleep?" He dished up three plates then set them on the table, ignoring her question.

"Most likely better than you." She poured tea for everyone. "You're very good at changing the subject."

"I haven't slept. Spent the night thinking and part of it sitting on the swing outside. Most of the families try to keep their children away from Annie because of her mother."

The bombshell he dropped stopped her heart. She didn't know where to begin but decided the questions about Annie should wait until she knew him better. "Thinking about what?" Her stomach growled as she eyed the food.

"You and me. Our bargain."

She didn't want to remember what she let him do to her last night simply because she wanted him to do it again. He was watching her now, probably waiting for her to say something. "Perhaps you shouldn't do that, think. It always gets me into trouble."

"Perhaps we should talk."

"No." She was shaking her head again and was relieved when Annie showed up with two dolls in tow. She couldn't talk because she didn't know what to say or how she felt about him and the way he touched her. With every second her feelings changed where Jamie was concerned.

His expression was unreadable but she knew he would pursue this at the first available opportunity. He wasn't a man to take no for an answer especially when that no concerned him and what he wanted.

"Yes." He smiled pointedly in the direction of the sofa even though she couldn't see it through the walls. Perhaps it was her imagination. "We will talk and it will be sooner than later."

"Can we eat now, Papa? I'm hungry and my dolls want to eat." Annie set the dolls on separate chairs and found a teacup for each of them. "Are you and Tira arguing?"

"Of course we can eat. Do you want to give your friends something to eat too?" Jamie asked.

He reached to the counter and retrieved two small plates and placed potatoes on each one. "Thank you, Papa. They were very hungry."

While they ate inside, silence clung to the air. Outside, Tira heard the wind howling around the house. Even Annie was unusually silent. Jamie was right. They needed to talk but she didn't know what to say. No one had touched her like that before, and she didn't know what to make of it or what his intentions were beyond the obvious. The Duchess said no but Tira definitely said yes and what was she really saying yes to?

Finishing the dishes, they cleaned up and Annie sat in the parlor dressing her dolls and pretending they were going to school. The storm died down so Jamie decided to survey the damage.

"I'll be back in an hour or less. Keep Annie inside and hopefully entertained." With that said, the door closed behind him.

"Guess it's just you and me to idle away the time until it starts raining again. Do you want to take your dolls to the porch so we can enjoy the brief respite and a little sunshine?" Tira wanted to see what the hurricane had done to the homes around them, and she was thankful Jamie's house withstood the storm.

"I guess we can do that but I want to make Papa happy so before he gets back, I need to show him I've practiced my knots."

Tira was laughing inside. The two of them seemed obsessed with knots. Why couldn't he just let her be a little girl? "I'll tell you what, we can tie the chairs in the house together and you can show me how to do at least one knot."

"That will make it so much more fun. Can we do all the chairs?" She jumped up from the floor, clapping her hands and laughing.

"Of course, whatever you want. We have to idle away the time we are cooped up inside. Do you know why your father wants you to learn how to tie knots? I've got to say I'm baffled by this endeavor."

"He says it could come in handy sometime. I'd rather play with my dolls though." She shrugged with a silly grin on her face. "I don't know when tying knots will be useful."

"Neither do I."

"Then why does he make me do it?"

"Maybe because he really doesn't enjoy playing with dolls," Tira mused as she watched his precious daughter crinkle her brows in thought.

Tira stood inside the parlor, hands on her hips, carefully perusing the room. "Let's start with those two chairs. You can tie both of them to the side tables. What kind of knot are you going to use?"

"Papa wants me to learn a bow line and a clove hitch. He says they're the most important in sailing." She left for a minute and returned with about ten long pieces of rope.

"Is that what you're going to use?" Tira was amazed. In a matter of minutes Annie had all the tables and chairs in the parlor tied together. The knots didn't look like anything but a jumble, but what did she know?

"That was a lot more fun. You have wonderful ideas." She brushed her hands together as if she had just finished an important task. "Can we do the same in the kitchen?"

"I don't see why not. You do know you will have to untie all these when your proud papa returns."

"Papa will check them first and tell me how wonderful I am but also that I didn't tie them right."

They were just putting the finishing touches on the kitchen tables and chairs when the front door squeaked open.

Annie ran to meet her father in the hallway only tripping over a couple of her projects in her mad dash. "Papa, do you see what we did? It was so much fun. Tira knows how to make a game out of everything."

He dropped the valise he was carrying and scooped Annie into his arms, giving her a big kiss and hug, which the little girl returned tenfold.

"Games out of everything, hmm...that gives me some pleasant and interesting ideas."

"That's not entirely true," Tira defended her ploy seeing the dark look he shot her way.

Taking his gaze from Tira, "I see the two of you have been busy. Let me look at your knots and see how you did. Did Tira help you tie all these?"

"Hardly, I haven't any idea how to do these, and it seemed she tied each one a little bit different. There doesn't seem to be any rhyme or reason to her creativeness." Tira tenderly placed a hand on the little girl's head, wishing she could give Annie everything she needed. But Annie needed a mother and she wasn't in a position to do that.

"That's why I want her to practice." Jamie laughed studying the plethora of knots she created. "You're right. Not one of these is the same. I wonder how long it's going to take her to untie all these."

"We do mean to help her, don't we?" Tira wondered at Jamie's words. "Jamie, why does she need to learn something a man does when I can't by your dictate do the same thing?"

"She tied them. She can untie them," he said blandly, easily ignoring her question.

"Alright then, what are we going to do?" She gave up expecting answers from him about subjects he must feel uncomfortable with.

"You're leaving that up to me. I would have thought you knew I have a one-track mind where you're concerned." He leaned against the doorframe, arms crossed over his chest and seemed to study her. "If I had my choice, I'd sweep you into my arms and take you to my bed."

"It's your home. You always seem to have an agenda and you wouldn't do that with Annie in the house."

"I'm not worried about anything as long as Annie is close by and what you said is true. So, what are we going to do?"

He wrapped an arm around her and walked upstairs with her as if he meant to take her to his bed. "You need a bedroom to sleep in tonight and every other time you sleep here, since you won't share my bed. We're going to move everything that isn't mine or Lizzy's out of the bedroom."

"I'm sleeping here tonight too? I could go home right now before the storm hits again." Her entire body shuddered against his large frame and she didn't know why. Giving up on the notion she might gain his permission to return home, "You brought my valise. I certainly hope Aidan picked out the clothes and not you. Did she give you a hard time?"

"Yes and no and yes." He pushed open the door. "I'm going to put all the furniture downstairs and tomorrow when the storm has blown through, I'll have Mooney and some of my men move the items back to the other house."

"I'll look through the crates before you take them downstairs, maybe sort out a few items. Didn't Lizzy have relatives who might have liked some of her things?" She pried open the first box.

"No one, no family she wanted to acknowledge. Why don't you see if there is anything Annie might want in memory of her mother? I did give Lizzy a few pieces of jewelry that could be saved for Annie when she grows up. I think Lizzy would want her to have them. I know I would."

Tira sat on the bed, which was now devoid of the two end tables and a chair that had been piled on it. Searching through the crates she found a variety of odds and ends, really not much that would merit saving.

The jewelry box held some beautiful pieces, a diamond and sapphire necklace and matching bracelet and so much more. Annie would love all of this when she was old enough to wear them. Crate after crate, Tira looked through. Most she set outside for Jamie to take back to the rental house. A few she set close to the door for Jamie to look through and decide what to do with.

The jewelry put aside, Tira found a crate full of books. On top was a journal. Tempted to look through it she stopped herself. This could be something Annie could cherish, depending on what it said. She didn't want anything that might be written in the book to hurt Jamie.

Closing her eyes and thinking hard, Tira made up her mind. She wouldn't read all of it, just enough to make sure it was friendly to both Annie and Jamie. The words written on the pages were nearly indecipherable.

She squinted her eyes and strained to read the words. Lizzy had tried to put her thoughts on the paper, but it was apparent to Tira she had a difficult time and it occurred to Tira that Lizzy had made the best of her short life. When she thought of the jewelry, Jamie must have treated her like royalty. If not for Jamie, what would have become of Lizzy?

The few words she could decipher were friendly and told of a love Lizzy had for Jamie. She adored him and thanked him for all the good things that had happened in her life. Tira set the book aside, deciding she would show Jamie and let him determine when and if Annie would receive the journal.

Beneath the diary was a stack of five books. Tira picked up every one, opening each to the middle then reading bits and pieces. After perusing the books, she set them all, *Fanny Hill, Philosophy in the Bedroom, Therese the Philosopher, Margot la Ravaudeuse and The Indiscreet Jewels,* save one beneath the bed, intending to read each one.

What she read left her confused and curious about lovemaking and what went on in the bedroom. She thought of asking Jamie about some of the things that were penned but decided against it and settled for exploring what the books could teach her. If she was going to make love with him, she needed to understand a few things The Duchess never told her.

She heard Jamie's footsteps on the stairs. With trembling fingers, she stuffed the book beneath the pillow on the bed, realizing the sheets needed changing before anyone could sleep there. She would make sure Jamie didn't uncover her new treasures.

"I see you've separated some of Lizzy's possessions. I assume everything outside goes back to the house and everything on the floor in the bedroom you want me to look through. What have you saved out?" He stepped inside. "Why are you blushing?"

"Am I? I..." her hands flew to her hot cheeks.

"What aren't you telling me?" He sat down beside her, one hand resting on hers, the warmth permeating through her. "At least you have a bed now. If only it was larger, I would be tempted to join you."

"I found a journal Lizzy wrote. I think you should look at it," she said in an attempt to divert his attention from her heated cheeks and her focus from the lazy movement of his thumb against her skin.

She handed it to him and watched him open it, staring at the pages, a blank expression on his face before he finally looked at her. "I had no idea Lizzy could write let alone read."

She didn't want to say anything, just tried to keep her expression neutral. "I think Annie might want to see this when she's older. I don't know what you can decipher from it, but what has been written on these pages might tell Annie something about her mother."

"Anything else?" His hold on her hand tightened, squeezing slightly, his gaze riveted on her eyes.

"Just the jewelry you mentioned, nothing more." She handed him the box, which he set aside.

"What makes you blush? This time it wasn't me because I wasn't here. Show me what you found."

"Nothing. When you walked in the room it made me think of last night and your kisses."

"There was more than just a kiss," he reminded her pointedly.

She ran her tongue across her lips, looking away while feeling her body reheat and her cheeks flame anew. His calloused fingers created sensations on just her hand and good lord, she remembered the feel on her breast.

"You don't have to remind me. I remember it clearly." She could barely inhale a breath of air.

"Are you thinking about the beautiful things we can share with each other?" his finger on her chin, he turned her to look at him.

"No."

"I don't believe you."

"Well, you should." She rose, tugging at her hand until he let go. "I need to see what Annie is doing."

"She's fine." He quickly blocked her path, his hands on her shoulders, reminding her he was in control.

"How do you know?" She needed to get out of this room before she did something she'd regret.

"I checked on her before I came up here to check on you." His hands settled on her waist, teasing her emotions in too many ways.

"We have at least ten minutes before we should see to Annie. I want to know what heated your cheeks so beautifully. While I'd like to believe it was the memories from yesterday, I don't imagine that's the truth."

She was shaking her head and backing toward the bed where she abruptly sat down on it. He was beside her before she realized this was exactly where she didn't want to be. "I should go find fresh bedding."

"You should kiss me."

"The bargain doesn't start until the ship sails."

"It's only a kiss and has nothing to do with making love, smoothing the way is how I see it." He set hair behind her ear, allowing his finger to explore her ear, down her neck then her lips. "I want to give you new experiences every day. Your education, I suppose. A complete innocent in my bed might be nice, but I prefer a woman who can give as well as receive. So, one tiny step at a time I believe is best. Tira's education."

"What if I don't want to be educated?"

"Then you would never have agreed to the proposal, the bargain we made. Of course you can change your mind at any time. Do you want to do that?" His voice took on a stern note she'd never heard before.

"It's just that I'm afraid and curious at the same time. I don't know what to expect." Her hand rested on his chest.

"There's no need for fear. I won't hurt you or do anything you say no to even if it's The Duchess speaking in your head. I might try to convince you otherwise. Let me kiss you, Tira."

Her lashes fluttered closed and before she opened them his mouth settled on hers. A heated whisper of longing swept through her sending an inferno surging within. The pressure of his lips against hers was sweet and tender, seducing even as he leisurely stroked. Pulled against his length she tried to memorize the feel of his body touching hers. His scent permeated her senses.

On every level, if she admitted it to herself, she gave in to him and wanted everything he was willing to give. She pressed her tongue against his lips, tracing the seam and wondering if he'd let her explore inside. Rewarded for her aggression, he met her advance with one of his own.

The slide of his hands against her back drew her closer. She was sure she felt the beat of his heart against her breast, could hear each breath he inhaled.

"You're so sweet. You taste like you, just as woman should. It seems I'm hard pressed to stop but later tonight we need to talk about this, what we're doing here and what we intend to do. What do you really want, Tira Hepburn? Do you want me deep inside you?" His hand rested on her breast, cupping it and teasing the bud through the fabric of her gown.

She gasped at his words. *Deep inside me...* Her tiny moan seemed to give him reason to smile. She pushed away. "I need time to think."

The crash was earsplitting. Tira jumped at the noise, terrified. She found herself held tight in Jamie's arms.

~ * ~

"What was that?"

"Annie!" Jamie turned, racing from the room, taking the steps to the first floor two at a time, Tira following. "Annie!"

"Papa." Jamie found Annie huddling near the kitchen entrance, tears sliding down her eyes. "What was that noise?"

"I don't know." Jamie pulled Annie into his arms, hoping to soothe her shaking body. "I'm going to check it out."

"You shouldn't go outside in this storm. It's not safe," Tira said. "Let's just check out the house. It sounded as if a tree fell and hopefully it didn't hit the house."

Reluctantly, he agreed. "Stay here with Annie." Jamie headed upstairs to check each room.

Tira pulled the terrified little girl into her arms. "I suppose we should stay in the middle of the room. Are you hungry? It must be close to dinner. Let's go into the kitchen and figure out what we can put on the table. Unless of course there is a tree blocking the way."

"We didn't eat lunch. Papa got back and I'm hungry."

Jamie returned almost as quickly as he left. "Nothing hit the house."

Tira turned, her hand on Annie's shoulder. "We're going to find something to set on the table for dinner."

"There's eggs and bread. We could have another breakfast, this time for dinner. With the café closed, I don't have much in the pantry." Jamie searched for something he could fix, feeling as if he let Annie down for the hundredth time.

"Hope you can cook them," Tira said, finding the bowl of eggs and setting them near the oven.

"You can't cook." Jamie smiled at her, chuckling. "Something else I need to teach you." He'd much rather teach her how to make sweet love to him.

"If you expect that to be part of our bargain, I suppose. My sisters would never eat anything I prepared." She fiddled with the dishtowel, her eyes downcast.

"What is your talent, Miss Hepburn?" he asked, hoping the most brilliant part of her talents would become apparent in his bed.

She shrugged slim shoulders before replying. "Don't know that I have any. Ella can draw beautifully. Gossip has it she drew pictures of Drake. He was naked. I suppose I could try to sketch you, but I don't know what a naked man looks like. Well, I've seen statues but..."

"Thank God."

"You know things I can't even imagine," she said.

"That's alright. I think I heard about the nefarious sketchpad and drawings. Also heard there were drawings of them making love." He gazed at her, undressing her in his mind and imagining possible sketches of them in the nude, arms and limbs entwined, her mass of hair wrapping around him. He needed a glass of brandy, maybe three or four.

"My cousin, Storm, breeds horses and sells them to people who race them. I could try my hand at that, but while I can ride I don't really like sitting on a horse, and I wouldn't know the first thing about breeding them."

She was toying with him now, twirling a lose piece of hair around her finger. "If your cousin breeds horses, why do you seem so innocent to the ways of man and a woman. You should have some ideas."

She paled. "I've never been to her stables. I avoid them and have always pleaded a headache when the suggestion was made. I don't like horses. They frighten me."

"I see." He broke eggs into the bowl, scrambling them before adding a pinch of salt. Butter in the frying pan began to heat then to boil. He slid the eggs into the pan. "What else can your cousins do?"

"Eveleen paints landscapes." She made a face. "Everyone but Tavia and myself...none of us had mothers. Our fathers let us do whatever we wanted to do and cooking, sewing, singing, learning to play the piano...didn't appeal to any of us."

He wanted to laugh but kept the emotion in check. "An unruly lot of girls who refuse to learn the finer arts that were supposed to get them a husband."

"I suppose so." Looking down, she fiddled with her fingers. "I do climb trees, well, and masts," she reminded him with a hesitant smile.

"Do you think Annie will be unruly?" Jamie stared at her for a few seconds, waiting for an answer.

"I hope she has a mind of her own and will make good judgments," Tira said.

"Of course, an independent woman and strong woman." He didn't want Annie to make bargains with a man she barely knew.

"Father wasn't like you. He didn't care about us and perhaps we are strong willed, liberated and in being that way we can take care of ourselves. You love Annie and care so you will instill values in her that you want her to have."

His gut rolled. It seemed The Duchess was the only person in her life who cared about her. New respect for Tira's aunt filled him and subtly changed the way he thought of Tira.

"Eggs are done." Jamie set the table and they gathered to eat. "Would you like wine?"

Annie was strangely silent. Her dolls still had their place at the table. Annie had eaten half her meal. "Papa, I'm tired. Can you read me a bedtime story?"

He'd lost track of the hour. A quick look at his pocket watch, he discovered it to be past her bedtime. "Come along then." He held out his hand for Annie and she clasped his.

"Tomorrow the storm will be over and you can go outside. Will you like that?"

"I know but we won't be able to go swimming. You'll be helping everyone clean up and rebuild just like you always do."

"Tira will be here with you."

"I like her but she's not you, and she can't take me swimming," Annie pouted.

He wanted to laugh but thought better of it. "Get dressed for bed. I'll be right back." He left her for a few seconds to make sure Tira didn't run to her bedroom to hide.

He found Tira on the sofa, sipping a glass of wine. "Don't go to bed," he warned. "I'll be down as soon as I talk with Annie."

"I won't go anywhere," she whispered.

Upstairs he read a short story, tucked Annie in and after giving her a kiss to her forehead, left the room.

In the parlor he poured a glass of brandy and sat down next to Tira. "I'm sorry about your father."

"Don't be. He's been lost to everyone since mother died. You remember he didn't even attend Ella's wedding and if I ever marry and if he's still alive, he won't show up at my wedding either." A small tear slid down her cheek.

His heart went out to her and gently he pulled her into his arms. Her head settled against his chest. He stroked her hair. The silken mass filled his fingers and he longed to wrap himself in the dark strands.

"Do you still want to sail with me? It's going to be at least a week, maybe two before we can leave town. With the damage from the storm," he paused "and the burning of one of the workers quarters on my farm, I just don't know when the time will be right."

"I want to find out..." she hesitated, pushing away from him. "I want you to make love to me, no one else."

"But do you want to sail with me knowing the people in town will talk. Do you want to keep our bargain?" The question burned in his mind.

He needed to know she was doing this of her own volition.

"I guess Hepburns think alike. Ella didn't care about the gossip and neither do I. People who spread rumors, true or not, in time will find something else to talk about."

"But do you care?" He needed no regrets if they pursued this. What would come after the fact he didn't know, but he was willing to chance it just to spend a week with Tira Hepburn.

"A little."

"There are already rumors about you and me. I've heard some people are thinking to send messages to Damian. What do you think he would do?" He didn't really care. There were no threats that could dissuade him from the bargain if that's what Tira truly wanted.

"I don't know. It probably depends on what I tell him."

"You wouldn't want him to hurt me," Jamie laughed, placing a chaste kiss on Tira's forehead.

"You've touched my heart in ways I could have never guessed possible, Jamie Lundin. But I'm frightened I'm making the wrong decision. Waiting two weeks is just going to make me more nervous and apprehensive."

"If Damian shows up here before or after I take you away for a week, he'll likely keelhaul me."

She laughed softly, running her hand along his chest. "Damian won't hurt you."

"Why not?"

"I won't let him."

"You are his sister in law and I plan on making love to you. He'll want us to wed or he'll seek to damage me physically."

"After what he did to my sister? He married her against her will and hid her away in a castle near Dover with his paramour. For the longest time she loathed him. He has no high ground to stand on."

"Until Damian convinced Amorica to love him." Jamie wondered about the story. Over the years he'd heard several rumors, and he recalled other things about their rocky relationship. Amorica had been kidnapped and Damian had to fight to get her back. It was a fight to the death for the loser.

"Damian was a smuggler and it was a smuggler who killed mother. Amorica hated him because of that and she shot him."

"Didn't do a lot of damage, I gather."

"No, story is, it was a flesh wound." Her thoughts changed to another sister. "I don't know where Tavia is. I'm frightened for her. She set off on a ship to somewhere as a cabin boy."

"What about us?" He lifted her chin, kissing her softly, tasting the saltiness of her tears. "Where do we stand in this story?"

"I don't know because I don't know what I want where it concerns you. I know that if we go off together our relationship might not end well. I need the respect of my family, and I won't have it at the end of our fun together. But for some reason I don't understand and can't explain I want to be with you, intimately, and what other people are going to say doesn't bother me as much as I thought it would."

"And I'll give you all you bargained for."

"In the end, I don't know if that will be enough. I guess if I do this, it will have to be enough to last a lifetime." She paused to sip from her wine glass. "My mind keeps changing."

"I'm sure in London you'll find someone to love you." Thinking of Tira in another man's arms didn't sit well, a dark cloud hovering in his mind. He yearned to find a way to bind her to him.

"Once all is said and done, I'll go back to London. I want you to know that. I'm not going to pressure you for anything. Only those I care about will know what we did and they'll understand, and while they won't like my decision, they'll know it was mine to make and they'll respect me."

His gut tightened, not liking the gist of her words but unable to promise love or marriage. She touched his heart in ways no other person had, but she was aristocracy. Good god, she was related to a duchess. He could never ask her to marry him, a commoner. Not that he had any use for marriage.

"Perhaps I've asked you for too much," he told her, regretting his words the moment he said them.

"You've changed your mind then? You don't want me."

"You should go back to London before you regret what we're about to do. Because if you stay in Baltimore, I won't be able to stop myself. I want you too much."

"Enough, we keep talking about things that make no difference to me. Ravyn wed a commoner, a bastard. Are you a bastard?"

"I will be if I keep pursuing you." *She can't know what she does to me.* Thoughts of her sleeping in the room adjoining his kept him awake at night.

"Storm wed a commoner, a wealthy one, just like..."

"Like me?"

"I didn't mean to imply that you would marry me. I don't want a husband and you don't want a wife, so we're perfect for each other. There really isn't much more to discuss."

"But that's a lie, isn't it? You do want a husband and a family. Just not me." He was determined now to...to do what? He still wanted her so desperately, he didn't think he could ever let her go.

"You're wrong. My not wanting a husband has nothing to do with you. If I had to pick a man from any I know, I would choose you."

"It's nice to know I'm your first choice." Funny thing was, she was his first choice, too, if he was forced to marry.

Lost in thought and feeling the silence, he felt her slowly fall asleep in his arms. Holding her felt like heaven to his soul yet it brought back memories of another time he'd rather forget.

A long time ago, even before Lizzy, he'd had his heart broken. He fell in love with his childhood sweetheart. She was everything Tira was not. Her hair was flaxen and her eyes were the deepest blue, and she professed to love him until the day she died.

Kendall, his first and only wife broke his heart and he vowed never to let a woman in his heart again. Between the constant arguing of his parents and the pain he felt when Kendall left with another man, he vowed never to wed. Years had come and gone and if Lizzy had not come into his life, he might still be wallowing in self-pity.

He felt as if he had finally found home with Tira in his arms, and the thought he might lose her in a month or so made his heart stop. Imperative that he come to terms with what he wanted for his future, he had to decide if Tira held that kind of place in his heart. Yet he didn't know if he was ready to open up to someone and become vulnerable again.

Before standing with Tira in his arms, he lightly kissed her forehead then strode to her bedroom. He set her on the bed, loosening her garments before leaving.

Her long sooty lashes fluttered open. "Jamie?"

"You fell asleep. I just brought you to your bed. I'm leaving now."

Downstairs a quick glance at the grandfather clock told him it was almost five in the morning. The wind had died and rain no longer pounded on the roof. Unable to sleep, he strode outside to survey the damage caused by the storm and discover what caused the explosive sound last evening.

Rising water ran through the street in front of his house, expanding to near porch level. He walked the length of the deck then peering around the corner, he saw the source of the crash. The huge oak tree had fallen, uprooted by the wind and the rain.

He swallowed the lump in his throat when he realized how close the tree had come to his house and his daughter's room.

The storm surge sent water into the shipyard but seemed to be receding as he watched. He could see the masts of his ship standing proud and tall and suspected the vessel withstood the battering winds and rain.

Gripping the railing of his porch, he regarded the other homes in the vicinity. The café where he purchased most of his food had water flowing inside. But when he looked to Martha's home above the restaurant, she was waving out the window, telling him she was fine.

He needed to find a way to the Andrews home, but right now there was no way man or beast could navigate the rushing water. However, a boat could. When he turned his attention back to the shipyard, he saw Mooney waving to him. He was lowering a skiff into the water and began rowing in his direction. At first Jamie thought Mooney would be swept out to sea, but slowly he made progress and pulled the small boat onto the land at the corner of his house.

"You're pretty creative, Mooney."

"Just aimin' to please. I know you would want to check out the neighbors personally. When I saw you were up, that's when I decided to bring out the skiff and see if you were ready to dare the currents."

"Thanks, let me leave a note on the kitchen table for Tira so she won't worry then I'll meet you."

"She stay at your place during the storm?" Mooney's voice turned gruff and disapproving. "If you're not careful you're going to make life real difficult for her. People are already talking about you and her and what she's doing for you."

Jamie heard the censure in his first mate's voice, understanding it came from concern for both Tira and himself. "Didn't have much of a choice since she was here when the storm began, and I couldn't leave Annie alone in the house to get her home."

"You could have asked me to see Tira to the Andrews' place."

"Was I supposed to send up smoke signals?" he asked sarcastically.

"If that was the only way."

Jamie didn't want to argue, and he wasn't about to answer questions about his conduct. "Let's head straight to Andrews home then we can make our way back. I'm assuming they are fine since they're situated on a hill." He left, striding through the parlor then into the kitchen with a paper and pen in hand. He set the note under a cup close to the teapot.

Mooney was silent when he returned and Jamie was thankful his friend wasn't letting lose with a barrage of questions that would leave him thinking about things he didn't want to consider at the moment.

With both men at an oar, they battled the current and finally found a place to land close to the Andrews' porch.

Aidan came out to greet them, waving, "Would you two like a hot cup of coffee and a bite to eat?"

"Sure. You're up early." Jamie stepped from the boat and with Mooney alongside him, they pulled it out of the water.

"Always get up at the crack of dawn." She smiled. "Come on inside. Everyone here is fine. How is Tira?" The censure in her voice didn't go unnoticed.

"I left her sleeping soundly." Jamie's brows furrowed together at the sight of Aidan's expression. "She didn't sleep with me and I shouldn't have to tell you that."

"But you plan on doing that very thing. Why not seal the bargain before the ship finds water?" Her sarcasm did not go unnoticed.

"I'm not like that." He choked on his words, knowing if Tira were more experienced or more amenable he would have had her in his bed the first night she slept at his house.

"Good to hear. Now come inside and have a delicious scone Lilly made. I'm sure Tira hasn't had time to prepare many delicacies with her duties as a nanny, but she's a very good cook."

He paused, rubbing his chin and remembering her words, no one would eat anything she prepared it was so bad. "A good cook you say? That's not what she's told me."

Aidan nodded, smiling as she walked through the house to the kitchen. "The best of all of us, cousins included. She won't admit it but she has a way in the kitchen. She can make anything taste delicious."

"She told me she had no talents and she didn't know how to boil water," he said, his words whispering from deep in his throat.

"She lied," Aidan said flippantly with a small laugh. "I'm sure you've lied to her about your intentions. All men lie. You're still welcome to have coffee and a scone."

"I'm not Blade MacPherson," He retaliated through gritted teeth.

"Of course you're not. If you were you wouldn't be welcome here, and I wouldn't be serving you scones and coffee." She skipped away, seeming pleased with herself.

He was more than glad Tira was more amenable than Aidan McLellan. Although he knew Tira could be just as bristly at times, one of her more endearing qualities. He so enjoyed the way Tira stood up to him for herself.

The kitchen smelled delicious. Loaves of fresh baked bread were set on the counter and coffee brewed on top of the stove. Lilly quickly poured him a cup and set the plate of scones in the middle of the table.

"You two going to join me?" he asked as he set a scone on his plate and reached for the strawberry preserves.

"We've both eaten, but I'll sit with you and enjoy a second cup. There's not much to do as long as the streets are running with water. "She sipped the coffee Lilly set on the table for her, eyeing him critically over the rim of her cup.

"You have questions? I can see them brimming in your eyes." He tried to remain calm but his fingers drummed on the table and his foot tapped a rapid staccato on the floor.

"Since you got yourself here." She looked pointedly to him then Mooney, who seemed to be enjoying the small breakfast Lilly had set out. "I expect Tira here before nightfall."

Jamie toyed with his napkin. "That's not a question."

Aidan glared at him, her brows drawing together in disapproval. "No, it isn't. Well... I'm waiting for an answer to my statement." She drummed her fingers on the table, tilting her head to one side.

Clearing his throat before meeting her gaze, "That won't be possible unless the flood lets up. It took the two of us to get to your house. I can't leave Annie, a six-year-old, alone."

Aidan sat back, a scowl on her pretty face. "You need to find a way. Be creative."

"Not possible." This little slip of a girl was not going to dictate to him. Tira would return to the Andrews' home when it was safe.

"What are your intentions toward my cousin?" She leaned forward, her hands clasped together.

"That's not your business."

"It is because Tira has no one to protect her interests save me. I won't have you taking advantage of her. So tell me..."

He rose, knocking the chair he'd been sitting on to the floor, "Thank you for your hospitality. If you need anything, send Joshua."

"Wait," Lilly ran after him, two loaves of bread wrapped in dishcloths. "These are for you and your family. Don't mind Miss Aidan, she's just concerned for Tira. We all are."

~ * ~

"What is this? A messenger from town dropped it off a few minutes ago." Amorica walked into the stables, handing Damian a letter from some unknown person, Damian's name written on the back. "Do you think Aidan needs something? Or the storm..."

Damian leaned the pitchfork on the stall before opening the letter. "Your sister-in-law, Tira Hepburn, is being compromised by Jamie Lundin. You must come to town and fix this deplorable situation before it's too late. He is keeping her in his home in the guise of a nanny to his daughter. We

62

all know what he is doing to her. Come at once or it might be too late to save her from ruin."

He looked up, appearing puzzled and running one hand through his hair, "Did you know Tira was in Baltimore? No one told us, did they?"

"I knew, but she was staying at the house with Aidan so I wasn't worried. Do you know Jamie Lundin? Is he someone who would hurt her?" Amorica understood the rocky road that love and romance could take. She prayed Tira had a solid head on her shoulders and would not let anyone influence her. Yet from firsthand experience she knew love didn't always go along with what you planned.

"In passing and by reputation, which is very good. Do you think we should rush into town just to find another situation similar to the one Aric discovered with Fayth?" He couldn't do anything for the couple except let them find their way by themselves.

"Like we did."

"There was a time I didn't think you would ever be a willing partner or forgive me my smuggling."

Amorica understood the truth of his words. Perhaps Tira and Jamie would have an easier time than they did. "I'd like to know what busybody wrote this note before I overreact. It's a long way to go for no apparent reason, although I would like to see my sister. It's been a long time and we weren't given notification of Ella's wedding until it was too late to attend."

"The gossip will follow her if she stays in Baltimore. I didn't think Tira would be as impulsive as Ella. They are not at all alike. Why would she take up residence in his home when she has another place to live? Nothing is as it seems."

"There are men involved and so there are complications."

Damian laughed, drawing his wife into his arms and kissing her soundly. "We had our share of problems and created a scandal. I had to have you and you hated me. I would stop at nothing to get you into my bed. Thank God I didn't have relatives butting into something that was of no concern to them. And thank God I never gave up."

She poked him in the chest. "You married me first."

"I was noble."

"No one else knew that. All the good aristocracy understood was that you absconded with me. They never thought you noble."

"Unless you believe this to be an emergency, I can't drop everything for a week to find out what the rumor mill has spread. It's up to you."

Amorica sat on a hay bale, staring at the paper in Damian's hand. Then with a long drawn out sigh, "If the message was from Aidan, we would go check this out at once, but Tira will do what she pleases whether we show up on her doorstep or not. I know my sister and nothing I say will change her mind."

"I don't believe Jamie Lundin would force Tira in any way," Damian said, handing the note to his wife and going back to work.

"But he might seduce her."

"Most likely if she's what he wants."

"Then we're not going." Amorica stuffed the note in the pocket of her apron. "The biscuits will be ready in a half hour."

Chapter Four

Three weeks had come and gone. Jamie spent his time at the farm or the shipyard. Tira spent her time taking care of Annie and wondering about her future. She barely saw Jamie save sometimes he'd come home in time for dinner. Most nights she put Annie to bed and rarely waited up for him. Because he was out of town or late in coming home, Tira still spent most nights at his house.

To keep from being bored, she'd been reading the books she found in Lizzy's crate of things and was amazed and horrified at the idea that a man could point a magic ring at a woman's private parts and find out who all her lovers were. She read that in *Les Bijoux Indiscrets*, the indiscrete jewels. She wanted to ask Jamie if he would ever do such a thing to her, if the ring existed of course.

Now she was reading *Fanny Hill* and there was so much she just didn't understand. She wanted to ask Jamie about orgies and what he thought but didn't dare. Then there were the love scenes between just men and just women. Truly she didn't comprehend any of this, and she needed to know if some of the other things she read here he planned to do with her.

With Annie, she'd exhausted all their natural playtime pursuits. Tea parties, dolls and the swing on the old oak tree vanished when the tree crashed to the ground. Today they were expected to stay in the captain's cabin on board the new ship while Jamie worked to prepare the vessel for the journey. Time to collect on their bargain drew closer with each passing second. She was excited then terrified at the prospect of what would happen.

Annie grew uninterested within the first half hour. Tira was tempted to teach her how to climb the ship's masts but thought better of that endeavor when she remembered the look of disdain etched on Jamie's face when she did that very thing.

"Can we practice knots again?" Annie asked, holding what was left of the cloth Tira once used to bind her breasts.

"Of course, I don't see why not as long as you stay right here and let me read. I'm absolutely intrigued by this story." She held up the book, a smile on her face, knowing she blushed.

"What's it about?"

"Oh." Tira felt more heat rise to her cheeks, unsure what she should tell Annie. "It's about a young woman and her life which was very different from ours. She was only fifteen when she had to make her own way. Some of the choices she made were really very questionable."

Annie didn't seem too interested in Tira's answer. "Remember when I tied all the furniture in the house together? That was so much more fun than just tying knots."

Tira smiled, recollecting all too well the look of chagrin on Jamie's face when he saw what his daughter had accomplished. "I do remember that day." She enjoyed surprising the stoic man who seemed to have a sense of humor only when he was teasing her.

"There isn't much furniture in here. I have nothing to tie up." Annie let out a long sigh of frustration.

"No, there isn't," Tira agreed, a bit distracted by the book and the erotic section she was reading, "Just a few things and most can't be moved to accommodate your endeavor like you did at your house."

Tira came across a most interesting page and was focused on the words, trying to understand just how and why they did that and attempting to figure out the position that was being described.

"Can I tie your wrist to the bedpost? I promise I'll get it right."

"Hmm..." She turned a page, her mouth dropping open at what she read. "I suppose."

"You have to give me your arm." Annie indignantly put her hands on her hips, waiting not so patiently for the desired arm. "I can't tie your wrist if I don't have an arm."

Sitting against the backboard of Jamie's large bed, Tira let Annie take her arm.

"This is a bow line," Annie said, "and I'm going to tie a clove hitch on your other arm." Annie finished the first knot.

Tira turned a page. Annie scooted around to the other side of the bed, proceeding to tie her second wrist to one of the spindles on the bed. Tira scooted higher so Annie would have easier access. The book slipped to the mattress.

"Would you get the book for me? That's a dear, now flip through the pages until I find the one I was reading," Tira said, wondering what the couple would do next in the strange game they were playing.

"Okay." Together they found the right page then she propped the book up so Tira could read more easily.

"Your foot doesn't reach the end of the bed. Can I tie your ankle to this chair?" Annie asked.

"Why not?" Tira tried to shrug but found her arms stiff, blood flow seeming to slow. "Are you doing them right so your father will be proud of you when he sees them and so we can get them untied?"

Annie pushed her tiny delicate shoulders up and down before smiling. "He's always proud of me. That's why I don't care if I do it right."

"Just be careful and not too tight." She tugged on the ropes binding her wrists, suddenly feeling a bit claustrophobic as the bindings gripping her wrists began to cut off the circulation.

Annie turned another page before tying Tira's ankle to the chair. The little girl sat back on her legs, examining her handiwork. "You've got another ankle and I need something to tie it to." Holding up the cloth, she found a long piece. "I think this will reach the foot of the bed if you scoot down."

"Just turn the page sweety, and I'll try to scoot as far as possible." Tira realized she couldn't read if she was on her back so she gave up on the idea, realizing suddenly she wanted to be untied immediately. Her body quivered while sweat beaded between her breasts, on her forehead and everywhere else. She should tell Annie to stop.

With that last piece of cloth, Annie attached Tira's ankle to the foot of the bed. "All done," she said proudly, dusting her hands off, grinning at Tira. "I think Papa will be pleased. I might have even tied a few the way he taught me."

"Good, I'm glad. Now that you're finished, perhaps you can untie them." Tira truly didn't want Jamie seeing her this way. It was too much like some of the things she was reading about, her arms and legs spread apart making her more vulnerable than she'd ever felt before.

"Then Papa won't see my good job," Annie protested. "We have to wait until I can show him."

"No, Annie, untie me now. I'll tell him what a good job you did." Frantic didn't begin to describe the way she was feeling.

"Do I have too?"

"Start with my arms. They're beginning to throb." The blood pulsing painfully nearly brought her to tears.

Annie bent to the duty at hand, fumbling with the fabric and trying to dislodge one knot from the other. To Tira it seemed hours passed while the little girl tried to untie her. All Annie accomplished was tightening the knots.

Finally, she stopped, her hands at her side. "I'm sorry I just can't do it. I'm going to go find Papa and he'll fix everything. Just like he always does." She turned, starting for the door.

"No!" Tira panicked.

Annie stopped. "I can't untie them. I have to find him." The look on Annie's face appeared as terrified as she felt.

Tira took a moment to swallow her pride and inhale a long deep breath. "Go! Hurry," she said to Anny's back. Closing her eyes for a moment, she tried to think of something that would calm her splintered nerves. Nothing seemed to work.

Watching the little girl race from the room, Tira closed her eyes again and once more tried to calm herself and the horror welling deep inside. Vulnerable to anyone who entered the room, she prayed it would be Jamie even though she didn't want him to find her this way.

Time slipped by. Her breathing changed as she inhaled swift short breaths unable to take a long deep one. When she looked at the room, it seemed to swirl and dip, her body swaying. She closed her eyes again, counting to herself and trying for deep slow breaths that wouldn't come.

The feeling in her arms and legs vanished. "Help, please." The thin wail whispered in the room.

More time passed and her terror increased. She tried swallowing and praying. The room began to darken as the sun descended. Where on earth had Annie gone? Where was Jamie? She was sure she would die here before anyone found her.

Footsteps.

She tried to see who was there, but when Annie had tied her one ankle, she slipped down so she was lying on her back. "Who's there," she whispered into the darkness.

"What do we have here?" Jamie's voice came out of the shadows, invading her soul yet promising in silence that her agony would soon end.

"Jamie. You came for me."

"This picture is intriguing. My daughter have a hand in this?" Laughing, he sat down beside her, picking up the book on her stomach. "And what do we have here? *Fanny Hill*. You do know this book was banned in England and the writer went to jail? It's considered scandalous and immoral." He set it down long enough to light the bedside lantern.

"I don't know anything about its history. It was one of Lizzy's books and I was curious," she confessed, sure he would say something that would make her blush.

"Orgies, homosexuality, cross-dressing, masochism? How droll that you want to read this. Curious, you say?" He paced the room, reading one of the more graphic scenes out loud before regarding her as if he wanted to know what was in her head.

More heat rose to her cheeks but with her hands still tied, she couldn't cover them. She didn't know how to put into words her intentions. "I wanted to understand what we would do."

"We won't do any of this." He closed the book sharply then setting it on his desk, "But if you want to read the book and talk to me about these things, I've no objections. We might learn something invaluable." He sat down beside her, tracing the line of her bodice, staring into her eyes as if he still wanted to understand what she was thinking.

"I'm sorry I didn't tell you what I found in that crate." She paused, inhaling a jagged breath. "Jamie please, mock me later, seduce me another time, but I hurt. I can't feel my arms or my legs for that matter. Annie couldn't untie these knots so she went to find you, and it seems every time I move, they get tighter. I don't know where she is."

"I'm right here," Annie said, appearing suddenly from behind

Jamie. "I couldn't find Papa, but he must have gotten done with his chores sooner than he expected."

"Annie," Jamie said slowly, "Mooney is in my office getting things in order. Go find him and ask him to take you to his wife. You can even spend the night with her. I need to stay here with Tira until she feels better. No worries, I will untie her."

"Okay, Papa." She turned, racing from the room, quickly sliding to a halt. "Is this a sleepover?"

"Yes, sweetheart." He smiled as he watched her leave, already missing her then he turned to Tira.

Her panic was real and terrifying. "My legs first, please. They're so tight. I don't think I can breathe." She closed her eyes listening to his whispered curses. When she opened them, his knife was in his hand. "Jamie!"

"I have to cut them off otherwise they won't come undone." He slipped the knife between her leg and the bindings.

She felt the cold steel caress her skin. Then she was free. He turned his attention to her other leg.

She screamed, pain encompassing her.

"Did I hurt you?"

"No." She barely heard the words she uttered. "My feet, dozens of bees stinging them. Get them away." Tears slipped from her eyes as nausea rolled in her stomach.

He held her feet, massaging them. "It will pass. It's just the blood flowing back into the veins." He continued rubbing, gently easing the pain somewhat. "I'm going to cut the bindings on your wrists now that your feet don't hurt so much. You'll probably have the same sensations."

"Hurry." She moaned, terrified of the next few minutes.

He straddled her, reaching for her, slitting the binding on both wrists and when she cried out again, he helped her through the agony. When it was done, he held her, smoothing his hands along her back.

"I'm so sorry. Whatever made you agree to such a reckless venture? My daughter will be punished."

She didn't want to answer, didn't feel like answering questions. "Just hold me please."

In his arms she trembled, her body shaking with the fear and anxiety she experienced. He sat back, resting against the headboard, pulling her close. In his arms she felt protected and cherished and she supposed for this moment it was true.

He spoke and it wasn't to pass judgment. "When I first saw you on the bed, the book beside you, I was interested, curious, too, at what you were reading before I realized you had no idea about the differences in our world. This book was an education no innocent should ever get." He stopped to gaze at her. "Do you feel better?"

"Yes." She pushed away from him and gently placed her finger on his stubbled chin. She was always so amazed, curious at the differences between them.

"Good, then if you want, we'll begin the next part of your education." Idly he drew a calloused fingertip across the line of her collar, gently unfastening the first few buttons. When his warm moist lips followed the path of his fingers, she inhaled a swift breath of air, her head falling back to give him better access. No longer as gentle as he'd been before, she shuddered at the astonishing sensations his touch elicited in her.

"Jamie..." was all she said, and her voice broke on the word, her thoughts and feelings a jumbled mess. She couldn't think; all she could do was feel. Needing to touch him, she wound her hands around his neck, reveling in the way he felt.

"Hush sweet one, just let me please you and enjoy this first time. I want to make everything perfect for you. Don't rush this..." His voice shivered across her as more buttons were undone and moonglow slanted across them.

"Are we sailing then? Annie is..." She had thought this unholy bargain would begin when the ship was at sea, not before. His lips followed a path up her neck to her ear the moisture of his mouth and tongue sending shock waves pulsing to places she'd never thought of until she met Jamie and he touched her so tenderly and intimately.

"With Mooney's wife," Jamie muttered between kisses.

"Good."

"Can you feel the movement of the ship? We are in the harbor and before long we'll be on the ocean. Yes, we are sailing. There is no turning back now. We've both made promises." He told her as he kissed her again and she felt the palms of his hands push the fabric of her gown off her shoulders, pinning her arms but giving him more access to soft parts, tender and sensitive parts.

"I can't feel anything but you and what you're doing to me." Frantic to touch and caress more of him, she pulled the fabric of his shirt from his pants before running her hands up his chest, stopping at his nipples, touching then exploring, realizing she wanted to know everything about lovemaking, about Jamie Lundin.

He stopped her exploration, bringing her hands to his shoulders. "I want to kiss you first, see your lips swollen from our passion." His hands were on either side of her head as his mouth found hers, sucked and gently bit. He pulled her bottom lip into his mouth then swept his tongue along the soft curve. Once more he drew her lip into his, nipped and laved until her body arched into his. "Do the same to me," he whispered next to her ear as he explored the shell before his mouth rested atop hers.

She inhaled a sharp breath, unsure of herself and exactly what he wanted from her. "James, I..."

"Take my lip with your teeth then pull it into your mouth. I need to feel your heat," he whispered his breath fluttering against her.

She did as he instructed, found the softness of his lips incredible. While she drew him into her, he moaned, pushing his hips against hers as she arched to meet his. Then she thrust her tongue inside his mouth, discovered him as she found his advances an aphrodisiac she was hard pressed to control.

He moved away from her, his arms braced on either side of her. "That was very, very good. Trust me then. If you continue with so much diligence and passion, we are on our way to an adventure I hope you will love as much as I will. Now, shall we proceed with your education?" Not waiting for an answer, he finished with the buttons on her dress as he pulled her gently to a sitting position and slipped the dress over her head then let it fall on the floor. He gazed at her, his eyes shining with desire and passion, she assumed.

Now she wore nothing but her chemise and underclothes. He had seen her breasts, touched her there and had always left her wanting. Now he would look at all of her. More than anything she wanted to see all of him. He straddled her, bending to take a nipple into his mouth, her chemise still covering her while his fingers touched the other. It seemed with each passing moment he discovered more of her, sending an inferno of his making pulsing deep inside. She moaned and the sounds she couldn't keep to herself seemed to delight him.

He rose above her, touching her lightly, yet more heat swept through her as his fingers found the waistband of her underclothing and deftly drew them from her legs. She thought embarrassment should follow but it did not. Reaching out to him, her fingers rested on the fastening of his pants.

"Not yet, little imp, but soon. Your stockings have little embroidered flowers. Believe I want to leave those on you. They seduce without even trying." He spread her legs, staring at her for a moment before he brought his mouth to her legs. He kissed his way a long her inner thigh to her belly before doing the same on her other leg.

"James!" she cried out as her body assumed a life all its own. She arched and looked for something, a feeling, a release...

"Look at yourself," he spoke softly yet his voice was gruff. "Look at what I'm doing," he told her as he propped a pillow behind her back, and she was able to see him slip a finger inside her. "You are so small and tight."

She ran her tongue across her lower lip and watched. "What is that?" she asked as new sensations swept through her.

"You're wet and slick my fingers. Your body is telling me you're ready to take my rod inside you, but not yet. First, I'm going to give you a woman's pleasure then I will fill you, become one with you."

Her eyes were wide with wonder as he continued to touch her. He found a spot that sent more heat coursing through her and she cried out, a soft mewling sound while her hips rose again and again. It seemed she could not stop the mercuric heat sweeping through her, nor did she want to. No, she wanted this to last forever.

"That's it, Tira. Keep your eyes open. Don't close them, never close them. I need to see the wonder and the passion in their green depths when you climax. When your beautiful woman's parts fill my hand with crème."

Then without warning, spasms swept through her body, heat coursed and she cried out as more tremors spread through her, encompassed all of her. She closed her eyes for a moment before remembering his words and she let her lashes fly open.

"How do you feel?" he asked, his voice so very gentle and calming. It seemed to soothe and caress.

"Jamie," was all she whispered before sagging in his arms. "I don't think I can breathe."

Tenderly, he gathered her close, held her while her eyes remained shut tight. When her breathing slowed, she drew away so she could see what he might be thinking.

"Did you like what we did?" he queried, brushing hair from her face. "I enjoyed watching you. Your face is expressive and compelling."

"There is more. I know there is more," she told him, running a finger down his chest. "Do you feel as good as I do?"

"No, but I will as soon as we can continue your education. We must give you a moment to rest."

"There is more to this lovemaking. I know it," repeating what she'd said before now she looked down, shielding her eyes and realizing he would know why she spoke so confidently.

"From the books you've been reading, I presume," he said, laughing and grinning at her as if he knew a secret and would only tell it if he could have a prize.

She nodded, staring at him, holding her lip beneath her teeth, understanding she was that prize he desired. Then she blurted, "I want to see you naked too. It isn't fair that I'm nearly without clothes and you wear all of yours."

He let out a roar of laughter, seemingly pleased at his accomplishments as well as the pleasure he brought her. "Just like you are? But I want to see you with nothing on too. I believe it's another part of our agreement."

She looked at herself. While she wore nothing but her stockings, she was not completely naked. "One garment at a time. Your pants for my stockings."

"I'll go first." He pulled off his shirt, tossing it on the floor then resting his hands on his slim hips, "Your turn," he moved back, his gaze riveted on her breasts then slowly lower.

She could not help herself. She set her hands on his torso, reveling at the feel of his hard muscled body beneath her hands. Raking her fingers down his ribcage, across his nipples to his waistband, she was pleased at the low groan emanating from his chest. He placed a hand on hers, stopping her from discovering him intimately. She wanted to protest but held back.

She found the top of one stocking, slipping the silken fabric from her leg until it pooled on the floor, she then repeated the process with the other stocking. He set his hands on her waist then her legs, spreading them so he came down between them the weight of him atop her.

He kissed her furiously, stroking the inside of her mouth with his tongue. Unlike before there was no gentleness, just a fierce invasion that she longed for, understanding the purpose and the culmination. She responded, frantically exploring, running her hands along his back then raking her nails across his flesh as he pulled her against him.

"Jamie..." She had no words. She needed him, yearned for a fulfillment she was beginning to understand and wanted to know for the rest of her life. "I want to be part of you."

"Your words unman me," he gritted out as he seemed to hold himself back. "And I want to make this joining perfect because we are going to be as one when we come together. Yet I find I'm having a hard time controlling myself. You unman me."

"What do you look like, Jamie. Beneath your clothes..." He straddled her then, her fingers fumbled with the fastening of his buckskins until it seemed he would take matters into his own hands.

In seconds his feet touched the floor and he was kicking off all of his clothing to stand naked in front of her.

"You are so beautiful. I...I have no words."

"Not as beautiful as you, my sweet one. Soon, I'm going to come inside you, join with you."

She held her arms to him, wanting to feel the length of his body against hers. "You are not like the statues I've seen." She was staring at him, the pulsing part that amazed and intrigued her. Then she looked up and she saw the smile on his face.

"No, my shaft is not like the statues you've seen because I'm desperate for you and the way you'll make me feel when I'm deep inside you," he told her, sweeping her against him before falling on the mattress. He spread her legs again and came between them, her core wet and hot once more begging for his touch, pleading for him to enter inside her silken warmth.

"Are you going to really make love to me now?" She ran her hands up then down his arms, his muscles bulging then tensing when she touched him and she marveled that she could do that to him.

She didn't care that this would forever change her and cast her in a new light to all the people who knew her. All she knew, all she could think about was how he made her feel and how much she loved him.

~ * ~

"Yes," he whispered. He watched as her eyes remained open and she stared at him, framed as they were in the moonglow now slanting through the tiny window in the captain's cabin. Her lips parted in a soft gasp as he drew her to him. And still he stared at her, for the moonglow danced eloquently upon her body, outlining the firm fullness of her breast and defining the dusky rouge peaks, touching shadow at the slender ribbon of her waist, glowing full on the flare of her hips. The moon seemed a matter of temptation in itself, finding shadow again in the haunting juncture of her thighs.

"Then you must finish this now, please. I need you more than I can imagine."

"Even though I just brought you exquisite pleasure only a few moments ago?"

"Doesn't my education include everything?" She moaned as he touched the soft wet feminine folds and the tiny bud that would give her so much pleasure.

A deep, guttural cry came from him, startling her, causing her to tremble. Then his hands were upon her again, pulling her closer still. He felt the fever of her mouth upon his once more, and he drew her closer if imaginable, stunned by this new ferocity of passion emanating from her, yet more than willing to ride the soaring force of it. She met his lips again and again. He sought her mouth and tongue over and over, breaking away, finding her warmth once more. His hands began a bold foray upon her. As their lips met in searing fire, he stroked her shoulder and her breast, rounded her naked hip. His fingers grazed her belly and drew with startling purpose to the dark nest between her thighs.

She moaned softly, understanding what would come, but he drew her closer. He whispered against her lips as he explored her further. She gasped and shuddered, so weak that she fell against him as his touch surged intimately inside her.

"I cannot, will not, let you go," he muttered close to her ear. "This week can never end for us. I want you for a lifetime."

"I don't want to be let go, at least not now." She burrowed her head against him, and he covered her with the heat of his body. His lips seared hers again and again and still it was not enough.

He touched her with shattering liquid heat in intimate places, bringing gasps to her lips as he possessed her breasts with his touch and teeth and tongue, covering her belly with the ardent sweep of his mouth. Fire and need consumed him. Sensations he created in her were meant to bring her more pleasure, for he understood that each new touch was still new to her and evocative beyond measure for her and he gave her no time to register the one before the next began.

He was a practiced lover, and he prayed she didn't care that nothing he'd done before with others would matter to her now. He meant to cherish her with both tempest and tenderness while he initiated her into the realm of sensations she'd never before imagined with another human. He was with her not because of the damn promise but because he desired her, and tonight as well as this week he could let hunger rage, for he had shown her that he cared for her.

He moved from her, hovering over her, seeking out her eyes that were ablaze with tension and passion. Lightly he touched her breast, keeping his eyes upon her. He drew his fingers low over her ribs against her abdomen, down to her thighs. Her lashes fluttered close, seeming to enjoy his caress.

"No," he told her softly, and she lifted her gaze to his again as he invaded her more intimately. She drew her limbs together as the magic of the night touched her features then her body surged against his touch, searching for its sweet desire and he laughed with sheer pleasure and triumph and his lips seized upon her.

"What is it?" Her fingers moved to his neck, winding into his hair.

"Moonglow," he whispered to her. "Thank God, sweet one, that you entered into this agreement with me, for I hunger for the very sight of you and would die tonight for your sweet touch." His lips covered hers. In tempest and wild abandon, they traveled to her breast, to her belly, ever downward. Brazenly he touched her intimately. She cried out loud in stunned yearning, writhing against him, reaching for him to draw him against her.

For a moment he saw the fear of the unknown in her eyes. He did not let her know distress. He teased her no longer but fell upon her with purpose, cradling her tenderly into his arms before thrusting inside her.

It seemed the pain was astounding, wrenching her from the web of sweet desire that he wound around her. She cried out and bit into his shoulders, tears stinging her eyes. He held still within her, holding her, waiting for her pain to ebb.

"You did not tell me," she whispered fiercely.

"You didn't ask. I thought your book would have told you there would be pain." He responded with a tender understanding, and she nearly laughed then it seemed to him the enchantment he tried so hard to create seemed to override the pain, and he was astounded at the sweet smile curving her lips.

"You should have warned me," she murmured softly. "I had the right to understand. For your information, none of the books made any mention of pain, at least not the parts I read."

"I've never known a hunger so intense; I've never wanted anyone or anything so desperately," he told her, feeling a tenderness for her he'd never known before. "I could not think only feel and in my defense, I've never made love to a virgin." He realized and reluctantly admitted his wife of a few days had not been untried when they wed. Once more he began his ardent exploration.

Beneath him her form shifted and writhed and arched on her own.

She stroked his flesh and felt the constriction and heave of his muscle and the ever-greater strength of his body. It seemed to him she swirled. She soared. She reached for something more. Then it seemed as if she pulled him even deeper inside, and he felt the sweet spasms of her release as he stroked her.

He watched her close her eyes, nearly limp in his arms. She had found that pleasure he wanted for her, he prayed. She shuddered again and again against him while hot rapture tore through him. She opened her eyes to discover that he hovered over her, smiling.

He lay within the bed, drenched and slick, entwined with Tira. She looked away as if for some strange reason she wanted to hide from his gaze, perhaps from what they did here, and what she must have felt and perhaps the repercussions that would follow.

He pulled away from her, coming up on an elbow, smoothing the tangle of her hair away from her face. "Regrets?"

"No." But she turned away from his gaze, biting her lip, seeming to hide from him and what they did.

"I've none," he told her, wishing he could see into her head.

She nodded, seemingly uneasy with what they'd done. This time she did turn against him, burrowing against his chest. "This is too new for me. Can we not speak of this? I'm embarrassed and confused."

He touched her gently, letting her lie against him. "We will have to speak of this sometime."

With a long deep sigh and a soft shudder, "Can we talk candidly then?"

"Anything you want," he answered, more than willing to give her everything she fancied.

She paused thinking. "I've suddenly imagined that love is a grand and magical thing, for it is, perhaps, even more wonderful to lie against you so, to feel the ripple of your muscles and your soft touch upon me as you hold me close. And in so many ways this seems an even greater intimacy."

"Yes, I suppose." He'd never thought of just holding her in such a way.

He stroked her easily now. He did not touch her then to enflame her, but just to idly feel her flesh and soothe her. He rested his stubbled chin atop her head and sighed deeply.

"Was that a strange thing to say? I really have no idea, no past experiences, but I want to please you."

"No, just different. What shall you do now?" he asked her.

She shook her head against him, "I don't know what you mean?"

"Well, my sweet one, when you go to London when we are done here. What will you tell The Duchess?" He shouldn't challenge her or make her uncomfortable when all of this was new to here. She did make a life changing decision here today; one she would be held accountable for.

"Nothing!"

"Nothing?" he asked skeptically. The mood of the evening vanished suddenly, and he wanted her to admit she needed him and wanted to stay in Baltimore even though he knew he would never commit to anything permanent.

Eyes flashing with sudden fury, Tira pushed away. "We both know what this night means, what this week was meant to be and nothing more. I will not suffer your insinuations. This was supposed to be for pleasure only and my dreams. You are a cad to...to..." she broke off.

"If you are with child, what then?" He had not meant to bring that up just yet, but in light of her denials, perhaps confronting her with all possibilities was important.

Her face paled and she moved from him, her body shaking. Then she turned back, "I will not be and I don't know why you bring this up. You mock me when something momentous just happened in my life, and I just admitted feelings I should have kept to myself. You've taken from me all I have to give, and we both know we've only this week to enjoy each other."

"I want to make sure you understand the consequences of this agreement we've made, because I intend to collect all that is within you so I'll never forget the beauty of this short time we have as a couple." He was suddenly furious with himself and the wild tempest of emotions she single handedly created in him.

"I will deal with my own life. Just leave me in peace. I won't be pregnant. It won't happen. It just can't." She tried to pull away, pushing at him.

"I cannot leave you in peace because I cannot find it for myself.

This was an unholy agreement, but it was made with the best intentions. This bargain will be fulfilled."

"That makes no difference to me." Small fists tightened she pounded on his chest.

He drew her close, smiling his handsome debonair grin then pinning her beneath him. "It does to me."

"Get off," she insisted, flailing against him.

"No, my sweet one, I cannot. And I give fair warning. Forget the future and answer to the sweet whispers of the night. We need think of nothing but the present."

"Tomorrow—"

But her weak protest meant nothing to him. His lips seared hers anew, her body burned and trembled against his. He knew she could feel the hard swell of his sex and she gasped and strained to deny him or perhaps to accept all that he yearned to give.

He sank into her, filling her, and making her one with him. The mercuric heat of their passion could not rise so swiftly again and yet it did. Soaring, sweet, thundering, savage, it rose like a summer storm, brought her to a sweet and shattering climax and cast her down softly and incredibly to earth once more. He gave her no quarter and no mercy, now that he possessed her. Still holding her, still entwined with her, he rose above her.

"Say the word and we can extend this trip for as long as you want. We can sail north to New York or Boston then South to the warm Caribbean." He would run away with her, keeping her only to himself and the sweet heaven he felt when he held her between his arms.

"We cannot."

"And why is that? You have so many obligations to fulfill that you will not idle away the days and nights in my arms? Travel the world with me. See places you've only read about." Purposefully, he taunted her with a life of adventure and passion.

"It is not that easy and you know it. What about Annie? Who will take care of her or do you mean to bring her along and will she share the cabin with us? What kind of lessons will you be teaching her?"

His features shuttered against her questions and it seemed she hit a nerve in him as his mood quickly darkened. "Annie is not your concern.

Don't ever forget, I will take care of her best interests."

He left her, walking to the window and staring at the ocean or perhaps the lights of Baltimore as they slowly vanished. In reality he saw nothing save Tira in the throes of her climax. Gritting his teeth together he searched for a way to make what they did this day right and he could find no way to do that. This evening had not ended the way he imagined nor had it begun the way he planned. The reality of her leaving any time soon was not tenable. If he could find a way, he would never let her go.

On his back he felt the heat of her gaze, understood he hurt her feelings, but deep down he also knew she would break him. He could think of no acceptable way to stop Tira from sailing back to London where she would make a new life without him. When she left and he knew she would, the very depth and soul he possessed would break.

Marrying a second time was out of the question. He'd believed that for so long the notion had become ingrained.

"Jamie?"

Her voice reached out to him and he wondered if he turned and went to her again, if she would allow the tempest they created together to wash over her and sweep into him once more. They would have this week, he determined, and he would hold her to all her sweet promises. Then and only then would he allow her free reign to decide her fate.

"What is it?" He turned, his gaze riveted on her beauty, on the fall of silken black hair so thick and long it nearly hid her breasts from his view. While he watched, she tilted her head, slowly lowering her lashes before she gazed at him again, and he wondered if she understood just how evocative and tempting that tiny gesture was. He thought if he lived for the next hundred years this one scene would haunt him throughout.

"I don't know. This..." He watched her nervously swallow before moistening her lips. "After what we just did, this, this doesn't feel right. I feel as if some part of you has been changed and not for the better." She pulled the covers closer to her, covering what her hair did not.

"Don't hide from me."

"You can't expect..."

"We are supposed to be lovers now but we both feel estranged. I can see it in your eyes. What are you afraid of?" He yearned to draw her into his arms and make this disagreement between them evaporate, but he knew better. They wanted different things. She needed a commitment he could never give. He wanted her to stay with him forever.

"Like you and Lizzy were lovers? You know I can't do that, not for the rest of my life. This one week was all I could give you."

He heard the censure in her voice, but she didn't nor would she ever understand his feelings for his mistress. "No, what we have will never be like the relationship I had with Lizzy." He never loved Lizzy. She was easy going and made no demands. He could come and go as he pleased, and he thoroughly enjoyed her company. His paramour was every man's dream.

Quickly, she turned away from him. The length of her long slender back open to his gaze, she was bent over and he heard the soft sob of despair, saw how her body trembled. Then she squared her shoulders and when she met his gaze again, her eyes shown brilliant with fire and hunger. "I will honor our agreement as you will honor yours. After that, there will be nothing between us."

He should have felt pleased, elated. Instead an emptiness that left him reeling in despair invaded his soul. "I intend to honor our agreement also." He strode to the bed and stood over her for a few seconds. Her chin tilted high, he recognized pride dictated to her and in that moment, he knew in the future she might let him touch her, kiss her, make love to her, but she would hold some part of herself from him.

So be it.

The knock on the door startled him but he knew it had to be Mooney coming to give him some message. "Come in." He gave his attention to the intruder and heard Tira's tiny gasp as the door slowly opened. "Stay covered."

He heard the rustle of covers as she most likely slid beneath them as if to hide. It made no difference. Mooney knew she was in his cabin and his bed. He would know what they'd been doing since the ship sailed. His first mate would only seek him out in the middle of the night if he needed him.

"Captain?" Mooney stood silhouetted in the door, holding a lantern in one hand. What moonglow had once filled the room was gone now and except for the lantern light darkness held sway.

"Is there a problem?"

"Winds are pickin' up. Think we should head north and east. Don't want to get caught in the middle of a tempest blowin' our way."

He was in the middle of a storm and the winds wouldn't die any time soon. He sighed heavily, taking one last look at the bed and the beautiful woman who possessed it as well as his heart. "I'll be on deck as soon as I dress." He picked up the discarded clothing, remembering just how they came off.

"Where are you going?"

"On deck. No matter what you hear or what you think might be happening, you need to stay here." He hoped she'd obey his commands and he'd give anything if he had time to explain to her, but he didn't. She was too impetuous to be sure and a cold wave of terror swept through him at the thought of what could happen.

Dressed and on deck, he felt the brunt of the wind as he strode to the helm. Mooney had the spinnaker flying as they caught the tail winds and raced ahead of the storm and exhilaration claimed him. Thinking back to the woman in his cabin, he clenched his jaw. This respite from his escalating emotions left a brief calm in his thoughts. But when the sun rose and the peace outside returned, he would have to confront Tira and all his raging feelings.

The winds were stiff but nothing dangerous. When they out ran the storm they'd be in the middle of the Atlantic. He could take her to London and what...confront The Duchess with what they did? He'd be better off if the confrontation occurred with her brother-in-law. Either way both relatives would insist on marriage.

The ship dipped into a deep trough then rose; spray drenched the deck. He loved the sea and the dangers that came with sailing.

"Jamie?" She stood a few feet away, her feet wide, bracing for the movement of the vessel.

His heart lurched to his throat yet he somehow knew this would happen. Unable to let go of the wheel, he reached out a hand to her. She clasped it as if he was a lifeline and he drug her to him. "You shouldn't be here," he gritted out, fear for her suddenly overwhelming. "You should be in the cabin where it's safe, where a wave can't wash you overboard." His voice gruff, terror for her taking over all his senses.

"If it's safe for you out here then it should be for me too." She wrapped an arm around his waist, leaning into him. Resting her head on his chest, he held tight to her, savoring this tiny moment.

"That's a feeble argument. This is my life; ships, oceans, tempests, not yours. It has nothing to do with you as a woman but with physical strength."

"There are no women sea captains?" she queried.

He ignored her questions, knowing there had been women pirates commanding their own ships. "Now that you're here you have to stay until Mooney relieves me. I don't want you walking the deck by yourself."

She clung to him, her head still resting against him, her hand placed on his chest just above his heart. Yet she didn't speak for the longest time. Then, "I'm sorry I upset you. This is all so new to me. I never know what I should say or do. What does a person say after such an incredible experience?"

Of course it was. She was a virgin and he knew she'd never known a man before him in anyway, not even a kiss. An innocent from the moment he met her, he'd taken advantage of her physically as well as emotionally. Yet he had no regrets except that she would leave him, and he could not say the words that would keep her by his side.

The ship dove into another trough then rode the wave. "I see why you love this." She gazed at him, droplets of water coating her face, her eyes shining with excitement.

At that second, he understood they shared something deeper than life, something that transcended the years. He stiffened, unwilling to believe in such a connection, focusing his attention on the winds and the waves of the storm looming behind them. "You seek things that are meant for a man, not a woman. You overextend yourself in every way." The words echoed in his head, knowing how wrong he was but unable to correct himself.

"That's because father allowed us to run wild, to be ourselves in every way. He loved us but in such despair he couldn't seem to come out of the depression that consumed his life after mother died."

"Just be yourself." He kissed her chastely on the forehead, wishing they were in his bed. A beautiful woman with so much to share. A week with her would never be enough. Only a lifetime would do.

"But there are things about me you would change. I know it and I want to be more than just a beautiful woman." Looking toward him, she closed her eyes for a moment. "I can't be your mistress. I know that about myself."

"No," he said, shaking his head slightly, wondering what she would change about him. He could guess. "There is nothing about you I would change."

"You're stubborn, you know."

"And so are you." He hugged her quickly before casting his gaze to the horizon and the rising sun. "You should go back to bed."

"I'd rather be out here with you." She pushed away from him to look into his eyes. Hers shimmered with desire, "I can hear the beat of your heart, feel the tempest surging within your body."

Her words swept through him. "I have to stay here for at least an hour, maybe more. Mooney appointed a second mate who will relieve me. You don't have to keep me company."

"I would only lie in bed, eyes wide open, contemplating what you were doing and wishing I could feel the warmth of your smile, the sweet caress of your fingertips against my skin." She stepped away from him, walking to the railing, peering at the waves below. "What is it you think about when you're out here all alone? Tell me."

"Mostly Annie and what she is doing. Right now she should be sleeping and if I focus my attention on her, I can imagine her sweet little face and when she wakes up, the smile and her unconditional hug."

"When Lizzie was alive did you think of her?"

"No, not often. Before Annie...I don't remember. Probably what I would do when we landed; sex with her, really nothing more." This wasn't something he wanted to share with Tira.

"Did you have a lady waiting for you in every port? No, never mind, don't answer that."

"Yes, I suppose so." He mused thoughtfully, never really thinking about what Tira would believe.

~ * ~

Amorica sat at the kitchen table reading the missive from Aidan. They had received four notes in the last few weeks; ones coming from town about Jamie and Tira, but this was the first from Aidan, which made Amorica sit up and take notice.

Amorica,

I'm afraid for Tira's heart. She has given everything to Jamie Lundin; all that she is, to this man who treats her as his mistress. There are no commitments coming from him, and Tira says there will be none. She won't fight him or argue with him about this, saying if he wanted her for anything more permanent, he would have to come to that decision by himself.

Tira left almost a week ago with him on his ship. A bargain between them created this scenario. She traded her virginity for a chance to build a ship. I wouldn't ask if I didn't feel it was imperative, but if you had a chance to confront her, maybe you could talk some sense into her. I know I can't.

If you can't change her mind about Jamie maybe Damian will keelhaul the insensitive man until he has found his senses.

Aidan

With a huge sigh, Amorica set the letter on the table, looking out the window to where Damian worked. It was nearly harvest time. She didn't know if Damian could take the time to leave, but they no longer depended on the crops to make a living. Their horses and the breeding of them was now their main source of income. In any case, she'd told Damian if Aidan wrote to her, she would seriously consider going to town. She could talk to Tira, but she doubted her words would have any impact.

Drumming her fingers on the table, she thought about all she and Damian went through before they realized how very in love with each other they were. Perhaps what Jamie and Tira were experiencing was part of their path to find love. Interfering might not be wise.

She stood, stretching sore muscles. She'd spent the better part of the week helping with the horses, feeding them, brushing them down and cleaning the stalls. It seemed her body hurt from the tips of her toes to her head. Damian insisted she take this day off.

She had biscuits to bake. Dinner wouldn't put itself on the table. Venison stew was already simmering in the pot, and Damian would be washing up for supper before she knew it. She picked tomatoes and cucumbers from the garden for dinner. She would can tomatoes later in the week when the bulk of the crop was larger.

An hour later, right on cue, Damian tossed his hat on the table and pulled Amorica into his arms for a kiss. His hands expertly roamed her body, knowing the exact sensitive spots to linger and tease. In his arms she sighed, knowing if she gave him any indication, he would sweep her into his arms and to their bed before dinner.

She hit him on the shoulders, laughing and saying, "Let me go or your biscuits will burn."

"Be damned, I wouldn't want that to happen." He sat down at the table. His gaze tuned to her as she pulled the biscuits from the oven.

"How was your day?" She knew he was watching her and that he probably wanted to make love to her more than eat. What he didn't know is that she would let him after she removed the biscuits from the oven.

"What do you want to talk about?"

"How do you know I want to talk?" It seemed he could always read her mind, sometimes knowing her thoughts before she did.

"You have that serious expression on your face I've come to know so well. Is it Tira?" Damian asked, ladling the stew from the pot Amorica set on the table and filling the dishes for himself and the kids.

She set a basket of biscuits near him for easy access then handed the letter to Damian to read. After a quick perusal, he shrugged his shoulders, "You're worried about your sister. We have to go and at least try to make things right. By the way, I like the part about keelhauling him."

"You would, but we both know how important it is to let these two reluctant lovers figure this out on their own as I'm sure they will. They can't be forced. If they are, they might never make the right decisions." Amorica wished she had a magic ring she could point at them; say the right words and all would be right. Firsthand experience told her this tact would never work.

"Still, I can pretend I'm helping Mr. Lundin come to his senses. We both know a man will do what he wants, when he wants and not a moment before. Lundin must care about her because the man I know would never ruin a lady's reputation if he cared about her."

"The other notes," she paused, "I wasn't as concerned about. I knew when and if Aidan wrote us then it would be time to step in, Damian. When they return from this crazy voyage, Tira could very well be pregnant. Can you even imagine the gossip if that happens? She won't even be able to escape the rumors if she moves to London."

"Do you think that will make it easier for Jamie to make the right decision?" Damian asked. "Men have a way of seeing things more clearly if there is a child involved."

"No, probably not but one can hope. Jamie didn't marry Lizzie when she was with child. Pregnancy won't compel him to give her a ring. What would, I wonder? I also know Tira wouldn't accept a proposal if she sensed the only reason he was gifting her with it was because of a pregnancy." She didn't like the direction of her thoughts. An urgency she didn't feel before swept through her. "When do you want to leave?"

"Tomorrow morning should be soon enough. Do you want to take the kids or leave them at their friends' homes for sleepovers?"

"We can travel faster without them."

Chapter Five

Tira and Jamie stood on the deck of the ship watching the land slowly come into view. They'd spent a week, seven beautiful days and nights enjoying each other's company as well as exploring each other's feelings. All this was over now, and they would have to accept the reality of their actions. Well, she would have to face the gossip, none of which, she understood, would come Jamie's way. Most likely praise for his manliness would be the topic.

Tira didn't know how long she would stay in Baltimore or how she would leave without Jamie knowing. She was a coward, intending to slip away and never tell him. Goodbyes were not something she wanted to deal with. Would her leaving mean anything to him?

"Are you glad we're home?" Jamie's arm wrapped around her; he pulled her close. "I'm not but now it's time for me to make good on my part of the bargain. You can start work tomorrow morning. I promise you I will give you as many responsibilities as possible."

She gulped a long deep breath thinking of all the things they'd done together. She'd miss him so much her heart would never heal, but Jamie couldn't give her love marriage and a family. Now she wasn't even sure she cared if he fulfilled his part of their agreement. "No. I wish we could turn the ship around and head out to sea again."

He laughed, pulling her closer, "Neither am I. This was a long needed holiday for me. To spend it with the most beautiful woman on earth a bonus that can never be repaid."

"Facing everyone, Aidan anyway, will be hard. I don't want to go back and encounter the unknown," she whispered softly, wishing for things that could never be and yearning to have the last week returned. It would have to stay in her memories for the rest of her life. When she returned to England, she would go home and live with her father. At least her father would not censure her.

"Not quite that easy but if you want, we can restock and set out tomorrow with the tide." He pushed a strand of hair behind her ear, regarding her intently, his eyes smoldering with the heat of passion she was learning so well.

"Are you serious?" she asked, eager to leave Baltimore behind as well as the responsibility of accepting and dealing with the problems they created to another time.

"Whatever you want is yours." His grin was infectious and she found herself smiling as well. Standing on tiptoes she kissed him lightly on the mouth and he responded heatedly. They both knew turning the vessel around was not in the realm of possibilities.

"You know we can't. In case you haven't noticed, we both have responsibilities. Need I remind you of Annie?" She had few obligations and none that were binding or important but Jamie did. He had his daughter as well as two businesses to run.

"It wouldn't be the same with Annie along. We'd have to behave ourselves. School should be starting soon and she can't miss that." He swept her close, gazing into her eyes. She saw the passion blazing, ready to erupt at the slightest invitation. Once again his lips molded over hers, sweeping her into that tempest of delight he could always induce. An inferno raced through her, engulfing her heart and her very soul. She longed for a lifetime of this but would have to settle for a few months.

She pushed away as the ship drew closer to the dock, searching the small group of people for Aidan. "Jamie..."

"What?" he placed a quick kiss on her forehead, his hands around her waist. "We could go back to my cabin and have one last moment of delight, create that tempest again."

"Are you sure you can't turn the ship around right now. We could restock somewhere else. I'm not ready for the questions and the condemnation that waits for me in that crowd." At the site of her sister and her husband, chills swept through her as panic consumed her.

"I'm sure." His hand settled on her back as he stared at the group of people. "Who do you see that I should know about?"

"My sister is here waiting for us as well as her husband, Damian.

Aidan must have sent for them. Truly, I'm not in the mood for a lecture or allegations. Nothing they can say will change what has happened between us and how we feel. Nor can it change what we plan for our future." Her heart raced while a cold sweat ran down her back. Panic shook her to her core.

"Should I be frightened?" He laughed softly, his fingers pressing lightly to give reassurance. "Be assured, I'm not afraid of Damian Andrews or the truth. I'm not frightened that your sister or her husband can make us do something that isn't right for the two of us. We will set the course that is best for us."

"I don't want you to be intimidated into doing anything that would make you unhappy. We are perfect together just the way we are, and I'm not asking you to change your mind about marriage and never will." She would never let her brother-in-law force a wedding between them. She turned to him and lightly touched his face. "If we bowed to their wishes, we would end up hating each other. I won't allow that to happen."

I love you, Jamie Lundin. I didn't think it would happen and I didn't care either, but now that I've found you, I'm going to leave before you do something you'll regret. I couldn't live with that. I understand you don't want a wife, any wife, not just me. I have to put distance between us before... Before what?

"You should know that no one can force me to do something I'm not in total agreement with," Jamie spoke softly. "You've no need to worry about me. It's you I'm apprehensive about."

"My sister and her husband can be very persuasive."

They stood at the bow of the ship until the lines were secured and the gangplank lowered. With a stiff back and hand in hand they walked toward the couple waiting for them.

"Amorica. Damian." Tira hugged her sister but stepped away from Damian, seeing his dark look of displeasure slanted at Jamie. "This is Jamie Lundin, my friend."

"And lover," Amorica said quietly, looking to the other people near them to make sure they didn't overhear. "The two of you must take responsibility for that and the repercussions that might come with the pleasure you enjoyed together. You cannot ignore the fact there might be a third little person involved."

Tira saw a shadow cross over Jamie's face as his brows drew together. His hard visage matched Damien's. It seemed they silently challenged each other for dominance. "Even though you are Tira's sister, what we do behind closed doors is none of your business. I won't have you censure your sister or say things that might hurt her."

Amorica hissed out a breath of air then inhaled deeply before speaking, "I would never judge my sister when you seduced her. She was innocent in the ways of men, but you knew that and did what you pleased. You must take some blame."

"I can take care of myself as well as any unexpected responsibility that might happen," Tira stepped into the conversation, angry that she was being ignored.

"Perhaps we should take this home." Damian scowled at them. "This argument should happen behind closed doors."

While Damian seemed to be the one with common sense and patience, the dark look he slanted Jamie's way didn't bode well for either of them. Tira half expected Jamie to continue on his way, collect Annie before returning home and ignore Damian's invitation to their house. Indeed, she expected him to leave her right now. After all that would be the easiest course of action.

Their baggage was placed in the cart. Jamie helped her to the seat beside Amorica and both Damian and Jamie leapt into the back. While Amorica drove the wagon, Tira felt the heat of Jamie's scrutiny on the back of her neck. She didn't like this any better than he did.

Tira knew this wasn't going to go well, but she couldn't foresee what would happen. No one would dictate to her, and she vowed she would not become a victim nor would she allow that to happen to Jamie even though he professed no one could make him do something he didn't want to do. He didn't know Damian Andrews.

"This will turn out just fine. It might take some time," Amorica said in an attempt to encourage her, perhaps give her hope where there was none. "Everyone means well and I promise you Damian won't try to force either of you."

"Looking at Damian I hardly think this will be easy, and I don't see how you can promise something you have no control over." Her nerves thrummed and she could barely inhale a breath of air. Suddenly, her stomach rolled with nausea. The sensation so strong she was sure she would lose the contents.

"Nothing worth having is easy. Is Jamie worth having?" Amorica asked looking pointedly at her. "Can you live the rest of your life without him? Go to bed at night without his arms around you?"

Heat rose to her face, and she covered her cheeks with her hands. It didn't matter. Jamie would never be hers. "Yes but... I will have to live the rest of my life without him. He has no intentions of marrying anyone, and I won't stay here and be his paramour."

"But?"

"He was married once before and his wife left him for another man. His heart was broken. He refuses to risk it again."

"That must have been one hell of a man," Amorica muttered then, "What about your heart? Seems he's too arrogant and he doesn't think about anyone but himself. You've given yourself to him, making yourself vulnerable. Most men don't understand that gift a woman can give only once."

"I can put myself first, which I'm doing. About the trip we took, I've no regrets and I will hold the time I had with him close to my heart for the rest of my life. It's a memory that will have to last a lifetime because that's all I'm going to get. After we build this ship, I will leave."

"You're selling yourself short," Amorica said softly. "I know because I did something similar. The difference was that Damian married me before anything like this happened."

"No, he made himself clear. I knew all along his intentions as well as mine. I'll spend the next month or two working in his shipyard and learning then I'll return to London then to our family home," she repeated, trying to convince herself this was the best course of action.

"You don't expect anything from him then? Are you going to keep giving yourself to him?"

"I don't know." That wasn't true. She would if he seduced her. Tira knew she couldn't say no or deny him if he touched her. "Yes, I suppose I will."

"You know, I feel sorry for you and the pain that's coming your way. I remember those days when I thought I hated Damian, yet at the same time I wanted him to hold me and love me. In your case you know you love him, and you're going to deny yourself a lifetime of happiness because he's too stubborn to realize the treasure he holds in the palm of his hands."

"He won't marry me or anyone." She wondered how many times saying the words would convince everyone including herself.

"We'll see about that."

"You can't make him..."

Amorica pulled up in front of the Andrews' home, the cart slowly coming to a halt. Before Tira could climb from the wagon, Jamie's hands were on her waist lifting her down. "Thank you."

"Don't let them bully you," he whispered. "I will always support you and keep your best interest at heart."

If he thought that would encourage her, he was wrong. "I won't," was all she could manage.

Lilly and Aidan were at the door greeting them as they entered the house. Tira felt as if she walked to her execution. Other than a scowl Jamie didn't appear affected at all.

In the parlor Aidan and Lilly set out lemon bars then offered drinks. All politeness, yet what they would have to say would not be gracious.

"Brandy?" Aidan asked Jamie while she handed Damian and Amorica a drink.

"Yes." Jamie still didn't seem touched by the gathering of the clans nor did he appear intimidated.

"Me too." She swallowed hard, wishing she could breathe.

They sat down and Tira fidgeted with the glass of brandy, running a fingertip around the rim, smelling it then looking over the top. Silence terrified her and she wished something would happen, the explosion pending.

"So, why did the two of you come to town?" Jamie asked, leaning back nonchalantly and taking a sip of brandy.

Amorica appeared shocked and Damian's eyebrows drew together. "Why do you think?" Damian asked, his voice harsh.

Tira had never heard that voice from her brother in law. Once again she wanted to go back to the ship and sail away.

"You had crops to bring in for sale." His voice dripped with pleasantness. "You must hate leaving them to rot."

"We came." He looked to Amorica then back to Jamie, his jaw tightly clenched, "to make sure you do the right thing."

Tira wanted to melt into the walls, but Jamie's eyebrows rose. Slowly he sipped his brandy then set it on the end table. "It's time for us to retrieve Annie then go home." He stood, holding his hand out to Tira. "Do you want to stay here or come with me?"

Damian's fist clenched at his sides and his jaw tensed. Amorica frowned at him, shaking her head at Tira. Torn between her needs and wants and her families, she couldn't believe what she was about to do. She was leaving soon and would never see Jamie again. She meant to create a lifetime of memories with him.

"I'm sorry," she addressed her sister, tears clogging her throat. "This is what I want, to be with Jamie."

"We can't change your mind?" Amorica queried.

"No." she spoke softly. "I want to be with him as long as possible." *Until I return to England.*

Tira didn't know where the strength to defy her family and go with the man she loved came from, but she accepted his hand and walked from the Andrews' home.

Hand in hand they strolled through the town to Mooney's home where they picked up Annie then continued to Jamie's house. They exchanged no words about what just happened, and she silently thanked him for that. She simply didn't want to explain herself to anyone. These last months would be bittersweet, but she wasn't going to miss even one day with him.

"Annie." Outside the Mooney residence Annie ran to her father, wrapping her arms around him, hugging him then the little girl hugged her. "Did you have fun? I hope everyone treated you like royalty." Jamie asked, patting Annie on the head.

"You know I did. I played on the piano and with their grandchildren. We went swimming in the pond behind the Andrew home. Can we go soon? Before you left with Tira, you promised."

"Maybe tomorrow, well, maybe not, I've a new ship to begin working on, and Tira wants to learn what that entails." He looked her way grinning as if he knew a secret.

"Let's stop at the café and pick up something to eat. I doubt if there is anything in the house." He ruffled Annie's hair. "What would you like?"

"Can I have anything I want?" Annie asked.

"Yes, but you have to pick out a meal before you decide on a dessert." It seemed Jamie read Annie's mind.

"Here we are," Tira said in front of the café. This was the first step toward her future. She inhaled a long deep breath before walking into the store with Jamie and Annie.

"Well, you two are finally returned," Martha said a smile on her face then patted Tira's hand as if saying I'm on your side against the town. "You three need some dinner. Chicken stew and muffins is the specialty tonight. I've got a huge pot on the stove. Is that to your liking? If you ever want someone to talk to, stop by the café and we can have coffee." Martha looked to Tira.

"I thought I got to pick." Annie said, hands on her hips, looking a bit angry with her father.

"Sorry, Annie, that's all I've got left tonight. Next time stop by earlier and put in an order. I'll fix you anything." Then she turned to Tira again. "Don't forget about the coffee, girl talk, you understand."

"Thank you, I'd appreciate that," Tira said, picking up the bag of food Martha hastily put together.

Then Annie turned to her, eyes alight and shining, "What did you and Papa do? Did you have fun?"

Tira felt the color drain from her face then she stammered, "Y-yes, yes we did have fun. We saw dolphins and lots of seagulls. I watched the waves and felt the salt spray against my face." She ruffled the little girl's hair. "And I did miss you."

"Was it too hard for Papa to get you free? I didn't mean to hurt you."

Good Lord, she forgot about the knots. All the color that drained from her cheeks rushed back. She heard Jamie laugh as if he enjoyed her discomfort or perhaps the thoughts that raced through his head when he saw her. She was sure he was remembering the book and what came afterwards.

"It was very hard and I don't ever want you to tie anyone to anything ever again. I had to use my knife and all the blood flow to her hands and feet were cut off. You could have caused serious damage." Jamie chastised Annie yet he was still grinning.

"Oh." She hung her head. Then, "I'm sorry. I wasn't thinking."

Tira was beside herself. She never wanted to hurt Annie and it was after all her okay that gave Annie permission to tie her. "I told her she could."

"Neither one of you used good judgment," Jamie added, slanting both a harsh glare.

At Jamie's home, Tira sat in the parlor, a glass of wine in hand while she waited for Jamie and his daughter to talk about the week. She needed this time to come to terms with her decision to stay in Jamie's home, and she knew Amorica would probably be at her doorstep tomorrow morning, but she'd find her at the shipyard unable and unwilling to talk.

The room was dark when Jamie finally appeared, pouring a drink then sitting beside her. He placed her hand in his. "I know today was difficult for you, but you're mine, you know. I'm glad you came with me on your own accord. Not sure what I would have done if you said no." He kissed her forehead then sat back watching, his brows having drawn together.

Well, Jamie Lundin, for the next few months you're mine.

"I'm not going to change my mind," she reassured, knowing she had only a few months with him. "This is what I wanted and it was my decision to make. Even though I understand there are no commitments involved and the gossip will race all over town, I want to be with you."

"I hope you won't leave us, Annie and me." He rose, striding to a window, looking into the night, moonlight washing over him, reminding her of that first night he made love to her as well as their first disagreement. "The gossip will get worse every day you stay with me. Can you handle the whispers behind your back?"

"Yes, of course I can even though I would like to wish it away." The gossip surrounding Ella had been horrific, but they ended as soon as

Drake married her sister.

She wanted to run to Jamie, needed to have the same easy carefree nights and days they had on board ship and the gossip she would endure, knowing it would all end when she left town, left Jamie and Annie Lundin behind. The memories would always be with her and would remain bittersweet. She could not believe she would ever fall so completely in love with anyone else. "I..." She stopped, unable to speak, emotions rushing through her. Trembling, she brought a hand to her face to brush away the threatening tears.

He was suddenly beside her, holding her, cradling her in his arms. "I hope you never leave me, but I've no way to hold you here." His voice was deeper and gruffer than she'd ever heard it and it seemed to break. "Only what we have between us."

She wanted to yell at him that of course he had options but understood his mind would not be swayed. He'd endured a loveless marriage and would not repeat the mistake. "You shouldn't worry about me. I won't break. I'm tougher than I look." She tried to smile at him, but the smile wasn't sincere. A huge price was paid for following her dream, and she didn't have one regret about the past only the future.

"I will always worry about you. Just as I worry about Annie. Don't cry, please." He kissed tears from her cheeks. "I don't know what to do if you cry."

She placed both hands on the sides of his face. "That's sweet, but Annie is a child. I can take care of myself. You don't need to concern yourself about me." *And my heart if only for a short time.*

"You were completely innocent when I took your virginity. I was a selfish, arrogant bastard, and I understand that's how Damian and your sister think of me." He held her hands in his and bringing them to his lips, kissed them.

Laughing softly, "Yes," she agreed, "Perhaps that's a bit too strong, but I wouldn't want you to behave any other way. Your confidence among other things is what attracted me to you first."

Smiling, he waggled his eyebrows at her, "My dashing good looks too?"

"If you must hear the words, yes there is something so compelling

about your dark brown eyes. They seem to mesmerize in a haunting way."
She had looked into them and felt as if he drew her to his heart.

"Enough about me. Why did you decide to ruin your reputation more than it already was and come with me?"

She turned from him, her gut clenching in pain. Telling him was not part of her plan. Her shoulders moved in a silent way of telling him nothing. When she turned back, "I...no." She licked dry lips, wishing for a change of subject before she gave too much of her heart and soul to him. "I don't want to talk about those reasons."

"Your motives are something I'd like to know. Why, Tira? Why would you betray your upbringing for me? A selfish, arrogant bastard." His voice had gentled and took on a soothing cajoling tone. "Understanding your intentions are important to me." His words whispered near her ear then the heat of his lips sent shivers throughout. Tiny swirls of his tongue, teasing, enticing, exploring started the tempest that would end in a startling heat and sensations that would send her into the magical world only he could create.

"Jamie..." she sighed, pulling his shirt from the waistband before letting her fingers travel the width and length of his chest.

"Tell me," he implored while he used his lips to seduce, following a line down her neck to where her blood pumped feverishly then beyond to places that never ceased to arouse and provoke.

"No, I-I..."

"Please."

She pushed away from him, her breaths short gasps, her heart pounding frantically from the enchantment he incited. Swallowing hard and shaking her head, she tried to push away from him. "Jamie..."

His hands dropped to his sides, his brows drawing together in a frown, eyes darkening. "If that's what you want."

"It is." She stood in front of him, her lips drawn together, wishing the truth wouldn't hurt him. "The hour's late. Perhaps we should go to bed. Do you want me in the room next to yours?" Her voice wavered on the last words while moisture filled her eyes. "I'd understand."

With a low growl he swept her off his feet and strode up the stairs to their bedroom. "I'm not letting you create an excuse to stay out of my bed now that you've committed to me."

"You still want me?"

"I'll always want you. Don't let my curiosity about your reasons for staying with me dissuade you." Taking the steps two at a time to his bedchamber. Inside the room, he let her body slide down the front of his and his hands resting on her derrière.

"I want you Jamie," she said. "I want to feel the heat of your body next to mine." Her hands under his shirt, she lifted it over his head. His lips trailed slowly, provocatively across her bodice and with his teeth he tugged the fabric of her gown lower then lower still until she let her head fall back, giving him easy access to her breasts.

Together they fell upon the bed, her body responding to his urgency. With a pressing need, she felt a feverish intensity between them a physical need to become one with him.

She lay on his bed, wondering how much longer she had to enjoy the love she wanted so to share. She felt the warmth of his body next to hers, remembered the evenings on the ship and the moonglow slanting through the window. Everything had been perfect, but like everything else, the time passed, and the journey returned to the reality of the real world.

She felt his hands upon her, stirring and provocative as they had always been. The heat of his breath at her nape and the tender stroke of his fingers over her breasts enchanted her. She felt the length of his body, hard and as hot as molten steel.

He wove a web of magic and sensations, a dream in this paradise she never wanted to leave. His hand shifted, slipping beneath her skirt. His fingers stroked a fantastic dance upon the bare flesh of her thigh and formed over the soft tender curve of her derrière.

"Jamie." She murmured, and she would have turned to him to cast her arms around him, but he held her still. His touch was no longer gentle but demanding as his hands latched firmly upon her hips. Then she gasped, startled by the searing steel rod of his sex thrusting deeply into her.

"Hush," his whisper came to her, and he held her tight. The world erupted into life and vibrancy and tender passion. He moved against her with the force of the wind and waves, with the powerful, fearless tempest of a storm at sea. It swept her by surprise, but it enwrapped her entirely in its magnificence. It thundered within and around her, and it left her crying out softly. Reaching for the sunlight, reaching ever higher in a gasp of rapture. It burst upon her, as sweet as silken drops of honey, filling her limbs, her body, her very center with warm liquid ecstasy. She trembled and felt him, groaning and shuddering, and holding her fast one last time as his body drove into hers, seeming to touch the length and breadth of her in one sweep of magic.

Then he fell still. His hand rested upon her naked thigh exposed beneath her skirts.

She opened her eyes and heard the delicate sound of the wind coming through the open window. She looked outside and saw the same moonglow that had enchanted her the first night at sea. She felt his limbs entangled with hers still, the life and pulse of him within her still...

He withdrew from her and turned her, "Soon, I will have your reason for living in my home with me instead of with your cousin. I will know why you risk even more of your shattered reputation to stay with me. Soon, Tira, I will know the truth about why you gave up your status for me."

"No." He could never know how much she loved him, and she would never allow him to seduce the truth of her feelings from her.

~ * ~

For almost two months now, Jamie watched Tira struggle with each long day of work, his heart pounding while he watched her, needing to step in and stop this ridiculous bargain, his head yelling at him he'd collected his part of the bargain. It was her turn now and only she could call a halt to the pain he knew she endured each day and night. He had to let her do this even though she was physically incapable of performing the work.

"Need a break?" he asked, gazing at her as she worked on the lines, his heart in his throat as her foot slipped and she clung to the mast to keep from falling to the deck below.

"Not unless it's the regular time. I don't want any favors from the boss," she called down from above having secured herself.

Her smile appeared forced. "It's past time. Mooney brought over ham sandwiches for lunch and cold lemonade." He would do anything in his power to make her realize this was man's work and not something a fragile delicate wisp of a woman could do. If she had been built differently, if she had a man's muscles, perhaps this would be different. There were women who were built differently, who could work eight hours in the pounding sun or the pouring rain.

He wanted to close his eyes when she descended, but he couldn't just in case she fell and needed him on her journey to the deck. She landed easily on bare feet, her hands on her hips, smiling at him. "I am hungry, starving in fact."

"After these months of hard labor, your hands might never be the same again." He picked them up, turning them over before grimacing at the sight of the calluses and blisters as well. As much as he didn't like it, he'd put her on the masts so she wouldn't hammer her fingers again. Now they were filled with tiny slivers.

She withdrew her hands, hiding them behind her back, "I'm not very good with a hammer. Is that why you sent me into the sky?"

"That and to keep anyone else from ogling your breasts. Can you wear more clothes under that shirt?" His thoughts turned to her and the sweet pleasure she gave him, so innocent and pure.

"I could bind them again, if that's what you'd like."

He shuddered at the thought. "No. Whatever you do, don't bind them. Come with me. We need to get those slivers from your fingers." He held out his hand in hopes she'd give him hers and wasn't surprised when she stuffed hers in her pockets. When he turned to walk to his office, he was pleasantly surprised to know she followed him.

In his office, he offered her a chair at the small table. Without speaking she sat down, a tiny smile on her face. He heard her stomach growl. She'd not eaten much for breakfast if anything.

She clasped her hands together, catching her lip between her teeth. "How are you going to get them out? You shouldn't do this. There will be more talk if you treat me different. Everyone knows I'm sleeping with you now, if you're giving me favors..."

He pulled a pair of tweezers from a desk drawer. "I would do this for any of my workers. Most have callused hands and they don't get slivers.

Your calluses are tiny and just beginning to form. They are little protection. Drink this." He held a bottle of whiskey.

"Why?"

"At least half, it will dull the pain. Tweezers aren't going to remove all of these." He said as he lit a candle and sterilized his knife.

Gingerly taking the bottle, she sipped then coughed. "Is that enough?"

"One sip is not half the bottle. "Drink it fast and it will go down easier."

She stared at the bottle for a few second then tipped it to her mouth and gulped. Setting it on the table, she doubled over, coughing and choking, but she did manage to drink almost half. "There."

"I suppose that will have to do."

She handed him the bottle. "Thank God."

Sitting down he held one of hers in his hand and began to painstakingly remove the tiny slivers first. After he hoped the whiskey had taken affect, he moved on to the larger and deeper slivers.

She had closed her eyes, her body tensing in pain. He watched tears slip down her cheeks. When he finished, "This might well hurt worse than the cuts. I wouldn't do it if I didn't think it was necessary. Hold out both hands, palms up."

She didn't question him. Her hands extended he poured the rest of the bottle over the wounds. By the time he finished, her body shook but she didn't cry out as he expected. He pulled her into his arms, holding her until the shuddering stopped. He drew her onto his lap and held her, stroking her back.

"That hurt," she finally said.

"I know. I'm sorry. Do you want to eat now or see something special?"

"Something special? I don't want or need any favors. I think I told you that."

He grimaced. There wasn't much else he could do. "I will always pamper you. If you hurt, I do. But no matter, I want you to look at this." He nodded toward plans for the ship.

"What is it?"

"Designs for this boat. I think you might be more suited for designing than building. You've already made some suggestions that would create a more streamlined and faster sailing ship." He watched her back stiffen and her jaw clench and knew she was fighting demons she didn't understand.

"Can I see now?"

"Eat first. You're losing weight."

"Obviously, it's the work, but I'm not hungry any more, just curious even though my eyes feel as if they are crossing."

"Work I don't want you to do," he said with reluctance knowing this was the last thing he wanted for her. "You shouldn't be taxing yourself. No matter what I assign, it's too strenuous." He knew she'd take umbrage at his words but he didn't care.

She rose, leaving the food and drink behind, striding to the design. "Perhaps you're right about the physical work. I'd like to see the plans then I'll eat," she said, seeming to make concessions.

His hands were on her shoulders. "You need food."

"But I don't think I can eat. My stomach is tied in knots; has been for the longest time." She sat down at his bidding and picking up a glass of lemonade she sipped, her lashes fanning beneath her eyes. Her head nodded. "I don't think I can keep my eyes open another second."

"It's the whiskey taking affect." He helped her from her chair to the back room where he kept a cot then helped her lie down. "I'll wrap up your sandwich for later. Sleep well."

If she kept up this schedule, she wouldn't be able to walk in a few days. Shaking his head and wishing for some idea that would solve this predicament, he ran into Mooney.

"I never thought you were an evil or cruel man until you seduced that sweet little woman. She loves you and any fool can see that, but you keep her in your bed even though you can't return the sentiment. She deserves better from you and you know it, just won't admit anything to yourself. She's going to be pregnant if she's not already."

Jamie felt as if he slapped him in the face, understanding the truth of Mooney's words. "It's none of your business, Mooney. Keep your advice to yourself and we'll both be happier," Jamie growled, comprehending the words Mooney spoke but unable and unwilling to give her up.

"It is my concern. Someone has to tell you what an ass you are." Mooney slanted him a frown, his voice taking on an angry tone.

"I'm not going to marry." He'd never had to say the words so many times in order to convince himself.

"That marriage you had was years ago. Both of you were immature young'uns and didn't know what you wanted or needed. Not all women are cut from the same cloth as your first wife. Marry Tira or let her go."

"I'm leaving her to sleep off the whiskey. Will you check in on her if I'm not back in an hour?" Jamie strode from his office without a backward glance, his nerves pulsing. Yet he heard Mooney, every damn word and it wasn't anything he hadn't told himself a thousand times.

"You're a damn fool, Jamie Lundin. Mark my words you're going to regret what you're doing," Mooney called after him.

Striding down the street, he passed several women. The heat of their gazes searing his back, his name as well as Tira's were the topic of conversation. No matter how much he wanted, he couldn't put a stop to the gossip swirling around them. When he stepped inside the café, Martha greeted him with a frown. Not her too.

"What can I do for you today, Mr. Lundin?" she asked, her tone curt and to the point.

"You having a bad day? If you need more help cleaning up the water damage left from the hurricane, I can send Mooney and some of my workers from the farm." Martha had never acted like this at least not to his recollections.

"Everything's fine in my neck of the woods." She handed him two loaves of fresh baked bread. "What else can I get you?" she asked, finishing wiping down the counter.

He wasn't in the mood for another lecture. If he didn't have to buy something for dinner, he'd pay for the bread and walk out the door. "What's the special this evening?"

"Rabbit stew and biscuits. Enough for three?" she asked, tapping her fingers on the counter, the frown still plastered to her forehead.

He nodded, looking at some of the muffins that were set out and the apple pie. "Give me three muffins and the apple pie." Like all children Annie had a sweet tooth and he knew she would enjoy it.

"You going to marry that girl?" she asked while she put together his order. "The sooner the better if you get my gist. You've never done anything like this before, Jamie Lundin. Your actions are despicable, young man."

"None of your business," he gritted out, needing to leave before he said something he'd regret.

"I'm making it my business since your mother doesn't care and neither does your father. I've known you since you were knee high to a grasshopper, and I've never seen you take advantage of another human being. Why don't you just stamp the words *my whore* on her forehead and be done with it?"

Another slap in the face but this one sent his mind reeling backwards. Martha was brief and to the point. "You've got to understand the situation." Cornered by the only woman who had cared about him while he was growing up, he tried to defend himself. He could think of no defense for his actions.

She listened to him when he was a child, and when his wife ran off, she held his hand, telling him time would heal the wound and one day he'd find a woman he could love.

"I know what I see. She's beautiful and sweet and if I'm right, and I know I am, she lost her heart to you and where you're concerned, she'd do anything you asked. She loves you, Jamie Lundin. How do you feel about her? Make up your mind or let her go."

"She would tell me if she loved me."

"Would a deer tell a wolf she loved him? If she did, he might devour her." Martha snapped back, clearly displeased.

"What on earth are you talking about?" He ran his fingers through his hair, his gut telling him he was the wolf. "I'm not going to devour her." His defense of his actions seemed to be rolling downhill.

"You already have. You've taken from that sweet woman and given nothing in return. She doesn't deserve the way you treat her. Bet your last dollar she's already carrying your child or have you taken precautions?" Martha set the container of stew on the counter with a bang.

"I gave her the dream she asked me for. I treat her well and I'll never hurt her." Yet something wasn't right between them since they returned from the short voyage. She didn't give all of herself anymore, always holding something back, a part of her he could not reach.

"To build a ship?" Martha asked incredulous. "That's not what a woman dreams about, at least not all. I admit it's a bit unconventional, but Tira has more than one dream."

"If she does, she hasn't told me."

"Uh huh..." Martha paused for a moment, studying him, still holding on to the food as if that would keep him in the café. "What would you do if she told you she loved you?"

This conversation turned increasingly uncomfortable. He respected Martha and wanted to answer questions, but she delved into places he wasn't prepared to go. "Well..." he swallowed hard.

"Well?" she asked, hands on her ample hips. "Would you return the words and tell her you loved her. Because you do, love her. I see it in your eyes every time you look at her."

He couldn't think and after picking up his food, he stormed from the room listening to her muttering. "If you don't do the right thing for the both of you, you'll come to rue the day."

Tira didn't love him. She enjoyed his company, just like Lizzy had. He took care of her needs, just as he had Lizzy. But he set her up in his home, not as a mistress and she was aristocracy.

None of that mattered. Their relationship was exactly right for the two of them and what other people thought didn't matter. She had told him she didn't care about the gossip. They had expected the gossip and she knew her reputation would be shredded when she agreed to their bargain. She understood what he could and could not give.

It seemed his reputation was the one getting shredded. The people he cared about the most condemned him and his actions. It's none of their business, he told himself again and again.

What if she was carrying his child?

When he stepped inside Mooney's home, Annie ran to him. "Papa, Papa," she cried out flinging herself into his arms in expectation of a huge hug. The bag of food fell to the ground.

"I'm glad to see you too, pumpkin." He laughed, tossing her in the air, enjoying the giggles. "We're going to swim this afternoon. Will you like that?" Jamie set her on her feet.

"Can Tira come too?"

"If she wants." He hoped she would tag along and that he could find a babysitter for Annie while they spent some time alone.

"You should be spending the hours moving that sweet young woman you've been taking unholy advantage of back to the Andrews' home," Mooney's wife spoke up. "Do what's right for that young lady."

Good Lord, was the entire town up in arms against him? What had his first mate been telling his wife? His patience was nearly at an end. "What Tira and I do is no concern of yours or Mooney's."

"I don't want Tira to move back. I like her right where she is, in my home," Annie said, her voice pleading while she tugged at his hands. He liked Tira right where she was too. "She plays with me. Tells me stories. I love her Papa."

"In your father's bed? I'm sorry I shouldn't have said that around your little girl, but the question is viable."

For a moment he thought Mooney's wife would back off but he wasn't going to chance it. "Go outside and play but stay in the yard." He wanted to keep Annie by his side to keep the barrage of condemnation from coming his way, but he supposed he needed to answer a few questions and perhaps make a statement she couldn't refute.

"Tira is an adult and where she lives and whose bed she sleeps in is up to her. I don't make her do anything she doesn't want to do. She can move back anytime. All she has to do is tell me." He tried for a calm he didn't feel. Anger was far too close to the surface. His hands fisted at his sides in an attempt to control himself.

"Tira Hepburn is sweet and innocent. I'll wager you took her virginity on that horrible trip to sea. She deserves to be treated like a lady, not your whore. From what my George has told me, she's an aristocrat. You haven't even had the decency to set her up as your mistress, not that anyone would approve of that status either."

Inhaling a long deep breath, he thought of all the things he could say but needed to refrain from speaking them, "I'm giving her what she asked for. If she wants to move out, I won't stop her."

"I suppose she's asked to be pregnant and unmarried. You do know it's only a matter of time if it hasn't happened yet."

Her words gave him pause then gave him the first reason to feel better since he put Tira to bed on his cot. "If it happens or perhaps when, I'll take care of both Tira and the baby."

"What about her feelings? What about the child? Do you want the good mothers in town to keep their children away from your second child, too, simply because they think of Tira as your whore? They'll call your second baby a bastard just like they do Annie."

So much for feeling better. "Like I said earlier, it's not your concern and your advice or condemnation isn't appreciated. I get enough of that from Mooney and the other people in town."

"Well, then my Mooney has more common sense than I give him credit for. He knows just as I do that Tira wants more than to learn how to build a ship. That was a childhood dream, one she held on to for lack of something better to dream about. At least she held on to it until she met you."

"How do you know all this? You've barely spoken to her."

"Mooney, he's told me she loves you." It appeared she was going to stand her ground. "He says you love her, too, but you're too damned stubborn and arrogant to admit to yourself let alone to Tira."

"It's time to collect Tira and go swimming." *And end this conversation.* He picked up his bag then strode from the room, his gut churning while he mulled over everything that had been said to him.

"You'll regret not telling her you love her, Jamie Lundin. Tell her before it's too late and she finds another man to love."

Another man to love, not while I can breathe.

Outside, "Annie," he held a hand out to her. "Come along."

"Where we going?" She skipped, trying to keep up with her father's longer strides.

He slowed, "To my office to wake Tira up."

"Why's she taking a nap in the middle of the day?"

"Had to give her some whiskey so I could dig the splinters out of her hand. She might wake up with a headache and a sick stomach. Wait here."

Annie sat down behind his desk, pulling out the drawers, searching for the little candies he kept there just for her.

"Tira?" He knelt by the cot, gently touching her cheek and thinking about the conversations he had since leaving her.

With a small groan of pain, her eyes lashes fluttered open. "My head aches," she whispered. "Everything is pounding and the room is spinning."

"It's the whiskey. How are your hands?" He picked them up and unwrapped the bandages to look at them. "No infection, that's good." He put the bandages back on.

"They hurt a little but not as much as my head."

He handed her a glass of water, "Drink the whole glass. It will help then I want you to finish that sandwich that's still waiting for you on the table. Water and food will make you feel better."

She closed her eyes for a moment before sitting up and accepting the water from him. Taking small drinks, she finished the liquid. "Doesn't feel any better."

"I promise in a little while you will."

She rose from the bed with Jamie steadying her. "Weren't we going swimming?"

"Do you want to go with us?" He hoped she would. "Swimming in cool water might help the headache too."

"I won't feel any worse if I go than if I don't. The breeze should be cool, but I don't have anything to wear. Wait, Aidan has a bathing suit she would probably let me borrow."

"You could swim in this, your shirt and britches."

"Really, and you want more rumors to circulate."

"No one will see you."

"I'm not going to give anyone, a chance passerby, more fuel for gossip. Now where's that food I'm supposed to eat?"

In a little over an hour, Tira was dressed in the cumbersome bathing suit Aidan gave her and they were sitting by edge of the small lake near the Andrews' home.

Annie waded in up to her knees and splashed water at Jamie, giggling while he made faces at her. Then he dove, gliding through the water just below the surface.

When he came up for air, he stroked closer to Annie. With his feet on the bottom, "Swim to me." He encouraged.

Her head out of the water, she dog paddled toward him. "Put your face in the water and use your arms."

She nodded, her head bobbing up and down as she tried to swim. A few arm strokes and she came up for air, reverting to the dog paddle. She reached him and he tossed her into the air before letting her fall beneath the water.

When she came up, "More, Papa, more!"

He obliged laughing then he turned her onto her back to help her float. "Put your head back, relax," he told her.

The lesson as well as the games continued for over thirty minutes. "Time to get out before you look like a prune. Tira and I are going to swim for a little while and Aidan's going to keep you overnight. Would you like that?"

"Yes, a sleep over." She clapped her hands together. "She likes to have real tea parties, just like Tira."

"And there she is, right on time." Jamie ruffled Annie's hair then gave her a kiss on the forehead. He wrapped a towel around her. "You have extra clothes at her house. Enjoy and behave."

He stared at Aidan, wondering if she would start a tirade similar to the ones he heard earlier in the afternoon. There were no words forthcoming. Silently, Aidan took Annie's hand in hers and walked home.

~ * ~

Kendall lounged on the sofa in her personal suite, relaxed and enjoying Mathew's company. He always had a way of making her feel special. Until Mathew she'd never felt that way. He had another girl in mind for the position of Madam in another brothel. She'd never thought selling sex could be so lucrative. Closing her eyes, she imagined the hell her life would have been if she hadn't left her husband of a few days for this adventure, if Mathew hadn't found her and taught her the seamier side of sex. Her ex-husband was a prude, too full of himself and what was proper.

"You look pretty smug, my sweet Kendall." Mathew handed her a piece of chocolate cake. "Happy birthday, darling, in more ways than one."

She savored a mouthful of the sweet confection. "Thank you Now what is it you want from me tonight?"

"Just your sweet body as well as your understanding." He sat next to her, pulling her into his arms. "Kiss me now."

She pushed herself against him, enjoying the slide of his hand along the length of her leg and the exquisite way his lips and teeth against hers unraveled her. She gave a tiny cry of delight. Yet she felt reservations in his movements.

"Mathew?"

"Hmm..." he said nipping at her ear.

"You want the girl. Go get her. Why waste time here with me?" She didn't like making love to him when he was thinking about someone else. Kendall pushed his hand away.

"At the moment she's unattainable. Lundin has a strong hold on her emotions."

"You can change that."

"Not so easy. She needs some kind of catalyst to change her mind about the man. From everything I've heard she's enamored of him. I'll bide my time." He returned his attention to her lips then, "Do you expect me to remain celibate while Lundin digs a grave for himself?"

Chapter Six

"How's your head feeling?" Jamie sat down next to Tira before pulling her into his arms and he laughed when she slapped him away.

"You got me all wet. Stay away."

"Isn't that your intention? Swimming? Water? Wetness? The last thing I want to do where you are concerned is stay away. It doesn't matter what we are doing. I want you."

Smoothing the bathing suit she borrowed from Aidan and feeling insecure, "I really don't see how anyone can swim in something so cumbersome. Look at this..." She held up the hem of the long skirt, "It's weighted with something, stones of some sort. Why would anyone sew weights into a garment you want to swim in? Is it some nefarious plot to drown someone?"

"Have no idea. Where you come from you don't wear one? A bathing suit? What do you swim in?" He held her hand, rubbing lazy circles on the underside of her wrist and looking at her as if he wanted to consume her.

She slanted him a quirky smile and raising one eyebrow, she said, "We don't wear anything." She loved the look on his face and could guess what was going through his mind.

"Buck naked? What did your neighbors say?" he asked, grinning and looking as if his imagination worked overtime. "I'd like that. Should we risk it all? Take off all our clothes and shock everyone? By my way of thinking, swimming nude would be safer than in that garment of yours."

"No." She swallowed, knowing she didn't want to create more talk yet laughing at him and the wicked smile he was giving her. "I'll try out the bathing suit. If it doesn't work, I'll get out of the lake, but if we're going to swim again, I'm going to need to think of something practical that will cover me."

"Shall we go swimming then?" He rose then gallantly held out his hand to her and helped her from the blanket she sat on.

She hesitated, unsure of the bathing suit and seriously concerned about her ability to swim given the ache in her arms and legs. When she tried to take a step, every muscle she possessed cried out in pain. Grimacing, she supported herself on Jamie's arm and stepped into the lake, stopping when it reached her knees.

"It's cold." Playfully, she splashed Jamie.

"You'll get used to it." He laughingly returned the favor.

Tira turned her back to him. That tiny movement caught her off guard and she let out a tiny gasp of pain, her leg cramping for a second before she could work it free. "I'm fine." She anticipated his questions.

He was beside her, "The water will relax you. I hope."

Together they waded into the lake. When the liquid reached her waist, she pushed off the bottom, swimming a few strokes. Turning onto her back she floated while Jamie swam circles around her.

"This thing is really heavy," she said grimacing at the weight and wondering if she dared swim any farther. "I'm not thinking this is a very good idea. Perhaps I should go back to the shore."

"Are you a good swimmer?" he asked, treading water beside her.

"You worried about me?" She laughed while she kicked her feet, moving into deeper water against her instincts. She wanted to prove herself to him so she didn't listen to the voice inside her head telling her everything was all-wrong.

"I should have asked sooner and now that you've thrown in your swimwear..." he paused, treading water. "Yes, I am worried. I don't want anything to happen to you."

"I've been swimming, it seems, since I could walk. My sisters drug Tavia and me down to the lake near our home and taught us when we were about three. We started out dog paddling of course, but soon we could swim." Cautiously she stroked toward Jamie, feeling the dress pulling her legs downward. She tried to maneuver the skirt so it would rest around her waist but wasn't having a lot of luck.

"Good, then I won't worry too much." Jamie swam with hard sure strokes before turning back to watch Tira for it seemed a quick look then he was swimming again.

"Jamie!" Tira called out, waving an arm, but his head was underwater and he couldn't hear. She struggled for a few seconds, trying to turn herself on to her back. Every muscle in her body cramped, moving them to keep her afloat nearly impossible. She gritted her teeth, trying to stay on the surface, keep her head above the water. The pain was so intense she couldn't move despite her frantic efforts, efforts that seemed to do the opposite, sucking her underneath the surface.

Just float on my back. All I have to do is turnover.

When she couldn't bring her feet to the surface and turn onto her back, fear swept through her as she slowly slipped under, her hands fighting to push the water upward. She saw him. *Thank God. Jamie, help me.*

He was beside her and tried to pull her to the surface, but the weight of the dress seemed too heavy for him. Kicking hard again and again he managed to get her head above water for a second. She gasped for air, a second breath just as she went under again. Curling into a fetal position in hopes of easing the pain, she cried tears blending with the lake.

Jamie tried again and once more he was able to give her a breath of air before she slipped beneath the top of the lake. It seemed to her he was trying to get her closer to shore where she could stand. But she knew the cramps wouldn't allow the added pressure to her muscles. She was going to die here in this pond in this damned contraption all because pride wouldn't allow her to swim naked.

Once more she was above water, and she heard him say, "I'm sorry, imp, but I'm going..."

Sorry about what? She slipped beneath the water again, but this time she saw a knife in his hand. Panic swept through her. She tried to struggle away from him but to no avail. What was he planning? The cold steel of the knife rested on her back then she was free. The top of the bathing suit including the heavy skirt slipped to the bottom of the lake.

She was above water and in his arms, breathing deeply. "Jamie."

"You're safe now. Try to relax, I've got you."

The air in her lungs gave her hope but she couldn't move. He swam with her until he could stand then he carried her to the blanket. Wrapping a towel around her, he dried her off.

"My legs...cramping."

Quickly covering her with a towel, he gently massaged her limbs but she screamed, tears sliding down her face. Low moans of pain emanated from her. Never before had she felt anything this debilitating.

"I'll get you home." He picked up his shirt and replaced the towel he'd wrapped around her then helping her, put her arms through the sleeves.

"Cramps..." She closed her eyes, curled tight trying to keep the pain away. "I'm so tired and I hurt everywhere. Make them go away," she pleaded.

"As soon as I get you home."

Leaving everything behind Jamie carried her to their cart and carefully set her in the back. She tried not to moan but her body writhed in pain, her muscles shrieking for relief.

"I'm hurrying," he said, setting the small buggy to a fast clip.

At the house he rushed upstairs with her in his arms then set her on the bed. Tears slid down her cheeks, and she couldn't stop the whimpers from radiating from her. She had no words for the searing pain.

"I have liniment. Don't move. I'll be right back" He rushed from the room and was back sooner than she expected.

She couldn't move if she wanted to, couldn't breathe either. He undressed her, cursing as he pulled the last remaining part of her swimwear, the woolen pants, from her legs. "Who the hell would ever think a woman or anyone could swim in this? It's a death trap."

With the ointment in hand he turned her so she lay on her stomach. She felt the warmth of the salve as he gently began massaging her thighs, moving from one to the other then beginning work on her lower legs before moving to her feet. The agony slowly began to ease. She let her lashes close, trying to will all the soreness away.

Then he gave his soothing attention to her arms and her shoulders. She closed her eyes, feeling almost normal for the first time since the garment nearly caused her death.

"Try to relax, Tira. Please," he told her, his voice whisper thin, filled with concern and fear. "Now that the muscles are no longer cramping, I want you to enjoy this massage. It won't work if you tense up on me." Once more he moved from one leg to the other, her arms and her shoulders, giving his tender attention to every part he could reach.

Jamie didn't stop. His hands swept over her derrière and between her legs down to the soft flesh below. An odd sound squeezed from her throat. She wanted him now. The craving for intimacy seemed a reassurance of life. She could never tell him no, never wanted to say the one word.

"Do you feel better?" Jamie asked blandly as if his hand didn't touch her in a familiar way.

Even though she couldn't see him, she felt his smile and self-confidence, knew he gently seduced, and she liked the sensations but wasn't sure she could respond without the terrible cramping of her limbs.

Tira made another small sound. Yet this was so unexpected and so amazing. She didn't want him to stop.

"Yes?" he asked.

Heat rose to her face and she felt as if the warmth covered her entire body. "Jamie, please."

"Please what?"

Bracing up on her elbows and turning sideways so she could see his face, "What are you frowning about?"

"I was thinking about Aidan's bathing suit lying at the bottom of the lake. Then I thought you might have ended up with the garment." He inhaled a huge breath letting it out slowly. "Thank God I always carry a knife with me. I'm just not sure I could have found a way to get you to a place where I could touch bottom."

She shuddered, thinking much the same way. "But Jamie..."

"What?"

"I don't know. You're touching me, you know. And I...well..."

"Do you want me to remove my hand?" he asked, his voice soft yet gruff at the same time.

"No," she said, shivering, with heated pleasure, "but I'm not sure this will work. My body, I'm so weak and I feel as limp as a rag doll. Almost every part of me feels as if it is on the verge of tightening again."

"If you're unsure of what you want then maybe you should unclamp your legs so I can, you know, take my hand away." His voice flowed easily. "I've only got so much control where you are concerned."

"I don't know if I can move them," she whispered as her body shuddered a cramp beginning once again then shimmering up her leg until she cried out.

"Then don't I love being pressed into the secret velvet heat that's you." Yet it seemed he noticed her discomfort.

Exhausted, she shifted back to her stomach, releasing his hand in the process. The slow withdrawal of his fingers and the hint of a sleek, intimate caress made her ache for release she hoped he felt the sweet intensity.

"You should rest," Jamie said in a matter-of-fact tone. "I know I've overworked you the last few weeks, and this evening's near drowning proves the fact. I don't want you to get sick or die because of my stupidity."

Tira nearly wept and watched wide-eyed as Jamie turned her onto her back and once more began the same slow massage of her muscles.

"I'm not sure I'll ever get used to you staring at me while I don't have a stitch of clothing on. It's easier when you're naked too."

"I thought you would like me to watch you. I enjoy seeing you naked."

"It's just that..." she paused, her body stiffening against her will.

"Tira, quit worrying. You're tensing up again. If this is going to make you feel better, you have to relax."

She reached up and touched his shoulder. "You should undress so I can look at you."

"That would be nice," he said," but I wouldn't finish the massage. It wouldn't be pleasant for you if you woke up in the middle of the night with more cramps." He didn't undress for her. Still he enjoyed the silken feel and the fine porcelain texture of her skin. When it seemed he tried for indifference, it didn't work. His fingers found familiar erotic places and she understood he'd like them to stay and explore.

"If I woke up, you could give me another massage."

"Have you forgotten the pain you were in?"

"Of course not. I just thought once my muscles relaxed, they wouldn't come back and cramp again."

"If I make love to you." He shrugged broad shoulders that she wanted to touch, "you might."

Jamie closed his eyes and she watched the slow smile form on his lips as if he was imagining something. "I don't think this is working. Your mind is going places you just told me you don't want to go."

"I believe it's working quite well. Do you have a better idea?" he asked unemotionally.

"No—"

"Then let me finish and we'll get some of the stew and apple pie I bought for dinner. After that I'll put you to bed and if you're relaxed, we can see what happens from there."

She didn't know what to tell him knowing how much she wanted him to continue this slow gentle seduction. He'd never made love to her quite this way. Before she left, she wanted to understand as much about him as possible.

Within seconds, "Tira, this is a bad idea and a good one. The feel of your small utterly feminine body beneath my hands, fully relaxed, inflames me as much as anything ever has." When he moved to her shoulders, he let his palms roam across her nipples. He gasped for air as the sensation affected him as much as it seemed her.

"There, I'm fine now," Tira said finally. "Everything is fine. If what you told me is true, you need to stop now before neither one of us can end this. I know you, we, don't want regrets and there is always tomorrow."

"Good Lord, I don't know whether to be glad or sad this lovely torment is finished. Don't move, I'm getting dinner," he told her as he turned his back and left the room. He returned in a few minutes, a tray filled with two bowls of food and two plates of apple pie, a bottle of wine tucked under one arm and two glasses between his fingers.

"I'm amazed," she sat up brushing damp hair from her eyes. "That's quite the balancing act. You're very good at that."

"Put on my shirt and come sit by the fire with me. I want to pamper you," he said, watching her move slowly to dress herself. "I'll see if I can make your stomach feel as good as your muscles."

Longing for a lifetime with her, Jamie looked at her as she slowly walked to the fireplace, mesmerizing him. Naked but for the enormous shirt she wore. Thoughts of regrets and a lifetime without her by his side tore at his insides.

"Those pants must be uncomfortable. Shouldn't you put on something that's dry? I wouldn't want you to get sick." She parroted his earlier words.

Shamelessly, he grinned at her and slipped from his breeches, slowly making his way to his wardrobe to pull out another pair. "I really don't want to put anything on, but if I don't..." He let the thought hang in the tense room. He would make love to her and eating would come later.

"You would make love to me and you don't think I'm strong enough," she said, her voice faint. "I'm not as fragile as you seem to believe I am. I'm really very strong."

"I don't deny the fact you're capable of a great many things yet I feel guilty for what I've done to you. All the hard work and in the end you almost..." He didn't want to speak of what just happened at the lake. If he'd not had his knife with him, she very likely would have drowned. The image of her flailing arms and the terror in her eyes haunted him.

Tira gave him a startled look. "What you've done to me? I knew what I wanted and you gave me my dreams. What happened at the lake was not your fault."

"This is all so new to me. The feelings I have for you and the person you are. You unman me from the depth of my soul." *I love this woman with all of my heart. She touches me so very deeply.*

"It is? You do?" She didn't know what to think. "You've had a wife and a mistress. This can't be too new."

"I've never massaged a woman before, never worked one to near death, to a place where..." He turned away, momentarily his voice taking on an emotional edge. "You could have died."

"You gave me what I asked for."

"I was a damn fool." Moisture in his throat caused him to choke, brushing tears from his eyes he determined he would never treat her so callously ever again.

In silence, Tira walked to the fireplace and sat down on the white fur throw. She inhaled a sharp breath at the way it felt on her bare skin.

"What is it?" Jamie asked, sounding impatient as he threw on a shirt, leaving it unfastened.

Tira shuddered. "It's so soft. It feels strange to have nothing against me but this. The sensation reminds me of swimming naked and the silver glide of the water against my flesh."

He inhaled a sharp breath, his muscles tightening with her words. "You leave me speechless and needing you more than I ever have before. Strange to me that I even thought I wanted to make love to you in your condition. I'm going to resist my baser instincts."

She let out her breath and shifted slightly. A shivering little sigh escaped her lungs. "I don't want you to have so much control where it comes to me. We both understand that when I finish with the ship, there is nothing left for me here in Baltimore."

Without realizing what she was doing, she moved again, stroking her legs against the luxurious fur. She stopped when she saw the strained look on Jamie's face as his jaw tightened.

"Guess you don't know what your throaty little sighs can do to a man." He sat down on the hearth as if he needed the small distance from her. Yet he reached out tentatively seemingly unable to resist touching her again.

"I didn't mean..." She closed her eyes, understanding all too well what he was feeling. She was experiencing the same physical arousal, the same ache that could only be quenched by sexual contact. He also had no idea what the sight of him naked did to her, how her body needed him, craved to feel his weight above her. Even now when they'd made love so many times, the effect on her was the same as the first time she saw him naked, and she imagined it would be the same for the rest of her life. Only she wouldn't be with him that long.

A moment later he seemed to brighten as if he put all thoughts of making love to her to the side. "First, I think some wine is in order for you," Jamie said thoughtfully. "It will relax you and help you sleep. You need to rest, and I'm not going to wake you up in the morning to go to work." He held up his hand, stopping her. "This is preferential treatment, and I'm not ashamed of it.

She was shaking her head, laughing, not even thinking about her refusal of special treatment. "Wine?"

"Yes," he rumbled. "We could say for medicinal purposes or just because we both need to be able to sleep tonight. Whatever you want to call it."

"Medicinal?" She couldn't help but smile. "Yes, it will help me sleep. I'm sure of it."

"I'll get another glass for the parrot too."

She laughed softly and ran her fingers through the fur, wishing she could entice him. She had this unholy urge to seduce him, realizing for the first time the power she held over him. "The fur has the most heavenly texture."

Jamie stood for an instant, seemingly transfixed by her. Abruptly, he turned and walked out of the room. When he came back, he carried two small snifters of brandy in his hand. "I needed something stronger, and I thought you might want more too."

She reached out to take the snifter from him, but when she did the shirt started to slide off her shoulders. It was never meant for her. It was too big by far. She made a startled sound and instinctively grabbed. Her reflexes were slow. The shirt fell below one breast before she caught the edge and brought it back up to her shoulders.

"Sorry," she said, wondering why she was apologizing when she'd just had thoughts about seducing him. She watched Jamie close his eyes for a few seconds, his jaw clenching tightly once more.

With a stifled curse, he opened his eyes and pressed the snifter's rim against her lower lip.

"Drink."

Jamie's voice was thick with what Tira was coming to know as desire, but there was no mistaking the command in it. Watching him over the rim, Tira opened her mouth, drank and swallowed. The heat of the liquid burned a searing path down her throat. There were times when she and her twin stole into the parlor and drank their father's brandy. Overtime, she'd learned to love the taste and the fire as well as the feelings that followed.

He sipped his drink. "You surprise me."

Tira nodded, "You surprise me, too, but I'm sure it's not for the same reasons."

"Now," he handed her a bowl of stew and a spoon, "eat. I insist."

The food was a nice compliment to the brandy. She was hungrier than she had thought. Tira watched in fascination as Jamie ate. His lips intrigued her as did every movement he made. She couldn't imagine life without him even though she knew she had only a few more weeks to enjoy his company. She meant to make the best of every moment.

"I guess I was hungrier than I thought," she said, eyeing the apple pie that waited for them with anticipation while she dug into the stew.

He groaned and seemed to choke back his words. Then he said, "None of this food will quench my hunger tonight. Not in the least."

Tira had the strange feeling he was talking about something other than food, and the way he looked at her she was sure he spoke of making love to her. "You can have my pie."

He stared hard at her, his gaze seeming to penetrate through the soft fabric of the shirt she wore. And she remembered all the times he lavished sweet hot kisses on her breasts. She blushed and muttered.

"Blushing again, Imp? Are you thinking about *Fanny Hill* and the different positions you read about in that book? We could talk about them and try them out at another time, a different day."

She looked at him, slanting him a narrow look. "You're taunting me," she accused. "I've never—" She stopped, unable to think of anything to say. Instead, she inhaled a long deep breath, praying for courage and remembering that day he discovered the book.

Jamie turned away but not before Tira saw him smile. He picked up the plates holding the pie and gave her one.

"Be careful," she said. "You might not be able to keep me away from you. What would happen if I seduced you? I could tie you to the bed. You would be under my control."

He sucked air, the muscles of his gut tightening. "You could try but I'm determined that tonight you get your rest. I won't be the man responsible for your pain."

She laughed softly and confessed, looking into the fireplace and watching the leap and dance of the flames. "I know you've got more control than any person I know. I've always admired you for your strength of character."

Smiling, Jamie coaxed the stopper from the brandy and poured them both another drink. "You know how to find a path straight to my heart.

Too bad the rest of the people in town don't think I've an iota of strength of character. They believe all I've done is take advantage of a sweet young innocent. I suppose Martha as well as Mooney are ready to tar and feather me then run me out of town."

She sipped, fascinated by the slow burn filling her while mulling over his words. "And you have a place in my heart. I would never let them hurt you." She ignored his other comment thinking what he said to be a bit strange. Some other time she'd ask him what he was talking about. The people in town thought her to be a whore. They loved and admired Jamie Lundin.

"Tell me what you want." Jamie traced her collarbone with a fingertip. The touch was feather light, almost as if a soft breeze floated across her flesh. "Not just learning how to build a ship but what else? Martha told me you wanted a family. Is that true?"

She nodded her head, closing her eyes. When she felt the pressure of his fingers moving along her shoulders and down her arm, she let a tiny groan emanate from her. What she yearned for wasn't what he wanted to hear. She would never make him feel guilty for not being able to give her what she needed.

"I don't know what to say."

"Whatever is on your mind."

"You don't want to hear it." She sighed, uncurling her fingers from the fur rug and letting her head fall back, giving him access to more of her.

He laughed softly and traced a line back to her shoulder, placing a gentle kiss on her neck. "I do. I've been barraged by incriminations all day, and I need to know that I haven't hurt you."

The gentle glide of his hands across her felt amazing, and she wanted it to go on for the rest of her life. She had to enjoy the moment, and if he wanted to seduce her tonight, she wouldn't say no. She reveled in the sensations he evoked and wished this moment could just go on forever. As he moved from side to side, his hands kept brushing between her arm and her body, floating softly across her nipples. "I thought you wanted me to rest."

"I do but I can't bring myself to stop touching you."

She forgot about her muscles and the threat of pain. His touch was simply too wonderful. Then the back of his fingers brushed the sides of her breasts, her ribs, the inward curve of her waist, and the swell of her hips. It seemed he touched her everywhere, and she had no words to tell him to stop simply because she didn't want him to.

~ * ~

Watching her and touching her, Jamie realized her breasts were larger and seemingly more sensitive to his touch. The color of her nipples had changed, just like Lizzy's when she was pregnant.

He paused, suddenly grasping the truth of his thoughts. Tira nurtured his baby in her womb. Tender feelings assailed him in rapid speed. If he didn't misunderstand, Tira didn't have any idea about her condition. He would enjoy telling her and watching her eyes when she realized she carried his child.

He lay on his back beside her, trying his best not to touch her intimately. "What do you want to do tomorrow?"

"Something that takes no energy at all."

"I can pamper you." He thought of all the things he'd like to give her, wanting to take her dress shopping for her growing body. Ah, but she was clueless and if he hadn't noticed her breasts, he wouldn't have known either. Unlike Lizzy she hadn't been sick and he tried to calculate just how far along she was.

"Another massage?" she asked, bracing on her arms so she could look at him, her breasts touching his chest, enticing him in every way. His body hardened even more, his need for her intense.

He groaned a little, wishing he dared pull her into his arms and show her how much he cared about her.

"How about a picnic. We can stop at Martha's for sandwiches and take Annie. She'll enjoy playing in the stream." He touched her lips, traced the fullness with a fingertip, reveling in the soft silken texture.

"Tell me about your comment a little while ago." She cuddled next to him, idly running her hands down his chest then roaming dangerously close to his arousal. He forced the groan to the back of his throat.

"What comment?" He placed his hand over hers, stopping the slow hot torment she inflicted.

"About your strength of character, I thought it an odd comment. Why would anyone, especially your friends, want to tar and feather you? Doesn't make any sense."

"Yes, well, it seems we thought wrong about the gossips and the way the people in town would think about us." He smiled, knowing he liked it better that his friends did not blame her for the decisions the two of them made.

"We thought wrong?" she asked, clearly puzzled by his strange words. "I've not heard anything consequential, but I know they whisper behind my back."

"This afternoon when I left the shipyard to run errands and collect Annie, everyone made a point to tell me what they thought of me and my treatment of you."

"I don't understand. You've been nice to me."

"Neither did I but I'm coming to comprehend that they love you." As did he, so why couldn't he tell her? Because he was a coward, too afraid of losing her if he committed to her. If he didn't tell her he loved her, she couldn't hurt him. He enjoyed what they had right now, no commitments and no lasting obligations. Each was free to do as he or she pleased without hurting each other. That wasn't true though.

"And not you?"

"They blame me for keeping you in my bed and they've told me I'm going to regret my actions." He paused to feel the length of her hair. "Tell me am I going to regret having you in my bed?"

"No," she told him, shuddering with the words and sucking her bottom lip between her teeth. "I know I'm not going to ever regret what we've shared with each other.

"Then why don't I believe you?" He gently pushed strands of hair behind her ear, reveling in the texture, needing to wrap the silken lengths around his body. This woman he was falling in love with was so much more than just a pretty face.

She shrugged slim delicate shoulders and he was reminded how close he came to losing her this night. "I don't know. What have I done to make you regret your actions?"

He chuckled, watching the strands of dark hair fall around her breasts. "You turn it back on me. What have you done? Nothing. All the choices you've made are exactly what I wanted. No regrets for me."

"We thought my reputation would be ruined." She posed the same thought running through his head. "And the townspeople would crucify me. Some do believe I'm your whore."

"We did, instead it is my reputation on the line. Enough," he kissed her soundly on the lips. "You need your sleep and I've work to do."

"Who did you talk to that told you those horrible things?"

"Not sure I should tell you, but I'm going to anyway. It started with Mooney. As soon as you left, he laid into me. When I stopped at the café, Martha gave me an ear full, and when I picked up Annie, Mooney's wife repeated pretty much Mooney's thoughts."

"Those are your friends and they have your interest at heart. I'm surprised Aidan wasn't one of them. What about the rest of the city?" she asked.

He didn't want to tell her the gossip but she knew most of it. "Probably the opposite. You can't forget the people who sent the messages to Damian and Amorica."

"Were both pariahs then, one and the same." She lay back, closing her eyes. "Perhaps we should move away and start again somewhere where no one knows who we are."

"We are outsiders it seems. Now go to sleep. I'll be up as soon as I finish a few things." He kissed her again and rose then finished dressing before leaving the room.

In his office he poured another glass of brandy before sifting through the papers on his desk. He had a letter from Clay about the farm's status. Several years ago, they switched from corn to sweet weed, tobacco. Now they were going back to corn. He didn't like the way sweet weed treated the earth. The plant seemed to rob it of all nutrients

The change was a good one and the farm was prospering even without slaves. Clay wrote that there were no more incidences. Perhaps the fire to one of the outbuildings was not arson, just a bad accident. He should take Tira to the place to meet his parents.

He paused in thought, understanding the meeting of parents had more significant meanings to the people involved. The commitment would be assumed, and it wasn't something he was ready for despite the fact a child was most likely on its way. The baby would be their first grandchild.

Turning the paper over he decided the picnic on the river would be the best bet for a relaxing day, and maybe he could find a way to break the news to her. He sifted through the remaining papers on the desk. The next ledger contained the earnings on his last shipment to India where he sold tobacco and bought fabrics and tea to sell in London.

Morning sunlight slanted through the window. He didn't realize he had spent so much time in his office. On the porch he sat on the swing, remembering another time, a windy night not too long ago. What did he want from Tira Hepburn? He needed to figure it out.

He let out a heavy sigh, rising and heading for the café and a loaf of fresh baked bread and an order of sandwiches for this noon. When he entered, the bell above the door chimed merrily. He braced himself for another lecture.

"Good morning, Mr. Lundin, you're up early. Did you have a nice evening with Miss Tira?" Martha said casually as she arranged the fresh baked goods on the countertop. "You do any thinking about our conversation yesterday? The clock is ticking, if you get my drift."

"The bread smells good." Jamie turned away, looking over the room. He didn't want to acknowledge anything and disliked being put on the defensive yet again. She made it her business when the way he conducted himself with Tira wasn't. Tira was an adult and she told him many times there were no regrets.

"You can avoid my questions, but you can't avoid the inevitable. If you keep on as you are, she will be pregnant before you know it. What are you going to do then? You best come up with some answers." She poured him a cup of coffee. "It's on the house," she told him sweetly. "Think about what I've said."

"Thanks." He picked up the coffee and smiled, "This smells good too. Believe I see a friend."

"Don't waste time, young man. You might not have a lot left," Martha reminded him as she wiped the counter clean. "Tell her how you feel and give her your last name. Don't let that baby the two of you are trying your darndest to make be born a bastard."

Coffee and package in hand, and trying to ignore the last comment, he strode to a table. "Blade MacPherson?" He didn't wait for acknowledgement but sat down. "Aidan know you're here? If she doesn't, I'm obligated to tell her."

"She might," Blade answered nonchalantly. "And I'm sure your code of honor demands no less. I'm not trying to hide anything from her, just not sure of the reception she's going to give me."

"There'll be hell to pay when she finds out you're in town," Jamie said, studying the man who seemed to cause chaos in Aidan's life, so much so, she fled London to get away from him.

"For me, hell started nearly a year ago. What happens today or tomorrow won't change the past. Where Aidan is concerned, I've made a lot of mistakes and have a lot to answer for. Mean to do just that."

"That bad, think my hell started a few months ago," Jamie admitted to himself, tapping his fingers on the table.

Blade leaned back, crossing his arms over his chest. "I'm going to fix things with Aidan. Don't know how quite yet, but if I have to get down on one knee and beg, well then that's just what'll happen."

"Why did you say she might know you're here?" Jamie sipped, watching the man who stole Aidan's heart when she was barely thirteen. Strange that he never wed, just followed Aidan, making his presence known in her life for all those years.

Martha stopped by with a scone and jam for both of them. "Compliments of the house. Didn't mean to eaves drop but couldn't help overhearing. Both of you need to wise up and fast. Your ladies are worth fighting for."

Blade fiddled with the silverware, his eyes downcast. "Thought she saw me yesterday. She looked straight at me so I backed into the shadows. Not ready quite yet to confront her."

"Was she with anyone?"

"Why do you ask?"

"Just giving you some food for thought," Jamie said, knowing Blade wasn't going to react well to the information.

"Aidan had her arm locked with a huge blond fella. It was all I could do to keep myself in the shadows. I want her to know I'm here on my terms. If you're going to tell her, I better up my plans."

"That would be Samuel P. Jackson, better known as Sam. He's the local blacksmith. He's a nice guy, sweet, gentle. She's also been seen with Baxter Hooley."

Pausing in thought before he spread strawberry jam on his scone, "Sam and Baxter Hooley, what the hell kind of name is that?"

Jamie almost laughed. "Baxter works at the bank and he's a pompous ass who's full of himself. Sam's a huge guy but gentle as a kitten. I think Sam figured out Aidan was too much for him the first time he took her out. Lilly makes a basket of food every Sunday so Sam can bid on it. I think Aidan enjoys having someone to talk to."

"Who's Lilly?"

"She works for Damian Andrews."

"Friend or foe?" Blade asked. "She didn't come to Ella's wedding, did she?"

"Friend if you're good to Aidan. Foe if you hurt her. No, that's why Drake needed someone to fill in for him and Eric. Which is why I was there."

"Good to know. Aidan needs people like that around her, good people. Maybe I'll pay a visit to Sam. Find out more than you can tell me about their relationship. I'm not going to hurt her if that's what you're worrying about," Blade said. "This time I'm going to do things right where Aidan is concerned."

"What are your intentions? You going to stay at the boarding house, I assume that's where your living until you reveal yourself?" Then he'd move into the Andrews home and the situation would be much the same as the one he found himself in with Tira. A sudden rush of guilt sped through him.

It seemed Blade was more aware of the gossip about him than he wanted to acknowledge. "I'm going to stay at the boarding house until she excepts my proposal of marriage and I can take her back to my home in Scotland. It's about time I married her and make up for all those bad times."

"You won't compromise her then?" Jamie asked, feeling overly protective. Perhaps someone should have stepped in and protected Tira from him. Problem was someone did try but Tira chose him and he was more than happy to go along with her wishes. He was a selfish bastard.

"I can't make any promises on that front. She has a way of provoking me beyond my control. She doesn't know it but the way she looks at me causes my blood to surge, and all I can think of is taking her into my arms and..." Blade slammed his fist on the table. Coffee sloshed from the cups. "And, I'm not going to let any man, Sam or Hooley, take what is mine, take what I've not so patiently waited years to claim. I didn't know it then but ever since I set eyes on that thirteen-year-old lass, I've known she was my destiny."

"What about Aidan do you think is yours, Blade? Her virginity? Shouldn't Aidan be the one to decide that?" Jamie knew Tira had given him hers by choice. Or had it been because of the damn agreement? He wanted to believe it wasn't because of the unholy bargain they struck. His lecture to Blade suddenly turned into reflections on his past.

"She would have let me make love to her that night in London if we hadn't been interrupted," Blade said looking thoughtful. Turning from Jamie to gaze out the window, "It's going to be a beautiful day. I'd like to find a way to spend time with Aidan, court her like she deserves."

"In your defense that's true but a lot has happened since then. You called her a little girl, if my memory is correct, and you didn't take advantage of her. Could you court her?" Jamie asked. "She left because of your cruel words, and she's determined to make you beg for forgiveness. Can you do that?"

"You don't have to tell me what an ass I was. I mean to make it up to her as soon as possible."

"The way I see it, the sooner the better."

"True words, but I've been a coward and every time I think about her, I remember how she feels in my arms. Can't get her wild red hair and the beautifully freckled face from my mind."

"Then how do you propose to make it up to her? You have to remain the man she fell in love with, an arrogant son of a bitch, but you have to show her another side too." He realized he was talking about himself as much as Blade. They had way too much in common.

"Confident," Blade countered.

"Thoughtless."

"Stupid," he disputed once more. "And I'll be the first to admit where Aidan is concerned, I've been an idiot. I'm not a thoughtless person. In fact, I've put too much thought into my relationship with Aidan. I've waited for her to grow up. Perhaps I waited too long. That's the definition of stupid, not thoughtless."

Jamie finally laughed, feeling empathy for the man. "We're both doomed, I believe. These cousins can wrap any man they choose around their little finger, and the funny thing is they don't even know the power they have. I've been tied up in knots for months now trying to do the right thing but too much of a coward to actually say the words."

"Nor do they understand it," Blade added with a long sigh that seemed to cover years of frustration. "She's had me turning somersaults since she was eighteen and tried to seduce me. I knew then it was just a matter of time until she succeeded then I made a grave mistake for which I've paid dearly. For Aidan, I've even remained celibate since that day in Scotland."

"Tira did the same to me when I saw her in the crow's nest barefoot with a shirt on that showed off all her curves. When I yelled at her to come down, she scurried down the mast just as if she were a little monkey. She landed on the deck, hands on her hips, grinning as if she'd done nothing ill-advised and had no idea I could see everything beneath her thin shirt."

"And the gossip mills are ripe with innuendos about the two of you, unflattering inferences. I understand if I'm not careful the same thing will happen to Aidan and myself. Difference is, I'm not an upstanding member of this community. No one will defend my actions. If I do anything wrong, I could be tarred and feathered and run out of town."

"I can always look on the bright side. If they have someone else to talk about, they might forget about Tira and me." Jamie stood holding out his hand in friendship. "Take care and I wish you luck. From everything I've heard from Tira, you'll need every ounce you can find."

They shook hands, "It was nice talking to you. Gained a little insight into myself. I have you to thank for that," Blade said thoughtfully, rubbing his chin as he looked out the café's window.

"I'd invite you to breakfast but I've a feeling Aidan will be showing up with my daughter, and if she does, your work will start perhaps before you're ready. The two of them would happily gang up on you, I've no doubt."

"Thanks anyway. I don't have a plan of attack so I'd just as soon bide my time until I understand the situation better. I've spent too many years invested in her, to do the wrong thing now and lose her."

"Even when she was thirteen, you were invested?" Jamie asked curious as to what he'd say.

"I didn't know it then, but I was. I had this urgent need to keep her safe and oversee her childhood until I could court her. Messed it up royally, if I do say so myself."

Jamie left the little café, whistling and for the first time since yesterday afternoon feeling good. In his house he stopped, looking to the top of the steps. Tira sat on the first one, her head in her hands. She was so very still it frightened him. He paused for a second.

When she heard him, she looked up and lifted her shoulders, a quirky smile on her lips. "I don't think I can walk down these by myself. I'm pretty shaky and when I move too much, all of me seems to tighten in pain."

Jamie dropped the bread. Racing up the steps, his breath catching, he helped her stand. "Your legs?"

She smiled sending a quick nod. "Just hold my arm, please."

"I'll carry you."

"No, I think movement is good for me. If it starts to hurt, I'll tell you." She moistened her lips, gazing at him with her huge green eyes.

"You sure?"

Clearing her throat, she nodded again and placing her hand on the bannister, stood.

Together they walked to the kitchen where Jamie pulled out a chair for her to sit. "Aidan will probably have Annie here soon. They're both early risers and I've got something I need to tell both of you." He thought on the surprise conversation he just had with Blade, hoping all would work out for the couple.

He broke eggs into one frying pan while he put bacon to cook in another, expecting Tira to question him. He paused, staring at her, deciding to confront her about her cooking skills. "You told me you couldn't cook. Aidan said you were the best cook among all the cousins. Which is it?"

"Are you calling me a liar?" She frowned at him, sucking her lower lip into her mouth as she appeared to contemplate his question. "Truth of the matter is that none of us can cook. I just don't burn everything and most of what I cook taste alright. So, I'm the best of the worst."

He chuckled, thinking she was feeling better. He circled around behind her and kissed her cheek. "Of course I didn't think you were lying. I knew there was more to what the two of you said, but you can tell me now if it's true and why you told me you couldn't cook."

"You didn't get any sleep last night. Aren't you tired?" She tilted her head slightly, a silent invitation for him to explore the length of her neck. "Insatiable hussy," he teased, pleased with the offer, but he didn't oblige her. If he did, the only breakfast they'd have would be burned.

"Not at all but you're dodging the question, quite conveniently if you ask me. You've lots of practice in this art?"

"I am avoiding the issue. It seems cooking and baking are my only not so good talents, but I enjoy watching you in the kitchen. I didn't want to take over your space."

"Yoo hoo, anyone home?" The front door banged open. Aidan followed Annie into the kitchen, waving her hands in greeting and smiling.

"Papa." His little girl ran into his arms. "I had so much fun. Aunty Aidan is almost as much fun as Tira."

"Aunty Aidan, is it?" Jamie cocked an eyebrow then smiled, ruffling his little girl's hair.

"Yes, we decided last night after the swim that was what I should call her," Annie said.

"What did you do with Aidan that was so much fun?"

"Well, we baked cookies last night with Lilly. She's funny. Then we got out real tea and Aidan put lots of milk and honey in it."

"Mostly milk," Aidan said, defending herself.

"That's good. Now." He turned to Aidan, "would you like to join us for breakfast?" He wanted a chance to tell both women about his conversation with Blade, but something held him back. He supposed the pair needed to find their way in their time just like he and Tira.

"I'd love to. I'm starving and Tira and I have some girl talk waiting. I'm sure you understand." Aidan slanted him a pointed look.

He grabbed a chunk of bread. "I'm going to let Tira finish breakfast and the three of you can talk your hearts out. Meanwhile, I'm going to take a bath."

His conversation with Blade and the accusations from yesterday began to change his aspirations for his relationship with Tira. Martha and the Mooney's opinions were right. If he didn't ask Tira to marry him, he could regret it for the rest of his life.

What he'd learned about the cousins was that they were stubborn and strong willed. They would never let anyone take advantage of them, at least not for a lifetime. If he didn't act fast, Tira would leave him of that he had no doubt.

Tomorrow he was going shopping and find a ring to put on Tira's finger. He wanted to claim her for everyone to see. Tira Hepburn was his.

~ * ~

Blade walked toward the blacksmith shop intending to meet Sam and find out the man's intentions toward Aidan. He'd seen the look on her face when they walked arm in arm, watched her laugh at what he said to her. Aidan didn't look smitten, never saw the spark in her eyes when she gazed at him. Yet the man might present an obstacle to his plans.

"Samuel Jackson," Blade extended a hand, ulterior motives in mind. "Blade MacPherson. I believe we have someone in common. I'd like to know your intentions."

"Ah, you know of me but not nearly as much as I know about you." Sam laughed, a boisterous sound.

"Not all good I presume." Blade crossed his arms over his chest studying the big man, wishing he could read Sam's mind.

"Ye ken you hold the wee lassie's heart in the palm of your hand." Sam concentrated on his work then returned Blade's stare.

"Thank the good lord. She holds my heart and has the ability to crush it if she so chooses. Where Aidan is concerned, I've made a few mistakes and I'll be the first to admit to that fact." Blade realized Samuel was not as he seemed, and he also realized he didn't have to worry about Sam as a suitor.

"A few mistakes?" One bushy eyebrow rose in seeming speculation. "Not to hear her tell the tales," Sam said, laughing again good humoredly. "If you treat her right, you'll have no problem winning her hand. You will need to beg forgiveness though. Get down on your knees, maybe plead a little."

"What has she told you?" He prayed she had not divulged everything. So much of it was private and he needed to keep those facts between them.

"Enough."

"You're not going to tell me." He respected Samuel for his loyalty to Aidan, yet he needed to know.

"No, but Aidan might. Be assured she didn't tell me anything that was private or intimate between the two of you." Sam slapped him on his back, sending him backward a step. "Just your transgressions."

"What did she tell you?"

"You think she's a little girl." Samuel went back to work. "That's absurd. How long did it take you to realize she's a woman grown?"

"I've known her since she was thirteen and even then she stole my heart. I had to do everything in my power to protect her from myself."

"No longer thirteen." Flames from the fire flared as he pumped air into the furnace. "What are you going to do about her heart?"

"I'm going to win her over."

"I won't let you hurt her," Samuel said as the fire grew hotter. "She's no interest in me except as a friend, but I'll step in as if I'm her father if you overstep your bounds."

"If you're meaning to intimidate me, it won't work." Blade knew the man just meant to let him know how he felt but Aidan was his.

"If I were you, I'd check out Baxter Hooley. That man has lied to Aidan, and he's not who he seems to be. You should protect her from that fool of a man."

"And you know who he is?" Blade challenged.

"I know he masquerades as a good person, one who is an upstanding pillar of the community when he is not."

"I'll take your advice in stride."

"Don't hurt her," Samuel warned one more time.

"Or I'll have you to answer to?"

"Aye, ye ken it well."

"I'm glad you care about her but if anyone hurts Aidan, it won't be me."

Chapter Seven

Tira poured Aidan a cup of tea then set the sugar bowl on the table before returning to the pan of eggs that needed her attention. She finished the meal Jamie started then dished up plates of food before setting the remainder on a warming pan for Jamie.

"So, what do you want to talk about?" Tira asked, helping Annie with her napkin then taking a bite of eggs. "Needs more salt."

"I saw Blade yesterday," Aidan blurted, spilling her tea in the process. "I was pretty sure this time would come, but now that it's here I don't know what to do." She methodically wiped up the spill.

"Follow your heart." Tira gave advice she'd channeled for the past few months but could no longer do that very thing. The pain surrounding her heart was too much. She wanted nothing more than to stay with Jamie, follow her heart, but he had to commit to her and he wouldn't do that.

"Is that the bad man you told me about, Aunty?" Annie asked, scrunching up her face. "You've got to make him pay for what he did to you or you won't be happy. Remember, you told me that. Don't ever let a man break your heart."

"I feel sorry for any man who courts you, little one. He's going to have to be perfect or you'll tell him exactly how you feel." Aidan smiled and ruffled the little girl's hair. "They're going to have their work cut out for them. And Blade's not really a bad man. I love him but he hasn't been very nice to me, and I'm not going to forgive him just because he showed up here with a smile on his face and perhaps a bouquet of flowers and a box of candy. While those things are nice enough, in the long run they don't mean anything. He has to prove something first."

"A man has to be nice to you before you give him your heart or anything else," Tira added, knowing that quality was not always enough. Jamie had always protected her, treated her with a gentleness that amazed her, but he couldn't give her the one thing she needed more than life itself, his love. She couldn't make herself any more vulnerable than she was.

"Papa's nice to you but I've heard people talking. They think you're a bad woman and I just don't understand. You're not what they say. You make Papa smile and laugh; no one has been able to do that ever. Why would they say those things about you?"

Tira didn't want to know what Annie had overheard. Before she answered she inhaled a long very deep breath, hoping she would say the right things. "Whatever you heard is just gossip. People should learn not to listen to it."

"They should learn to keep their noses out of other people's business," Aidan piped in, sharing her opinion.

"Whore, that's what they said you are. I know Papa kept a mistress, my mother, and people think that was bad but not as bad as a whore. That's not a very nice word. It's an ugly word." Annie crossed her arms in front of her, pursing her lips in annoyance.

Tira's heart caught in her throat. In a sense that's exactly what she was. She sold her body for her dream, agreed to a bargain that cast her in that role. What could she say to Annie? Nothing the little girl would understand or probably even accept as fact.

Tira stood, walking to the kitchen window and gazing outside, wishing she could change Jamie's mind. She'd come to love this land, Jamie's home as well as the man and little girl who lived here. Leaving this place and the man she loved was inevitable even though it was the last thing she wanted to do. He didn't love her and never would. She had to stop dwelling on that fact and look to her future.

"Hush, Annie, Tira's not a whore. She loves your papa and that fact makes all the difference in the world. Whores don't love the men they're with." Aidan brushed a tear from Annie's cheek. "Don't cry. The rumors just aren't worth your tears. We all need to rise above the inferences. Love is such a powerful emotion, people act crazy sometimes."

"Why don't you go upstairs and bring some of your dolls down here. We can play in the parlor," Tira said, watching the little girl who had become so dear to her rush upstairs seeming to have forgotten everything they talked about. Yet somehow Tira suspected Annie didn't forget anything.

"I'd like to play dolls with you," Aidan said.

"Too bad I can't forget all the horrible things people are saying about me," Tira told Aidan with a wistful little sigh. "Every time I walk past, they say those very things by the way they look at me. They stare at me and I feel their gaze burning me inside and out."

Tira assembled a tray with a teapot and honey along with cups. Aidan followed her from the kitchen into the parlor.

"What are you going to do?" Aidan asked, "You can't keep on like this and you know it. What would The Duchess say?"

"Unfortunately, The Duchess left my head a long time ago." Tira told her. "I didn't want to listen to her, so I shut the door to her voice. I wish she'd come back to me and tell me what to do."

"When he seduced you?" Aidan asked.

"I suppose that's when it happened. He knew I was thinking about everything The Duchess told me and I pushed her out of my mind because everything he was doing to me felt..."

"Too good to be true?" Aidan asked, taking Tira's hand in hers. "I know exactly how a man can make you wish for something more than you know you should give. They all know how to control you so you can't think and all good sense soars out the window."

"They make us feel things we've never even dreamed existed." Tears slipped from Tira's eyes. "When he touches me..."

"We have to say no but it's hard. I know I would have let Blade ravish me that night in the gazebo. I hope I can stop him next time he tries, but I'd be lying to you and myself if I thought I had control to do just that. Men know just where to touch you, kiss you. They know how you'll lose any conscious thought while melting into their arms."

"What are you going to say to him when he finally shows up, and you know he will? Right now, it seems he's hiding in the shadows biding his time. Do you think he knows who you've been seeing?" Tira knew their circumstances weren't the same, but she could always hope for advice.

"I haven't figured that out yet." Aidan poured the tea for everyone. "And yes, I know I need to do that soon. If he's been watching me, well, then he's seen me with Baxter and Sam."

"Here, I've a doll for each of us and clothes." Annie appeared in the parlor, smiling then plopped down on a chair between them. "Are you two talking grown up stuff again?"

"We are and we can always use your opinion. You seem to have insight into our issues. How does a six-year-old know so much?" Musing, Tira accepted one of the dolls and Aidan another. Idly Tira finger combed the dolls hair and thought about a little boy or girl of her own. She wanted a family but if Jamie didn't change his mind about marriage, it wasn't going to happen.

"I think," Annie paused then told them with amazing insight, "that both your friend and my papa are doing something wrong, and from everything you both have said, you both need to stand up to them. Tell them what you think and how you feel. Your opinion counts. You're both good catches. You could have anyone you wanted. Perhaps you chose wrong."

"And how do you suppose I should do that, stand up to your father?" Tira asked, believing The Duchess was speaking for the little girl. Annie's advice sounded so familiar.

"I've watched you and you give him everything he asks for," Annie said in a pointed way. "You should make him work for what he wants and he'll appreciate you even more."

"And he does the same for me," Tira spoke up in his defense and wondered how on earth she could ever make him work for anything?

"No, he doesn't," Annie said, carefully undressing her doll. "He takes advantage of you every day."

"How is that? What are you talking about?"

"I don't want to lose you and if you have to go away for a few months, at least it's better than not seeing you for the rest of my life. You need to leave him so he sees what he's missing." Annie methodically redressed her doll in a pretty pink outfit.

"You think I should leave?" Tira asked, feeling as if she'd been hit in the chest and all the wind had been knocked out of her. She had always known it would come to that, but she wasn't ready for such a rash action.

"Yes," Annie said matter of factly and with an emphasizing nod of her head. "You need to show him he can't take advantage of you. If you go away, he'll come after you and bring you home to me."

"Why would you think leaving him is the best course?" Tira felt stunned by Annie's statements. She meant to leave him but never expected him to run after her.

"When Papa has to go away for a while, when he comes back, he always tells me how much he missed me. Then he treats me to special things like new clothes or toys. I know if you left and he had to go after you, he'd figure out how much he needs you in his life. That's what he tells me. He needs me in his life." Annie put the doll on the sofa and smiled at them, appearing content with her statements.

"I left Blade and now he's here. I wonder if he'll tell me how much he needs me in his life and how much he misses me," Aidan said with a shallow laugh, shrugging her shoulders as if Annie's assessment was correct. "No, he'll probably just demand something or reinforce the fact I'm still a little girl."

"It was a risk for you to leave, but at least you got your answer, Aidan. If Jamie doesn't come after me, I can assume he doesn't care and that I made the right decision." At that thought her heart stopped. She would risk losing him. It was a huge gamble.

"That's if you discount the fact he probably still believes I'm a little girl," Aidan said sarcastically. "I'll disappear again if he continues with that approach. I won't stand for it. I don't know where I'll go, but I'll figure out some place he'll never think of."

Well, there was more to her problems than what they discussed here. Jamie Lundin didn't want a wife, yet Tira believed he truly didn't know what he fancied. "At least Jamie has never thought of me as a little girl, and I don't have anything to prove to him." She let a long sigh cover the discomfort she felt right now. "That just isn't our issue, and I don't see how the chasm between us can be solved. His mind is fixed. He's perfectly happy the way things are."

"A little girl?" Jamie sauntered into the room. "Who's a little girl, besides Annie that is?" Jamie sat down next to Tira, picking up her hand and gallantly kissing the back.

"Always the proper suitor," Aidan said with a hint of disdain in her voice.

"You're letting your feelings out, I see," Jamie said, smiling at

Aidan as if she hadn't just put him down. "Is this about Blade? I suppose I should tell you, he's here in town. I talked to him this morning. Told him I couldn't keep his presence here a secret."

Tira wanted to jump in and diffuse the situation but understood Aidan had feelings she needed to let out. Whatever problems were between Aidan and Blade were not hers to solve. She had a big enough problem herself.

"I am aware. I've watched for months now and hoped Tira would come to her senses and leave you but she hasn't. I think what you forgot in your seduction is that she might love you. You do have an obligation to make your feelings known to her before continuing with your amorous intentions. You know there are consequences to what you're doing." It seemed Aidan left none of her feelings unsaid and most importantly wanted to ignore the fact Blade had reappeared.

Jamie visibly bristled, his voice curt and to the point. "It seems you said more than you should have. You've no idea where our relationship has been or where it is going."

"No, you're right. I don't understand what is between Tira and you, and the most important fact is that neither does Tira. You need to tell her how you feel about her," Aidan went on to say. "She deserves at least that much respect. Really," she paused. "Tira deserves more."

Tira stepped in, unwilling to be talked about in such an intimate manner as if she wasn't even in the room. "He's told me he doesn't want to marry me. I know exactly how he feels about me. From his standpoint there's nothing more to say." Even though she desperately wanted to hear the words that would keep her in his home as well as his life.

"I don't think you do know his true feelings. For that matter I don't believe he knows them either," Aidan said, setting the doll she was dressing in her lap and staring at Jamie.

"I haven't agreed with your cousin the entire time you've been in my home until now. You've no idea what I feel for you, and I take full accountability for that. I mean to change that but in private. This matter is far too important to me. I don't want the whole world to know my plans before you. Mark my words, I'm going to make this right."

"Perhaps Annie should go to her room. This is not a conversation I want to have around her," Tira said, tears clogging the back of her throat, understanding he might be thinking about kicking her out or even setting her up in Lizzie's house. She could never survive if he did that.

Jamie nodded to her daughter. Annie collected her dolls. "Yes, Papa." Then she stood, seeming unable to leave. "Don't you hurt Tira, Papa. I love her and you know you do too."

"Perhaps I should leave. You have a lot to talk about and I'm sure you don't want a third party listening in and sharing their thoughts." Aidan stood, nervously smoothing her dress while staring at her as if she expected an invitation to stay.

Tira wanted the lifeline Aidan tossed her but understood the need for a conversation with Jamie; just not right this instant. "I'd like you to stay, if you wouldn't mind."

"And I'd like Aidan to return home," Jamie bristled, his gaze moving from one woman to the other. "Annie, go on to your room. I'll come get you when we're done here. We're going for a picnic. Martha is making sandwiches and fried chicken. I mean to enjoy this day with my girls and nothing is going to put a shadow on it. We'll take the buggy. I've got the perfect spot in mind."

"I'll see you soon. You can tell me about the picnic later, tonight or tomorrow." Aidan picked up her bonnet before giving Tira a hug and leaving.

Nervously, Tira turned her attention to Jamie. A picnic she knew would be nice, but all it would do was delay the inevitable and make her even more vulnerable where Jamie was concerned. Every additional moment with him would make it even more difficult to leave him.

"After that do you still want to have a picnic?" Tira asked Jamie. She cleared her throat, waiting anxiously.

He drew her into his arms, swinging her around in a circle before setting her on her feet and kissing her soundly. "Of course, why wouldn't I? I've been wanting to do something special for you, and now I have the opportunity. Annie will enjoy the outing just as much or more than the rest of us. It will give us a chance to relax and enjoy the sunshine."

"I don't know. It's just you wanted to have a conversation privately. If Annie is with us, we can't talk." Insecurities assailed her. She might be leaving on his command.

"The perfect day awaits us. I couldn't ask for anything better than spending time with my two girls. We can have that discussion tonight after dinner when Annie goes to bed. I've made certain major and important decisions about the three of us and our future." He wrapped an arm around her waist, escorting her to the door as Annie raced down the steps to join them.

"I'm ready." Annie wore a simple lightweight frock, one that wouldn't be too hot, and she held a bonnet in her hand.

Tira had a moment of thought about changing her dress but what she wore would have to do. She didn't know what she would change into. Everything she owned seemed to be getting tight even with her corset synched as far as it would go. Before long if this continued, she would have to buy some new things.

With the wind blowing her hair and the sun shining down upon her, Tira was determined not to worry about the upcoming conversation with Jamie. He pulled up at a grassy knoll, a stream winding its way merrily to the ocean.

Tira helped herself from the buggy while Jamie set Annie on the ground. With blanket and basket of food in hand, she spread the blanket under a tree, a soft wind whistling through the leaves, which had started to change color.

"Can I go wading in the creek?" Annie asked, already sitting to remove her shoes and stockings.

"Of course, I'll go with her." Jamie took his boots off and rolled his buckskins as high as he could.

Tira giggled at the sight of the father and daughter pair, wishing with all her heart she could be a part of this forever with perhaps a couple of their own. "I'll set everything out. You two enjoy yourself. Don't let your feet freeze."

"Ooohh...! The water is cold," Annie cried out as she moved deeper into the creek.

"That's far enough. Didn't plan on swimming today," Jamie told Annie as he picked up a rock, idly skimming it across the water where it formed a small pool.

Looking into the basket, Tira was amazed at the food Martha packed for them. "Fried chicken, homemade biscuits, potato salad, ham sandwiches and lemonade. There were also freshly sliced tomatoes and cucumbers. "This is a feast. We can't possibly eat all of it." Her heart was right where she wanted it, with Annie and Jamie. Closing her eyes a moment then lifting her face to meet the sun's rays, she thought about Annie's wise words. *Leave him and make him miss you.*

Could she do that?

Despite what Martha told Jamie the other day, she still seemed to look at him and regard him as a preferred customer. Martha spoiled him. She wanted to do the same.

Tira waited, watching them, sipping her glass of lemonade still pondering the serious talk they would have tonight. Fear caught her, holding her breath and going over every possible scenario. She didn't think things had changed between them to such an extent that it would merit a serious talk. Perhaps it was something in his working life. Sometimes he had to leave town to visit his farm.

Jamie sat down beside her, slipping her hand into his. "Your head is in the clouds. What were you thinking?"

"Not much." She tilted her head slightly, watching him and wishing she had some way to read his mind and wishing also she dared tell him how much she loved him.

"Tell me." He urged tracing lazy circles on the underside of her wrists before bringing it to his lips. "You look worried."

Even now he seduced. The gesture easy yet he knew what he was doing, just as Aidan had said. Annie wouldn't understand what he was about and how little resistance if any she had to his amorous ways. His touch was enchanting and magical.

"Tell me." His breath whispered across her neck, sending shivers of desire and heat inside. He created that tempest again, and if he continued, she'd wilt in his arms as soon as they had privacy. Then there would be no conversation, only the heated tempest he never failed to create within her.

"Nothing, just wondering what you wanted to talk about that was so serious." She tried to see into his mind again, find a way to read his thoughts.

"You'll just have to wait." He laughed softly, "You must have patience. Although I know how little you have."

Angrily, she removed her hand from his, amazed at his shocked expression. "I don't want to wait. You're playing with my emotions and..." She couldn't say more. Instead, she became more determined to take Annie's advice and leave before he broke her heart. She needed to find out how he truly felt about her.

"What if I promise you'll like what I have to tell you? At least I hope you will." He held her hand again, turning it over before kissing her palm and biting gently each fingertip. She shuddered in his arms, trying to stay mad at him an impossible feat.

She withdrew her hand from his again, her breaths coming in large gulps. It was all she could do to fight the tears back. "You don't play fair, Jamie. I think it's time to eat. Annie," she called needing the respite the little girl would give them. "Annie, you hungry?"

Annie appeared and asked, hands on her hips, "Are you being nice to Tira? I'll be mad at you if you're not."

"Of course I am. Why would you ask that?" Jamie looked totally confused by her question.

"Sometimes you hurt her feelings," Annie said, sitting down and accepting the plate of food Tira dished up for her. "I know you don't mean to but I've seen her crying after you left her too many times."

"How would you know that?" Jamie asked.

Annie picked up a piece of chicken then holding it in one hand as she spoke, "I just know things and I listen to the gossip. I know I shouldn't but..."

"I'm being very, very nice. Truly you don't have anything to worry about." He told her as he lay on his back, his hands behind his head. "What can you see in the clouds, Annie?"

Annie finished and wrapped the bone in a napkin. "I see a dog over there in that one. Do you see it too?" She pointed skyward.

"Absolutely, that's definitely a dog."

"You changed the subject, Papa. Is that because you know that you do hurt Tira?"

"What do you see," he asked Tira, still ignoring Annie's questions.

She closed her eyes for a second, relieved the conversation had changed from her fears and Jamie's actions toward her to the clouds. "I see an angel and the sun is shining behind her just like she has a halo."

She watched as Jamie inhaled a deep breath before closing his eyes. He must be tired, no exhausted. She stood, extending her hand to Annie, "Let's go for a short walk. Put your shoes on. We should let your papa rest. He didn't come to bed last night."

They strode in silence down an animal trail that paralleled the water. Seconds turned to minutes. "What's Papa up to?" Annie asked. "He seems different somehow."

"I don't know." Tira lost track of the time. "And for some reason I can't figure out, I'm terrified of what he might be up to. I'm afraid he's going to ask me to do something I won't like." She stopped gazing over the river. Tira was so afraid he wanted to move her into Lizzy's old house. "We should probably walk back."

"Okay, my feet hurt anyway and my legs are tired."

By the time they returned, the sun was only feet from the horizon and Jamie was sleeping soundly. "I don't want to wake him, but I know he'd want me to do just that. It's time we left for home."

"You have to," Annie told her.

"I suppose so," she said with a huge sigh as she sat down beside him.

"If we don't, it's going to be dark before we get home. I know Papa won't want that. He doesn't like me out when it's dark. He says sometimes bad things happen at night."

"Wish we could let him sleep." Tira picked a piece of grass and trailed it along his neck then across his cheek. She touched everywhere with it, tickling him and hoping he would wake.

Suddenly she was beneath him. "Jamie!"

"Thought you'd tease me, did you?" His lips pressed against hers, his large body between her legs then he must have realized Annie was with them and he rolled off her and drew her to a sitting positing. "Sorry about that. Shouldn't wake a man from a sound sleep. You never know what will happen."

Tira swallowed, shrugging her shoulders and smiling, "I didn't know how to wake you up. That's all I could think of."

"I'm glad you did. Time to go home. The sun is going to set soon." He put items of food into the basket. "On the bright side we've got enough food for dinner, so no one has to cook."

"Mr. Lundin."

Jamie stood, "Dutton." His voice was curt and his smile changed to a frown. "Both of you get in the buggy, now."

Tira had never heard him sound like this. His voice was harsh and the words were a command of some sort. She watched, curious at Jamie's strange reaction to this man.

"Nice day," the man said, seeming to ignore the blunt greeting while his gaze remained on her.

"What do you want?"

"Just passing through. Saw your buggy. Thought I'd be polite and say hello," Dutton said, tipping his hat.

"Keep passing." Jamie moved so he blocked Dutton's view of her. "Get yourself and Annie in the buggy," he repeated.

"Jamie," she stepped to the side. "You're not being polite. You could introduce us."

"No," he said.

"I'm Mathew Dutton. Pleased to meet you and your name?"

"Tira Hepburn, pleased to meet you. How do you know Jamie?"

~ * ~

"That's no concern of yours." Angry, Jamie interrupted Dutton's reply. "Best you keep right on going to that brothel of yours in town. We've no reason to keep you a moment longer."

He heard Tira's swift breath of air and understood he'd have to tell her the whole story, but not tonight. Tonight he meant to ask her for her hand in marriage. Right now the diamond seemed to burn a hole in his pocket.

But it appeared Dutton meant to ignore him. He leaned so he could see around Jamie. "Who's the pretty little girl?"

Rage filled him with a fury he'd never known before, "Leave before you regret stopping," Jamie gritted out.

Once again, Dutton tipped his hat before turning his horse down the road, his laughter slicing a hole in Jamie's heart. "Nice meeting all of you. Hope to see you soon, Tira Hepburn. You too, little Annie."

Jamie looked to the sky, searching for the control he needed to change the environment he helped create to something calming and filled with laughter and good feelings. With the appearance of Dutton, his light mood vanished and the exhaustion he'd been feeling all day settled in his gut.

Tira rested a hand on his back. The tiny gesture gave him hope where there had been none, and he reminded himself Tira was nothing like his once upon a time wife,

"What was that all about? You're not usually so curt with people. The man seemed nice enough."

"Just a man I despise." Jamie gritted out his voice harsh. "No need to concern ourselves further."

"Who is he?"

"Annie, Tira, stay in the buggy. I'll collect the basket and blanket." He couldn't talk about this now, needing to get the words right the first time. "Have patience and when we're alone tonight, I'll tell you the whole sordid story. That man is a viper."

"Jamie."

"Later," he said. "I just told you that I'll tell you everything." Really, he should appreciate Dutton a little more.

"I'm going to hold you to that," Tira said as she watched him, hands on her hips, a strange expression on her face.

He smiled, wishing he could pull her into his arms and erase the gut wrenching fear and the tension from the last few minutes. "I had something else planned for this evening. Even though Mathew Dutton is the last person I want to talk about, I'm going to have to get this out of the way. I'm afraid the information will put a damper on my plans."

"What you did and how you acted does need an explanation, but I'm sure I can wait since you promised, sort of, to tell me everything." She cast him a wary smile.

Jamie retrieved the basket and blanket. Then, "It does but it doesn't change the fact that I wish we hadn't seen that man. The reminders, for me, are not pleasant. Until today I've been able to leave those memories in my past where they belong. There is no room for them in my future or yours."

"I suppose you have no reason to explain anything to me. It is only how you deal with those memories and how they might affect me." Her soft sigh and the moisture he saw forming in her eyes startled him.

"Of course I need to clarify my actions. You deserve to know the truth about that man and how he changed my life, for the better I'll add." He didn't understand the sudden alteration in her demeanor and he cursed himself if he caused it. Tonight, he would change all that.

"I don't deserve anything from you." She was shaking her head and looking away from him. "Nor should I make demands. I've no rights here. A woman has no rights."

Where had those thoughts come from? He'd never given her any reason to say she had no rights where he was concerned. "Tira, what the hell are you talking about?"

"We need to get Annie home. There's a chill in the air. I wouldn't want her to get sick." Tira spoke stiffly holding her tightly clasped hands in her lap. She looked away from him when he needed to see into her eyes.

"Of course."

The ride home was met with silence. Even Annie's happy chatter was stilled by the somber mood surrounding her. It seemed the little girl sensed the tension between Tira and himself. The sun settled on the horizon as he pulled up in front of his home.

"Go on you two. I'll see to the horse and be right in." He was happy to have a few moments alone, unsure now about the marriage proposal or the explanation. Matthew Dutton had been a thorn in his side for almost a decade and it seemed, coincidence or not, he was back harassing him.

It appeared he could put the inevitable off only so long. Telling her the details of his failed marriage with Kendall was not going to be pleasant. For so long he blamed himself and thought if he had only done something different, she might have stayed with him.

When he heard about the brothel Kendall and Dutton established, he knew she was cut from a far different cloth than most people. The failed marriage was not his fault. Yet that marriage had given him pause, and he'd avoided any serious relationships until Tira strode into his life, dressed as a man and cocky as all get out.

What he never understood was why Kendall agreed to wed him in the first place. He laughed at himself. What had driven him to ask her was another question. She held herself back for months, barely letting him kiss her. Her passion was nonexistent, at least where he was concerned. He supposed it might have been the idea of marriage that she liked.

Once they were wed, she changed. What she wanted he couldn't give her. Bondage was not something he expected or wanted with lovemaking, and there were other things she seemed to crave that were just wrong to his way of thinking.

Ironic that before he made love with Tira for the first time, she'd been tied to his bed by his daughter. He chuckled thinking about her beautiful body on his bed, and he was so thankful she'd not been hurt.

The sight of her tied on the bed did provoke some enticing thoughts and what he could do with her. Then the book she was reading, *Fanny Hill,* gave him more ideas, ideas he didn't act on simply because they didn't excite him. Most disgusted him and he assumed those were the reasons Kendall left him. In her mind he wasn't exciting enough sexually.

Finished with the horse and tack, he leaned against the stable doors, watching the sun slip beneath the horizon. The sight was beautiful. He would have liked to be sitting on the porch swing and watch the display of colors with Tira nestled in his arms. Yet here he stood trying to stay away from her as long as possible and in the process, delay the explanation that revolved around Dutton and his ex-wife. In the end he was also delaying the marriage proposal.

With a heavy sigh, he pushed away from the door, striding to his home only to find Tira sitting on the swing. She was the most beautiful woman he'd ever had the good luck to know, beautiful inside and out. He prayed she would agree to his proposal then she'd be his forever.

Sitting beside her, he wrapped an arm around her, still unsure of what to say and dreading the conversation to come. He meant to put off asking for her hand in marriage. Tonight, today, there were too many memories he'd rather leave in the back of his mind where they belonged.

"I gave Annie dinner and sent her to bed. She was yawning and her eyes were drooping shut while she ate. What took you so long?" She let her hand rest on his chest.

"Didn't want to have this conversation so I put it off. I'm a damn fool." He kissed her forehead, pulling her closer and enjoying the feeling of her soft curves nestled against his chest.

"You don't have to tell me anything. Whatever happened had to be in your past, and it truly has nothing to do with me. We need to make this evening as pleasant as possible." She pushed away from him, looking into his eyes with a longing he'd never seen before.

Perhaps she was right but it had everything to do with his adversity to marriage. "What happened with Dutton and Kendall have everything to do with you and my feelings about marriage. Why I haven't asked you to marry me even though my feelings for you transcend anything I've ever felt before. No woman has touched my heart as you have."

"Me?"

He gazed out at the darkening sky and slowly nodded, "You."

"I don't understand."

"Kendall was my wife and Dutton was the man she ran off with."

"I see."

"Not everything."

"I understand if you don't want to explain. It's really none of my business." She pointed out again, "You've told me enough to satisfy my curiosity." She rested her head on his chest. "Did they marry?"

"No."

"Then..." She looked at him, her beautiful green eyes shining with tender concern. "What happened?"

"Dutton put Kendall in charge of a brothel. She is the madam there still. You see she likes sex with everyone but me, and she doesn't like it in the usual ways." His words were clipped but he suddenly realized he no longer cared. The pain had vanished.

"I have a hard time believing she didn't like making love to you." Tira gently touched his lips with a delicate fingertip.

"She likes things different than most."

"Like what things."

"Think about that book you were reading, *Fanny Hill*."

He gently touched her suddenly bright red cheeks. "I don't want to. They were truly embarrassing in places."

"Together they own several brothels in the surrounding communities, all expensive. They cater to the wealthy and many politicians make special trips. I've heard there is blackmail involved at times. Just to go inside, a man has to hand over one hundred dollars."

"It never bodes well when a wife finds out about an indiscretion of this type. I'm sure they collected even more money in those circumstance or they hold the knowledge so they could collect favors. That's what The Duchess does. She has dirt on almost everyone in London, but she only threatens. Don't think she's ever had to tell what she knew."

"Or your constituents," Jamie added, drawing her closer, adoring the warmth of her tiny body against his. He ran his hand along her spine, pressing her closer and appreciating the feel of her full breasts against his chest. Only Tira could touch his heart so completely.

She tilted her chin upward and let him kiss her. In his arms, she was soft and compliant, excepting him completely. The primal dance they always played exploded inside with heat and fire, enchantment and magic overpowering all his senses.

She pulled away from him, touching his cheek with her palm, tilting her head and staring at him as if she tried to commit the way he looked to her memory. A wave of fear swept inside as his brows drew together.

What was it about this day that was so different from the others he'd had with her? She was unlike herself, distant and wistful, her mind somewhere it shouldn't be. She was strangely aloof from him.

"A penny for your thoughts?" he asked, smoothing her hair behind her ear, reveling in the silken strands running through his fingers and never wanting to lose her.

She smiled at him, breathing deeply. "Are you hungry? I didn't put the food away."

"You're changing the subject, I see."

"I don't want to talk about the emptiness in my head. I really wasn't thinking about anything except getting food into your stomach and making sure you get an entire night of sleep."

"Why don't I believe you?"

"Because you're a stubborn man, a very tenacious man who thinks he knows everything."

Who loves you. "I can be that way at times."

"At times? All the time." She laughed then standing and extending her hand to him, "Let's eat."

In the kitchen, she busied herself setting out plates and he dished up the food. "I still want to know what you were thinking about." Truly, he didn't want to let this conversation end.

"Wine?" she asked, moving into the dining room to search the wine rack.

"You've never been this elusive. Did I do something?" he asked watching her as she dodged his questions.

"You've done nothing," she said, her voice whisper thin.

Her tone stopped him. "What does that mean?"

"It means it's time for you to eat and go to bed. I'm going to stay down here and sip my wine until I'm sure you've gone to sleep."

"I'd sleep better with you in my arms." It seemed he gave in to her ploy and let her change the subject.

"No, you wouldn't." Her smile was infectious and touched his heart.

"Perhaps you're right. I want to make love to you, right now." *And I want to feel our child kick, feel the babe move beneath my hand and spend every night possible with you in my arms.*

"You see. Come sit in the parlor with me for a few minutes. I'll let you kiss me. Then you need to go to bed."

He wanted to find a way to do more than just kiss her. "Has The Duchess returned to your head to torment me?"

She followed him into the parlor and curled up next to him, her head on his chest, the wine glass in her hand. "The day with Annie was fun. We should do it again sometime before the weather changes. The leaves are already turning color. Before long it will be too cold."

"Did you have a good time?" He took her glass from her hand and set it on the end table. His lips molded to hers before she could answer. Beneath him she was warm and soft, giving almost everything that was hers to give, yet he felt a hint of reservation. Tonight, she was still holding something back and he meant to discover why.

"Annie enjoyed the picnic. She wants to go on another one tomorrow." Tira closed her eyes, running her finger along his neck and stopping at his pulse point.

Everything about Tira was soft and tantalizing. He silently berated himself for taking such terrible advantage of her innocence as well as her dreams. While he'd known what would happen, she'd truly had no idea the extent of the repercussions. Annie was right. He treated her horrible, but that was going to change.

"I know Annie enjoyed herself. She always does." He turned to her, "Did you? Enjoy yourself?" Insecurities where Tira was concerned assailed him.

She moistened her lips, pulling his head downward to meet her. He felt her tongue glide along the seam of his lips. When he drew her inside, she met him with the expertise he taught her.

His fingers sifted through her hair, loosening all the pins. The long black strands fell around her shoulders, and he felt the silken fire, wanted to wrap it around him and bask in the heat. In the back of his throat he let out a low growl of pleasure, molding his lips to hers.

He drew her closer, loving the scent surrounding her. The inferno they created together encompassed him, and he held her in his arms, intending to make love to her tonight before he slept. He wouldn't take no for an answer.

"Jamie, you need to stop so you can sleep."

"Not now, I can sleep afterwards." If she didn't actually tell him to no, there was no way on earth he'd stop loving her.

"I promised myself, I wouldn't..."

"Hush." His lips closed over hers once more while he swept her into his arms intending to carry her up the steps to their room.

"Mr. Lundin. Mr. Lundin!"

The loud pounding startled him. He turned and set her on her feet. "Clay? What the devil is it?" This didn't bode well. He had an uneasy feeling this would mean bad news.

"Your father, he fell and he isn't doing so good," Clay said, tipping his head toward the farm. "Your mother's asking for you to come."

"How bad." Jamie pulled Tira close, knowing his plans had just been changed and not wanting to let her go.

"Doc doesn't think he's going to make it through the night. You've got to come now."

"Go saddle my horse and get a fresh one for you. I'll be right with you."

Tira's hand rested on his arm. "You need sleep."

Jamie turned to Tira, realizing nothing tonight happened the way he intended. "I'm sorry. I have to go. I'll try to be back tomorrow morning. If not, I'll send a message."

"Do what you must." She stood with her hands clasped in front of her, eyes wide. He wanted to ask her to come with him. For some reason, he didn't want to leave her tonight, more so than any other time. She didn't like horses, least of all riding them.

He pulled her closer, kissing her hard and fast knowing it would have to be enough for tonight and possibly the next few days. "Take care of yourself and Annie. I'll be back as soon as I can."

"And we'll have that talk you promised me."

"I want that more than anything."

He left her standing in the middle of the room, a haunting faraway expression in her exquisite green eyes. Fear he didn't understand swirled around him. He met Clay in the stables and finished saddling his horse.

Thirty minutes later he left the reins with Clay, and he took the steps to the farmhouse two at a time.

"Jamie," his mother met him at the entrance, her body shaking from fear or fatigue, possibly both. Her eyes were dark circles in the candlelight. "I'm glad you could make it in time. He's in the downstairs bedroom. I think he's holding on just so he can say goodbye to you."

Heart in his throat he strode into the room. His father lay on the bed, eyes closed, his breathing slow and labored. "Dad."

His father, with a frail shaking hand, reached toward Jamie who sat beside the bed and took it into his. He didn't know what to say to the man who sired him and created a living hell, lived out during his childhood. The love and respect he was supposed to feel for his father just wasn't there, yet he cared for him, was sad that he was dying.

"Son."

"Don't talk. You need to rest so you can heal," Jamie said as exhaustion threatened to claim him.

"I wasn't a very good father." His voice was whisper thin. "But you turned out to be a damn good man. I love you. I've never told you that." He closed his eyes, his breathing slowed and the man Jamie called father was gone. Jamie pulled the sheet over his face.

"Mother." She stood in the doorway, wiping her hands on her apron.

"You got here in time. I wasn't even sure if you would come. You always despised him. A man should not despise his father, but I understand what he did to you." Tears slipped from her eyes.

Jamie strode to his mother and wrapped an arm around her. "He did it to us, both of us. Never forget that and remember I came for you."

"Never for your father. I wish it could have been different between the two of you." She exhaled a long breath of air.

"He didn't ever treat you right but you stood by him. I don't love him and never respected him." Struck by his words, he understood now how horribly he treated Tira. He vowed once more to make it up to her.

"When we first wed, I loved him. He was like no other man I'd ever known. Then everything changed." She let him wrap his arms around her as she leaned into him for support.

"Not for the better, I'm guessing. He didn't want a child. He didn't want me," Jamie said the words bitterly.

"No, he was pleased when you were a boy, but he had different ideas about bringing up a son. You had to be tough, tougher than the next boy. That's when we started arguing about everything, not just how to treat you but how I cooked the meals or cleaned the house, what I wore."

He drew her closer, wishing their lives had been different. Wishing he knew the words that would mend her heart. He couldn't do either. "I'll send Clay for the coroner."

Jamie strode from the house. "Clay!"

"Boss." It seemed he'd been waiting. He tipped his hat back waiting for Jamie's order.

"Send your best man to town to retrieve the coroner."

"He's gone then," Clay said.

"He is." *And good riddance.*

"I'll go," Clay said.

"You don't have to do that, seeing you just came from town."

"I'd be happy to go for you. With any luck I'll be back in an hour or so."

"Suit yourself."

Jamie turned, making his way back to the house and the downstairs bedroom. His mother was bent over, sobbing, her face in her hands. He marveled that she missed him that much. The last few years he'd been one mean bastard.

"Mother, you need to go to bed. There is nothing more you can do here. Clay went for the coroner. If you want, I'll wake you when they get here."

She looked up, patting him on the hand. "Thank you." He helped her to her room before striding down the stairs to the parlor.

Pouring a glass of brandy, he tucked the bottle under his arm then stood in the doorway looking over the farm. The fields stretched farther than he could see. With his help, his parents built the farm to a point where it was one of the best in the territory. Now it was all his and the thing about it, he didn't want anything to do with farming. He couldn't sell it because his mother loved the house.

The alcohol burned a path down his throat. When he closed his eyes, he saw Tira, naked, stretched out on his bed. He longed for her in the most elemental ways. She was his enchantress, magic to his soul. She was his everything. He wanted to race back to the house and tell her exactly how he felt.

He wasn't going to make it home tomorrow. After the coroner took care of the body, his father would be buried in the family plot. He drank the contents of his glass then poured another. He'd have to stay for his mother and make sure she had all she needed. Perhaps he should move her into town. She could live in Lizzie's old house and she'd be close to him. He could take care of her. Who would live in the farmhouse she loved?

Inside he sat on the couch he'd never been allowed to sit on when he was a boy. The brandy was making him sleepy, hell, he was exhausted and he should be asleep upstairs in his old bedroom.

Would God take his father into Heaven or would he be denied? Hell, probably wouldn't take the old man either.

Striding into the office where all the ledgers were kept, he found paper and pen.

Tira,

I won't make it home until late tomorrow night or the next day, most likely the next day. Take care of Annie while I'm gone. I miss both of you so much. When I get home, we're going to have a private talk, just you and me. I've got something I want to ask you.

Make sure you get bread from Martha and anything else you might like. Of course you could show off your cooking skills to Annie. I'm hoping to see them someday soon.

I forgot to tell you why I can't come home just yet. Father passed away just after I got to the farm. Have to stay and help mother bury him.

I'm thinking of you and Annie.

Jamie

He almost wrote I love you but held back. The words he wanted to say to Tira needed to be said privately to her.

~ * ~

From the front porch of the brothel Mathew Dutton watched Tira Hepburn stride purposely to the docks and enter the office. She appeared determined; her hands fisted at her sides. A ship had come into port last night and he was curious what she was doing. Leaving Lundin perhaps? That thought gave him a good reason to smile. He'd heard all the gossip about the couple. Perhaps she was putting a stop to the rumors by leaving.

She was inside the office for the longest time, and when she left, she went straight to the Lundin home and escorted the little girl down the street. He assumed to Andrews' home where Aidan McLellan was staying. He couldn't see quite that far.

Taking it upon himself to find out why, he strode to the office and entered, waiting for the clerk to look up from his work.

"Good morning," he said, taking his hat off and smiling. "Nice day outside. I see a ship came into port this morning."

"What can I do for you?" The man set his pen on the paper-clogged desk.

"Would it be possible to find out why the young lady, Miss Hepburn, was here? She's a friend of mine and I wanted to see if there was something I should know. She didn't say anything about leaving Baltimore."

"Booking passage to London." The man went back to work, scribbling on a paper in front of him.

"What ship?" Dutton set his hand on the man's paper work, stopping him.

"Ah, that would be the Sweet Folly. It's one of Hadden Johnston's ships. I believe the man is a brother-in-law of some sort to the girl. That family's damn confusing, too many girls and not one boy among them."

"Is there room for one more passenger?" His plans for Tira were beginning to take shape. A trip to London on board for months with Tira Hepburn, ripe for seduction. He would do his damndest to train her for work in the brothel, and by the time they reached London, she would fit right into the role of madam.

"There is. Need the money up front. Ship sails at three o'clock sharp. Be there or it'll go without you."

Dutton pulled out his money clip and slipped the required payment on the desk. He returned to the brothel and found Kendall.

Pulling her into his arms, he kissed her soundly, enjoying the feel of her pliant body next to his. He wanted to draw her to the bed and make love, but if he did, that he'd miss the ship.

She pulled away smiling. "You're amorous today. Why? What has you kissing me in the middle of the day?"

"Tira Hepburn is leaving Lundin. She booked passage on a ship sailing to England. I plan on being on that ship. Tira is a perfect madam for our brothel in London. She's beautiful and has that innocent air about her men love. Since she's only been with one man, the men can teach her things she could have never dreamed of."

"One man that you know of," she corrected him. "Any way, it's fitting. I'm glad she's left him. He doesn't deserve her." Kendall laughed, her smile infectious. "You going to have sex with her?"

"I'd like to. Perhaps in time, but for the moment, I should tread carefully, win her to my side first." He walked around Kendall and lifting her hair from her neck trailed a line of kisses down it.

She leaned into him, silently telling him he could do whatever he wanted. "I'll miss you."

"If Tira proves to be a willing partner, well, I probably won't miss you too much. Do you mind?"

"I'll have to find someone to take your place while you're gone. Maybe Jamie will be so distraught over his loss he'll come looking for solace in my arms. He did fall in love with me once. Maybe he'll do it again."

"In your arms? I doubt it." Dutton laughed, swatting her on her bottom. "Ran across him yesterday. Make no mistake he loathes both of us."

She shrugged her lily-white shoulders. "Stranger things have happened. Perhaps I'll pay him a visit in a few days and see for myself what he thinks about me. Maybe I can be a stepmother to his little girl."

Chapter Eight

Tira read the message from Jamie then reread it aloud to Annie. With shaking fingers, she let it slip to the floor. Her hand on her chest, she tried desperately to breathe.

"You have to leave today," Annie said matter of factly, her little hands on her hips. "You might not get another chance. Papa won't ever know how much he misses you if you don't go. I'll help you pack."

"I understand, sweetheart. I booked passage on a ship earlier this morning and I packed my trunk. I comprehend it's what I have to do in order for me to know how he feels." She looked around the room, her mind reeling. Was she really doing this? Her stomach rolled as a bout of nausea ripped through her.

"I miss you already." A tear slipped from Annie's eye and she wiped it away with the back of her hand. "He'll come after you. I know it. Don't be afraid."

Breathing in a long slow breath and wiping her tears away before she spoke, "I really hope he's as predicable as you say he is. In either case it's for the best. If he doesn't care enough to follow me to London, then I will know for certain he doesn't love me."

"Come, I'm going to bring you to Aidan and get Joshua to take my trunk to the ship. It leaves at three so we should hurry. I don't want to miss it. Don't know when there will be another one out of here. This is one of Hadden's so I know it's safe." Tira looked around the room again, realizing she might never see it again. This was her home and she didn't want to leave. What would Jamie do when he found she'd left?

"Did you leave him a note?"

"I will, right now." Truly she didn't know how to explain her actions. The thing was, she couldn't live as his whore. If she tried, she would die a slow death inside until she was nothing.

With pen and paper in hand she began.

Jamie,

I can never be your whore and that is what people are calling me. I thought the gossip wouldn't bother me but it does. In a sense I am a whore. I sold my body to you for my dream, for that bargain we made. Living like this is eating away at my soul. I need love and a family. I want a legitimate child more than anything. You can't give me either of those things."

Now, I'm going to London and I'm hoping The Duchess will allow me to stay with her for awhile. After that I don't know what I'll do, maybe return home. I won't be a burden to Aunty Charlotte for the rest of my life. I have to find my own way sometime. Perhaps I'm not meant to have a husband. After what I've done with you, who would want me? Possibly I could get a job as a governess in some wealthy man's home and teach the little ones.

Annie is staying with Aidan. She will be fine for the one day you are gone. The ship I booked passage on is one of Hadden's. I think it's called the Sweet Folly and I'm sure it will be safe. When I get to London, I'll write you and tell you I've arrived safely as well as anything interesting.

I love you Jamie Lundin and I wish with all my heart you could have returned that love. I guess I wanted more than just my dream. I also wanted a husband and a family with you and Annie. You can't give that to me.

With all my love,

Tira

Gathering Annie close, they walked through town to Aidan's home. "I'm leaving," Tira said with a heavy heart, moisture pooling in her eyes. "One of Hadden's ships is in the harbor and it's heading for London. I have to go now. It all seems to be happening too fast and it makes me terrified I'm doing the wrong thing."

"So, the ship will be safe and you will be safe too," Aidan said, taking Tira's hands in hers. "I know it wasn't an easy decision, but if he loves you, he'll come for you. At least this way you'll know how he feels about you and you won't be second guessing everything."

"I suppose, but we both know there are no guarantees." At the moment she felt lost and adrift. She was re-sorting her intentions every second, thinking about turning around and going home.

"We both appreciate the fact you need to do this," Aidan said, taking her hands in hers, trying to give support.

"It doesn't mean I'm pleased about this decision of mine. Since last evening, I've changed my mind more times than I want to admit." Her heart was breaking. She didn't think she'd ever feel happy again.

"No, we won't know what the future will bring. All you can do is make the best of bad situations," Aidan said, her voice sounding wistful. "I saw Blade this morning. He was eating breakfast at Martha's café. I don't think he saw me but I started shaking so hard I had to sit down on a bench."

"I may never see Jamie again." Tira tried to hold back the tears threatening. "I already miss him and Annie. How will I ever survive without him? He has to come for me."

"You really do love him, don't you?" Aidan asked as if she could read her mind and didn't really need an answer.

Tira pushed hair from her eyes. "Doesn't matter anymore."

"Of course it matters."

She plopped down on a couch in the parlor, letting her head fall back. "I have to get my things on the boat."

"Joshua will be more than happy to take your trunk." Aidan left the room for a few minutes. "It's all settled. I told him it was upstairs in the master's bedroom. He'll make sure it's loaded and in your room on the ship."

"Thank you." Tira breathed a heavy sigh. She wasn't sure if it was relief that someone was helping her or that she had truly made the decision and at this point she wasn't going to turn around.

"Then you are going."

Tira was nodding while she tried to remember all the things she wanted to tell Aidan before she left. Then, "Aidan, I keep forgetting to tell you. Your swimsuit is at the bottom of the lake."

"It's where? What?"

"I was lucky to have Jamie with me. It was so heavy I couldn't swim in it. I almost drowned the other night. Jamie had to cut it off me." Remembering those terrifying moments, she inhaled a shaky breath. "Whatever you do, don't you dare wear that torture device to swim."

"Why didn't you tell me sooner? I don't care about that awful thing, and it doesn't surprise me. Now I have every reason to swim in as little as possible." She laughed, clapping her hands. "I'm so glad you didn't drown."

Aidan's laughter was contagious. Tira laughed so hard now that the terror had passed more tears formed in her eyes. "I'm relieved I didn't drown too. What if Blade wants you to go swimming with him? He must know we always swam naked."

"I'm not going to worry about situations that haven't developed yet. If I did, I wouldn't be able to eat or sleep. All my nerves would be stretched so thin I'm sure they'd snap."

"I wish I had your attitude, Aidan. Right now, I'm worrying about everything; the ship, London, time without seeing Annie. I don't even know if I'm doing the right thing by leaving. Don't know if The Duchess will help me."

"Of course Aunty will help you. Don't you think otherwise."

"Are you sure/" Once again Tira began to vacillate.

"You are doing the right thing and he'll find you wherever you go, just as Blade seems to find me. Aunty Charlotte will help you no matter what. Come, Annie and I will walk you to the ship. Everything will be fine, you'll see."

When they reached the harbor, the gangplank was down and after giving Aidan and Annie a hug, Tira reluctantly yet determinedly walked onto the ship. With each step forward she wanted to turn and run. She found herself into something she had no control over. It seemed this process had taken on a life of its own.

The first mate led her to her room where her trunk had been placed in a corner. Tira lay down on the bed. Tears turned into sobs of despair then more tears. Jamie had to come for her. She'd die if he didn't. She needed him to find her before the ship left port, but that wouldn't happen. He was still at the farm.

What if she never saw him again? The question reverberated in her head, sucking her into a fierce depression. She let a six-year-old talk her into a desperate act.

Slowly the ship began to move and all hope of a quick reunion died.

She wanted one last glimpse of Baltimore and his home. On deck with the wind in her face and tears streaking her cheeks, she clung to the railing as the city slowly disappeared from view.

The railing seemed like a lifeline grounding her. Frozen to the spot, she couldn't move, her emotions escalating into debilitating anguish. As the sun began to set, a chill swept through her. She was shivering but couldn't bring herself to leave the spot where she stood. Cold wind whipped around her, tearing at her hair, seeming to tell her she was wrong in this.

Second thoughts, doubt at the viability of her decision assailed her, but she couldn't turn around, retrace her steps. A life with him, even as his whore or mistress was preferable to a life without him. She had given him her love and he couldn't return it. She told him in the letter she couldn't live that way.

Tira inhaled the sea air, knowing she would be smelling it for some time. This was one of Hadden's antiquated older ships. It would take some time for them to reach London, months for her to regret her decision, months to find some peace within and come to terms with this hasty decision.

Jamie's ship would have reached London in half the time. She needed to stop thinking about Jamie and the first time they made love on that very ship. Her virginity was hers to give to the man, the right man, and she had. Tira had no regrets except the resolution that caused her to walk onto this ship.

The nights and days for the one precious week they were aboard his ship were straight from heaven. Those first days she'd given her heart to him, and he held it in the palm of his hands. What would he do with it? He could come for her or he could crush it.

Good Lord but she hadn't thought of Tavia for the longest time. Perhaps she would be in London when the Sweet Folly arrived. She would love to see Tavia, find out how her adventure went, hopefully better than this escapade. She was returning in disgrace but of course, if she didn't say anything, no one would know. There was some consolation in that fact.

Ella would be there, and she would be someone to confide in, her marriage a happy one still. This was all so bittersweet. She was returning home in shame, knowing why The Duchess had told them so much about her life and romance with her duke. Aunty Charlotte had given herself to the man she loved, but in Charlotte's case the Duke returned her love. He was willing to wed her.

"Miss Hepburn, you look pensive or is it sadness I see in your beautiful green eyes?" He rested his hand on her back, insinuating himself in a way she didn't want.

She swallowed her fear, telling herself this was a moment in time, nothing more. Tira backed away. "Mr. Dutton. I don't think I should be talking to you."

"I'm harmless." He leaned on the railing, letting his arm touch hers. "You're returning to London I see."

She moved farther away. "I doubt that you're harmless and where I'm going is none of your concern."

"Trouble in paradise?" He leaned into her, his breath touching her cheek. "I can offer a solution."

"I'm not interested in anything you have to propose, Mr. Dutton." She tried to move away but he wrapped an arm around her, pulling her close. He turned and she felt his arousal pressing against her.

She stiffened, pushing on his chest, knowing he would do what he wanted, still... "Let go of me." Fear swamped her.

"You have no protector. I can be that for you. All you have to do is be nice to me and I'll make sure you are pleasured and pampered." He smiled, letting his thumb trace a lazy circle on her neck then followed the path with his lips.

She tried to slap him but he caught her hand, his expression changing to one of anger. "That's not wise, sweet one." His mouth closed over hers, his tongue slipping inside.

Tira heard the anger in his voice before he kissed her. She bit him hard and he jerked away.

"Feisty little thing. I promise you that you'll regret that move," he told her as he used his handkerchief to wipe blood from his mouth.

"It makes no difference if Jamie is on this ship or not as the case might be. If he finds out what you're doing, he'll kill you. If you try that again, I'll kill you and feed you to the sharks."

He grinned, seeming to pay no attention to her words, tracing her lips with a soft fingertip. "You're high spirited. I like that but you cannot overpower a man of my size and strength."

"Don't..." She stepped away from him, looking for a way to run, but he backed her into a corner.

"Ah, but he's miles away and the distance is growing. It will be in your best interest to go along with my plans. They are very lucrative for both of us. I'm sure you'll enjoy it. But you have to pass a test first."

"What is that?" She shivered in disgust, loathing the feelings he provoked in her.

"You have to make love to me." He stroked her cheek again, trying to seduce her.

Bile rose in her throat. "Never."

"When you're starving with no roof over your head, you'll change your mind. I'm a patient man." He sneered and stepped back, looking pointedly at her belly. "After the baby is born, you'll have another reason to come to me."

"Baby? What did you say?" She didn't mean to make herself more vulnerable. "There's no baby."

"Believe what you want. Time will tell." He stepped back, a strange expression on his face. "I'll leave you to your thoughts however dreary they are. Remember my proposition."

Tira watched him leave wondering what he was talking about. Baby? Maybe he was guessing. She leaned on the railing, wishing she could have a bath and wash the stench of Matthew Dutton from her body.

"You need to get inside before you catch your death."

"What?" Tira swiveled, seeing a woman she'd never met standing beside her.

"I don't mean to startle or bring any harm to you. Not like that awful man who just left. I heard what he said. Oh, I'm Genevieve." She held out her hand in friendship.

"What part did you hear?" She cringed away, afraid to trust anyone after what just happened.

"Pretty much all of it. If you are pregnant, I want you to know I'm a midwife and I can take care of you. Come to me anytime you want. Even if it's just to talk. You will know soon the truth of his words if you don't already."

"I'm Tira." Somehow last names didn't seem important. "Why would you think I'm pregnant?" Curiosity stirred inside and she rested her hand on her abdomen. What did people know that she didn't?

"The glow on your lovely face. That man obviously does not cause the gorgeous coloring, so it has to mean you're carrying a beautiful child. While I understand why you wouldn't want to admit such a thing to that awful person, perhaps you can tell yourself the truth," she said.

"I don't believe..." She paused thinking of the days since her last monthly and she certainly couldn't remember when that was. "I couldn't be pregnant." Yet she understood what she and Jamie did had repercussions.

"Because you've never been intimate with a man?" she asked a pointed question, one that gave Tira pause.

"I..." Tira suddenly felt tongue-tied. "I suppose anything is possible."

Genevieve tilted her head. "You paused, what did you remember?"

"More than I wanted to think about, and Dutton knew it. I'm sure of it. He is just goading me and making guesses he has no answers for."

"That dreadful man who was taking advantage of you?" the lady questioned.

"No, the father of my child. He bought me these dresses. I didn't understand why at the time because they were huge, but I'm wearing one and the bodice fits while the voluminous folds of material... I just didn't understand why he'd buy me these."

"Men have a way of sensing the changes in their woman's body. Your man was very thoughtful and without them you'd have nothing to wear on this impulsive trip of yours."

"He was thoughtful and I left him. There was nothing impulsive about my decision even though I regret it almost every second since I made it." Tears streamed from her eyes. She wiped them away with the backs of her hands.

"Why?" Genevieve reached into her pocket and handed her a handkerchief.

"He couldn't tell me he loved me, wouldn't marry me. Townspeople called me his whore. I couldn't live like that even for the man I love." She felt the tears rise in her throat once more. Nothing she did could hold the wracking sobs back.

"But he showed you he loved you every time you were together, didn't he?" Genevieve asked, her voice soft with knowledge. "Once a long time ago I had a man like that."

"He did, but I..."

"I'm assuming you couldn't handle the gossip. Am I right?"

"He has a daughter I adore and in her infinite wisdom she encouraged me to leave, even though she would miss me." Tears changed to heart wrenching laughter. The irony didn't escape her.

"The little girl knew her father would miss you just as much. She told you he would come for you, didn't she?"

"Yes, Jamie always told Annie how much he missed her and loved her when he had to leave. She assumed he would do the same for me. So, I took a six-year-old's advice and ran off."

"Do you have a place to live when you reach London? If not, I'd be happy to let you stay with me. Sometimes I get lonely wandering around my townhouse with only the servants to talk to."

"The Duchess," Tira said, trying to see the humor. "She's my aunt and I'm sure she'll welcome me with open arms even if I am pregnant. She told me only kisses. Never let a man touch you in any other way. But did I listen? No."

"When it comes to our hearts, few of us listen."

"Perhaps she will even help me find a suitable husband. The debutant balls are obviously out of the question." Tira ignored the woman, thinking only of her future.

"The Duchess, you say. I wouldn't want to get on her bad side." Genevieve laughed softly, her eyes taking on a strange hue, almost as if she was remembering something. "Her reputation for righting all wrongs done to her family goes beyond the pale. She helped me once a long time ago, and I owe her more than I can ever repay. If you give birth before we reach London, I'll be there for you."

"And I truly can't believe she still has favors to call in. If the truth be told, I'm a bit afraid of her too, at least when she's The Duchess. When she's my aunty she's sweet and patient, the most kind and motherly woman I've ever known." Tira said, thinking about the fun times she spent with Aunt Charlotte.

"So, how far along are you?" Genevieve asked, studying her. "I'm guessing about four months. If this is your first child, you won't show as quickly."

Tira thought back to that first trip on his clipper, the moonlight slanting through the window. His body bathed in the silver glow. Truth be told that first sight of him stole her breath. It had been the middle of July. When she left, autumn leaves were redolent on the trees now. The first of October had come and gone. It was the twenty-fourth today. Where had all the time vanished?

"I'm guessing about four and a half months. If I conceived the first time we made love." She looked down, her hands pressing on her womb. "Am I really carrying his child?" Wonder and awe swept through her. Instinctively, she wanted to run to him and tell him the news.

"You could have this tiny one before we dock in London. We should get busy sewing. This child will need some clothes to wear. We can't have the wee babe spending his or her life naked. Can you sew?"

"Not very well. We always purchased our clothing, and I never enjoyed sitting still that long." Hit hard by her lack of feminine skills, she didn't know what to do. "I've stitched a few seams. I've no idea how to make baby clothes. We'll need tiny blankets too. Truth be told I spent more of my childhood climbing trees than learning how to do feminine things."

"I will help. First thing tomorrow morning we should go through your trunk and see if there's any clothing that would be suitable for a baby. What do you think it is, a boy or a girl?"

"I don't have any idea. Should I?"

"No, but some women have dreams and sometimes those dreams prove correct and sometimes they don't. I was just curious."

"I'd like a boy, one who looks just like Jamie."

Four and a half months to the day, the Sweet Folly was just off the coast of England and Tira had given birth to a beautiful baby boy. Now, a few weeks later she stood with Genevieve at the railing of the ship, watching London come into view.

During the voyage they managed to sew several rompers for the child and a few tiny blankets to wrap him in. Luckily, they had only been a few weeks out when the child was born and now she could purchase suitable clothing.

The trip had taken longer than anticipated. They had been plagued by storms and tossed off course more than once. She smiled, relieved she would step on solid ground after so many months at sea and looked forward to seeing Aunt Charlotte.

"Do you have coin to hire a carriage?" Genevieve asked.

"I do. When I left London for my adventure, Aunty made sure I had enough money to last a year if necessary. I made sure I emptied most of my account and had the rest transferred to London."

"She'll be pleased to hold your son. Have you named him yet?"

"No, and I understand he needs a name but..." she stopped, thinking of Jamie and how he'd love his son. He'd known of her pregnancy. Now if he came for her, she wouldn't know if his arrival would be for her or for his son. The easy solution to her problem changed.

Dutton suddenly appeared next to her. "I see we've finally arrived. You reconsider my proposition?" he asked her, his hand resting possessively on her elbow. For some reason the awful man kept his distance during the trip and she'd been utterly grateful.

Tira flinched away from him. "I've not spent one moment thinking about you and that ludicrous proposition. I will never let you touch me that way. I loathe you and the very thought makes me nauseous."

"You will reconsider. I promise you. It won't be long before you grace my brothel and my bed."

"Never."

He gazed at the baby, moving closer. "Heard you had a boy. Did you name the little fellow after his father?"

She held herself rigid, knowing he would leave when he was ready and not a moment sooner. "You're a despicable man."

"Ah, but that's one of my better qualities. And you should know, I always get what I want."

"Not this time." What he didn't know was that she wasn't alone and vulnerable here in London. She had family and friends to protect her, The Duchess as well as Drake Montgomerie. Individually they were forces to be reckoned with but together they were invincible.

"You will come to love me or at least welcome my love making, so much more creative than what you've known before." He smiled, walking away from her, twirling his cane.

"Thank the good lord he's gone. I pray I never see that man again." Tira let out the breath she was holding.

"You should take care where that man is concerned. I've a feeling much of what he's saying is the God's honest truth. Guard your child and keep him close to your heart. He could use the baby to make you do what he wants. Because like most women, you would even compromise yourself to keep that wee one safe."

Tira shivered knowing what Genevieve told her was true. "If he does anything, The Duchess will find a way to make him pay." But that might be too late for her.

"Not if he has your child. Don't let him touch the baby and whatever you do, don't leave the child alone."

Genevieve's harsh warning sent a wave of nausea through her. She moved the blanket away from his face so she could see him better. *He's fine and secure.* There was no way she would ever let that man close to him. She would kill Dutton if he tried anything.

The lines were thrown out and the ship secured. A few minutes later the gangplank was in place.

Tira hesitated, her hand to her throat. Fear, love, desperation the emotions swept through her. "Dear God in heaven."

"What is it?"

With a shaking hand, Tira pointed to the Warf. "That's him. That's Jamie." She clutched her throat, barely able to inhale a breath of air. "He's come for the child. I know it. He can't mean to take him from me."

"If he cares anything for you, he won't hurt you by taking the child, but he might use the babe to control you if you don't give him his way. Have you figured out how you feel about him? Keep in mind no argument or stubbornness is worth the problems you might create just to stand your ground."

"I betrayed him, left him with only a short note to explain myself."
She pulled the child to her body as if the tiny gesture would keep all harm
from the little one.

"He's here ahead of us? I'm having a hard time believing that,"
Genevieve mused.

"The clipper is fast. His ship is fast. He must have used the storm
winds to get more speed." She kept the baby close, holding him tightly and
praying he wouldn't take him from her. He wouldn't be so cruel. Trying
for air she inhaled a ragged breath.

Genevieve touched her back. For a moment the gesture was
reassuring. Then she saw his face. His brows furrowed, his eyes dark and
shuttered, angry looking. She'd never seen him like that.

~ * ~

The day of the funeral was hot and humid. Jamie wiped sweat from
his brow as he watched the dirt fall on his father's casket. More than
anything he wanted to ride home, take Tira into his arms and feel her life
beat meld with his. He needed to take her into his arms and tell her how
much he loved her. Then he would get down on one knee and ask for her
hand.

Instead, he had to stay at the farm until tomorrow afternoon. He
promised his mother and knew she needed his support and love. She
grieved for the man she married many decades ago. The man she had loved
for those same years despite the hate his father harbored inside for just
about everything.

He spoke to her about moving into town but she adamantly refused.
This was her home she told him, and she would leave when she died. They
finally agreed on a younger companion to see to the things she couldn't do
herself. The next day he found one in a nearby village. The woman had
agreed to live in the house, and Clay was charged with supervising the new
employee.

In truth, he tried to do that very thing several years ago, but his
father would have nothing to do with his proposal. The man kept telling
him he could do everything himself when he could barely leave the couch,

nodding off while talking to people.

At least he had the means to help his mother now. Dinner that evening was food left by family friends coming from nearby farms. They ate from an array of stews, biscuits and even desserts. There was so much, he made sure all the farm hands ate.

A storm blew in the next day. Rain pelted the earth, the roads sloppy with mud as he traveled back to town. Before going home, he checked the office to see how the building of the new clipper was coming along. Then whistling a cheery tune, he walked into his very quiet home.

"Tira. Tira! Annie?" He strode through the strangely silent house, which was usually brimming with chatter and laughter. Annie's dolls still sat in the parlor, some dressed some not so much. The teapot held tea and there were still scones on the tray. It appeared as everyone left at once. Fear for his girls swept through him.

"Where is everyone?" He strode through all of the rooms, baffled then realized they must be visiting Aidan, his relief was palpable. Poking around the kitchen, he grabbed a slice of bread before setting his sights on Aidan's home.

Inside Aidan's house, "Papa, you're home! Did you get Tira's letter?" Annie ran into his arms, hugging him fiercely.

"No, there was a letter? Where was it?" He set Annie on the floor then turned his attention to Aidan who was moving at a more lady like pace, her expression wary and he knew she was holding something back he wouldn't like.

"You've returned home. How are you doing?" Aidan asked, her hands folded in front of her.

"Growing more curious by the second," he said, watching the myriad emotions flit across Aidan's face. "Where is Tira? Upstairs perhaps? Visiting her sister? You need to tell me."

"You didn't see the note. You should go home and read it. I'm sure there is nothing I can tell you the note from Tira doesn't say."

"Papa, she loves you and you're going to go after her." Annie's excitement confused and baffled him. He did believe Tira loved him.

Jamie ruffled Annie's hair. "Calm down, maybe, that remains to be seen. I don't know anything right now." A dark energy swept through him, fear for Tira escalating. Nothing good was happening here.

"Get your things," Aidan said. "I'll talk to your papa while you're finding everything."

"Where did she go?" His gut knotted painfully. He hoped it was just a quick trip to visit her sister.

"I'm sure the note will fill you in when you read it. She returned to London," Aidan said, her voice shaking.

"London? Why on earth would she do that? I thought she was happy with me and Annie." She carried his child and she left him. Long ago memories assailed him. Kendall had left him too.

"She wasn't happy. Tira was very sad and afraid of living the rest of her life unloved." Aidan spoke softly, her voice whisper thin in the small entryway. "Happy has not been a feeling she had for a while. Do you want to know the truth?"

"Of course I do," he gritted out, bile rising in his throat. Why didn't she tell him about her feelings and how could she pretend for so long?

"Tira doesn't want to be your whore or anyone's for that matter. She wants a husband and a family to call her own."

"She is the farthest thing from a whore."

"It's not what the good people of Baltimore believe, Jamie. Haven't you been listening to any of the gossip or even the uncensored advice of your friends?"

Pacing, he traveled the length of the room and back. For a moment he paused then, "Can Annie stay with you for an extended length of time?"

"Yes, are you leaving? Don't go after her if you don't intend to marry her. She deserves better than to be called the town whore whether it's here or in London. She needs a safe place where love and respect is offered."

"What I intend with Tira is not your concern." Yet he'd been on the verge of asking her to marry him. Now he wanted to throttle her and drag her home. If not for unfortunate circumstances, she would have been his wife within a week or two.

"She's my cousin and her feelings are very much my business. I love Tira. Can you say the same?" Aidan challenged him with every ounce of strength she possessed.

"Then you should have found a way to persuade her to stay," he insisted pushing his hair around with his hands, his frustration mounting. The fear of losing her escalating, almost debilitating, he put his face in his hands, holding back the tears.

"I talked her into leaving," Annie said scrunching her face and stepping into the middle of the fray. "I don't think she would have done it otherwise. She longed to know how you felt where she was concerned."

"Why?" This was all beyond his comprehension. "I thought you loved her and wanted her to be your stepmother."

"I do but I want you to love her and miss her too. It was the only way to make you come to your senses," Annie said, her intense determination weakening in the onslaught of his questioning.

"Do you want her for a stepmother?" he asked, watching her little face light up with joy at his question.

"Yes." She clapped her hands jumping up and down. "I knew her leaving would be for the best. Now you can go after her, tell her how much you miss her and bring her home. Everything will be wonderful."

Slowly Jamie pulled a small box from his coat pocket. "I bought this before she left meaning to ask her to marry me the day of our picnic."

"Why didn't you?" Annie's face fell.

"Because my father, your grandpa, passed on and I was called away. I was going to do it tonight over a nice dinner and a bottle of wine." *Then I was going to make love to her.*

"But she's gone. I talked her into it. Will you ever forgive me?"

"Yes, she is and now my proposal will have to wait. You should not interfere in the ways of adults. We create enough trouble all by ourselves." His anger grew. She should have trusted him to do the right thing. She should have known he'd come around.

"Are you going after her?"

"Yes, so you'll have to stay here, with your aunty Aidan, until we return. I guess now you have to go unpack your bags." Frustration at the horrible timing and with his daughter filled his soul. She was a precocious little thing and most of the time he admired her spirit. Not this time.

"I don't mind. Aidan and Lilly will help me get more things from the house as I need them."

"Give me a kiss so I can be on my way." He pulled his daughter into his arms and kissed her soundly on the cheek. "You behave yourself. It might very well be a while before I'm back. You're going to have to go to school with out me by my side. I hope Aunty Aidan is up to the job."

"Do you know which ship she sailed on?" He turned to Aidan for the answer.

"One of Hadden's older ones. I believe it was the Sweet Folly. I didn't tell her about the clipper that sat waiting for cargo and passengers. Thought you might be able to catch up with her in a day or two. That way no one would have to sail all the way to London."

He groaned. "A very slow ship." Aidan was right. He would have to see if he could intercept it. If he didn't, he'd be in London at least a month or maybe more ahead of that ship. "I don't know why he doesn't retire that one from his fleet."

Aidan shrugged her shoulders, making a face to go along with it. "I'm sure I've no idea. You're a ship captain. Maybe you can figure it out."

"Annie, I'll see you as soon as I can and hopefully, I'll have Tira with me." With that said and not wanting to waste any more time on idle conversation, Jamie left.

A few minutes later, striding into his office, "Mooney."

"Aye, sir." The man grinned at him as if he knew exactly why he was here.

"Pack a bag. We're leaving as soon as the tide turns."

"Where we going?"

"You don't mean to tell me you don't know where Tira went? If not, you're the only one in town who doesn't know she left me and returned to London."

"Haven't heard a word." He chuckled, scratching the back of his head. "Told you that you were going to regret treating her the way you were. Mark my words, I told you. Guess you've got some quick talkin' to do. When you catch up with your little lady, that is."

"Had a ring in my pocket. She just didn't know it. I did mark your words and everyone else's who lectured me including your wife and Martha," he said, the anger at his stupidity building.

"Well, my wife will be pleased to hear you've finally come to your senses. The boat should be stocked and ready with the tide. I'll see to it myself."

"Good." Then he left for his house and packed a trunk, eager to be on his way and fix this catastrophe. He prayed his child would not be born on board the ship with no one to help Tira.

A few months later the wind at his back, they sailed into London. He realized several days past, he would arrive well ahead of Tira's ship, the Sweet Folly. Once they docked, he hired a buggy to visit The Duchess.

"Well, well, well," The Duchess greeted him. "I've heard things over the last months from Aidan as well as Amorica, and I certainly hope they aren't true. Come in and sit and tell me where Tira is. Shouldn't you be retuning my charge safe and sound then asking me if you can marry her? I can have a minister in this room within the hour."

Jamie cleared his throat remembering some of the stories he'd heard about this formidable lady. "Tira sailed on one of Hadden Johnston's antiquated ships. She's on her way here as we speak. She left me just before I intended to ask her to marry me, before you begin your lecture."

"Why would Tira leave you, young man? On someone else's ship is not an answer I can accept." She tapped her cane several times on the floor. "Well? You waiting for the coming of summer to talk? It's April now, so we'll have quite a wait."

He truly understood why The Duchess had been in Tira's head when they first met. What was hard to believe was how easily he'd been able to erase this formidable lady's voice.

"She left me without a word. One day she was in my house and the next she vanished. I went after her as soon as I knew."

The Duchess pointed her finger at him accusingly. "You kept her in your bed and didn't give her a ring. What the bloody hell did you expect? She's a lady and deserves more than that from a gentleman."

"Guilty as charged, but I intend to make it up to her. I just have to wait until that antique ship she's taking to London docks." He had to admit some of his anger cooled during the last months.

He followed The Duchess into the parlor and sat as far away as possible.

"Lemon bar?" She held out a plate, smiling.

He was suddenly terrified of that grin. She was holding something back from him. "Is there something you're not telling me? Is Tira here?"

"I wouldn't tell you one way or the other." His heart caught in his throat. He'd heard stories about how she held out on the men in her charges' lives. She refused to tell Logan where Eveleen had gone and she also refused knowledge to Blade as to Aidan's whereabouts.

"What I do know is there is no damn way the Sweet Folly could have arrived in London before me. She's still on that ship, and I know for a fact you're not hiding her somewhere." Frustration bit into him as he watched the older woman. He wanted Tira now, needed to hold her and make sure she and their child were all right. Lizzy had died in childbirth.

She bit into a lemon bar, powdered sugar coating her lips then she delicately removed the sugar with an embroidered handkerchief. "I suppose I can't pull one over on you. You're right, of course. What do you plan?"

"Wait at the docks until the Sweet Folly is moored. Then I'm going to find out, in her words, face to face, why she ran away. I'm also going to find out if she's given birth to my child." He didn't know how far along she was when she left. Hell, she didn't even know she carried his child when she took such drastic charge of her life. The look on her face when he gave her the maternity clothes had been amazing, one he etched in his mind.

"So, she's pregnant. You know that for a fact?"

The Duchess' pointed question stopped him, nearly stole his breath. He needed time to recover. What he did understand was that he couldn't lie to her and he'd not intended to let go of that fact. "I believe so."

"Don't you know for sure, young man? Of course you do."

"When Tira left, she didn't know. She must by now though." He coughed, clearing his throat.

"And you didn't tell her? Why the bloody hell not? She was an innocent, still is I'm sure, and you held her heart in your hands. You abused her. Got her pregnant and didn't have the decency to tell her."

He wiped sweaty hands on his pants legs. "Didn't have time to tell her. I was waiting on the right moment. Truthfully, I wanted to ask her to marry me before I told her she was pregnant. I had no idea she would bolt."

"I see. You never got around to telling her you love her either, I suppose," she paused for a couple of seconds, seeming to study him. "Or do you? You have not performed very well, young man. It seems you've only thought with your cock and not your head. For the future, you need to remedy that."

"I knew I loved her from the first time..." He stopped, running a finger around his collar. The Duchess was living up to everything Tira told him about her. This unequivocally was her intimidating side. This lady was no Aunty Charlotte.

"I know what you did to her. Just fess up. You made love to her and more than once." Her cane started tapping again, sending an intimidating message.

"Yes, I was too damn stubborn to admit to loving her." He wished like hell things had been different. Now he had a lot of explaining to do. Explanations he didn't understand himself.

"My girls, too much trouble." She was shaking her head, a sad expression on her face, moisture in her eyes. He understood just then the transformation from The Duchess to aunty. One was formidable, the other gentle and sweet. "I didn't do right by them. Each has their story of love. For none of them was it easy. It was my job to protect them. I failed all of them. Now Aidan is all alone on what seems like the other side of the world. I was actually happy that Tira journeyed there to live with her."

Where Aunty was concerned, he suddenly felt defensive. "Tira is strong and independent. That's why she left and why I admire her enough to come after her. I believe you instilled those qualities in her. She didn't have a mother so you played that role in her life."

"Will you do right by her and wed her?" she asked, tears slipping down her pale cheeks.

"If she'll have me. If I can convince her I came for her and not the baby." He hadn't meant to remind the lady. "She can be very stubborn."

"Keep me informed. I'm assuming when she arrives, you'll want to keep her with you. I want to know if she had the baby." She tapped her cane on the floor again. "Go on, do what men do, whatever that is. I need to take a nap." She sat back, resting her hands on her lap and closing her eyes.

With a quick backward look at Charlotte, Jamie left. The meeting with The Duchess had been something he hadn't looked forward to. Now that part was over and all he had to do was wait for Tira to arrive.

A couple months later, pacing the deck as he'd done every day since he landed, he saw what he'd been waiting for, the Sweet Folly. His heart in his throat. It was all he could do not to run on board and challenge Tira. He held back, resisting his impulse to confront her, hoping he had enough sense to treat her gently and not terrify her. He wasn't angry, just worried.

He inhaled several long deep breaths, forcing himself to a calm he didn't feel. "Mooney, she's here."

"'Bout time. Don't think I could've taken many more days of your caustic behavior."

Jamie wasn't about to give credence to Mooney's words even though he knew the first mate was right. He watched the ship, not knowing if he was angry or relieved the boat was finally in London.

The vessel made port several berths away from him. Striding down the dock, he walked up the gangplank, noting the shocked expression on Tira's face and the bundle she held in her arms. Matthew Dutton's presence next to her did not go unnoticed. The sight of the man who'd run off with his first wife standing vigil next to her, sent a raging fury bubbling up inside.

The man's hand rested possessively at her elbow. Rage filled him. It was an anger he never experienced before, not even when Kendall left him. He had never wanted to greet Tira in anger, but today after the long absence that was what he did.

"Tira." He boxed Dutton out, moving in to take the baby from her arms. An awe he'd never felt before swept through him. "You had our child." When he pulled the blanket away and looked at his beautiful baby, tears formed in his eyes.

She smiled, "A boy. Broc. I named him Broc, but if you don't like the name, we can call him something else."

The expression on her face and the feel of his child in his arms softened his feelings a bit. He didn't have time to reply.

"Handsome little boy," Dutton said, further antagonizing him.

Any softening he felt vanished. "Tira." He headed down the gangplank with his child in his arms, not waiting to see if she followed. He knew she would. Tira would never let him walk away with the child and he realized if she refused to marry him, he could use the child as leverage.

"Good luck with your man," Genevieve said, giving her a quick motherly hug. "Go after him and tell him what is in your heart. You can't lose. The truth is always the best."

"Remember my offer," Dutton called after her. "I'll stay in touch and when the time is right, I'll have you."

His pace quickened. "Jamie, wait." Tira rushed after him.

He paused to see Tira picking up her skirts to race his way. By the time she reached his side, she was breathless, her hand clutching at her throat, gasping for air. "What are you doing? You can't just take my son."

"My son, and I can do whatever I want with him. The law will be on my side." He turned again, his anger filling him with pain. This time he didn't stop until he was inside the cabin on his ship. The very place where this little boy had probably been conceived.

He settled the boy in the crib he purchased several months ago before he left Baltimore. It had been impulsive. but he was glad he thought of it in time,

"Jamie, we have to talk. Please."

"Now you want to talk. Why not before you left me while carrying my child?" Months of worry and fear for her and this infant overwhelmed him. He was lashing out at her when he wanted to ask her to be his wife.

"I didn't think you'd let me go and I didn't know I carried him. Jamie, he's crying. I have to feed him." She reached out to him with her arms, silently imploring him to do the right thing.

He discovered he was blocking the crib from her. "Go ahead." He stepped aside then sat down behind his desk. "Mooney!"

The door opened, "Send someone to tell The Duchess Tira arrived unscathed with a little boy she named Broc."

"Captain." He nodded with a smile and was gone.

She picked the baby up then lowering her bodice and sitting with her back to him, she let the babe suckle.

"You're suddenly shy?" he asked. "Now you forget how many times we made love and you hide yourself from me?"

"It's been a while and you're angry. I'm afraid. I've never seen you like this. I'm not sure I know who you are or what you intend." She stroked the child's cheek.

"I want to watch you feed my child. I've missed out on so much. I would have liked to be there when he was born. You deprived me of precious time with my son, precious memories." He realized that, more than seeing Dutton touching her, caused his anger and frustration. The site of Dutton created a deep fear in his gut.

She rose, moving to the bed where she could lean against the headboard and prop her arm on a pillow. "Why did you come after me?"

"Why did you leave with Dutton?"

"I didn't know I was pregnant. Had I known I would have stayed. I suppose I was a bit naïve."

"Would you? Even after Annie talked you into something so stupid."

"Yes, and Dutton had nothing to do with any of this. It was a coincidence that he was on board that ship."

"With Dutton, nothing is a coincidence," he growled, realizing there was something else going on here. "What did he want?"

"He gave me an offer which I turned down."

He needed to put the conversation about Dutton off to another time when his anger wouldn't cloud his judgment. "Annie said you wanted to leave so I'd realize I missed you."

"By your reaction I can tell you don't miss me. You came for the baby. Well, you can't have him." She stroked the baby's cheek, watching the little boy's reaction. "He's going to stay with me forever."

The sight of Tira nursing his child awed him. He'd never been able to watch Lizzie nurse Annie. "Of course I can take him. I've the means and I'm bigger and stronger than you," Bloody hell, he didn't understand where that statement came from.

"You can't feed him," she blurted, moisture forming in her eyes. "You can't feed our child." Tears flowed even while little Broc suckled.

"I can hire a wet nurse. It won't be hard. It's what I did for Annie when her mother died in childbirth." Damn, he goaded her and was behaving like a five-year-old. He had to put a stop to this useless banter before he lost her.

"How dare you," she said, her body shaking with emotions he knew he could never understand. "I carried him inside me for nine months, gave birth to him. It was a beautiful pain you, a man, can never understand. How dare you threaten me and the life of my son."

"All you have to do is come home with me." Gently, he touched the curve of her breast and was shocked when she flinched away.

"All you have to do is stay here." Her angry voice didn't surprise him.

He needed to start over. "I'm sorry. Seeing you with Dutton at your side, his hand on your elbow unraveled my mind. Brought back memories better left in the past."

"There is nothing..."

"He always has an agenda." He waved a hand in the air. "I don't want to talk about any of this. Dutton doesn't deserve our time when we have other things we need to discuss."

"The truth, Jamie, why did you follow me?" she asked, the hopefulness in her words gave him optimism.

"I came for both of you. If you weren't pregnant, I would have come for you and you alone."

"I just don't know if I can believe you. You still want me in your bed without benefit of marriage. I'm not going to live like that."

This was his opening. One he wanted to capitalize on. He walked to his trunk and rummaging in it for a few seconds he produced the box with the ring inside. He swallowed nervously moistening his lips.

"Remember the night my father died and I had to leave?"

"I do."

Those were the words he needed to hear from her in front of a minister. "Good, then you recall, I wanted to talk to you privately about something."

"Yes," she said, removing the baby from her breast and covering herself.

He was disappointed. It seemed it had been a lifetime since he seen and touched her breasts, made love to her. "I bought this the day before." He opened the lid and a sparkling diamond rested inside.

Her eyes widened and her gaze lifted to his. "You knew I was pregnant."

"I did but that wasn't why I wanted to ask you to marry me. I didn't marry Lizzy when she was with child."

"Why then?" She put the child in his crib. He closed his eyes, peacefully sleeping, unaware of the milestone his parents were about to embark upon.

These were the hardest words he'd ever said, and he truly didn't know if he could commit to them yet. "The rumors, the gossip, I needed to put an end to them. You never deserved to be called a whore."

"So it was the only way you could think of to ask for my hand when you don't love me. You want to marry me because the name, wife, sounds better than whore." Her words were bitter and hollow sounding.

He swallowed the words, letting them linger in the back of his throat. "If you wore my ring, the gossip would vanish."

"I'll have to think about it. In the meantime, I need a carriage to take me to The Duchess' townhouse. If I stay here with you the rumors will abound in London, and there will be no where for me to hide."

~ * ~

Dutton paced the front room of the brothel he owned in London, searching his brain for some way to convince Tira to accept his offer. He reached the conclusion there was nothing he could say that would change her mind. He would have to coerce her to his way of thinking. The only way he could do that was with the child.

"If I possess the baby, she'll do whatever I want." He spoke out loud to himself while a grin stretched across his face. "I'll have a room on the third floor prepared just for the little tyke and perhaps a wet nurse."

"Who are you talking to?" Eliza purred, her heavy breasts resting on his naked chest. Her slick core touched his shaft.

"Just myself. Nothing you need to worry yourself about," he told her pleased with his plans for Tira.

"You still trying to figure out how to get your lady friend to manage this place?" she asked, running a fingertip along his chest, stopping to explore each nipple. "I could do it. Then you wouldn't have to bring her all the way across the ocean."

"You can do a lot of amazing things, sweet Eliza, but manage a place like this is not one of your skills. You can't read let alone calculate and keep track of the money coming in. Besides, she is here." Life would be so much easier though, if she could. It still wouldn't ease the obsession he had with the Hepburn chit. If she gave herself to Jamie Lundin, she should be begging him for his attentions. For some reason he couldn't explain, he was obsessed with Tira.

"Ah." She licked his lips before leaning farther so he could suck her nipple into his mouth. "Mathew," she purred.

Grasping her by the waist, he lifted her so she could settle on him. A groan of pleasure slipped from his mouth. "God, you're so sweet. I think I might keep you for myself."

Slowly she rose then moved down. "That wouldn't be good for business and you know it. Besides I'd get bored. The men who come here pay handsomely and most are good lovers. They bring me expensive baubles. You could never take the place of all of them."

"You're right of course." He rolled her over, sliding inside her farther until he touched her core then out harder and faster he drove until she cried out his name. Then he emptied himself into her.

He moved off her, idly tracing circles around her nipples, thinking about Tira and how it would feel to bury himself deep inside her. He would too and she would be hot and tight. He would find a way even if it meant holding her son hostage.

"Prepare the front room for Tira. It's always been the Madam's room. Give her all the amenities possible. Shower her with expensive trinkets. Give her anything she asks for except her freedom." He paused, thinking of Eliza. "When that is done, go buy yourself something special. You don't know how much I'll appreciate you doing this for me."

"You want her bad, don't you?" she laughed, rising above him. "You should have her too. You deserve the best in everything. I'll take care of anything you ask for."

"Fix a room on the third floor for the baby. We'll have to hire a couple men just to guard the child. Lundin will try to get to him and Tira once I have her here in my home."

"You want to keep the child from Tira too?"

"No, just from the child's father. He's a dangerous man and if I'm going to keep Tira for myself, I have to keep Lundin from the child. Tira's access will have to be limited though. Just when the boy needs to eat and if she's available."

"Of course, some of the bodyguards here will know more men who can help with this problem. I'll speak with a few this afternoon," she told him.

"They have to be loyal to their employer. Me." He cautioned. "Make sure they will swear their fealty."

"Sometimes that's hard. Men will sell themselves to the highest bidder, and their loyalty will be there until a better offer comes along."

"Make sure they know I will meet any price offered to them." He rose from the bed, standing naked at her window and looking over the city.

"That will be part of the contract offered."

"Good then Tira Hepburn will be mine."

Chapter Nine

"You would be safer if you stayed with me," Jamie said, "On board my ship. In my cabin, where I can protect you from Dutton. I don't trust the man."

"I'll tell The Duchess everything. She can increase the security around the house. Knowing The Duchess and her standing, I'll probably be safer in her home and my reputation won't be ruined for a second time."

"Perhaps I should stay in one of her rooms," Jamie said, looking over the ocean as if in serious thought. "I don't want to be away from Broc anymore than I have to be. I've already lost too much time with him, time I'll never get back."

"You still don't get it." Shocked would never completely describe her feelings when he pulled out the ring. While she wanted to believe he'd come for her as well as the child, she wasn't about to make this easy for him. Eventually, she would agree to his proposal even though he'd not said the three words she longed to hear.

"Get what?" Truly he did look confused now. "I understand everything you're telling me."

"You are not naïve, Jamie Lundin. Do you care so little about my status and what people think about me? I've told you too many times to count that I'll not be your whore. As for marriage...I don't know if I want to live in a loveless relationship. You're just going to have to put your passion and desire for sex on hold for the time being."

At her words he turned pale, his jaw tense. "Don't go outside alone, ever," he warned through clenched teeth. "You can't trust Dutton. If he wants you as his Madam at the London brothel as he told you, he'll do everything possible to get you there and once you're under his thumb, there are a myriad of things he can do to make you have sex with him. The thought of him possessing you... I'll kill him."

191

"You won't because I'll never let him touch me. I loathe and despise that man. There isn't anything he can do that will change my mind." Jamie was the only man who would know her intimately.

He helped her from the carriage. Her trunk had arrived earlier. Hadden's captain seemed to know where to send it. "Promise me you won't go outside without a bodyguard."

"I've no reason except to take a walk with the baby in the stroller." She didn't think Dutton would go to such lengths, and she wasn't about to promise something that might not be possible.

"Promise me, Tira," he persisted, his visage grim.

"Sometimes the only thing that will get him to sleep is a walk. I'm not going to walk up and down the stairs. The house is just too small to put him to sleep. I made it clear to Dutton I didn't want anything to do with him. I don't think he'll pursue this farther."

"Now you're naïve. A man like Dutton doesn't take no for an answer. In fact, if you say no to him, he'll make sure to exact a price in addition to taking exactly what he wants. He's planning your abduction as we speak." He opened the door for her before following her inside.

Scarlett, Charlotte's companion, greeted them, ushering the pair into the parlor. "I'll take the child and put him in your room. The Duchess wants to see you. She'll be down shortly. The two of you should make yourself at home."

"Nothing has changed." Tira strode around the room, picking up items then setting them back, feeling at home and wanted. "I always loved this room. We had lots of talks in here."

"The Duchess' voice in your head?" Jamie chuckled softly, a far away expression seeming to grace his features. "I had a devilishly hard time getting rid of that voice."

"Yes, and so much more. We laughed and cried in this room, reminisced about our childhood. At times we planned our future."

"You and your cousins?"

"And sisters too. I wonder if Tavia is in town." She looked wistfully to the door as if she hoped Tavia would rush inside and hug her. "Would you like brandy?" she asked, one hand on the brandy bottle. This was such an awkward situation she was so unsure of herself.

"Please," he said, "but do you think you should," he asked when she set two glasses on the counter.

"Why ever not?" She poured both glasses and handed one to Jamie without waiting for an answer.

"The baby?"

"What about Broc?" Really, he could be so obtuse. "What are you trying to tell me?"

"Do you think it's healthy?"

"I've no idea. What I do know is that the alcohol relaxes me. I've not noticed any change in Broc. However, I will admit until now, I only have a drink when I'm nursing."

Jamie seemed to be thinking about all she said, turning it over in his head. "Babies are new to me. I was so busy when Annie was born, I had little time to learn about them, about her. I want to have time with my son, if you'll let me. I want to see him smile, take his first step and there is so much more."

"You want to diaper our son also? Perhaps you can have your first lesson today." She laughed, watching the look of chagrin cross his handsome face.

"Any time you see fit." He sipped the brandy, closing his eyes as the warmth of the alcohol slid down his throat.

"Ah, I see you have made yourselves at home." Aunt Charlotte entered, a smile on her face. "Pour me one too, please."

"We did, Aunty."

"I'm thankful you understand the medicinal value of alcohol while you're nursing. Sometime it can be very difficult." Jamie handed her the asked for glass of brandy.

"Genevieve taught me a lot about my personal needs as well as those of my child's."

"Who's Genevieve," they said in seeming unison.

"A midwife I met on the Sweet Folly. I never learned her last name. She delivered Broc and without her I don't know what could have happened. No one else on board had any idea what to do. In my mind she was heaven sent."

"I'm thankful to her then," Jamie said. "I'd like to gift her with something appropriate."

"I'm sure a thank you note and perhaps some flowers would be most appropriate. If Genevieve is who I'm thinking about, she's a bit of reclusive," The Duchess said thoughtfully, tapping a finger on her chin.

"She offered me a place to stay telling me she would love company. Sometimes she gets tired of rattling around in the house alone. I think she's lonely. She also told me she owed you a debt, one she could never repay." Tira remembered the countless discussions they had during the long tr ip.

"Perhaps the two of you could visit her with the baby in a few days," The Duchess suggested. "Now before the conversation switches to anything less important, what is your status?"

"Our status?" Tira choked on the words.

"Yes, my sweet child woman. You've arrived with an infant in tow and no ring on your finger. Are the two of you wed or perhaps the better question is can I plan a wedding for you?"

"I've proposed and now I'm waiting for an answer, sooner than later I hope." Jamie looked pointedly at her.

She couldn't meet his gaze. Having wanted marriage and a proposal for such a long time she wasn't ready to say the words and commit to a man who would not tell her he loved her. She needed to know if he loved her or was just asking because of the child. What did that matter? She loved him and he treated her with tender concern. Wasn't that more than a lot of women had? It might have to be enough for her also.

"What is your answer, Tira?" The Duchess tapped her cane on the floor as if the rapid staccato would make her more decisive. "You must decide before the gossip begins so we know how to handle this."

"Broc needs his diaper changed and a feeding." Scarlett appeared downstairs, interrupting the discussion. "I assumed you would want to feed and change him upstairs."

Relief swept through Tira. At least for a few minutes she was saved from an answer to The Duchess' question. Then she turned to look at Jamie, "Were you sincere in your wish to learn how to change a diaper? If so, now's your chance." She smiled sweetly, expecting him to back down from his suggestion.

The Duchess tapped her cane, "A man who wants to be part of his son's life from the beginning. I like that. What are the two of you waiting for, go on with you but don't think I'll forget the question."

"Well?" Tira stood, waiting for him to take the lead. She'd known before The Duchess said anything she wouldn't forget.

He proved true to his word, striding up the steps, appearing eager to see to his son's diapering. In the nursery, Jamie lovingly picked up his son, cradling him in his arms. "What now?"

"Put him on the changing table. You have to undress him. Make sure he doesn't fall off." While he was following her instructions, she retrieved a clean diaper from the cupboard.

Naked, the baby cooed happily, waving his little arms and legs. "Now what?" Jamie looked to her for an answer.

"I suggest you put the diaper on as quickly as possible." She laughed when a stream of pee hit him in the chest.

He sputtered, quickly covering his son's little penis with the clean diaper Tira handed him. "I suppose this is one of the drawbacks of having a son versus a girl."

"Tira! You're back." Tavia ran into the room, her arms opened wide for a sisterly hug.

"I am and so are you. Oh my gosh, I missed you so much and worried over you. Your hair is growing out. You have to tell me everything that has happened to you."

"How are you?" Tavia stepped back, looking her sister up and down. "You've had a child. Me too. And look at that, Jamie Lundin is changing a diaper. My James is very good at it also."

"When can we talk? I mean really sit down and talk?" Tira asked, wishing things weren't so complicated.

"As soon as possible. I've so much to tell you," Tavia said.

"I need a clean diaper and a shirt," Jamie muttered, standing over the baby with a silly grin on his devilishly handsome face.

"The diaper I can furnish but not the shirt. You're going to have to wait until you get back to your ship." Tira retrieved a new diaper, handing it over and not giving him the chance to back out of the chore.

He finished with the diapering then handed the child to Tira. She sat on a rocker, nursing while she chatted happily with her twin.

Finished, she brought Broc into the parlor then handed him to The Duchess who smiled with delight, cooing nonsense words. "I consider this wee lad my grandson. Best you two treat him right and give him a proper home and name, or I'll have to call out some favors."

"I intend to do just that," Jamie said, his voice gruff. "All we need to do is convince Tira to say yes."

"I mean it, Tira, this little child needs a mother and father. I also know that you wouldn't have let him make love to you if you didn't love him. Just say yes and we'll happily plan the wedding," The Duchess said, still cooing nonsense words to the baby.

"Yes, you must wed this man." Ella swept into the room, her arms outstretched for a hug. "You can have the ceremony at the Montgomery estate and make it as big or small as you'd like."

The pressure and stress of this moment didn't escape Tira. "I...suppose...maybe..."

The girls gathered around her, hugging and chatting about the now upcoming nuptials.

Jamie cleared his throat. "Was that a yes? If you ask me, the answer was rather subdued." It seemed he wanted an answer that was bit more definitive.

For a fleeting second, she looked at the floor before tilting her chin to gaze at him. "Yes."

"Thank you. Annie will be pleased and perhaps a bit disappointed that she missed this. We'll have a reception when we return to the states, that is, if you like."

"So, you've committed to each other. If we have the wedding at the estate, perhaps the two of you will break the curse." Ella chatted happily with her sister.

Ella's words gave Tira a moment of thought and a tiny shiver of fear, remembering Ella's nuptials and Drake's brother nearly ruining everything. "Was there another incident besides your wedding?"

"Mine and Eveleen's and Addie's. It was horrible. I'll tell you more about it another time," Tavia said.

"Perhaps a nice tiny wedding in the parlor would be nice," The last thing Tira needed was more drama circling around her.

"Or we could elope." Jamie tossed in his thoughts. "Not looking forward to a large wedding."

"The weather isn't nice enough to have it outside. We'd have to have the wedding and the reception on the third floor," Ella said. "Only family if that's what you want."

"I don't have any friends here and neither does Jamie. So, just family will be invited."

Ella clapped her hands together, "Good then it's been decided. We do have to have time for a dress and flowers. We can make sure the dressmaker hires enough seamstresses to get the job done."

"A cake would be nice," The Duchess added.

"Of course, a cake and food, lots of good food," Ella continued, completely overwhelming Tira.

She looked helplessly at Jamie, "Should we set a date?"

"The sooner the better," Jamie said, "I'm eager to give our son my last name and make a real home for both Broc and Annie."

"In that case," The Duchess said, "Two weeks from today should be plenty of time to put everything together. I'll get you to the dressmaker's first thing tomorrow morning."

"This is all happening so fast. I can't breathe," Tira said, her hand on her chest, gasping for some elusive air.

The Duchess continued as if nothing was amiss. "Yes, you can feed the baby before we leave, Scarlett can put him down for a nap and we should have plenty of time. If necessary, I'll have the seamstress come here. Perhaps we should have Scarlett come too and she can take care of the baby."

"I'd like you to wear my ring." Jamie stood beside her then going down on one knee, he drew a box from his pocket. Opening it he asked, "Will you do me the honor of becoming my wife?"

She watched him, mixed feelings rushing through her. This is what she wanted for so many months. She'd already told him she'd marry him. With a shaking hand she held it out to him, "Yes."

After slipping the ring on her finger, he pulled her into his arms. "Thank God, Tira, I don't know what I would have done if you refused." His lips met hers, hard and demanding. It seemed he wanted so much from her, and despite her hesitation to his question, she was willing to give him everything he asked for.

When he drew away, she realized her sisters and The Duchess were clapping their hands in approval.

She wanted to hear three words from Jamie, but she also knew he wasn't going to say them.

"Broc needs a father and a mother. If I'm on this side of the Atlantic and you're on the other, he won't have one." She shrugged, needing more than this for the rest of her life. "The decision was the best for our child." Her heart wept for what she lost with this choice and even what she gained. Perhaps something could be salvaged from this strange relationship.

Jamie stayed for dinner and two more feedings. It seemed he didn't want to leave, even going as far as letting her nap while he walked the baby. She rose at six, noticing he'd taken his leave, but he left a short message.

Tira,

I'm so happy you agreed to the marriage. Please believe me, I crossed the ocean for both you and Broc. As you noted he needs a father, and I intend to be the best father a little boy could ever want. I swear I'll be the best husband for you also. I won't let you down.

I will meet you at the dressmakers in the morning. I don't want to see the dress, bad luck and all but I want to make sure Broc as well as you are guarded. Dutton will not get his hands on either of you.

Looking forward to our future.

Jamie

Sleepy-eyed, Tira set the note on her dressing table. She sat in front of the mirror, noticing the dark shadows under her eyes. Taking out her makeup she powdered her face and used a few subtle enhancements.

Sighing, she was not in the mood. No, she didn't have the energy to pick out a wedding dress. She set the brush on the table, closing her eyes. Broc was crying again. She'd just fed him and walked him. He was supposed to be sleeping. Her head on the table she drifted, remembering the better times with Jamie. Then she jerked awake. No more than a few seconds could have passed.

Someone was in the room with them. "Jamie?"

"I knew you'd need some help. I stayed away as long as I could." He held Broc in his arms. The child looked so small, fragile next to Jamie's huge frame. "You have an hour before you need to get up and run your wedding errands. "Go to sleep. I'll take care of Broc. If I have any questions, I'll get Scarlett. She let me into the house."

"I..." She didn't know what to think. "Thank you." But when she tried to sleep, her mind raced with so many scenarios, remembering Jamie's cautions to her about Dutton.

She didn't know if she fell asleep. She must have.

Jamie stood over her, "Sorry to wake you. I changed him and now he needs his mama."

She rose, brushing hair from her eyes, holding out her arms for Broc before adjusting her gown so she could feed him. Jamie backed away, sitting on a chair in the room, watching and smiling.

"It doesn't seem as if it could have been an hour." She closed her eyes with her head on the back of her chair. She tried to breathe deep and evenly, but she was so tired. "Can you shop for my wedding dress for me?" she asked, knowing he'd be amused at the question.

He let his head fall back, roaring with laughter. "And just how would the fittings go on?"

"You are a little bigger than me." When she spoke, Broc stopped nursing to stare at her with large brown eyes.

"A little? Has he finished?"

"No, he's just curious. I think he wants to know what his mother and father are talking about." Gently she ran her fingertip along his cheek, reveling in the softness.

"I'm going to have two men go along with you and The Duchess for the fitting. You and the baby have to stay safe."

"I wasn't planning on taking Broc. Is there anyone to stay at the house?" Her concern seemed to escalate now that Jamie seemed so anxious. "What if someone got inside and took Broc?"

"Drake has provided men to guard the house. I don't have enough people at my disposal and neither does The Duchess. With your brother in law's help no one's going to invade this home."

He stood, pacing the room, seeming to think. Standing at the window and looking out at the front street, he held his hands behind his back, rocking on his heels.

"What are you thinking?"

"I'm going to go with you to the dressmakers, just to take every precaution." He turned away from the window, his gaze riveted on her.

"But...it's bad luck for the groom to see the dress. You shouldn't." She didn't think his presence there was wise and she didn't want bad luck.

"I won't look. I promise and if it makes you feel better, I'll stand outside. Now, if you give me Broc, it seems he finished, you can get dressed and meet The Duchess downstairs."

She handed the little boy over and Jamie vanished through the door with the child in his arms. If she'd only stayed in Baltimore one more day, just one day was all that would have made such a huge difference in their lives. Why had she been in such a hurry to assert her independence?

Dressed and sitting in front of her mirror, she finished with her makeup and hair. Heaving a deep sigh, she rose and made her way downstairs to the parlor where The Duchess and Jamie were waiting for her.

Jamie gave the baby to Scarlett, who had somehow found a wet nurse in case they didn't make it home in time for Broc's next feeding. All Tira could do was accept the resourcefulness of her aunt and Jamie.

At the dressmakers, she settled on a fashion plate much the same as the dress Ella picked, except she chose an off-white fabric with all the Belgium lace in pale yellows. The old measurements were all wrong, so the fitting took longer than expected.

Jamie, true to his word stood outside, guarding the door from all intruders, and another man secured the back door.

"Tira." The Duchess poked her head inside the dressing room. "A message for you. Must be from Jamie. How sweet." Aunt Charlotte smiled and endearingly patted her on the hand. "Hope he's not too bored. Men don't like to stand around and wait for their woman to shop. They need things to occupy themselves."

Glancing at the back of the envelope, Tira knew this message was not from Jamie. A shiver of fear snaked down her spine, goose bumps rising on her arms. Slowly, she opened the message.

Tira,

I have your baby. If you want to see him again you must come now. Make some excuse and head out the back door of the shop. I made sure the guard is indisposed. I'll have a carriage waiting for you. Do it now and don't tell anyone. Your child's life is at stake.

Mathew Dutton

Feeling all the blood drain from her face, Tira dropped the letter. Her body shaking, she leaned against the wall. Her body tightened. She couldn't breathe, couldn't think, couldn't put one foot in front of the other. Gasping for air, she tried to calm herself and plan.

She stepped from the dressing room. "Aunty, I need a breath of fresh air, and Jamie said he was in the back of the shop. I'm going to meet him for a moment then I'll be back."

"That young man of yours just wants to steal a kiss. Pshaw..." She waved her hand in the air. "Go on with you. Gift him with that kiss he wants. As long as he is there, you'll be safe."

Nothing The Duchess thought was true. Jamie was surely still guarding the front door, oblivious to the fact she was about to go with a man they both loathed. Mathew Dutton was at the back door. How was he able to kidnap Broc? Hesitating then breathing deeply her hand on the doorknob, she stepped into the alley.

The moment the door shut behind her, a voice whispered from the shadows. "You came. Somehow I knew you would." Before she could respond, Dutton's hand gripped her arm and he pushed her to the buggy waiting for them.

"Where is my child?" She didn't mean to leave with this man until she saw her baby.

"At my home." He gave her no way to protest. His hands on her waist, he lifted her, making sure she was inside the carriage.

"I don't trust you."

"Of course you don't. Here." He held out the child's baby blanket. "Now do you believe me?"

Nodding, tears forming in her eyes, her fear for Broc escalating she lost track of the time. The sway of the carriage, the sounds of the city, all did little to soothe her tattered nerves and fears.

"You should try breathing," Dutton said. "I won't hurt your baby. After all he's my leverage over you. You see, my darling, I always get what I want, and I've wanted you for a very long time. From the first time I saw you, actually."

He spoke the truth. She would do anything to protect her baby. "I want to see him."

"Of course, he'll probably need to nurse soon. Unless of course you'd like me to find you a wet nurse. That would be much more convenient for me, but I want you to know I have your best interest at heart. As long as you comply to my wishes, your child will not be harmed."

"You're pure evil. How dare you use a child for your nefarious purposes. No matter what you think, you can't have me without a fight." She wiped the moisture from her cheeks. Jamie would come for them. He wouldn't let Dutton have his way.

"How dare I?" He roared with laughter. "I dare what I want." He leaned over, touching her cheek, tracing her jaw line then let his finger trace a path down her neck.

When she jerked away from him, he grasped her chin. Holding her, he pressed his mouth on hers, forced his tongue inside her mouth. She hit him and struggled against him until he drew away, his brows drawn together, clearly angry.

"No!" she cried out. "I don't want you or anything else to do with you. You can't have me."

"If you care about your son, you'll be more than willing." Once again he touched her, ran a finger across the line of her bodice. "You will allow me to have my way or your son will suffer."

"You'll have to force me."

"How drole, force you?" One eyebrow lifted in speculation. "Force is such a nasty word. Perhaps coerce would be more appropriate. Your son for your virtue seems a fair trade."

The carriage rolled to a stop and within seconds she stood inside the brothel. The large main room was strangely quiet. She hadn't expected that, but it was still before noon.

With his hand on her elbow, he guided her to a first floor room. A fire blazed in the fireplace, and it seemed there was a sitting room and a bedroom. Was this supposed to be her home?

He drew her to him, kissing her again, forcing his tongue inside her mouth. She bit him hard.

He pulled her close, his hand clasped around her waist. "She devil! You'll regret that. I have ways to make your life a living hell." Then he pushed her away and striding to the door, "Eliza!"

A small dark haired woman quickly appeared. They whispered but Tira couldn't understand what was said. A few minutes later another woman appeared with Broc.

"I believe he's safe, sound and bawling to be fed. Do it now. You won't be able to feed him later because you'll be otherwise engaged."

Hearing her son's cries, her milk let down. Quickly she gathered him close, never intending to lose sight of him again. Clinging to the baby, she turned her back on Dutton, adjusting her bodice so she could feed Broc.

He laughed, walking around her so he could watch. She closed her eyes, knowing there was nothing she could do about this situation. When she finished, he took the child to the door.

"What are you doing? I thought he'd stay here, with me."

"Never. You'll get to see him when you cooperate. Take off your dress. I want to see all of you."

"No."

"I've another dress for you to wear. One that is more suited to your new role as Madam. If you don't take it off, I will. I would probably ruin it." He watched her with glint in his eye she didn't understand. It seemed he studied her but there was more to the way he looked at her, something that puzzled her.

His threat was more than clear to her but she couldn't bring herself to disrobe in front of him. "Give me the dress and if you leave, I'll change."

He was shaking his head, grinning and clearly enjoying her discomfort. He handed her the dress and stepped back, arms crossed in front of his chest. "Of course you'll change. Every minute you wait is one minute longer I'll let your baby cry when he's hungry."

Once again she turned her back to him. When the new dress was on, she turned around. "It scarcely covers me." Her nipples were just barely concealed by the fabric. A slight breath and they would come free. "I can't wear this. It's indecent."

"Mathew?" The door opened. "I brought what you wanted. The wine to help Tira relax."

"Thank you, my dear." He took the tray. Two glasses of wine sat on it as well as a bottle. Dutton handed Tira a glass.

"No. I don't want anything you have to give. The alcohol might hurt the baby." She groped for some way to stop him.

One dark eyebrow rose. "Two minutes now. Drink up and I'll pour you a second. You would be wise to obey my wishes. I don't want to fight you."

For a moment she looked at him over the rim of the glass. Gingerly, she sipped.

"All of it," he commanded, his voice gruff, seeming to anticipate something.

She drank it down, realizing that drinking the wine or not wasn't her fight. He poured her another and one look from him told her she needed to do his bidding. She swallowed all of it, wishing to get this over with. When he poured her a third glass, her hand shook when she downed it.

Heat simmered within and a fierce pounding inside her body forced a groan from her lips. "Hot..." She waved a hand in front of her face watching his all-knowing smile. Her skin felt as if it was prickling from the inside out.

"I like you hot. Your face is flushed and your beautiful green eyes are sparkling with passion. Desire for me perhaps?"

"What have you done to me? This isn't normal."

"Good, the wine has done its job just as I planned." He pulled her into his arms and for a second, she was compliant. His hand settled on her breast and pulled the fabric to her waist then his mouth closed over her nipple. He sucked, biting down and she cried out.

"No." She hit him and pushed away, running to the opposite side of the room. He followed slowly. "Don't do this to me. I don't want you to touch me." She was trying desperately to pull her dress up.

"You still mean to deny me? The only way you'll feel better is if you let me make love to you. Otherwise, this condition you find yourself in will continue."

"No." She held her hands out. "No. I loathe you. What did you do to me?"

"Just a little aphrodisiac. I'll wait. In a few minutes you'll plead for me to give you your release then it will all start again and I will spend the entire night making love with you. Perhaps by morning you'll carry my child."

~ * ~

Jamie leaned against the wall to the dress shop, watching all the people strolling past and wishing he dared check on Tira. Something nagged at him, a feeling he didn't like. He ran a finger under his collar. Sweat beaded on his forehead. For a late day in April it was rather warm.

This stint at guard duty was well worth the time, keeping Tira safe of the utmost importance. The baby was well guarded if he stayed inside the home. Jamie didn't think Dutton would dare break into The Duchess' house.

Finally understanding why it took him so long to realize how important Tira was to him, he felt relief. Still, telling her he loved her was something he was having difficulty with. He did love her though, with all his heart. Why couldn't he say the damn words?

Ah, but Annie loved her too. Annie would be so excited to know she had a sibling. First on his list of things to do was to write his daughter and tell her about her new little brother, Broc, and how much he missed her, wishing she were here with him and Tira. He also needed to tell Annie they would be married when they returned home.

"Mr. Lundin, Sir." One of Drake Montgomerie's men stood in front of him, rousing him from his musings.

He stiffened, realizing the man wouldn't be here unless there was bad news. "What is it?" he asked his heart racing.

"Sir, we have to hurry. Scarlett took the child outside in his stroller because he couldn't sleep."

"And..."

"Scarlett was knocked out as was the man guarding her. The child was taken before anyone else could get there to help."

"Go to Drake. Tell him what happened." Telling Tira would be hard, but finding the child alive was his most important task. Truly he didn't believe Dutton would harm the only leverage he had over Tira.

Jamie strode through the door, "Tira. Tira! Where are you?" The Duchess sat on a chair, chatting with one of the dressmakers. Tira must be in a fitting room.

The Duchess stepped in front of him. "What game is this? She went outside to meet you. She's only been gone a few minutes, well, maybe more. You surely know where she is."

"She didn't come to see me." Fear swept through him as well as the realization Dutton now had the upper hand. He wouldn't get away with this.

"You were in the alley. At least that's what she said."

"Why would she do that?" Dutton was behind both abductions. At least he knew where Dutton would take her. The man made it clear what he wanted with Tira.

The Duchess appeared from the fitting room. "This was on the floor." She handed the paper to him.

"Bloody hell. He has Tira and Brock." It was the worst possible scenario. Even though he expected this, he was still shocked the man outwitted him. He believed both Tira and the child were well guarded and would be safe, simply because there was no alternative. Tira needed to play the game Dutton instigated until he could get there.

The Duchess sat on a bench, her face white, fanning herself. "It was my fault. I should have taken more precautions. We should have brought the seamstress and fabrics to the home. It's not like I couldn't afford it."

"Don't be ridiculous, Charlotte. None of this is anyone's fault. I'm going to the brothel. You go home and wait for word. She might need you when I bring her back."

"Take someone with you." The Duchess implored, her hand outstretched. "You can't go there alone."

"No time. Send a message to Drake for me. Tell him to employ the constables. If we are to get the two of them out of that place, we might need their help. On second thought, Drake's men might be more competent."

His heart in his throat, he hailed a carriage, giving directions before he jumped inside. The ride seemed to take an eternity. Dutton either wanted to humiliate him or he just wanted Tira more than he wanted to take his next breath. The man had a reputation for pursuing beautiful women, Kendall probably not his first.

The carriage was still rolling when Jamie jumped from the door. "Wait here." Running up the steps he threw open the door to the brothel. Inside two burly guards greeted him. Quickly, the men ushered him outside, tossing him on the ground.

He supposed he should have tried a different approach. Most likely he would be met the same way when he attempted again, but it wouldn't hurt to try. Dusting his pants off, he strode up the steps, trying one more time. Before the men threw him out again, he pulled out his money clip.

"I'd like to see a woman."

"I'm Eliza." A petite dark-haired lady appeared in front of him a smile of greeting on her face. "How can I help you?" She extended a hand, which he took in his, and she escorted him into the main room.

"The woman who just arrived with a baby. She doesn't belong here." He searched the opulent room not expecting to find anything. "She's going to be my wife."

"Ah, you must be speaking of Tira. She is being prepared for her debut and not for you. Maybe I can introduce you to someone else. We've a lot of beautiful women who would be more than willing to see to your pleasure. You are a very handsome man." She smiled, tilting her head at him. "Perhaps you'd like to explore the rest of the evening with me." She ran her hand up his chest, pressing herself against him.

"I'll wait for the girl." He sat down on a red velvet chair, his fingertips drumming on the table until Eliza brought him a whiskey and sat beside him.

"What's your story, handsome? Why only this new girl?" She watched him over the rim of her glass. "I can see to all your needs, pleasure you in ways you've never thought of."

Jamie smiled at her, wishing it were that easy and wondering how much she knew and how much he should tell her. "No, I doubt that," he said.

A scream sent Jamie to his feet and he headed toward the room where it came from. Two men blocked his way. He stepped back, running his hands through his hair. "Just wanted to help," he said before turning back to his seat and Eliza who hadn't moved. She patted the place where he'd been sitting.

"You mustn't concern yourself with what is going on in the room. Mathew has everything under control and would never hurt her. He has only her best interest as well as her baby's at heart. If she is to take over this place, there are few pertinent things she must learn first."

His fists tightened, frustration eating at him. "If he's not hurting her then why the scream?"

"No." The thin wail penetrated his frayed nerves. Tira needed him and all he could do was sit outside her room.

"We have to help her." He stood again, his jaw tightening while he tried to hold his protective instincts in control.

"I'll check and see if there is a problem if you promise to wait here." Eliza stepped quickly to the room then opened the door.

Jamie didn't keep his promise. He followed Eliza and stood behind the girl, peering over her head at the scene enfolding in front of him.

"What is wrong?" Eliza asked.

"She won't accept my help. I think you gave her way too much." Dutton strode to Tira and trying to pick her up from her place on the floor was met with her pummeling fists.

"Get away from me. I hate you. I won't be your whore." She moaned, backed up against the wall, sobbing. "I won't let you touch me no matter what you did to me, gave me. I'll fight you until I die if I have to."

"What the hell?" Jamie pushed past Eliza, nearly knocking her down and to Tira's side. He picked her up, cradling her in his arms. "What are you doing to her?"

She wrapped hers around him, moaning and sobbing. "Jamie, help me. I..."

"What did you give her?" He ran his hands down her back and she arched into him, seeming to beg for his caress. In his arms her body was hot, her face flushed and while he held her, she moaned softly, not pain but desire, passion.

Mathew smiled, seeming to enjoy the discomfort of the couple. "If I can't have her, then the two of you will find hell tonight."

"What did you give her?" He would find out. "Where is the child?"

"One question at a time," Dutton laughed, slowly crossing his arms over his chest, seeming to enjoy the little seen unfolding in front of him. "I thought this would workout for me. Would never force a lady though. Little hell cat that she is, she's all yours, Lundin."

"Dutton," Jamie set her on the couch.

"What?" he paused, stroking his chin.

Suddenly Jamie's hand wrapped around his neck and he pushed the man against the wall. "What did you give her?"

"An aphrodisiac. She's going to be that way all night. You can pleasure her but, in a few minutes, she'll need you again. You should have one hell of a night. Not the least bit romantic or comforting. Yet, I'm sure you'll never forget the evening because it will seem to go on forever."

From outside Tira's room, he heard the constables then Drake's men and orders being shouted out. "Everybody stay where you are. We need to know where the baby is."

Drake looked in, "Dutton, where is the baby?"

Dutton rocked on his heels, "Are you going to press charges?"

"Not if you give up the child," Montgomerie said behind him, "and get the hell out of London."

"Third floor second room on the left."

"Take care of Tira, I'll get your baby." Drake vanished.

Jamie cradled Tira, unable to give her what she needed with everyone watching. "Tira, stay with me. I'll help you soon. Hush sweetheart..."

Drake reappeared with Broc in his arms. "We can go to my estate."

"No, take the baby to The Duchess. She and Scarlett can look after Broc. I'm taking Tira to my ship. It's closer and she's in so much misery I have to do something soon."

Drake directed his men and Jamie brought Tira to the ship. Next to the ride to the brothel, it seemed the longest ride of his life.

Striding by Mooney, "Need lots of cold water in my cabin."

The pulse at her neck seemed to beat too rapidly, her breathing came in short pants while she moaned softly. Arching into him, her fingers kneading his chest. "I'm so hot and my skin feels like it's tingling. I can't think. I can't breathe. Please, Jamie. Do something."

"I'm going to make this alright. I promise," he whispered against her and even that simple gesture was met with a moan of anguish. Yet he understood the night would be a never-ending hell.

"I don't feel well," she stammered. "What did he give me?"

"I'm going to finish undressing you then I'm going to set you on the bed. Try to relax."

"Oh..." she began but the whisper became a low moan of despair. She wrapped her arms around herself, rocking back and forth, crying out with need.

"I'm going to make you feel better," Jamie said, his voice seemed to touch her flesh a rosy glow shimmering. "It's just the wine. You drank too much. You'll feel better soon," he tried to give comfort even though it was useless.

"No, there's more. He put something in it. I'm so...skin hot, itching. Too hot and I want...you. I need you to touch me and make me feel..."

Clothing fell away from her. Cool breeze wafted in from the window teasing her hot skin, now revealed.

"Hot?" he said. "You look ill, Tira. Here, you have to help. Can you sit up? There, that's a good girl." He finished undressing her.

The door creaked a fraction. He settled a sheet over her while Mooney walked in with the water. "What the devil? An aphrodisiac? You didn't."

"No, of course not. I'll explain later."

Mooney backed from the room muttering curse words.

She was naked now, and her moan sounded so distant and far away. "Jamie, please...do something."

"Oh, sweet imp, you've no idea what this night still holds. I'm so very sorry. No one should have to go through this. Dutton will pay for this hell he's created for you."

"Do something," she pleaded. Her eyes huge, luminescent spheres gazed at him unquestioningly and with so much faith in him, it nearly unmanned him. And he'd never seen her look so vulnerable and trusting.

He ran his fingers through his hair, a quick silent prayer. Lord, he only began to guess what was happening inside her body. Skin so flushed, breath heaving, and her hair spilled across her white shoulders, the silken curls circling her breasts. Son of a bitch, he felt it too. Eliza had spiked the whiskey.

"Tira, there's only one thing I can do that will help, and I don't think you'll appreciate the gossip and the innuendos in the morning, but there is nothing else we can do. You have to spend the night here with me and in this room."

"Please, Jamie, I'm on fire."

"I know, honey. It was the wine."

He sat next to her, drawing her into his arms. She ran her hands beneath his shirt and across his chest. He pulled his shirt off, letting her explore him. The flames, the inferno raged, and nothing he think of would stop it. He felt the nightmare begin to flame within him. With each subtle caress of her tiny fingers, his blood began to boil and he fought for control, hoping to ease this night for her without hurting her.

He tensed, "Dear God, please give me control," he prayed. His body shuddered and strained with the effort.

It seemed he lost the battle somewhere between the golden rays of sunlight slanting through the tiny window and his tormented soul, his control slipping away with each beat of his heart.

"Sweetheart..." He gritted his teeth against the heat rising within.

She cried out once more, seeming to tremble with the intensity of the raging wildfire he knew burned within her. He hungered, needed, longed for the sweet bliss she could give him, but not like this. His mind seemed detached from his body.

"You can fix this, Jamie. I know you can." In his arms her body writhed uncontrollably, pushing Jamie to his limitations. Tira tugged at his clothing, as if wishing for the feel of his skin meeting hers, naked flesh joining together. He was helping her rip his clothes away. Hard bronzed muscle rippled beneath the tips of her fingers, and she explored the width of his chest, down its length, stopping only when her fingers met his belt. His hand clamped solidly around her, holding her against him. The warmth, the heat, surrounded them. Filled his soul, yet overwhelmed too.

"So beautiful, Tira. I didn't want this for you. Truly I tried to protect you, but the wine, the drug. I can't stop what it's doing to us and what it's going to keep doing. We are in this hell together." He let her unfasten his pants before he shrugged out of them.

His mouth descended, softly, brushing against hers then harder. Control came then, momentarily, his tongue teasing her lips apart, tasting, pushing against them urgently now. His tongue swept across her lips. He trembled from the scorching heat and the hunger. Now he surged on, pushing within, sweeping the sensitive recess of her mouth, dueling, parrying each thrust. She shivered and cried out his name. He had to make sure he didn't hurt her, yet the sensations between them pushed him to his limits.

Sunlight shimmered through the open curtains of the room, glanced across the lovers. It was hot, so very hot achingly hot. The tempest created by the drugged wine, escalated. She rose high above, looking down at him, seeming detached, her eyes vague.

Jamie, he had come to her to help, and he eased the discomfort then it grew, the power soaring out of bounds, beyond the horizon, limitless. It seemed nothing could stop the agony or define the mystery that encompassed them. She clung tightly to him; a lifeline she didn't dare lose. Even in her wildest imaginings she had never thought such sensations existed, the swift spiraling of heat, low and so deep inside her, so different from their previous sweet lovemaking. Not until he had fallen upon her, teasing her with his caress. The fire, the agony, ever-increasing heat to result in a climax.

Jamie, she loved him and she wanted him. Hard as steel, potent, inflaming and she trembled from his heated touch upon her. Jamie caressed her, stroking her intimately.

She writhed beneath him again, she burned and wanted, and still there was no easing of the constant heat and raging desire. He should come inside her, should stop this burning.

Jamie.

His mouth, tongue, tasted her. Fingers touching, needing, the soft brush of his thumb across the crest of her breast. Feathery kisses exploring the smoothness of her flesh and the whisper of his breath sighing so close.

This was Eden, enchantment and paradise, a fire burning, a longing she would never deny. She moved against him, begging for so much more. He pulled her close, finding heavenly delight. His teeth rubbed against her nipple, lips closing over, swiftly tugging, setting the tempest raging wildly. And still he teased her with the promise of fulfillment.

She didn't want to be teased. She craved him inside her now and the ensuing climax.

Now his lips demanded hers again then moved to her eyes, gently closing each one, exciting, intriguing, seducing. A caress, which left no room for denial, claiming her as his own.

His fingers threaded through her hair and his grip closed around her neck, pulling her closer still. It seemed they had become one and she moaned, soft sounds, unrestrained.

"Jamie..."

Fire spiraled from the depth of her, commanding once more. Demanding everything she had to give and so much more.

He moved. The weight of him bore down upon her, rubbing against her flesh. His hands stroked everywhere, his mouth following, giving no respite. Sweet Jesus, her skin had never been this sensitive her body so responsive.

His hands slid over her waist, her hips, lower. The provocative allure of his mouth followed, feathering heated kisses, whispering fire. She moaned, writhing mindlessly.

She gasped as his fingers stroked the inside of her thighs. Moving intimately against her, pushing them wider. He shifted, falling between her legs. She was powerless, melting, his kiss paralleled his fingers, touching, heating, setting the fire burning hotter, hotter still. The stroke of his tongue. A gentle touch, lingering then exploring higher, hotter.

Her heart pounded and she closed her fist over his chest, willing her heart to calm. His mouth charted familiar territories, so intimate, so commanding, so fervent. Liquid fire exploded within, hotter than she could withstand. The wild hot tempest blasted her, swept hotter, higher and coming harder, swifter, unyielding. She cried out and he was inside her, moving with her as one. Feelings, violent, shuddering, claiming, consuming, she shattered down upon her until she thought nothing would be left of her. The tempest calmed, but it was only the beginning. The peacefulness was nothing but an illusion conjured by her imagination, for suddenly the coolness vanished and once again she felt the slow burn begin anew.

Then a moan ripped through him. Her hands ran the length of his torso.

"No," she cried out. "Not again."

"I'm so sorry, sweet heart. So sorry." He swept his hands across her body and once more she burned with pleasure and desire so intense she didn't think she could withstand it again. Heat wrapped around and within, shocking, dousing her from the sweet reverie she had just enjoyed. She cried out, but his mouth descended swiftly and covered the sound. The sweet agony didn't end, the heat, the tempest ripped through her. Tears slid down her cheeks and she responded to his touch, moving in rhythm until pleasure consumed her and the burning head dissipated.

"What did he do to me?" she asked while she could think.

"An aphrodisiac," he whispered. "I'm trying not to hurt you, but Eliza spiked my whiskey also. We are both under the spell."

"They exist?" She moaned again. "Why won't it stop?"

"Not until the drug is out of our system," he whispered softly. "For now, we have no choice but to follow its course and ease the burning the best we can," his breath feathering her ear then following along the column of her neck. "I won't come inside you until you're ready for me."

She felt him shift above her, gently now. So very tender and slow before she was on fire again. His solid length pinned her to the bed. Now he touched her, magically, the warmth, the mystery returned. Purposeful, sure, so defiantly. More and more he gave to her. He bit her lips then licked them. Her muscles tensed. Suddenly, she wanted to look at him. Intense, hot, the movement of his hands upon her, the tender care he took with her. Her eyes opened, memorizing him, the sheer masculine power that dominated, commanded then coaxed her senses to unparalleled heights. On the brink once more, the culmination of magical secrets, the force of it all, the sweet, restful, bliss following.

He surrounded her, encompassing, unrelenting. His body rigid, he poured himself into her.

She cried out, shuddering, gasping for a breath then relaxed against him, still enjoying the feeling of his body close to hers.

It seemed an eternity he lay heavily on top of her. Her thoughts traveled back to Dutton, the abduction, their child and the heat. Even when she needed to ask him about the baby, the sensations began to build again and she moaned, moving beneath him. Her body exhausted, sore, yet still she craved him, more and more...

And so, the night wore on. Her eyes closed, the wine, the drugs, the heat, but she no longer cared. Again and again he brought her to a magical climax. Then everything would start anew.

~ * ~

Smiling, Baxter Hooley helped Aidan into the small curricle, his hands around her waist, sliding higher than appropriate. Aidan decide to ignore his advances for the moment. A warm sun heated the ground of early summer and a cerulean blue sky with a few clouds gave Aidan a lilt to her step. The promise of a beautiful day was ahead and she didn't want to ruin it.

"I see Lilly packed us a basket of food. What's in it?" Baxter asked, setting the lunch on the seat.

"You're so impatient. I'm sure you'll like everything. We spent the better part of this morning preparing the meal. Where are we going?" She had the strange feeling Baxter intended something far different than a simple picnic.

"What do you say to my question first?" With a flick of the wrist he started the curricle. "You need to learn to answer me and not ask questions. Changing the subject just will not do. I don't like it."

Aidan sighed, her patience for this man had worn thin on their last outing and now she regretted this trip. It's just when she figured out he was pompous popinjay, she couldn't figure out a good excuse to refuse his company when she had already accepted the invitation. "I bought fresh salmon at the fish market this morning..."

"I cannot eat salmon or any kind of fish, for that matter. Makes me break out in hives. I hope you had the good sense to pack something else.

You will have to eat all of the fish." He regarded her with furrowed brows.

Even from Baxter she had not expected this type of rudeness. She had thought the salmon a delicacy most people liked. "There is fried chicken."

"I suppose that will have to do this time. For future reference, I prefer roast beef or ham."

She didn't know what to say or for that matter she didn't want to talk to him. If she could think of the right words, she'd have him turn around and take her home and there would be no next time or reason for a future reference. The less she thought about him the better. "There is wine."

"Ah...good, you must remember I prefer white wines."

"I guess you will have to forego the wine then. I purchased a Bordeaux." Her voice began to shake from anger. Actually, the wine came from Logan Maxwell's winery, and she could have picked up a Chianti instead.

"I didn't say I wouldn't drink the red wine." His voice took on a harsh indignant tone. "But you must remember my preferences. There is much you need to learn about me if we are to continue as a couple then wed."

We will never continue as a couple or wed. "There are cheeses and freshly baked bread. I hope at least that is to your liking."

"Of course." He set one hand on hers, which were clasped in her lap.

She didn't know how to extricate herself. His hands were clammy and hot. She had an urge to wash hers. "Look." She pulled her hands from beneath his and pointed to the sky. "Oh, it's gone. It was an eagle."

"I don't like what you're wearing, Aidan." He managed to change the subject to another one she didn't like. "It's far too revealing. You mustn't leave your neck and arms unclothed. I don't want any other man to see you this naked."

Her jaw dropped. "It's a hot day and I'm hardly naked. And you, sir, are not going to see me anywhere near naked."

"Makes no difference. This is far too revealing for my tastes. In public you must dress appropriately. You can wear nothing at all when we are alone."

She fought back the retort and sat still, nearly biting her tongue in the process. "You could answer my question now. Where are we going?"

"We are almost there." He turned the vehicle off the road and followed a narrow path toward the river. The spot was far too secluded for her taste, and she wondered how long she would have to put up with him before he grew tired of her and brought her home.

He pulled up beneath the trees then sat watching the river flow before he climbed down.

She declined his help and landed on the ground on the other side before walking around the buggy. Pausing a moment, she looked around, feeling as if someone watched them. Strangely the feeling didn't give her a shiver of fright but it was one of relief and seemed familiar.

"Are you going to set out the blanket?" he asked, hands behind his back and rocking on his heels. "I don't like waiting for you to do your chores."

"I thought you would." But she decided not to wait for a reply and did as he asked also taking the basket. She supposed she would have to feed him too. The thought made her shiver with revulsion.

"When you are my wife, you'll be more complacent and do my bidding without question. I'll make sure you know all my wishes before hand. If you disobey or do something I dislike, there will be punishment of course."

She stopped midstride, her blood pounding inside her head. "Baxter, I'm never going to be your wife. I want you to take me home right now." Stamping her foot to put emphasis on her statement seemed appropriate but too much like a little girl.

He grinned at her and the sight sent a shiver rushing down her spine and goose bumps on her arms. "Aidan, Aidan, Aidan...why did you go with me today? Didn't you realize I intend to have you? I'm going to make you mine today. When I take your virginity no one else will have you."

"At first I thought it would be a fun outing someplace close to the house. I never expected you to take me some place like this. You'll never have me, Baxter Hooley, and I will never be yours."

"But you chose to go without a chaperone, and when we're done here you will have to become my bride."

"You sir, do not know me very well. Even if you rape me and I conceive a child, I will never be your wife and condemn myself to a lifetime of misery with the likes of you." She turned toward the narrow path and began walking but was stopped, brought up short by the sound of clapping.

"Bravo, Little Fire."

She knew that voice. When she looked up Blade McPherson sat his coal black stallion, clapping his hands in approval, a wide grin on his handsome face. She never knew she'd be so happy to see him.

"Who is that?" Baxter strode beside her, wrapping an arm around her shoulders as if he claimed her.

She shrugged him off. "Once a long time ago, I called him a friend. This is Blade and Blade this is Baxter Hooley."

Blade leapt from his horse letting the reins fall on the ground and strode, hand extended in friendship toward Baxter. Blade grasped Baxter's hand and held on too long, squeezing until Baxter's face turned red.

When Blade finally let go, Baxter backed up a few steps, a look of pure terror on his face. Aidan had rarely seen the hard, unyielding expression on Blade's face. She suddenly realized it was Blade who she felt watching her and that was why she felt comforted.

"I'm going to leave. If this...this man is your idea of a friend, you would never be a suitable wife for me." In less than a minute Baxter was in the curricle and headed home.

"That's exactly what I've been trying to tell you." She yelled at his retreating back, her hands determinedly fisted at her sides.

With mixed emotions she watched Baxter leave. Her heart in her throat, hands tucked beneath her chin, she kept her eyes down. She heard movement as Blade led his horse to the river for a drink. When the horse was finished, he brought the stallion to a spot in the shade.

"Whether it matters to you or not, I like your dress." Blade's smile reached her heart and reminded her how easily he could seduce her. "Although I do tend to agree that I only want you naked in front of me.

"What are you doing in Baltimore?" She tried to ignore the less than subtle innuendo.

"Two things. I thought Jamie would have told you I was here."

"And what would they be?" she asked reminding herself she wanted an apology from him before she could relax her guard.

"You," he paused to look at her, "and I brought horses from Storm for Damian to breed."

"You can't have me."

"Of course I can."

"You're just as arrogant and unfeeling as Baxter but in a different way." Her anger rose with each word and each memory that had been severely etched in her mind. Clearly, she recalled all the times he called her a little girl.

"I don't know why you're so angry."

"Don't play naïve with me." It would not take much for her to lose control and throttle him. She'd wanted to take her anger out on him for a long time.

Her breath was coming in ragged gulps. "A man doesn't take advantage of a little girl." She repeated his line from that horrible night before Ella and Drake's wedding. The words that sent her running to America to hide from him. The hiding was over.

"It was the truth at the time," he said in a deep voice. "I'm not proud of hurting you though."

Anger overcame all common sense if she ever had any, where Blade was concerned. She charged him, her fists tight and when she reached him, she hit him as many times as she could before he grabbed her wrists.

The force of her onslaught sent them to the ground. When he hit the blanket he rolled, pinning her beneath him, his hands holding hers. "If you promise not to hit me again, I'll release your hands."

Her lip quivered and she wanted desperately to keep punching him until she felt better, but she nodded her acquiescence.

"Why did you come back here? I don't want to see you and here you are."

"I wanted to apologize and see what might materialize between us." Blade smiled at her, melting her heart in that one tiny gesture.

"Liar, you just told me it was the truth. I'm not a little girl!" She hit him and immediately regretted her impulsiveness when he seized her hands again.

"Let me see if your body is still one of a girl's." He slowly began unfastening her bodice.

"What are you doing?" Passion and desire rose within, touching her, tempting her. She remembered all too well how he could so easily create an inferno she couldn't deny.

"Just checking. Remember when we were at the MacLaren castle and you stood naked in my chamber trying to convince me you were a woman? Do you remember that night?"

"Yes." She caught her lip beneath her teeth, completely utterly mortified one more time. How on earth could she ever forget?

"While I appreciated your efforts on my behalf, your breasts were tiny buds, barely a woman's. And when we, well, I lost control and took advantage of you, yes they almost filled my hands. Well, I suppose you were a woman then but I was too terrified to admit anything, afraid I'd do something we'd both regret, and of course I had to save face so I just blurted out what came into my head."

She squirmed beneath his hard body, suddenly wishing she had never pursued him so diligently all those years.

"You have no right to do this." She tried to pull her hands from his large one but failed.

"Then tell me no. One little word and I will stop." The last button sprung free and he pulled the fabric as low as it would allow without ripping. He cupped her breast in one hand, watching her and it seemed he waited, paused for her to speak. "I wonder if the texture is as nice as the size." Gently he slipped the strap of her chemise over her shoulders and tugging the sleeve of the dress over her arm, her breast was barred for his eyes.

"Blade..." her voice wavered, her bottom lip quivering. "What are you doing?" she asked as his lips descended and pulled her nipple into his mouth. Her hips rose against his, craving something indefinable.

"I do like the way you taste. Your beautiful white flesh and rosy nipples are just as I remembered. And yes, Aidan, you are no longer a little girl. I believe I've had a tremendous amount of patience waiting all these years for you to mature. Another man might have taken advantage of you a long time ago."

She didn't know what to think or how to feel. His words were what she'd waited to hear for more years than she cared to remember. Even while she was thinking about all the ways she should tell him no, he explored, his moist lips caressing her flesh, his teeth nipping wherever he pleased. She moaned softly in the back of her throat.

"Are you going to tell me no?" he asked as one hand settled on her leg, pulling the fabric of her dress higher so he could see her legs. He caressed her inner thigh as he pulled her undergarment off. Now there was nothing between his hand and her body. She was his to explore.

And he did.

Very slowly all the while his gaze riveted on her, his hand rose until it rested on her abdomen, his long fingers spanning her hip bones. She gasped, her body arching to meet his bold forays. He let go of her and she wound her fingers into his hair, holding on to him for strength. This had to be a dream, a magical fantasy of her making.

He touched her intimately and she cried out, a soft cry, yet he paused to watch her and wait, it seemed.

"Hush, Little Fire, only pleasure, a woman's pleasure. Keep your eyes open for me and I will give you a sweet hot agony you've never dreamed of. Something you'll crave and I, a gentleman, will give you anytime you ask."

He parted her and touched her in ways she'd never dreamed of before. "Blade." All she could do was say his name yet her voice shook.

"You are wet and ready for me." His finger slid into her and she tightened while he pulled it out then moved deeper. "You are soft velvet and fire."

He touched her in unfathomable ways and she never wanted him to stop. She closed her eyes. The sensations were incredible. She felt her hips lifting to his demand, felt his hand slide beneath her hips to hold her.

She felt a throbbing pleasure, ebbing then washing over her with greater and greater strength, right where his fingers were caressing. She knew she was hot and damp. She could feel herself, and if she weren't so filled with the anticipation of something she couldn't quite yet imagine but something she she'd kill to have, she would have ordered him to stop that moment. Instead, she moaned. Moaned again and arched her back. Her legs trembled then stiffened.

"That's it, Aidan," he murmured, his fingers stroking her. "Relax let go. Just let me give you your woman's pleasure. Yes, that's it. I can feel your legs tightening, tensing. Just a moment...ah, there, do you like that?"

He'd slipped his finger inside her again, pushing inside and pulling back.

Aidan's head fell back against the blanket. She cried out, unable to help herself; tearing, harsh cries. Her thighs tightened and she felt a spasm of such unexpected force that she wondered if she could survive it. The thing was, though, she didn't care. She just wanted those incredible feelings to keep pounding through her, and she cried out again and again.

Chapter Ten

Two weeks later, the sisters and cousins who could make it to the wedding were decorating the third floor ballroom in preparation for the coming nuptials. Many different kinds of yellow flowers adorned vases that were put in strategic spots. The men were at Whites celebrating the last night of Jamie's bachelorhood with a little drinking and gambling.

Ella and Tavia were attendants along with Drake and James Macmurra standing up for Jamie. Sometimes when they were both in the room it got confusing. The McLellan had come and seemed to be smitten with The Duchess. Every so often they could be seen cuddling in a corner and more than once Tira saw David steal a kiss. That seemed terribly strange to Tira, but everyone needed love and they'd both been without someone for so long, it was nice to see them together and she wondered if they would eventually marry.

All of the McLellan Clan was there except Aidan who was still in Baltimore along with Blade. The Graham family minus Ravyn had also assembled to bear witness to the nuptials.

"We have a case of Bordeaux and one of Chianti from Logan's wineries. The finest Italy and France have to offer," The Duchess announced, holding up a glass of wine in a salute to Logan.

Aunty Charlotte oversaw the pouring of the wine then offered a toast. "To Tira, may she have a long and happy marriage. Thank God the children are tucked sweetly in their beds. While I love them all dearly, they create such chaos everywhere they go," she inhaled softly, "and they exhaust me just watching them.

The group of mothers laughed, agreeing with Charlotte wholeheartedly. They were all nodding their heads.

"We have a slight moment to relax," Ella said, picking up a glass of Bordeaux. "Wonder what the men are talking about?"

"I don't think I want to know," Tira murmured, hoping the conversation would have nothing to do with her or the aphrodisiac she and Jamie had been given. Yet she was sure the men would speak of it. That was one memory with Jamie she didn't ever want to recall again.

"Let's ask the bride questions," Eveleen said with a quiet chuckle. "It's always fun to find out things about the relationship and how it evolved."

"As long as whoever asks the question has to answer it too," Tira said feeling more vulnerable at the moment than she wanted to be and perhaps a bit picked on as well. There were too many questions she knew they might ask that she didn't want to answer.

"I'll go first," Storm volunteered. "I don't mind sharing my most humiliating moment. So," she began. "What was your most mortifying moment concerning Jamie."

"You all probably think it has to be the aphrodisiac but it's not. I didn't have any control over that. I was a victim as was Jamie. No, the most humiliating experience is when Annie tied me to the bed while I was reading a copy of *Fanny Hill*."

"No." The one word was chorused around the room. "*Fanny Hill*? Not really. What was in it?" They all seemed so very curious.

"I'd rather not say. I didn't read all of it just enough to understand people have some really strange quirky ideas about sex."

"Now you don't have to elaborate, but did Jamie find you?"

"Fortunately, and not so happily, he did. I was getting claustrophobic and the bindings were biting into my wrists and ankles cutting off the circulation. Annie tied both arms to the bedposts, one leg to another and the other to a chair. She tied me with the bindings I used..."

"I suppose when he discovered you were a girl and not what you masqueraded as was humiliating too," Tavia said. "That was my most awkward moment with James. When he finally told me he knew who I was from the moment I stepped into his cabin."

"At least Jamie told me the minute he knew, well, almost the very first moment he knew the truth. Said even Annie knew I was a woman. Our disguises weren't very good. Since you asked the question, Storm, what was your most embarrassing moment?"

Storm sipped her wine, pensively looking out the window as if remembering her past. "I proposed to Hadden and he refused me. I suppose there were other humiliating events but that one was the very worst. I wasn't very smart when it came to Hadden. In the end he couldn't refuse the offer."

Eveleen paused a moment, "What's your greatest fear. Logan asked me that and I lied. I do know now what it is though."

"My greatest fear... I do have two. I don't know which one is greater. Drinking something dosed with an aphrodisiac again or never hearing Jamie say he loves me." Tira's eyes welled up with liquid as she tried to keep the tears from falling.

"He's never told you?" Tavia asked, sounding astonished even though Tira knew her twin's journey had not been smooth.

"No." Tira shrugged, pushing away the moisture welling in her throat, threatening to change this evening amusement. "I love him though and even though he doesn't love me, I still want to spend my life with him."

"Be patient. These men of ours just aren't quick to say the words, but when they finally do, there is nothing sweeter. My Drake didn't tell me he loved me until little Ashcroft was born."

"Well, Jamie is obviously slower than your Drake. Broc was born over a month ago and still not a word about love."

"More wine?" Charlotte asked, holding up the bottles, smiling as if she wanted to change the subject to something that would put smiles on their faces. "We need to keep this on a happier note. Your Jamie loves you more than life itself. The words mean nothing if the action isn't there. Anyone with eyes can see he loves you with all his heart."

"*Fanny Hill*," Fayth mused, appearing pensive. "Is that the book that was banned? It seemed I heard the man who wrote it was imprisoned."

"That's what Jamie told me. But there were other books too. His mistress was reading them."

"Mistress? We never really heard about a mistress," Christel said.

"It was nothing really. Lizzie...where do I start?" Tira sipped at her wine, wondering about the questions. She supposed her cousins and sisters should know everything yet some of the things seemed just to private to share.

"At the beginning," Charlotte said encouragingly. "The beginning is always the best place to start. Your sisters and cousins know very little about what happened to you."

Tira told them the story then waited for the comments.

"How awful." Tavia wrapped around an arm around her twin. "Annie's mother died in childbirth and his wife ran off with another man. They own several brothels. I'm sure Jamie would have left her eventually."

"She did. It was Mathew Dutton she ran off with. The man who kidnapped and drugged me."

"We should move on. Does anyone have a humorous moment?" Charlotte asked.

Allura spoke up, "It doesn't seem that humorous incidents stand out in our lives, but looking back, my attempts to disguise myself by wearing matronly clothing, drawing my hair tight against my scalp and acting the shrew could be considered funny. It was stressful though. I didn't want to be forced into marriage which was exactly what father was doing."

"For me, now looking back, I suppose the fact that I tried to seduce Jarrett when I had no idea how to do it could be considered funny. I think he knew from the start I had no idea what I was about, and that I definitely wasn't the kind of woman he was looking for that night," Fayth spoke up. "When he found out who I was, he nearly swooned. Well, no he cursed. I guess that isn't swooning."

"Food is here." Charlotte clapped her hands together. "Hope everyone is hungry. Scarlett has made sure there is enough here to feed an army."

Servants entered with trays of cheeses, meats, spring peas, breads and cakes among a few things. The girls gathered, heaping plates and chattering among themselves.

"Eat up. It might be a long time until you get food again. The wedding is scheduled for noon," The Duchess spoke.

Tira wished it was scheduled for this very moment. She didn't want to wait another second to be with Jamie. Since that awful night on board his ship, they had barely seen each other, had not shared a bed for two weeks now. More than anything she needed to feel his arms around her.

"Ah, are you thinking of your handsome groom?" Ella asked with an infectious grin on her beautiful face. "I'm curious, didn't Auntie Charlotte make you promise not to sleep together until after the wedding?"

Tira nodded. "She did."

"And it will make the wedding night more memorable." The Duchess smiled methodically, searching through the trays of food until she founded her favorite, lemon bars.

"It made the days we had to wait tension filled. He said things he never would have and a few times he provoked fights with Logan. I've never seen Drake like that and haven't since," Ella said, sipping her wine while grabbing a slice of cheese. "If you have my vote, the two of you should find a way to..."

"Pshaw." The Duchess interrupted, waving her free hand in the air. "Don't be giving them bad advice."

"I think you make us promise just to play with us, perhaps torment the men," Ella said.

"It doesn't matter. I won't see Jamie tonight. I'm sure the men will be returning long after I go to bed." She agreed with Ella and hoped perhaps Jamie would find a way to sneak into her room. The Duchess was most likely playing games with them and testing to see how long they could keep their hands to themselves as well as their promises.

"Maybe not. I heard Drake say they weren't going to make it a long night since the wedding is so early." Ella nibbled delicately on a piece of bread. "If I were you, I'd go to just about any length to entice my man into my bed."

"Don't you go putting ideas into Tira's head. She and her beau have almost made it two weeks. It would be a shame to ruin it now." The Duchess cackled happily.

"You wouldn't know if they did sleep together," Tavia said, seeming to question Charlotte.

"She would know but it wouldn't change what they did," Ella said, slanting her aunt a strange expression.

"How?" Tira didn't understand what Ella was trying to tell her.

"I know because I look at people." The Duchess answered the question. "Why, when Ella and Drake were celibate, it was clear to me when they broke their promise. For the first time since the assurance, Drake had a smile on his face and his demeanor changed to a man well satisfied, one could even say relaxed. Don't think I don't notice those things."

Tira stifled a yawn. "Like I said before, it doesn't matter. I'm going to bed and I'll see you all come morning." Tira stood, smoothing her skirts before finishing her glass of wine. "Is anyone else going to bed?"

"Not yet. We've a few finishing touches here and there before the wedding. You get your beauty rest and we'll see you first thing in the morning." The Duchess waved her away. "Go on, everything will be ready for your wedding."

Thinking about Jamie and tomorrow night, she walked down the steps to the second floor. Stepping along the hallway, she was lost in thought, oblivious to her surroundings.

"Tira, hush." Jamie pulled her into his strong arms. Kissing her he turned her so her back was pressed against the wall. "Wrap your legs around me," he whispered close to her ear.

The heat of his voice sent a tempest raging within. Why was he here so early? Surely, he should be arriving later. She did as he asked and wondered if he was going to make love to her here, on the stairway, for anyone walking down the hallway to see. "What are you doing here?"

"What do you think?" One hand molded over her breast, his thumb rubbing her nipple, heat growing inside.

"I've missed you so much," she whispered into his mouth before his tongue entered, exploring and promising so much more.

She heard his low groan of desire, his hands cupping her derrière, squeezing. Closing her eyes, she knew this was right. Understood what Ella had told her about the tension emanating between them.

"Duchess made you promise?" Drake stood beside the couple, laughing at them while he watched unembarrassed, his arms crossed over his chest. "Did that to Ella and me too. Think you should find your bedroom and spend the night together. It'll make tomorrow so much easier."

"Good God, but I'm tempted." Jamie said, pulling away from Tira long enough to talk. She wanted his arms around her, had to have him now and didn't want to wait until tomorrow night.

"If you think The Duchess won't know, she will," Drake said, laughing. "Doesn't matter, in any case she wouldn't stop the wedding. It's my solid belief that she does it on purpose just to make the men as well as her charges squirm. She knows we bedded them before the wedding, so she's figured out a way to make us pay. Our punishment, you might say."

"Ella told me she could see it in the lines of Drake's face as soon as we broke the promise." Good Lord, but Tira wanted Jamie to make love to her. She wanted to feel his arms around her and his sex deep inside, and she needed the reaffirmation without the damn aphrodisiac.

"Do you care if she knows? I don't." Jamie asked while feathering kisses down her neck even though Drake stared at them, grinning broadly, and totally enjoying himself.

She was so hot she couldn't even speak so she shook her head, trying to take a breath. She wanted him so badly. She felt as is she was unraveling one tiny strand at a time. It was good thing he was holding her up because she didn't think she could stand.

"Promise I won't tell but she'll know when she sees you in the morning." Drake whistled as he walked away.

Not wanting to break apart from Jamie long enough to walk to his bedroom, she kept her legs wrapped around him while he strolled with her, his mouth molded against hers, his hands around her waist.

The door was ajar so he kicked it open then closed it with his foot. He leaned against the door while he let her body slide to the floor. "My God, you're so sweet, so beautiful. I can't live without you."

Tira was hoping to hear the three words she waited for all this time. *I love you, Jamie Lundin.*

Without care for her clothing, it seemed he did his best to remove her dress and underthings but managed to tear a few items. They were both in such a hurry. The night ticked by, moonlight filtering through the window.

She woke up to his kisses and tender caress. "Jamie?"

"Hmm...did you sleep well?"

"No, and you know you kept me awake most the night. What time is it?" She yawned, stretching her arms trying to focus on the clock.

"Time for you to sneak back to your room before anyone misses you." Jamie pulled her into his arms and beneath him.

"Get off me," she laughed, pounding his shoulders. "We don't have time to do this again."

"Just one more time."

"No, I need to be in my room before the wedding party comes in to dress me." To no avail, she tried to wiggle out from under him.

"Before then, so I concede." He stood, then kneeled beside her, pulling back the bedcovers so he could look at her one more time.

"Do you think we ruined the wedding night?"

"No, not at all. I must admit making love to you last night when we weren't supposed to be together was perhaps sweeter because we've been apart for so long, but it will be just as glorious tonight. I'll find a way to make it different," he promised.

"Different?"

"Yes." He lifted his eyebrows, his grin infectious.

"As in *Fanny Hill* different?" she laughed as he ran his knuckles across a nipple. She wanted him again.

"No, never that."

He pulled her to her feet. "Let's get you dressed." He laughed again seeming to explore her even while she tried to rise from the bed.

"I think Aunty will know."

"You don't plan on telling her, so..."

"You look different, happy, content, at ease with yourself, just like Ella said you would." She slipped on the garments he tossed at her. "Heaven knows half the strain I've been experiencing has vanished.

"I'll see you at the wedding." He kissed her, patted her on her derrière then opened the door with a silly grin on his face.

Quickly, she navigated the halls to her bedroom, relieved no one saw her and when she opened the door, she was met with slow clapping then a roar of laughter.

"You really didn't think you would get away with that?" Aunt Charlotte asked with a pleasant smile gracing her features. "The two of you slept together last night. I can see it in your eyes, the decided lack of lines and the sparkle."

"As well as the fact you weren't in your room this morning when we arrived here," Christel said.

"Drake told." She didn't care if he had said anything. They'd done what was best for them. Promises be damned.

"Drake never said a word, not even to me," Ella seemed to pout. "I didn't know until I got here this morning and you weren't in your bed. Good thing the two of you chose to sleep in his bed not yours."

"Then..."

"I woke everyone early just to get them here. I knew you couldn't refuse him if he came to you. And I was right." Charlotte sipped her morning tea. "You do look a bit more relaxed. Is Jamie better?"

"Yes, we both are," she spoke slowly, searching the room, trying to read their minds.

"You must get something to eat. It's going to be a long day. Your bath has been prepared. Let's spend the morning getting you even more beautiful than you already are and ready for the wedding." Ella seemed to take charge as well as diverting the questions bombarding Tira.

"We've more wine. But don't drink too much, you'll regret it later," Tavia said.

"The water is steaming and ready for you." Allura emerged from the bathing room connected to Tira's bedroom. "We'll leave you alone until you're finished with the bath." Allura handed her a glass of wine to take with her.

Thank you." Tira wasn't sure what to think any more. Slipping into the hot water she had time to reflect on the past events as well as think about the future, her future with Jamie and the two children, Annie and Broc. She set the wine on tray near the tub and with sponge in hand she washed.

"Are you ready for your hair?" Ella arrived with a smile on her face. "You have this far away look in your eyes. Must be thinking of Jamie and tonight."

"Yes. How did you ever survive all those months not knowing if Drake loved you?" Tira asked before she ducked her head under the water.

Ella put soap in her hand and began to wash Tira's hair. "It was hard. I loved him so much. I think if I had told him how I felt, he would have said the words I craved sooner."

"Why didn't you?"

"Why don't you? We probably have the same reason. I was too

afraid all he wanted was my passion and my body and love would never be a part of our lives."

"But Drake never told you he wouldn't marry you, did he?" Tira mulled over all the things Jamie told her over the months they were together. "He told me too many times to count that he'd never wed me."

"No, he didn't but there was a time I thought he was going to do just that. Done, I'll get the rinse water."

"What did he do to make you think that?" Tira asked as Ella poured the warm water over her hair.

"Nothing wrong as it turned out." Ella handed Tira a huge bath towel as she stepped from the water. "He was talking to Logan about the wedding and I thought he was planning on marrying someone else. I ran off and created more problems for both of us."

Once she was out of the bath and in her underwear, the girls gathered around her, chatting happily, each with a specific job to get Tira ready for her big day. It seemed to take hours for her hair and makeup then once it was finished, they put her in the gown.

The Duchess clapped her hands together, "You are so beautiful, Tira Hepburn. He will swoon when he sees you."

"Now," Ella took charge once more. "I'm lending you the pearls I wore at my wedding. So, sit down and Allura will wind them in your hair. She is so much better at this sort of thing than I am."

"I've brought you a blue garter for your stocking." Tavia handed her the delicate blue lace garter. "Keep the other one on so your stocking will stay up when Jamie takes it off."

Tira pulled up her skirt and tied it around her leg. Fayth handed her a bouquet of yellow rosses, calla lilies and dahlias, thanks to Logan's conservatory. She then presented Tira with a small bouquet of yellow roses.

"Thank you, all of you." Tira tried hard to keep the tears from falling.

"Now, don't you dare cry," Ella said, "The teardrops will ruin your makeup."

"We're not done yet." The Duchess opened a tiny box and inside were diamond earrings. "They are yours, dear. My duke gave them to me on our first anniversary. I have no need of them and they will look beautiful on you."

"Stand up and let us see how breathtakingly gorgeous you are," Christel said, stepping back with the others to appraise the bride.

"A toast!" Storm and Eveleen entered with two trays filled with glasses of sparkling champagne.

"It is your job, Ella," the Duchess said smiling proudly as she looked around the room at the girls she helped raise just a little bit.

"Well, Aunty, I'm not very good at these things." She cleared her throat, raising her glass. "To my beautiful little sister. May your marriage bring you all the happiness you've ever dreamed of." She breathed in, "As did mine."

"Here, here," they chorused.

"Shall we go? I seem to hear someone knocking on the door. I think your father is here to escort you."

~ * ~

Jamie stood with Drake at the back of the ballroom on the third floor waiting for Tira to appear. Shifting from one foot to the other, he wasn't sure why his nerves seemed to be splintering. He didn't have second thoughts about this marriage, just needed to get the damn thing over with. Good God, he'd weathered storms with more ease than he felt now while he waited for the ceremony to begin.

Drake nudged him in the side. Laughing, he said, "You shouldn't have that frown on your face when your bride walks through the door. That scowl might scare her off. She'll turn tail and you'll never see her again."

Music began to play as the little flower girl, Allura's daughter if he remembered correctly, walked down the aisle tossing yellow petals on the runner that led to the small arch set up for them to say their vows beneath. Then the ring bearer appeared, Allura and Hunter's son, followed by Ella who slanted Drake a piercing grin.

When Tira stepped through the double doors, his heart caught in his throat as did the air he inhaled. He always knew she was beautiful, but today she stole his heart for a second time. Mesmerized, he couldn't seem to remove his gaze from her. By the time she handed her bouquet to Ella to hold during the ceremony, he knew she was as nervous as he was.

Her father gave her hand to him before turning to sit down in the front row next to The Duchess and the McLellan. Her hands shook within his and when she met his gaze, her green eyes sparked with love and admiration. He knew she loved him. Then why couldn't he tell her how he felt?

The sermon seemed to take a lifetime. He didn't hear any of it. When the minister finally said he could kiss the bride, he wanted to jump for joy. With his hands on either side of her face, his lips found her, his tongue lightly tracing the seam of her mouth before pulling back. She was his now for all eternity. No one could ever change that.

She would be with him for the rest of his life or hers, and he was the happiest man in the world. "You're my wife now," he whispered.

"I give you Mr. and Mrs. Jamie Lundin." They walked down the flower-strewn runner to the applause of their family. In reality he heard very little of what the minister said and now had no idea of the promises they made to each other. He hoped they were the same vows he listened to in other weddings. In any case he would give her anything she wanted, promise her the world and everything in it if that would make her happy.

On one side there was a group of Scottish musicians who now played some lively tunes. The opposite side of the room was decked out with platters of food, more than they would eat tonight, and in the front was a large cake.

"Are you hungry?" he whispered to her, suddenly aware that everyone watched them. "We should get something to eat."

"I believe they are waiting for us to have the first dance." She smiled at him before she caught her lower lip beneath her teeth. "They are all tapping their toes in anticipation, and they can't do anything until we go out on the dance floor. Can you dance?"

"I have two left feet. Just thought you should know I'll probably trod on yours more than once before the dance is finished," he said.

"I'll endure, besides I don't believe you." She laughed softly, holding on to his arm as he led her on to the dance floor.

"You're most likely correct, Mrs. Lundin." He stopped midroom and held out his arms. She stepped into them before he whirled her around the dance floor. Once the song was over, he felt a soft tapping on his shoulder.

"I believe I get the next dance," her father said, a grin on his face. "It's been way too long since I've been a part of my girl's lives."

"I'm so glad you came. You truly surprised me. I was afraid you'd still be mourning mother." She let her father lead her into the center of the room.

Jamie couldn't make out the rest of the conversation. He stood back watching her dance, her skirts swirling around her slender ankles. Every few seconds, he caught a glimpse of them.

What to do now?

They would sail back to Baltimore as soon as she wanted but if he had his way that would be tomorrow. He missed Annie more than he wanted to admit. If he took a southerly tack, they might make it back in just a few months or less.

Tira and her father stopped in front of him as he handed her back to her husband. "Take good care of her. I don't want to find out you hurt her. Remember, I'm not too old to sail to America."

"Papa," Tira said, "you don't have to worry about any of that. Jamie has always been the nicest man I've ever known except you." She placed a quick kiss on his cheek. "I love you."

"I know. It's just I was thinking of Sadie. I still miss her terribly but with the help of The Duchess, I've come to realize Sadie wouldn't want me to give up on life or my girls. You two enjoy now. I might come visit you just to see another part of the world." He stepped back, arms crossed, still smiling at them.

"Shall we enjoy another dance?" Jamie offered her his arm. "I'm feeling restless and I'll take any excuse to hold you in my embrace."

"Of course." As they began to dance, he realized there was more depth to Tira than he'd ever imagined. She'd been through so much and still she looked on life with an optimism he admired. Her sisters too. Amorica had seen her mother murdered. Still she found a way to fight through her fears and marry a smuggler.

The tune changed to a haunting slow rendition of a song Jamie couldn't quite remember. As they slowed, he pulled her closer, wishing they were alone in the bedchamber, naked her softness against him. Ah well, the night would last longer than he hoped but then he could be with her for the rest of their lives.

"Jamie?" She gazed at him through her haunting green eyes. He realized in this light they were flecked with tiny bits of gold.

"Hmm..." She startled him from his musings, tugging on his sleeve.

"Is that The Duchess and Laird McLellan behind the curtain? Look over there." Tira turned him so he caught the same view as she did. He stumbled, losing time to the music.

"I believe so." He wanted to laugh out right. The man's hands were definitely not above the waist. He had no trouble remembering the first times he kissed Tira, touched her, as well as her words to him that came straight from The Duchess' sitting room.

"And I can't believe what I'm staring at. I never thought Aunty would do anything like that, anything so adventuresome, so outrageous. I know she and her duke, did, well, she admitted they made love before the marriage, but the McLellan is not her duke."

"Should we leave them alone or remind Charlotte that she is letting the McLellan break all her rules." Jamie felt a wicked delight in what he was seeing and by the looks of it, he and Tira weren't the only ones feeling that way. He wondered if the two lovers would spend the night in separate rooms. For that matter, had they spent last night together?

"Allura is moving their way. I don't know what she's going to say. No, Hunter has wisely sidelined her." Tira's laughter surprised him. "Perhaps this wedding will end with everyone finding happiness."

"She's completely under his spell. Look, his hand is on her breast. I'm sure Aunty would be mortified if she knew we were all watching them." Tira thought she might double up with laughter if it wouldn't cause embarrassment to Charlotte.

"Then we should go get a bite of something to eat. Did you have breakfast or were you like me too nervous to get any food down?" Jamie bent over to whisper close to her ear, taking advantage of his position, tracing a line around the tiny shell.

"You were nervous?" Tira appeared shocked by the confession, turning away from him.

He grinned at her, smoothing a lock of hair into place while enjoying the look of astonishment on her face. "A little but not nearly as much if I had not spent the night in your arms. I just wanted to get the ceremony and reception over with so I could be alone with you."

"Me too, but I was afraid that if I ate, the food would never stay down. The wine Logan sent was nice though. Other than that, I've had nothing in my stomach since last night. Hear it rumble?"

"Look, the amorous elders have come up for air. If my eyesight is not failing me, her lips are a bit swollen from his arduous attentions." He had to give credit to the older couple. They weren't giving up on life. If their original partners still lived, he was sure they would all be stealing kisses any and everywhere they could find. No balcony crevice would be available to the younger crowd.

"I wonder if the Duke is looking down on them with approval or disapproval," Tira said softly touching the tip of his chin tenderly. "They meant so much to each other."

"You don't suppose he would approve?" Jamie had sudden reservations about the older couple and their lovemaking.

"From everything Aunt Charlotte has told us, her duke loved her so much he would want her to be happy. I'm sure though he'd be tapping his foot impatiently, ready to claim what he deemed his once they meet again. But then maybe the duke is having a dalliance with Gracie."

"And I'm sure she will have to answer a few questions in heaven when they finally meet each other again," Jamie said, thoughtfully rubbing his chin. He never thought about Lizzy and what her feelings would be but that was different. Lizzy had been his mistress and he never loved her, cared for her, yes. For the first time since she died, he really thought about her and felt a brief moment of nostalgia then guilt.

"I don't really want to talk about death." She looked away from him, her slim shoulders taking on a downward turn. "We're only just beginning our lives together. When we were drugged and trying to find a way to find peace, I wished for death a few times."

"Never that. Don't ever wish for death. It can come far too soon, but I do agree with you. No more talk about death at our wedding when we should be rejoicing, dancing and looking for a way to steal a few kisses."

No matter what happened he wanted to live this life as fully as possible.

"I'm glad they are getting on with their lives. Aunty deserves to be happy. She's sacrificed so much for her nieces. Now with only Aidan left to find a suitable husband she can do what she wants."

"As does the McLellan. Come, let's find something we can eat that will fill our empty stomachs. While I'd like to dance the night away, I'd rather eat, drink, cut the cake and take you to bed." Jamie pulled her to him, gazing into her eyes for a moment before kissing her soundly.

Filling their plates, they strode to one of the tables set on a balcony overlooking the Montgomerie estate. The night was dark, the clouds so thick not even a sliver of moonlight shown through, and he could hear the soft sound of raindrops hitting the roof. Jamie took off his coat and wrapped it around Tira's shoulders.

"Don't want you to be cold." He grinned, thinking of ways to make her hot and passionate.

"Thank you." She inhaled a long breath of air, closing her eyes briefly, "Do you think about the curse on the weddings at the Montgomerie estate?"

Before he could reply.

"I took the liberty of bringing you both a glass of wine." Ella appeared beside the table. "Did you see Aunty and David?"

"That was sweet of you," Tira said, accepting the glass with a smile. "Do you want to sit and talk about them?"

"You're welcome but I really did have ulterior motives."

"And what would those be?" Jamie asked, assuming he knew the answer to his question. Since she'd already broached the question.

"Did you see The Duchess and the Laird? They were kissing as if they were young and in love. And his hands," Ella laughed, "they were definitely below the waist several times."

"I think Hunter is officially the Laird but yes, we did see them." Tira said, looking at Ella over the rim of her glass. "What do you think about them finding a little pleasure in this time of their lives."

"Well, Allura is beside herself with worry and Hunter says he wants to be kissing her like that when he's their age and Allura just replied, what if it was with a different man. Then Hunter growled, I mean he really growled. I'd better be dead if you're kissing another man at any age," he told her.

"What did Allura say to that?"

"She laughed and told him she'd kill him if she ever caught him with another woman."

"Oh my," Tira said. "None of that really answers the question at hand though."

"Oh my, is not harsh enough," Ella said laughing. "I have to tell you I feel the same way about Drake. I really don't think he would ever take a mistress or kiss another woman, but if he did, I'd cosh him on the head, beat him with a cane until he was black and blue."

Jamie cleared his throat, grinning at the two sisters. "Hardly the conversation for a wedding. I'm hoping the Montgomerie wedding curse does not come to haunt us and the way you two are talking, it just might."

"There is no one who wants either of us dead. We're safe and nothing untoward is going to happen." Tira said smugly.

"Dutton could show up just to put a damper on things. Drake did set up security at the front of the house just in case." He might be tempted to end Dutton if he did appear here. Now he had more than one reason to despise the man.

"I hope not."

"He won't show his ugly face." Jamie clenched his fists, hoping beyond anything his words would prove true. "If he does, he risks everything and he's not a stupid man."

"I don't want to speak of him or that night." Tira's face had turned a ghostly shade of white. "This is supposed to a happy event."

"Should we cut the cake?" Jamie asked, needing to put a rosy glow back on Tira's features as well as bring them one step closer to his bed.

"If it's not too soon. Our guests are still eating."

"I suppose we should finish. You need your strength for tonight."

A bolt of lightning slashed across the sky followed immediately by rolling thunder. The few raindrops falling turned into a dance of ice pellets on the roof, clattering nosily.

Both Tira and Jamie stood transfixed by the sight of a repeat performance. This time the lightning hit the gazebo and it burst into flames.

Everyone gathered at the balcony to watch the raging storm. While the ice falling into the gazebo doused the flames.

"My God," Jamie breathed, stunned by the ferocity he was witnessing as wind gusts whistled bending foliage to the ground.

For a third time lightning hit the ground, lighting the gardens in a spectacular display. A man appeared out of the shadows silhouetted in the light then his features became apparent. Briefly, Jamie thought it was Mathew Dutton appearing to renew the curse and haunt his wedding, continuing the horrible tradition.

"Grisham..." Drake whispered then with fists at his side, he strode to the edge of the balcony, leaning over despite the ghastly weather in an apparent attempt to gain a better view.

"Wasn't your brother sent to the penal colonies in Australia?" Ella stepped beside her husband, gripping his arm.

The ice turned back to rain as the storm seemed to be moving in a northerly direction. As they watched, two men appeared from the shadows and took hold of Grisham's arms.

A slight scuffle in the hallway turned everyone's attention to the entry door. Jamie reached for the knife he always kept in his boot only to realize not only wasn't he wearing boots, but the weapon was non existent.

Logan, on the other hand, had knife in hand and was poised and ready for a fight before most in the room could inhale a breath.

The man entering held his hands out. "Constables," the man said.

"Was that Grisham down there?" Montgomerie asked, sounding very nearly incredulous. "Thought he was on a ship to Australia."

The runner shrugged his shoulders. "The ship he was supposed to be on was full. We were putting him on the next available vessel and he escaped. Just wanted you to know."

"You are going to keep him in chains next time," Drake said, his visage a dark scowl.

"Plan on it, sir. Will that be all?"

Drake nodded, watching the man leave through the entry door. Then he swiveled, directing his words to Jamie. "You should cut the cake."

It seemed the Montgomerie wedding curse continued, yet this was not quite as bad as the other stories. No one was getting shot and there was no blood on the floor.

"Everyone should get a glass of champagne." Ella lifted her drink high, waiting for the guest to comply.

The sisters, cousins and spouse all gathered around the champagne table until everyone had a glass. Toasts were made and laughter outshone the tempest simmering outside.

Jamie sipped, staring at his new wife. She was beautiful, her green eyes sparkling, her dark brown hair, alight with the pearls entwining through the locks. She was his now.

The cake was cut and with drinks in hand, the musicians began to play again. Jamie held Tira, his hand on her waist, wishing they could leave. A carriage waited for them outside, and Drake let them have free run of his townhouse for the next few days.

"How long do we have to stay," he whispered close to Tira's ear then feeling the slight shudder of her slender frame. "I wouldn't want to break any aristocratic rules."

"Here, here," The Duchess tapped her glass several times with a spoon. Everyone stood still, watching her.

Jamie held his breath then slowly let it out as The Duchess began to speak. "The couple wants their wedding night. Shall we escort them to the waiting carriage and let them get on with it even though they disobeyed last night's rules."

"I'll get the rice," Ella called out and picking up her skirts, she raced to the entry where the bags sat waiting for the revelers.

Everyone gathered at the porch and the walkway to the carriage with the opened sacs of rice. The rain stopped but the night was still pitch black except for the gas lanterns adorning the front. As Jamie and Tira ran through the throng, rice rained down on them. Jamie helped Tira inside.

The decorated carriage with cans trailing along behind them began to roll. Jamie pulled her into his arms, his lips finding her soft ones, molding his to hers. She leaned into him, her hands running up and down his back.

"I want to be inside you right now and feel you close around me. I want to be one with you." He touched her ear with the tip of his tongue.

"You don't mean to..."

He wasn't at all sure if she was surprised. Wasn't sure if she was trying to tell him no or if she was in agreement and saying she wanted this as much as he did her. He ran his hand up her leg until he reached the waistband of her underclothes. In a sudden movement and with a little help from Tira, he removed them stuffing them in his pocket.

"Jamie, please, hurry."

She was swollen wet and so very soft when he stroked her. He worked his magic as he made her wild with pleasure. She arched her back as he caressed her most intimate and feminine parts. His fingers on her swelled woman's flesh, probing her, teasing her, knowing her body so well. She reared up. He grinned. Lifting her skirts, he positioned her a top his swelled hard sex then let her settle on him.

So deep inside of her he touched her womb and still it seemed she tried to draw him further inside her velvet soft walls as they were clenching his sex tighter. "I want to hear you scream with pleasure," he whispered.

Her head was back and she was moving on him. He gritted his teeth, trying to control himself. He pulled back bringing her close then easing away before he brought her to that point where she climaxed.

She screamed his name and he grinned, emptying himself inside her and enjoying the moment and the manly pride of a job well done. He hoped the driver didn't hear the shriek. Ah well, he was Drake's personal driver and it would shock him if Drake had never done the same with Ella while the man was driving.

It seemed the ride was shorter than he thought it would be. When they stopped, he pulled her into his arms, carrying her up the steps to the house. The butler must have been waiting for them because he opened the door for them.

"Welcome, you are to use the guest room on the second level. I'll show you the way and I'll have someone bring in your personal items as well as a bottle of wine and something to eat."

"Leave them outside the door and knock, please. We don't want to be disturbed tonight."

Epilogue

"Stay right here," Jamie said as he took Brock from Tira's arm. "Don't come inside until I can carry you over the threshold."

She watched him stride inside their Baltimore home and set Broc in a safe place. This felt like her home, their home. after all it was now. The trip from London was short and uneventful.

Grinning, Jamie reappeared and swept her off her feet. "I have to carry my wife over the threshold. Bad luck if I don't."

"You don't really believe that nonsense, do you?" She laughed as he set her on her feet inside the house.

"Don't want to take any chances with lady luck or any superstition."

She wondered if he knew she was pregnant or if she should wait to tell him. Brock was barely six months old. The child in her womb was maybe two months along. At least she was sure the babe wasn't conceived on that wild night of drugged lovemaking.

I love you, Jamie Lundin. "When are we going to retrieve Annie and let her know we're home with her little brother and another one on the way?"

"I wondered when you would tell me." He grinned at her.

"I assumed you knew before me. When were you going to tell me?"

"Wasn't. Figured you'd know. Still not a day of sickness, and from what I've heard that's very unusual."

"So, when are we going to get Annie?" she returned to her original question.

"As soon as you want. We can take Broc and introduce him to his auntie, Aidan, or we can wait until nap time and I can go by myself to get Annie."

"I've missed her. She has a way of creeping into your heart and staying there." It was so true, the precocious little girl who never failed to tell the truth as she saw it was deep in her heart.

"Hello. Sam saw your ship, and he sent a message to me." Aidan opened the door for Annie who ran into her papa's arms.

Jamie picked her up, twirling her around until she started giggling. It was then the baby started crying. "You brought me a little brother."

He set her down. "We did. Do you want to meet Broc?"

She nodded, "Sit down on the couch and I'll let you hold him," Tira held the baby in her arms who was now cooing softly. It seemed Broc knew there was competition and just wanted attention.

Annie sat down and Tira gave her some directions before she placed him in her arms. "He's beautiful. Do you think he'll like to play with dolls?" She smiled that stunning smile that always made Tira's heart skip a beat.

"Probably not, Annie. Little Broc will undoubtedly like to play with ships and trains," Jamie said, grinning.

Annie stroked the dark hair on the top of his head. "I think I can teach him. Did you know he's beautiful? Just like you, Papa."

"Yes, very beautiful," Jamie said, still grinning. "Now you should give him to his mother. He probably needs to have his diaper changed."

"Oh, no, his father will do the duty. It's his turn after all. Because he was busy sailing his ship, he didn't share the duties where Broc was concerned on our journey here. If I remember correctly, you promised to help." Tira smiled, letting her hands rest on her hips and feeling a bit proud of herself. Jamie told her he would share responsibilities.

Jamie's grin changed to a frown. "I remember the last time I..."

"Which was the only time you've changed his diaper," Tira finished. "You just have to learn to duck."

"Papa, what's Tira talking about? Why do you have to duck when you change his diapers? Did you have to when you changed mine?"

Tira grinned, wondering just what his answer would be. "I suppose you'll find out soon enough. Come with me and I'll teach you how to change his diaper and exactly what Tira means for you to duck."

Fondly, she watched Jamie take Broc in one arm and hold his daughter's hand in his as they walked up the steps.

Then she turned to Aidan, her curiosity overwhelming. "Blade?"

Aidan shrugged her shoulders, staring out the window, clearly disturbed. "He left about a month after you. Told me he was going to New York then Boston. Said it couldn't be helped and he'd explain the trip to me later."

"Did he tell you if he was coming back?"

"He said he was. The horses he brought for Damian are still in the stables behind Sam's blacksmith shop. I check on them and they're doing fine. I don't understand anything that has happened here."

"Damian didn't come to pick up the horses? That's strange. All this time." Tira mused. "I wonder why?"

"I don't know what to think." Aidan studied her hands, which rested in her lap. "I thought he sailed to America for me and it doesn't seem that's true."

"He said he'd be back."

"I haven't heard from him in months. Why couldn't he send a note, something to reassure me that he cares?" Aidan wiped the tears away with the back of her hand before sitting up straight. "Enough of this. I'm not going to waste any more tears on that awful, inconsiderate man. I thought he changed but he hasn't. He's just as arrogant and self-absorbed as he always was."

"Good girl." Tira reached out to her cousin, holding her hand in hers. "You have to stand up for yourself and what you want in this lifetime."

"You did and now you have everything you've always wanted."

"If he loves you, he'll be back for you."

"I shouldn't burden you with my problems. Has Jamie told you he loves you?"

"He hasn't, but I think in his own way he does love me," Tira said, praying some day he would say the words she needed so badly to hear. Ella received the words of love when he bore Drake a son. Well, she gave Jamie a son and now there was another child on the way. She didn't want to think about it.

"Have you told him you love him?"

Shaking her head and gazing up the steps hoping Jamie wouldn't suddenly appear, "I promised myself I wouldn't say anything until he did."

"You don't want to be hurt. I certainly understand your thoughts. I would never make myself so vulnerable before Blade said something to me."

"He's all yours." Jamie strode down the steps with his daughter next to him. "I explained everything to Annie."

"Everything?" Everything could mean anything or nothing and she wondered just what Jamie meant. She accepted Broc into her arms, lowering her bodice so she could feed him."

"We, Lilly and myself, have planned a party to welcome the two of you home for tonight if that's alright?" Aidan said. "Just a couple of friends."

"Of course, and what we didn't tell you yet is that we are married. Didn't quite erase the Montgomerie wedding curse, but no one died and there were no guns drawn."

"What happened?"

Tira explained while Jamie left to take a look at the shipyard and perhaps say hello to Martha.

"I'm going to put Broc down for a nap."

"Come by as soon as you can. Lilly will have dinner on the table and your friends will be there."

"My friends? You mean Jamie's. It seems when I left, I was the town whore."

"We'll come to dinner, but do you mind terribly if we spend tonight alone and forego the party. I think I've something to tell my husband and rather than postpone it, I think I'd like to get this over with. I'm not quite up to seeing his friends."

"You're going to tell him you love him?"

"If I find the courage."

"I'll see you as soon as Broc wakes up, an hour or two I assume." Tira gave her cousin a hug then watched her leave.

She closed her eyes, bringing a pillow onto her lap before settling on the sofa. Before she fell asleep, Jamie was beside her, pulling her into his arms, kissing her softly on the lips, nipping little kisses.

"Annie?"

"Exhausted, she's asleep. I'll wake her up after Broc finishes his nap if she isn't awake before then."

"All I want to do is curl up next to him and sleep for twenty-four hours, but we both know that's not possible."

"Hush, I brought you a glass of wine. Take a sip." He held it out to her.

She sat up, looking at him over the rim of the glass. "This is just going to make me fall asleep."

"You do need your sleep, but I've got something I want to say to you first."

"What is it?" she asked, suddenly afraid. "Should I be concerned?"

"No, love."

She brushed hair from her eyes, her hands shaking so hard she needed to set the wine glass down.

"Jamie, I need to tell you something. I swore I wouldn't tell you until you..."

"And you won't have to," Jamie interrupted. "I was going to tell you before you ran off, just as I was going to ask you to marry me. You left me and that changed everything."

"Oh," she didn't want to think about what he might say.

"No, it's not what your thinking. Tira Lundin, I love you with all my heart and I've prayed each day you return that love."

Tira couldn't help herself. Tears flowed from her eyes as she wrapped her arms around Jamie. "I love you too. That's what I was going to say. I love you."

"We've been pretty stupid, haven't we?"

"No, just cautious. We've both been hurt in all kinds of ways. It's done now, all the hurt. Only love is left for us.

"I love you so much," Jamie couldn't help but tell her again.

"I want to tell you over and over again every day our lives. I love you," Tira reached up and pulled Jamie to her, accepting his lips as they molded against hers.

"Tira's education, my love. It started so long ago, but every installment was worth the wait."

Coming by the Author
September 2019
from
Rogue Phoenix Press

Aidan's Love
Twelve Dancing Princesses Book Twelve

Chapter One
Baltimore 1822

Aidan saw Blade leaning lazily on the light post across the street. With no doubt in her mind, he watched her. Her heart thundering in her chest, she picked up her skirts and increased her pace, fleeing from him and the real threat to her peace of mind he created. She knew he would catch up to her if that was his intention, yet she continued without looking back.

Before he spoke, she felt his presence looming beside her. Tilting her head a bit she kept going, trying desperately to ignore him. Acknowledging his presence after he embarrassed her and humiliated her then had the gall to depart Baltimore for parts unknown without leaving a message meant he didn't deserve to be recognized. She would make him explain himself but not before she took a moment to rebuff him.

"You can't out walk or out run me, so why don't you slow down a mite before you swoon from exhaustion or fall flat on your face?" His voice was gruff sounding as well as impatient with her.

Her pride wouldn't allow her to give in to his request. Where she was concerned, he had no rights, none at all. She meant to fight him the only ways she could. Keeping her sights set on her home, she continued on, her breathing coming now in short gulps. Damn and blast, she shouldn't have worn the corset. She rarely did so why today? Didn't know why she had Lilly help lace it this morning. There was no one in Baltimore she cared to impress.

Except Blade.

"Foolish woman, this isn't good for you. I understand you're just trying to make a point. I'll acknowledge that point. I've not been a gentleman to you, but I mean to change that. Slow down, I'm not going anywhere." His hand rested on her shoulder as if he meant to stop her midstride. Automatically, she brushed it off.

Foolish woman, she had a few choice words to say to him about that, but not until he apologized at least a thousand times. First, for what he did to her in London before her cousin's wedding and second, for leaving town without telling her where he was going or when he'd return.

Chin held high, she resisted the temptation to stop and give him a piece of her mind. It seemed he fell back a step, still shadowing her but understanding she wasn't about to talk to him in the middle of the street or acknowledge his existence.

A gust of wind caught her skirts, tangling them between her legs. She fought for balance but knew when the struggle was over. Whirling her arms, she felt his hands at her waist, keeping her upright, pulling her against his hard body. She felt his entire length against her, every muscle.

Then, "Bloody hell." He caught her in his arms and holding her close, he carried her down the street to her home.

"I don't need your help, Blade," she protested, beating his chest with her fists even while she wanted to melt into him and enjoy whatever he might want to give.

"Appears to me, you do, Little Fire." He chuckled softly, seeming to appreciate her discomfort, while cradling her protectively in his arms.

"I can walk by myself." She gave up hitting the stubborn man. He'd do exactly what he wanted and there was nothing she could do about it.

"If I hadn't come to your rescue, you'd be sitting on your sweet little backside in the middle of the road," he told her, pleasantly grinning from ear to ear. "I don't want to see you hurt; only want to see to your pleasure," He paused seeming to think, "Now that you're a woman grown."

Her breath caught in the back of her throat. She knew exactly the pleasure he spoke of. He'd treated her to sexual fulfillment before he vanished, and without a note she reminded herself.

When they finally reached the porch, he set her down to open the door. Still not wishing to talk to him, she strode inside, pulling her hat from her head along with a few pins that left her hair in wild strands before setting it on the coat tree. She blew the errant pieces of hair from her eyes.

"I didn't invite you in." Ignoring him further she left for the kitchen, needing a cup of tea laced with whisky, knowing all the while he'd follow her. Lilly always kept a pot of hot water on the stove and tea leaves close by.

"Smells good. Lilly must have baked cookies this afternoon. I believe I hear my stomach rumbling." He stood behind her now. If she turned, she knew he'd have his feet spread and hands on his hips looking as if he owned her.

"Help yourself." She poured her drink before taking it into the parlor knowing he would trail after her. If she didn't talk to him now, he would stay forever. Damn and blast, with the permission of her cousin's husbands, he moved in months ago. All his clothes were here. It's just that he hadn't been here.

In the parlor, he relaxed, sipping his whiskey, studying her. A few cookie crumbs had fallen into the stubble on his chin. She tried to focus on anything but Blade, his broad shoulders and steel blue eyes, the way his muscles flexed when he moved. Tried to concentrate on anything but the way his hands had touched her, every part of her, aroused her in ways she didn't comprehend.

Rattled by enchanting memories of the time he seduced her, she ran her tongue across her lips while a searing heat rushed through her, reminding her of things she'd rather not think about. Against her will, he could do that to her; create a tempest swirling inside she was hard pressed to deny.

At times she didn't want to reject any advances he might make. If she gave in to his ploys, she would find herself in his arms and his bed before she could blink. After all, she'd been in love with him since she was thirteen, seven long years ago.

Inhaling a long deep breath and setting her cup on the table beside her, she asked and with a patience that was rarely a part of her character, "Where were you? All this time..."

"Ach lass, I was enjoying the silence." He rose and poured himself more whiskey. Returning, he sat next to her. Placing a hand on hers, he watched her carefully, his muscles tense.

"You don't want me to talk? Fine. I won't then. Be that way if you enjoy the sound of silence rather than my voice." She wanted to bait him, needed to erase the all-knowing smirk off his face. This isn't at all what she expected when and if he returned.

"Why are you so angry with me? I don't believe I've done anything to deserve your wrath." He brought her hand to his lips, placing a kiss on the palm of her hand, allowing his tongue to glide across her skin.

"Where were you?" she repeated with a little more force this time, tugging her hand to no avail while he drew circles on the underside of her wrist with his thumb. He wasn't going to seduce her so easily, she determined. She could and would resist him.

He lifted his shoulders, before nonchalantly speaking, "I left you a note. You should have read it. Then you would comprehend where I went and why along with the gravity of the situation. Truth be told leaving you was the very last thing I wanted."

"It's been three months and I had no idea if you were even alive." She succeeded in pulling her hand from him then she crossed her arms over her chest, trying to calm her escalating nerves. Lord, but he could bring her to anger just as quickly as he could create a storm of desire she couldn't control.

He picked up her hand again, brought it to his lips. Gazing into her eyes before kissing the tips of each finger, he continued to explore the palm of her hand then her wrist. When he stopped, "I told you in the note I left on that table." He motioned to the one by the door.

Thinking, breathing, even sitting straight was nearly impossible when he brought his lips away. "A-a note?" she whispered, enraged at the masculine smile on his face and the way she melted with a tiny kiss on her hand. The man knew what he did to her. For a second time, she pulled her hand away.

Instead of conceding defeat and withdrawing, he picked up her other hand and sucked each finger into his mouth, his teeth nibbling on each tip. This time he continued his path of discovery and exploration up her arm, kissing, biting. His tongue was warm and created its own magic against her flesh.

When he paused, "Yes, a note. Over there. It explained everything. Where and why. The gravity."

"I never saw a note." She stood, intending to show him there was nothing there. He let her go. Before she reached the table, she faced him, and in a huff clearly confused by his seduction, "Regardless, you could have answered my question. You didn't have to—have to..."

"Make you breathless with passion and desire? We could go upstairs. No one is home."

"You did no such thing and no we can't. Lilly will be in the kitchen fixing dinner any time now."

"Make you breathless or write a note? I can assure you, I wrote one." Still his voice was too calm, too sure of himself, his smile self-assured.

It didn't seem he believed she didn't see a note. Even if she didn't find one, it didn't mean he lied. Bending over and on all fours, she searched the floor below the table then tried to reach behind the nearby chair, stretching, moving her hand along the floor. She sneezed from the dust.

"I can't find anything."

His hand settled on top her back. "Let me help."

His mouth was close to her lips when she turned her head to reply. The warmth from his hand sent a whirling dervish of sensations spiraling to places he awakened a few months ago. A tiny whimper she had no control over made his grin broader.

She moistened her lips, "I don't want your help." Any more assistance from him and she'd drag him against her and make him give her those wonderful sensation he called a woman's pleasure. *Ninny, he would never let you take control*. Yet perhaps he would.

"But you can't reach as far as I can." His lips brushed softly against hers then in a blink they vanished.

"You're doing that on purpose." She closed her eyes, reveling in the touch of his hand as he slid it up her back then down to caress her bottom.

"Looking for the note I left you? I need redemption. Of course, I'm doing it on purpose."

"Then stop touching me and look for the bloody note so you can be vindicated. Or better yet just tell me where and why and I'll take you for your word." If he didn't stop soon, she'd end up a mindless, spineless puddle on the floor.

"I like touching you, hearing those tiny mews of pleasure and the soft flush that stains your cheeks when I do. Why should I settle for anything less?"

She'd wanted this for so long and now she tried to rebuff the potent attraction between them. Trying to move away, his body stopped her as he reached farther behind the chair.

"There it is." When he loosened his hold, she scurried away and standing, smoothed her skirts brushing off a few dust motes in the process. With a broad grin on his too handsome features, he held the object of her search high. "I believe this is what you were looking for."

"So, you found it. Care to tell me what it says?" As he stood and stepped toward her, she backed up, needing the physical distance between them before she did something stupid like throw herself into his arms.

It seemed he didn't mean to remain separated from her. Closing the distance, he read, "It says, my sister's youngest child was ill and she needed help, more than her husband could give her." He shrugged broad, masculine shoulders, "Since I was so close to Boston, I decided to visit another sister also. There you have it, proof of my sad tale as well as my vindication." He held it out for her to take as if he still wanted her to read it.

"I'm sorry I doubted you." There it was; she wanted an apology from him and she was doing the apologizing. Of course, she was. Women always apologized when it seemed the man should be doing that very thing, begging forgiveness.

"Come here." He stepped toward her again and when she moved back, her knees buckled as she hit the back of the chair.

"Stay where you are." She held her hands out, a tactical mistake he took advantage of.

"I need a proper welcoming kiss from the woman I'm now officially courting." He held her hands and bringing her to a standing position, wrapped her arms around his neck while his hands bracketed her face.

"Hardly courting..." she tried to say more but his lips found hers, his hands at the small of her back pulling her closer, so close she felt the hard angles and planes of his body against hers, the rising heat and strength.

The slow hot kiss reminded her once more of all he could do to her, all he made her feel when he touched her in certain intimate places. Yet she responded, letting him pull her tongue into his mouth, allowing him the freedom of exploring her body, with his mouth and hands.

Suddenly, he pulled away, a grim look on his face and with a soft almost regretful sounding sigh, "We should stop."

Stop? If he didn't hold her up, she would slide to the floor, melt in a pool around his feet. Her head fell against his chest while he ran his hands up and down her back, a soothing motion that calmed her nerves and eased the tension in her body but did nothing to eliminate the heat pounding through her.

"You can't do that," she whispered, barely able to speak.

"What," he grinned as if he knew what she meant to tell him.

With her hands fisted at her sides, "Make me feel all hot and wanting you then tell me to stop as if the kiss meant nothing to you."

He crossed his arms over his chest, studying her, meeting her gaze with the steel blue of his, "Would you rather I tossed your skirts and taught you a few new things about lovemaking here on the living room floor."

"That's a horrible thing to say." Yet she did remember the first lesson, the one where he confirmed to himself she was truly a woman grown, no longer a child. If she'd thought for a minute the size of her breasts would have established her womanhood, she might have padded her dresses.

"But so true."

"You haven't the willpower to stop before you ravish me?" She had no idea the effect of her words on Blade. A moment of apprehension swept through her when his eyes darkened.

"Where you and your sweet little body are concerned, I have no restraint. I used up all my patience where you're concerned years ago. With just that kiss, I was tempted to sweep you into my arms and take you to my room. If I did that, you would no longer be a virgin. Don't temp me, Aidan, unless you're serious." His threat was clear.

"I didn't know," she murmured, turning away from him and his piercing gaze. Yet she was thrilled he wanted her and even more thrilled he didn't revert to the excuses he used in the past, claiming she was still a little girl.

"Should we prepare dinner?" He led the way into the kitchen where Lilly had what appeared to be a meal simmering on the stove.

"You're back, Mr. MacPherson. Did you have a nice trip and visit in New York? Your sister must have been very pleased to have more help around the house and with the children," Lilly asked as she bent over to take something from the oven before setting the pan on the table.

"You knew where Blade was and you didn't tell me?" She couldn't believe what she just heard. "Lilly."

With spoon in hand and continuing to stir while looking over her shoulder, "Mr. MacPherson told me his plans before he left. I didn't mean to keep anything from you. He told me he left you a note. I thought you knew."

"I believed he got what he wanted from me so he disappeared." Aidan covered her mouth with her hands, appalled at what she just said when she saw the disapproving look in Blade's eyes.

"Excuse us, Lilly. Aidan and I need to talk privately before she embarrasses herself again. Is there a good place close by?"

"Walk down the path to the lake. It's part of the Andrew and Hepburn property and few go there. You should be alone," Lilly told them as if she surely knew his purpose. "I'll keep dinner warm for you."

"Many thanks," Blade spoke to Lilly then turned to Aidan, holding out his hand. "Come, Little Fire."

"Do I have a choice?" Mortified, she wanted to hide in her room, not go for a walk with him and what seemed to include a forthcoming lecture.

"I'm not going to hurt you or ravish you as you put it. We need to speak of something your innocence precludes you from understanding."

It was true, what he just mentioned. This courting stuff, if what Blade said was true was beyond her scope of knowledge or experience. She always had a way of blurting out her thoughts. This situation was no different.

She placed her hand in his before following him out the door. A cool wind blew in from the ocean. She shivered, wishing he could find someplace warm to talk to her.

"Wait here," he said and quickly disappeared. A few seconds later, he returned with a shawl for her to wrap around her shoulders.

They walked in silence until the lake appeared, her nerves unraveling one fine strand at a time until her body shook. So much had happened in the last hour. "Did you know my bathing suit is at the bottom of the lake?" She didn't know why she told him that.

His voice, dark and gruff as well as disapproving, he asked, "Just how did it get there."

She sat down on a rock, picking up pebbles in her hand and letting them slide to the ground one at a time. "The logistics of its fall to the bottom aren't known to me."

He sat next to her, placing her hand in his. It always amazed her how small her hand appeared inside his. Lazily, he traced small circles on the underside of her wrist. She inhaled a long swift breath. He was doing it again, making her hot and breathless.

"Did you have an affair last summer before I got here? Edwin perhaps or was it that Hooley fellow?" his accusatory words shook her to the core.

"Why on earth would you think something so despicable of me? I've never? Edwin? Baxter? Goodness no—never." She tried to tug her hand away, but he didn't allow it.

"An absence of swimwear denotes nakedness. If you were naked in that lake with me, I would make love to you." His low growl sent a shiver down her spine.

"Are you jealous or angry?" She'd done nothing like he implied and never would unless it was with him.

"Both."

"I haven't done what you said." He brought the back of her hand to his lips for a quick kiss.

"Thank God. I'd have to kill the bloke."

"You don't mean that."

He didn't answer. "How?"

"How what?" She'd forgotten the question somewhere between his kiss and the words, kill the bloke.

With seeming patience, he repeated, "How did your swimsuit find its way to the bottom of the lake?"

"I wasn't wearing it." There, she silently patted herself on her back, having finally put an end to this story that seemed to anger him beyond anything she'd seen from him before.

"You think to make me feel better, woman," he rumbled. If you weren't wearing it, you were naked."

"What? I wasn't. Not in the water." The tempo of her words increased. She spoke so fast she barely understood what she said. "Tira was swimming with Jamie and she nearly drowned because she'd been working so hard at the shipyard. She was so tired all her muscles cramped and she couldn't get to shore." She stopped a second to inhale a deep lungful of air. "Jamie had to pull her from the depths to keep her from drowning and the suit was so heavy he had to cut it off her. If he hadn't done that, she wouldn't be alive today."

Blade let a roar of laughter rumble from his belly. "Take another breath, Little Fire. I believe I've got the gist of what happened. Don't ever go swimming in this lake unless it's with me," he warned, pulling her close and giving her a quick hug. "Promise."

"Promise what?" She meant to be obstinate, didn't like the way he laughed at her.

"You won't go swimming naked in this lake, hell, any lake unless you're swimming with me. Promise." His hands rested on her shoulders, giving her a tiny shake. "I need to hear you say the word."

"I promise but Blade, I don't think I want to swim naked with you." She'd be so vulnerable.

"I hope to change that notion." He smiled, tenderly brushing a stray lock of hair from her face. "Now we have something else to discuss. The reason why we're sitting here in the growing darkness talking about dead swimsuits."

"So, why did you drag me out here?" She knew it was because of the words she spoke in front of Lilly, but what she didn't understand was why he seemed so displeased.

He slowly repeated the words she told him, "I believed he got what he wanted from me so he disappeared."

"I know what I said but what I don't know is why you have to talk to me about what I said."

Looking away from her, he ran his hands through his hair. "This innocent stuff is killing me."

She straightened her back, "I'm not innocent. You gave me a

woman's pleasure, or so you told me. So you know I'm not naïve."

"I haven't made love to you yet." He paused in thought, running a fingertip along her arm. "What you said implied as much, however."

"I did? I made Lilly think that? She wouldn't care." She felt as baffled as she supposed she looked.

"You implied I made love to you then left you to deal with any unwanted results. It will tarnish your reputation if you repeat such things in front of gossips. You're right about Lilly though. She would never spread gossip."

"Lilly won't say anything." She agreed with him still puzzled. "What unwanted result?"

"No, she won't but now every time she looks at you, she'll think we've been intimate. And if you think about it, you'll figure it out."

"Why can't you just tell me what you mean? Why do I have to think? I'm sure I don't know what you mean." She asked, fed up with the guessing games and needing honesty from him.

He sighed deeply then seemed to agree with her. "From what we did, you're not going to be with child. But if I had my way with you, you might be carrying my child as we speak."

"I can't think of anything much more intimate than the way you touched my body, the places, the sensations..."

"Hush." He placed a finger on her lips.

The wanton inside her leapt free. She licked it then pulled his finger into her mouth. She heard a groan emanate from deep inside him. She smiled, realizing she held some power over him. "Did you like that?"

"Too much." He groaned again.

Too much, what did that mean? "I like the way you taste, not just your finger but your tongue and I want to taste other parts of you."

"Bloody hell." He couldn't help himself. He pulled her into his arms, giving her a slow deep kiss that had her panting for more. When he finished, he set her aside, "We have to get back."

"Are you hungry?" She ran a finger along his chin. "Because I'm not at least not for food."

"Famished for you, that's why we should go eat."

~ * ~

"Your dinner is in the warming tray on the stove. Let me know if there is anything else you'll need. Enjoy," Lilly smiled at them as she walked from the room.

"Is that your stomach growling?" Blade asked as he dished up the plates of venison stew and set out the biscuits. "I thought you said you weren't hungry?"

"I guess all my blood was pumping to a different part of my body." She took the plate from him, setting it on the table, gracing him with a precocious Aidan smile. "Something you did to me."

Pure male laughter echoed in the room. While he knew Aidan McLellan would never bore him, had known that fact for many years, he'd never expected sexually laced comments from her, but did she know what she eluded to? "You can always say what comes into your head when you're with me, but you do need to curb your impulsiveness when you're around others."

"Impulsive? Don't know why you say that. If anything, I'm never impulsive."

"Sometime I'll show you, but I'm not about to explain anything while we're at the dinner table." The sooner he made her his wife the sooner life would be so much easier. Trouble was he was sure she was making him pay for past indiscretions. He'd pay whatever price she extracted from him to make up for his callous behavior over the years. Truth be told though, even as a thirteen-year-old, she overwhelmed him. From the beginning he'd understood denying her anything would always be difficult.

"Then we should move to the parlor," she said, picking up her plate, her hips swaying as she walked away.

He stopped her, "Not the parlor either. Would you like wine?"

"Why not? And yes, I'm going to the parlor. You can come if you'd like. Or not." She shrugged her small, delicate shoulders. "Your choice."

"Why not wine? Or why wine? It tastes good, relaxes, might...no never mind." He loved the myriad of expression flitting across her face and the way her eyebrows narrowed when she was trying to figure something out. She pretended to know so many things but he was learning she was more innocent than he'd ever believed.

She stopped in the doorway. "Why not the parlor. There you go again making everything more difficult than it has to be."

"Wine?"

"Yes, and you're deflecting."

Of course he was avoiding answering. He'd rather show her, pick her up and carry her to his big bed. Showing her would be so much easier. "Are you finished with dinner?"

He heard her huge sigh of frustration, he assumed, and watched as her eyes crossed for a second. "I'm done." She brought her plate back to the kitchen and to the sink.

"Let's take the wine into the parlor. You can sit on my lap and I can enjoy watching you purse your lips when you say something outrageous and I won't explain it to you." He grinned at the expression he adored, having only seen it a few times as she was growing up. During those years he kept his distance, hoping some day she would still have feelings for him. Some day was here now and he intended to relish every precious moment with her.

"I'm not sitting on your lap." She picked up her wine and flounced from the kitchen, her hips swaying and provocatively enticing him.

"Suit yourself." He grabbed the bottle as well as the crystal holding his wine before following her.

In the parlor and sitting in a single chair, she held her glass out for him. He obliged by filling it. "What do you want to talk about now?"

"Us." The entire night, if he could have it his way would be about them. "What did you do while I was gone? Go out with Edwin? Or was it Hooley?" He didn't know why he brought up the odious man, but his gut tightened at the thought of her keeping the man company.

"I went to church and prayed that some demon would rise from the sea and swallow you whole." She peered at him over the rim of her glass, seeming to watch for a reaction.

His laughter rolled from deep in his belly. Of course he understood. From her perspective he deserved that and more. "Anything else? You didn't spend seven days a week praying in church for my demise."

She sipped more wine, her eyes closing momentarily and when she opened them, they seemed to cross, her dark sooty lashes fluttering on alabaster cheeks. That gave him pause to think. Her lashes should be the color of her hair. When she opened them, their crystal blue depths never ceased to take his breath away, "No, I didn't. I spent the other six praying at home for your termination."

"I don't believe you." He stood in front of her. "Come, you don't have to sit on my lap, but I'd like you close to me. By the way, how did you make your lashes black?"

"As you've said any number of times, that might not be the wisest course of action." It seemed she ignored the last question and was thinking about where he was about to sit.

He picked up her wine and set it on the end table by the sofa then returned, "If I have to carry you to the sofa, I'll keep hold of you."

She didn't move, her breasts heaving as he sensed her panic. One moment she challenged him with sexual innuendos she didn't understand and the next, her eyes looked like those of a frightened deer.

"Give me a second to catch my breath."

"One."

"That wasn't nice." But she pushed herself from the chair and with what appeared to be wobbly legs, she made her way to the sofa. Sitting down, she drank the contents of her glass.

Taking his place beside her, he filled her glass again. "What are you, we, going to do tomorrow?" He wanted to spend the entire day with her, watching her and waiting for her to say something shocking she didn't understand.

"It's Sunday," she said, looking at her wine and frowning before twirling the contents around in circles.

"So, if you intend to pray, you're going to have make that sea demon something else." He put his arm around her, his hand on her shoulder, his fingers resting on bare skin. Pulling her to him, he made sure his chest was pressed against the soft curve of her breast.

"You're home now and all is forgiven. It's a church social and you will have to bid on my basket. Of course you'll have to bring a lot of money because Sam always buys it, and he makes sure he can outbid everyone else there."

"I have to bid on your basket?" He wasn't sure what she spoke of, having not attended church in years or a church social ever.

"Of course you do if you want to share it with me. The basket goes to the highest bidder. If you want my company, you have to spend the most money." She tilted her head provocatively, smiling. "All the money goes back to the church, who use it for good causes."

"If I don't then Sam will win it and you will spend lunch with him. Not a chance in hell. Still..." Given what he knew about Sam, he understood the man was no threat to Aidan or winning her hand, so he didn't understand the wave of jealousy he was experiencing.

"I spend every Sunday with him. I do believe he's sweet on me." She turned in his arms, smiling sweetly at him.

"He's just protecting you from other suitors you might not want. Sam prefers men." Now it seemed he was absorbing Aidan's habit of blurting what he thought.

"What does that mean? Prefers men?" Lines creased her brow as she concentrated. "I don't understand."

This was not what he expected or wanted. Leaning toward her, he ran his hands through her beautiful red hair, extracting the pins, hearing them clatter to the floor. The length fell around her shoulders. Then he kissed her, long and slow, exploring her, tasting the essence of Aidan. He could never get enough. For him it was a drugging kiss. When he finished, "We should go to bed."

"Together?"

"Do you remember the time when you stood naked in front of me in my solar? You offered yourself to me." The image had been etched in his head for all eternity. She had been slender, coltish. Her breasts barely beginning to grow, it had taken a will of iron not to toss her on the bed and make love to her. He'd understood then, if he waited for her to grow into a woman, sex with her would be heaven sent.

Slowly, she nodded. He placed a finger under her chin, keeping her gaze focused on him. "That was a long time ago. I guess you thought I was a little girl."

"Not a little girl, but a young woman just coming into her own and you still had a lot of life to live. I couldn't take advantage of you although God knew I wanted to place you on my bed and have you then and there."

"But you didn't."

"I waited and now I'd like to do that very thing." *Bury myself deep inside your warmth and give you a woman's pleasure.*

"Tonight?"

"If you want." Bloody hell why was he provoking her? "I wouldn't refuse you but by the look on your face, you're terrified. I'll walk you upstairs and we can go to our separate bedrooms."

"You don't want to talk anymore?"

"Are you relieved? It's late and I know you're an early riser. We can talk tomorrow after I buy your basket."

"Alright."

At her bedroom door Blade pulled her into his arms for another kiss. The passion she responded with left him grinning, knowing when they finally did make love, she would give all of herself to him. "Goodnight, Little Fire. See you bright and early in the morning."

When the door closed behind her, he stood in the hall for a few seconds before walking to his room. Spending the night with Aidan in his arms would be paradise, but not tonight.

In his room he slipped out of his shirt, folding it neatly and placing it on a chair. He unfastened his buckskins in an attempt for comfortable. After splashing water on his face, he lay down on his bed, his hands behind his head, thinking about Aidan.

Tomorrow the social and in a couple of days he intended to take Aidan with him to deliver Andrews' horses to his farm. Sam had been keeping them safe in the stable behind his blacksmith shop while he was gone.

He heard the knock on the door but didn't rise from the bed. When he saw her face peeking around the door, he smiled, knowing all along what she needed from him.

"Can I come in?"

"If you dare."

She stepped inside, closing the door behind her. Hands clasped in front of her, she looked at the floor then met his smiling gaze. Her hair fell in tangled disarray to her waist. He'd never realized how long it was.

"Are you going to make this hard for me?"

"I've no idea what you're talking about, and I don't want to make anything awkward. You're in my room, remember?" His gut tightened as he slowly rose from the bed, stepping toward her.

"I can't get my dress off. Lilly usually helps me but she's gone to bed, and I really don't want to sleep in it."

"Let me understand completely. I don't want to misunderstand you. You want me to take your dress off." The look of complete mortification on her beautiful face left him very nearly speechless.

"Yes, well no. I want you to unfasten the back then unlace my corset. As you can see," she moved so her back was to him, "I could only undo a few."

"I believe you've come to the right person." His nimble fingers worked their magic on the fasteners. As each one came undone, he couldn't help but leave an impression of his lips everywhere he saw naked flesh. Unlacing her corset, he helped the garment slip to the floor beneath her dress. For some reason she'd not donned a shift, and while she hugged the bodice of her dress to her breasts, she was naked all the way to her sweetly rounded derrière.

In his arms, he turned her, allowing his hands to slide down her back until he cupped her bottom in his hands, pulling her belly so she was positioned next to his pulsing rod. Only a thin layer of fabric and his buckskins separated them. Lord, but he gritted his teeth trying to stop himself. She could tempt a saint and he certainly was no candidate for sainthood.

"Thank you," she whispered, her breath wafting across his chest. The backs of her hands touched him, moved across him until she touched the hard buds of his nipples. "I like touching you. I like looking at you without clothes on too."

Holding her dress with one hand, she spread her fingers then moving lower stopped at the top of his waistband. He wanted to push his buckskins to the floor and let her wrap those slender very female fingers around him. He sucked in air, fighting the lust that was rapidly taking over his conscious mind and body.

"You're unfastened." His lips met hers in a gentle kiss. "Go back to your room before I do something I might come to regret."

She gazed at him, confusion in her eyes. "I thought..."

"That if you offered yourself to me, I would take advantage of the situation. You need to be sure sex is what you want before you give yourself to me. You must be sure the gift you're giving your first lover, well, that he's the person you want to give your virginity to. I'm not turning you away because I want to humiliate or embarrass you, or because I don't want you, but because I'm not sure you're ready."

"How will I know, how will you know if I'm sure? If I'm ready?" Her lips trembled slightly.

"Come, let's get you to your room." Blade walked the short distance to her room, behind her and made sure the door was closed tightly before he walked to his room.

Lying on his bed, Blade almost regretted sending her away. He didn't think he could sleep unless he found release. There were ways but he opted for a swim; exercise helped as well as the cold water. His little fire had no idea how difficult his actions this evening had been.

A few minutes later, with towel in hand, he strode down the dark path to the lake. He brought a lantern with him to light the way. For the end of April it was a warm evening. A sliver of a moon could be seen between a few strips of clouds and a slight breeze filtered through the trees. The croak of frogs and the hoot of an owl brightened the night.

Stripping to his small clothes he waded in until the water reached his waist. Then, inhaling a deep breath he dove. Swimming under water until his lungs felt as if they would burst, he finally surfaced. Sure, strong strokes propelled him to the waterfall that caught his interest. He found a path circling around the water and into a small cove behind it.

Trying desperately to think of anything except Aidan, he lost the battle. When he saw the secluded spot, all he could think of was Aidan and holding her skin to skin. He ran his hands through his hair, wondering if there would be any release for him tonight or ever, imagining a life in constant arousal.

He dove through the water into the lake. Making a list of things he needed to accomplish before he took Damian's thoroughbreds overland to the Andrews' farm, his mind strayed from the woman in the bedroom next to his.

They would meet Damian's men before the first evening. Camping out in the forest would be safer, so he'd timed everything with Andrews. If both parties left on the same day, they should meet shortly before six o'clock that evening. Nothing could go wrong.

When Aidan was involved anything could happen. Clear your mind, Blade. Keep thinking of horses and the food you need to bring with you. He desired good strong coffee, but Aidan liked her tea.

This wasn't working. Striding from the water, he found his towel. The lantern still burned. He tugged off his wet clothes and pulled his buckskins on then slipped his moccasins on his feet.

"Master MacPherson?"

"Yes." Blade reached for the pistol he usually wore.

"It's Joshua, Lilly's husband. But I suppose you know that. Saw you leave the house and head down the path. It's not always safe out here. Thought I'd stand guard for a few minutes. Figured you was havin' woman trouble the way you plunged into that lake. Not the right time of year for a swim, if you get my drift. It's mighty cold in there."

"Much obliged." Cold was what he needed. Blade towel dried his hair, looking to the house. No lights shown from the window of her room.

"We're too far away from both the main house and my cottage. You can't see lights. Sometimes drunken men from the bars stumble down here. I'll walk back with you."

"I wasn't thinking when I left the house." Well, he was but with the wrong part of his anatomy. "Left without my pistol or my knife. Had to get out of the house before I did something foolish."

With the silence of the night pervading his soul, he walked with Joshua "Take care and thank you again."

When he opened the door to his room, he stopped, traumatized by the site in front of him. Aidan lay on his bed, her wonderful red hair spilled across his pillow. She was curled up in a tight ball.

The vision of her was unparalleled. In his entire life he couldn't remember seeing anyone so beautiful, especially asleep on his bed. His gut tightened and the effect of the midnight swim in the frigid lake vanished.

"Aidan," he whispered, walking toward her.

The sound of her name in the silence seemed to wake her. She sat up, brushing hair from her face. "You're back. Where did you go?"

Once again he was nearly naked. He needed to rid himself of the damp buckskins but didn't dare. Not for one second did he believe she was ready to see him naked and fully aroused.

"Why are you here?" That sounded too harsh. "Aidan, you should be asleep in your room. Where you're safe."

She shrugged, pushing the sheet and blankets to her waist, her red hair falling in wild disarray around her shoulders. "I heard a noise and I was frightened. I was looking for you. I searched the house but didn't find anyone so I came back here. Somehow I felt safer in your room."

"I'm glad of that. Would you turn around? I'm going to take my pants off." He walked to his wardrobe and rummaging inside found another pair of buckskins.

When he looked to see if she did as he instructed, he found a set of blue eyes staring at him. I mean it, Aidan. Unless you want to see me buck naked, you need to turn around and close your eyes right now." At the moment he wasn't sure how he felt.

"You've seen me buck naked."

"True. Well almost. I never removed your clothing, but I did see certain parts of you." How could he refute something that was so accurate? Bloody hell, how could trying to be a gentleman and do the right thing be so fucking hard?

"No. You can't make me. I want to see you, all of you. I've never seen a naked man and I'm curious."

His breath caught in his throat. She sounded like a little girl at the beginnings of a temper tantrum that made him want to laugh. He wondered if they would have a girl, one who looked just like Aidan. He groaned knowing he was overstepping his bounds.

He had no words. Instead, he turned his back on her and slipped from his damp clothes then changing his mind, he pulled on a dry pair of underclothes and strode to the bed. "Do you want me to walk you back to your room or do you want to go by yourself."

"Neither." She patted the spot beside her. Aidan's angelic smile didn't fool him.

Two could play this game. He walked around the bed, settling in beside her and pulling her to him so her head rested against his chest. Her hand rose to caress him, and he prayed she didn't explore below his waist. He thought to scare her to her room, but he had the sinking sensation that tonight he would never frighten her away. Besides, if he were honest with himself, he wanted her in his bed and beside him for the rest of his life.

He closed his eyes, even while he kept his hands fisted tightly. A smile curved his lips while he thought of his first site of her this evening. In a virgin nightdress, she came to his bed to seduce or truly because she felt safer, he would never know. The gown was white and long, probably covering her beyond her toes.

He envisioned her in a filmy negligee, one he could see all her curves through, one he could...

She was asleep. The feel of her breasts against his chest, moving slowly with her breathing, caused such a wave of bliss to run the length of him. He would protect her always with his life. She was his through eternity and beyond.

She was asleep. He didn't dare wake her. This was something he never thought of before. His soon to be wife sleeping beside him and in his arms, the sensations more potent than sex and more enduring.

~ * ~

Laird MacPherson, Blade's father, sat up in bed willing his body to heal. He needed to stay alive until Blade returned with his bride, Aiden McLellan. It was too bad Blade scared her away, clear to the United States. If he died before Blade returned, there would be fighting over the land, MacPherson land. Blade's younger brother had always coveted this ancestral home for himself.

"Sir? You called for me?"

"I did, Angus, come in and help me dress. It's what I pay you good money to do. Besides I crave someone to talk to, a person I can trust. Then I need to have you help me downstairs. I must put in an appearance so the entire clan will know I'm alive and prospering. We must present a united front, you and I. Don't know how long it will be until Blade returns with his bride."

"You have a letter, sir. It's from your son."

"Ah, yes, it's about time. No, it's past time I heard from him. I pray this missive will tell me he's on his way home." The laird rose from his bed, extending his hand for the envelope. Quickly opening, he read.

Father,

I pray this letter will find you well and improving daily. As summer creeps closer, I'm sure the weather will heal what ails you. Take some time to sit in the sun and soak up the warmth of its rays.

As you know I visited my sisters so my return will be delayed a month or two. I'm now back in Baltimore, courting the lady I mean to make my wife and hoping to return before the end of the summer. I vow I will be home by the end of August if not before.

I've promised Damian Andrews I would escort the horses he purchased from the Graham's to his home inland. By that time, I do hope I've also convinced Aidan to become my wife. As a last resort we will handfast so my homecoming will be eminent. When that happens, I'll sail for home. Nothing will get in my way.

Stay well,
Your son,
Blade

The MacPherson sat down, head in hands, moisture clogging his throat. Truly he didn't know if he could hold on until the end of the summer. Pretending good health was taking its toll on his body as well as his mind. He looked at his valet and confident as if his old friend could give him the advice and strength he needed to do what Blade suggested.

"Help me dress. Something simple and I'll sit in the solar for a while before going downstairs to make my presence known. I need to regain their confidence and the only way that will happen is if they see me. Perhaps with the appearance of warm weather, my health will improve."

"Good, Sir, you must present a strong front for your son. You cannot show any signs of weakness. None of us at the keep want his younger brother taking over. Blade must get home soon if his brother's rise to power is not to happen and you must get well."

He coughed then cleared his throat. He really did feel better this week as the warmth of spring seemed to permeate his soul, giving health to his body. Winters here in this land were always harsh and difficult to endure.

Washed and dressed, with the help of his manservant, he sat in the solar, soaking up the warmth of the sun. Funny how this tiny bit of sunshine made him feel better. A dish of eggs and bread sat in front of him. His stomach rumbled. It was a good sign.

As soon as he finished eating, he'd go downstairs and visit with his people. They would relay the message to the second son that he was healthy and working. Yet the sooner Blade returned the easier this would be. He wouldn't have to spend the days looking over his shoulder for an enemy.

"Are you ready to make your appearance?" Angus asked.

The MacPherson groaned, understanding the importance of making his presence known. Each day he needed to go downstairs, mingle with his people, give them confidence. If he didn't, it would only be a matter of time before Blade's brother. Leod, rode into the keep, demanding he step down.

"Damn it, but this was his first son's birthright. He would not let anyone take it away from Blade, especially not his younger sibling." His fist pounded on the table, unwilling to give in to this malady possessing his body.

Other Books by Christine Young
Available at Rogue Phoenix Press

Catching Meara
Book One in the McKenna Clan Series

Meara Thorton was a feisty, world-class computer hacker—cornered by the FBI and shockingly given the chance to be their newly acquired technical analyst. Brilliant and intuitive, yet aching with the loss of everyone she has cared about, her restless heart led her to discover a love she fought and a world she didn't know could possibly exist.

Sweet Sexy Sadie
Book Two in the McKenna Clan Series

From the first time Sadie's eyes met those of Brody McKenna in the hot Sierra Madre Mountains, theirs was a potent attraction—not gentle, slow, and easy, but hot, hard, and all-consuming. The daughter of a dysfunctional family, Sadie had dreams no man could wrench from her with hot sex and an all-consuming passion. She'd challenge this alpha male with all the strength she possessed. But her red hair, fiery temperament, and indomitable spirit obsessed Brody...and he knew he had to find a way to show her he was more than he appeared and convince her to make a life with him.

Sweet Misbehavin'
Book Three in the McKenna Clan Series

Cast adrift after fleeing the home of Jokul, the ice demon, Atantsi, a firestarter, grew to womanhood as she moved through time to keep the demon from finding her. Though stubborn and courageous, she was ill prepared to use powers she had not been taught. Her first sight of the intoxicating Carr McKenna left her breathless, and her second encounter gave her hope for a future she never thought she had.

A playboy, a second son and a shifter, a man who thought his life would be carefree, Carr McKenna was shocked to discover the woman he'd paid as an escort is a firestarter who is running for her life. He is the leader of all the McKennas around the world and that he has multiple powers. His passion for Margo and the need to defend her might cost him his life as well as hers.

Sweet Talkin' Sugar
Book Four in the McKenna Clan Series

Lyonesse McKenna, was dreaming or was she? From the instant Lyn saw Deacon McClain across a black jack table in a crowed Las Vegas casino the unmistakable attraction sent Lyn's senses flying into overdrive. Her family of shapeshifters believed in soul mates. She'd always been skeptical yet she couldn't help but question the way her heart sped when he looked at her.

When Deacon appeared in Las Vegas he knew his first job was to save Lyn from a Sea Demon, but the next order of business was to convince her he would someday mean more to her than she'd ever expected. But her stubborn nature and unbendable spirit consumed Deacon...and he had to chase away all the demons real and imagined in order to win her heart.

Sweet Surrender
Book Five in the McKenna Clan Series

Ripped from her family at the top of Infinity Cliff, Kimi McKenna finds herself thrust somewhere into the future. Dark elements threaten to destroy the earth unless Kimi can work together with the white witch to stop the destruction. Confused by her mate's role in the conspiracy, she refuses to acknowledge the connection. But amidst raging fire and attacks on the people she is coming to hold dear, she allows Maska O'keefe into her heart.

Maska O'keefe has loved the beautiful shapeshifter for years. Unable to save her life years ago, he vows to watch over her as he is given a second chance to convince her that even though he is a witch and not a shifter, they are indeed soul mates. Kimi's divided loyalties between her family and the cause she is now a part of will determine their relationship. Only the part she plays as the messiah can bring this to a conclusion in the final battle.

Dakota's Bride
The first book in the Lakota/Pinkerton Series

When Emma St. John received her brother's letter imploring her to escape her stepfather's vengeful scheme and to trust Dakota Barringer with her life, she was willing to chance it. But the handsome, brooding riverboat owner Emma found in Natchez a danger of another kind. For Emma soon found herself surrendering to an unrelenting desire.
Raised by the Sioux when his parents were killed, Dakota had been betrayed once before by a white woman. He wasn't about to trust another, especially one claiming that her stepfather, a powerful U.S. senator, had framed her as a murderess. But he couldn't let Emma's intoxicating effect on him. Now Dakota would risk his very life to protect the innocent beauty who had seduced him with her tender love.

My Angel
The second book in the Lakota/Pinkerton Series

A BEAUTY IN BUCKSKINS
When her father decided to send her to a finishing school back East, Angela Chamberlain refused to be confined to stuffy drawing rooms. Instead, the

daring spitfire who could shoot like a man and ride like the wind longed for a life of adventure and romance—and she knew exactly who could give it to her. Devil Blackmoor was a hired gun with a dangerous reputation. But Angela was willing to go to the ends of the earth to capture the handsome devil's heart.

A DEVIL IN DISGUISE
He'd come to America looking for excitement, but Devil Blackmoor got more than he bargained for when he encountered a beautiful rebel who answered his kisses with a wild innocence that touched his very soul. Yet standing between them were more obstacles than either ever dreamed. For Devil had strapped on a gun for the wrong man. And that made Angela his enemy. Now he'll have to choose between his duty and the woman he loves more than life.

The Locket
The third book in the Lakota/Pinkerton Series

The year is 1894. Seeking revenge for crimes against his family, Misha Petrovich follows a path that leads straight to Ariel Cameron's boarding house in Mist Harbor, Oregon. A family heirloom in Ariel's possession leads Misha to believe she is guilty. The locket has been handed down to the oldest girl in the Petrovich family for generations. Ariel is innocent of wrong doing, but her father is not. Misha is torn by his feelings for Ariel and his need for restitution against her father. Knowing that the relationship between them is fragile, Misha does everything in his power to protect Ariel's father. His efforts are to no avail when her father is shot. Ariel comes to realize Misha's steadfast courage and determination to protect her and her father despite what has happened to his family. Ariel's love and devotion heals Misha's heart.

The Talisman
The fourth book in the Lakota/Pinkerton Series

Running from a marriage that lasted one night, Dr. Moriah McKeown discovers the land she has settled on is coveted by determined and lawless men. Yet the proud young woman who once vowed never to abandon her home has second thoughts when her adopted children are threatened. Her only recourse is to enlist the aid of a dark, dangerous gun for hire.

Haunted by the past and a betrayal he will never forgive, Ian Civanovich uses his fast gun and his reckless courage to forget the faithlessness of a woman in his past. He will trust no female—nor will he rest until the threat hovering over Moriah McKeown is put to rest.

Forever His
The fifth book in the Lakota/Pinkerton Series

Struggling to come to terms with the part she played in Jacob St. John's death, Etta Barringer resigns from Pinkerton Agency and seeks peace and solace in a Rocky Mountain Cabin.

Jacob has vowed to discover the reason Etta has betrayed him, sold him out to his enemy and left him for dead.

Isolated in their cabin, they discover their love for each other and learn to trust. But the trust is shattered when Jacob learns she is married to his sworn enemy; the man who left him in the desert to die.

Allura's Secret
Twelve Dancing Princesses Book One

Allura McClellan is horrified by her father's decision to take out an ad in the Times awarding her to the man strong enough and smart enough to win her hand and uncover her secrets. She's an intelligent young woman who takes great delight in the freedom allotted to her by her father. She's well aware that marriage would effectively curtail the adventures she's shared with her sisters and cousins.

Hunter Gray is nothing like the other men who've arrived to vie for Allura's hand in marriage and everything that goes along with it. However, he is the first to refuse to concede defeat and pursue her despite her attempts to disguise her true appearance. It's her temperament that is of more concern to him than her looks. Hunter has worked all his life with the hope of someday owning his own land. Now that it looks like there's a very real possibility that everything he's ever wanted is within reach nothing is going to deter him – including Miss Allura's disagreeable disposition.

Amorica's Wager
Twelve Dancing Princesses Book Two

Amorica Hepburn was sent to London to find a husband. Finding a man was the last item on her agenda. With her two cousins, Amorica wagers she can dissuade her suitor before the others. Despite her efforts she discovers a chemistry that cannot be denied. Suddenly she is the arrogant man's wife, pledged to a marriage neither desire. But swept off to his ancestral home above the Dover cliffs and into his strong embrace, Amorica is soon possessed by a raging passion for the husband she had vowed to despise… Damian Andrews couldn't afford to trust the emerald-eyed spitfire who happened upon his secret. Amorica's hatred of all men of his kind only inflames the war that rages between them. Still, he can not control the intense desire his stubborn bride inspires, or make her surrender to his will until he has conquered the headstrong beauty on the battlefield of love…

Ravyn's Marriage of Inconvenience
Twelve Dancing Princesses Book Three

A REGAL BEAUTY
When the duchess decides to wed her to a wastrel and a fop, Ravyn Grahm takes matters into her own hands and declares her engagement to another man. Instead of fessing up and telling her great aunt what she has done, she goes through with the pretense. Aric Lakeland is the bastard son of an earl and has a dangerous reputation. But Ravyn is willing to do most anything to keep the duchess from discovering the lie.

A DEVIL-MAY-CARE SMUGGLER

He'd bought land in America, looking to put down roots and end his life of adventure, but Aric Lakeland got more than he bargained for when he encountered a beautiful heiress who made a promise she didn't want to keep. But the promise could not be undone and standing between them were more obstacles than either ever dreamed. Aric had made plans to spend the rest of his life in America and that was at odds with Ravyn's plan of living in England and running her father's estate. Now, he'll have to choose between his dreams and the woman he loves more than life.

Christel's Sunrise
Twelve Dancing Princesses Book Four

He Made Her An Offer...

Life has thrown Christel McClellan some experiences that could have devastated a less determined woman. Beautiful, self-assured and fiercely independent, she is trying to forget the loss of her stillborn child. But is the child alive?

She Couldn't Deny...

Life is carefree for Ryder MacLaren who loves to see what is on the other side of the sunrise. Laird of Clan MacLaren, he is wealthy, handsome and happily unencumbered...until stunning Christel McClellan enters his life. When he hears her story, he believes the child she thought dead has been sold to a wealthy buyer.

Storm's Passion
Twelve Dancing Princesses Book Five

SHE MADE A PROPOSAL...

Life strikes Storm Graham a shattering blow when she learns her father has bartered her to a man she detests. Storm is beautiful, self−assured and fiercely independent, and refuses to be a pawn in her father's schemes, yet she can find no way out of this bargain made in hell. Going on the offensive she asks the wealthiest man on the eastern coast of England to marry her, never believing she might fall in love.

HE TRIED TO REFUSE...

For Hadden Johnston life has provided everything he ever wanted, including a sanctuary for homeless children. He is wealthy, handsome and happily unencumbered...until stunning Storm Graham marches into his life and proposes a marriage of convenience. Yet this type of marriage to a woman who inflames his senses is far from acceptable. If he's going to be tied down, he will move heaven and earth to have this woman warming his bed.

Gotta Have Fayth
Twelve Dancing Princesses Book Six

A regal beauty with raven hair and piercing blue eyes, Fayth Graham is unwilling to parade herself in front of the wealthy Lords of England during the season. Seeking a means to dissuade any man wishing to wed her, she seeks a way to ruin herself for marriage. When she unexpectedly meets a man with sparkling gray eyes and an infectious grin, she decides this is the man who will keep her from agreeing to obey.

He returned from six months at sea, looking for a few nights of pleasure with a willing lass, but Jarret Kinsley got more than he bargained for when he met a beautiful debutant who responded to his kisses with a wild innocence that touched his heart. Yet the obstacles looming between them might rip them apart. Both had vowed never to marry, so when consequences of their dalliances got in the way, Jarret would have to choose between the life he's always desired and the woman he loves more than life.

Ella's Pleasure
Twelve Dancing Princesses Book Seven

A WHISPER OF PLEASURE

Ella Hepburn was an auburn haired debutant from the harsh Scottish coastline—a wild innocent to be seduced and tamed. A spirited beauty, she captivated Drake Montgomerie's jaded heart—while succumbing to the smoldering desire she felt for her unyielding suitor.

A WHISPER OF DANGER

In Drake Montgomerie's glittering world of money and privilege, young Ella discovered passion and desire could overcome everything she'd been taught to resist—entangling Drake, the heir apparent, in a lethal coil of aristocratic family intrigue. But grave peril would only nurse the sparks of a love that knew no limits and a magnificent ecstasy that would not be denied.

Eveleen's Seduction
Twelve Dancing Princesses Book Eight

A WHISPER OF SEDUCTION

A brutal attack on Eveleen Hepburn's cherished island off the Scottish coastline leaves her shattered and bewildered. Learning a man she once trusted can kill as easily as he can breathe even though the deed saves her life, creates questions that need answers. An innocent beauty, she enchants Logan Maxwell's cynical heart—giving in to the raging passion she feels for her mysterious suitor.

A WHISPER OF INTRIGUE

In Logan's Maxwell's world of espionage and privilege, young Eveleen discovers truths about herself she never expected, and a need for passion and love can overcome all her fears if she learns to accept certain truths. She finds herself entangled in a lethal battle for land that was once owned by French nobility, taken from them during the revolution and sold to Maxwell. But grave peril would unleash the flames of love that simmers, creating a magical union that cannot be refuted.

Tavia's Deception
Twelve Dancing Princesses Book Nine

WHISPERS OF DECEPTION

When her father decides to send her to London for her season, Tavia Hepburn resolves to see the world instead. The raven haired beauty decides to disguise herself as a lad and find employment on a ship bound for Barcelona as a cabin boy. But she never bargains on finding passion and love to a red haired sea captain who rescues her from certain death.

WHISPERS OF MURDER

For James Macmurra, the world is black and white until he meets a young debutante, who turns his world upside down. He's unable to deny Tavia's intoxicating effect on him. In a match tense with obstacles, unwillingness to divulge secrets, and unforeseen peril, irresistible desire and passion grows into undeniable love. James would risk his life to shelter and protect the innocent debutante who seduces him with her sweet love.

Larena's Fascination
Twelve Dancing Princesses Book Ten

WHISPERS OF FASCINATION

Fiery, free spirited Larena Graham never wanted to marry a duke. She is thrilled to be in love with the fourth son of an aristocrat, Gavin Broon. But when it seems Gavin ignores her, she set her sights on politics and bettering human life. Unsuspecting intrigue and a plot against her, she continues her dangerous plans despite Gavin's wishes.

WHISPERS OF TRUST

Gavin has every intention of properly courting the beautiful Larena until he must leave the city in order to put his affairs in order. Returning to London, he finds the woman he means to make his own is embroiled in political protests that could lead to a prison ship. Larena must learn to trust the handsome Scotsman whose most pressing mission is to protect her and keep her from harm.

Twelve Days to Love

When Archer Steele shows up at Calanthe Durand's failing plantation with an alligator over his shoulder, Cali thinks she's never seen a more handsome man. During the war she had to defend herself and her servants from both union and confederate soldiers. Independent and self-sufficient, she vows to never marry.

But Archer Steele has different ideas. The first time Archer sees Cali in town, he feels an instant attraction. He decides he will do everything and anything to convince the beautiful Miss Durand he is worthy of her love. During the weeks leading up to Christmas, he gives her twelve gifts in hopes she will fall in love with him. Yet they are faced with challenges they must overcome before Cali can commit to a marriage.

Door to Heaven

Jessica Lawrence is the stepdaughter of a woman born in the twentieth century transported back in time to the year 1868. An acclaimed suffragette, she raises Jessica to believe in the equality of women. Jess Law believes everything she was taught, and when the time is right she becomes a private investigator. Courageous and impetuous, Jess finds danger in her quest to save all women from white slavery. Her passionate mission results in a wedding to Roc Newman, a man she knows can steal her heart...

Roc can't trust the sapphire-eyed spitfire who invades his home in search of secret papers and knocks him flat with her karate moves. Jessica's refusal to obey his wishes serves to inflame the war between them. Still, he cannot control the intense desire his reluctant bride inspires, or make her surrender her independence, until he has conquered the headstrong beauty on the battlefield of love...

Rebel Heart

HER REBEL SPIRIT DEFIED HIS OUTSIDERS SOUL... She was velvet and silk, eyes the color of a summer storm and amber hair. Victoria DeMontville, because of a promise and a codicil to her father's will, was forced to marry one man to protect her from another. She hated Cameron Savage with a fierce passion. But to hold on to her genetic research and find a cure for the deadly Signe virus, she must pretend to love the enemy at her door, come with weapons of fire to melt her icy heart...

HIS OUTSIDERS TOUCH IGNITED RAGING PASSIONS... He wore a mask, disguised as the Phantom, a true legend come to life. Even as war and debate over new genetic research engulfed them all, he would find his greatest adversary in the beauty who'd branded him an outsider and barbarian, the woman he was born to possess, his soul mate.

Safari Moon

Solo St. John, a wildlife photographer, is preparing for a trip to Alaska. Suddenly, Solo finds women of all sorts invading his privacy, his home and his office, all cooing nonsense words and blatantly throwing themselves at him. Solo doesn't know why, and he has no idea how to rid himself of the persistent women. He finally decides to beg a favor of his best buddy Nyssa Harrington.

In love with Solo for the past ten years and knowing he doesn't return her feelings Nyssa doesn't want to talk to Solo. She knows if she accepts his phone call, she will not be able to resist the temptation to hope again.

Straight to Heaven

Running from demons, Alexandra McMurdie stumbles into Forbidden Ground where up is down and elements of nature are contested. Though a strong independent woman in the twenty-first century' she is unprepared for life in the 1800s. Her first site of the formidable James Lawrence makes her heart skip a beat, giving her cause to reconsider her desperate need to find a way home.

Born with a silver spoon, James' life was torn apart during the War Between the States. Moving west he vows to put the life he once knew in the past. When he discovers a half-frozen woman near Gold Hill, his heart begins to thaw. His love for Alexandra and his need to keep her from a man who has pursued her through time might cost him his life as well as hers.

A Valentine's Anthology

The Lending Library-a fantasy by Christie L. Kraemer

Faeries try to fit into the human world when the forest where they make their home is destroyed by a mysterious enemy.

Chasing Rainbows-a contemporary romance by Genene Valleau

An eccentric aunt, an inventive uncle, a mother who wears poodle skirts, and a brother who wears pearls provide a hilarious backdrop for the courtship of a young woman who yearns for a "normal" family.

The Gift-an historical romance by Christine Young

A man and a woman on opposite sides of the Civil War get a second chance at love after one final battle returns soldiers to their war-torn homes to rebuild their lives.

A St. Patrick's Day Tale
by
Christine Young, C. L. Kraemer, Genene Valleau

Tumble through time…

…to Ireland in 1817, when tensions are high between Protestants and Catholics and faey people guide the fate of villagers. A lovely Catholic lass stumbles upon the weakly ritual fisticuffing between Irish lads. She falls into the lap of a handsome young Protestant. Family ties, grudges, and two conniving faeries threaten their budding love. But the faeries outsmart themselves when they hijack a time machine that has mysteriously appeared in their forest and are whisked to…

…Eugene, Oregon in the 20th century, amid a property feud between the local faeries and night elves. The conniving faeries from Olde Ireland try to stir up more mischief. However, a warrior gnome convinces the magic folk to control their own destiny, and forces the intruding faeries to take refuge in the time machine again, spinning their way toward…

…A modern day castle in western Oregon. An eccentric inventor is determined to reclaim his wayward time machine and save his beloved wife from her latest misadventure. If only they can travel safely past the black hole…

a May Day Anthology
by
Christine Young, C. L. Kraemer, Rosemary Indra, Genene Valleau

Highland Miracle -- Christine Young

HURTLED THROUGH TIME, Sean Michael Sterling, landed in the midst of a May Day celebration he didn't understand, assuming the role of Laird Sterling.

ILLIGITAMATE CHILD OF NOBILITY, Reagan Douglas searches for a way out of her half brother's house.

Defying the Odds -- C.L. Kraemer

The night elves on the hill aren't happy without their magic. They concoct a plan to punish those who were involved in the act that rendered them almost human. Meanwhile, Uther, the rogue night elf, has returned to woo the Librarian to be his eternal mate.

Love in Bloom -- Rosemary Indra

When childhood friends reunite it takes two fairies and a matchmaking daughter to help them admit their true love for each other.

No More Poodle Skirts -- Genie Gabriel

After drifting for years in the innocent age of the 1950s, a woman struggles to join today's world by finding a career and a new love, with some help from her zany family.

Once Upon a Christmas Moon
by
Christine Young, C. L. Kraemer, Genene Valleau

TWELVE DAYS TO LOVE

When Archer Steele shows up at Calanthe Durand's failing plantation with an alligator over his shoulder, Cali thinks she's never seen a more handsome man. During the war she had to defend herself and her servants from both union and confederate soldiers. Independent and self-sufficient, she vows to never marry. But Archer Steele has different ideas. The first time Archer sees Cali in town, he feels an instant attraction. He decides he will do everything and anything to convince the beautiful Miss Durand he is worthy of her love. During the weeks leading up to Christmas, he gives her twelve gifts in hopes she will fall in love with him.

BOOTS AND BLADES

An ancient evil from the old country has arrived in the high desert of Oregon. Gnome children are vanishing then re-appearing, showing various stages of traumatization. Tiamoon, warrior gnome, will put her skills to use alongside Killian, a handsome warrior, also in need of a cause.

CHRISTMAS PAWSIBILITIES

With their world destroyed and their space ship malfunctioning, the dogizens of Planet Canid have little choice but to crash land on Earth. They face tortuous experiments at the hands of the Geeks in Green...or they can trust an eccentric inventor and his zany family to deliver the Canine Queen's puppies and help them celebrate new lives.

**VISIT OUR WEBSITE
FOR THE FULL INVENTORY
OF QUALITY BOOKS**:
http://www.roguephoenixpress.com

Rogue Phoenix Press

Representing Excellence in Publishing

Quality trade paperbacks and downloads

in multiple formats,

*in genres ranging from historical to contemporary romance,
mystery and science fiction.*

Visit the website then bookmark it.

We add new titles each month!